Pathway of Dreams

Pathway of Dreams

Adam Bailey

PIATKUS

First published in Great Britain in 1990 by
Judy Piatkus (Publishers) Ltd of
5 Windmill Street, London W1

British Library Cataloguing in Publication Data
Bailey, Adam
    Pathway of dreams.
    Rn: Peter Rolls   I. Title
    823′.914 [F]

    ISBN 0–86188–978–9

Phototypeset in 11/12pt Compugraphic Times by
Action Typesetting Limited, Gloucester
Printed and bound in Great Britain by
Mackays of Chatham PLC, Chatham, Kent

For Milly

PART ONE

Chapter One

This was the moment she'd dreaded. She searched for words, and could only come up with: 'No! No! No!'

She paused and tried to smile, hoping to soften the stark refusal and spare his anguish. She failed. That was evident by the sadness on Simon's face. Sarah wanted to go to him, take him in her arms and nurse his bruised feelings.

Be strong. Don't give way now. If you do, you're finished. You can say goodbye to your hopes. Your dreams will go up in smoke. This is make or break time.

She resisted the temptation and moved so that she was standing behind a large armchair. It was like taking refuge behind the ramparts. She knew that if he were to take her in his arms, all her resolutions would crumble.

'You're not really surprised, are you?' she asked.

Simon collapsed into a chair facing her. He was a long time in answering, his fingers stroking his beard as if that helped the thought process.

'Well, you know me — I'm not exactly career-minded, myself. And I'm struggling to see the woman's point of view in this. I realise, of course, this is 1984 and things have changed over the last few years. I can understand the spinster type forced to look for a career. But you!'

'What about me?' she asked quietly.

'Well, I — ' He was floored. 'I mean, after all we've meant to each other. We can't just give it up because of this — this — '

'This what?'

'This aspiration of yours.'

Sarah could feel her anger mounting but tried to keep it in

check. 'Look, Simon, even now I don't believe you truly know me. Ever since Auntie Win brought me over from the States to get me away from Ella, I've had this ambition burning inside me. I must – *I will* – get to the top.'

He conceded a point. 'I can see if I'd had a mother like yours, I'd probably be the same, just for the sheer hell of making a rude gesture in her direction.' He stretched his legs and looked at the ceiling.

Sarah came out from behind the armchair and sat in it instead. She no longer felt she needed the protection.

He was speaking again. 'But what I don't understand is that you seem prepared to throw away all *our* happiness – as though the years together never happened. You're paying a damned heavy price in the name of ambition.' He looked straight at her. 'Your feelings haven't changed, have they?'

She was forced to admit they hadn't.

Needing no further reassurance, he nodded. 'Then why? Surely marrying me wouldn't get in the way of your career.'

'But it would! Don't you see? I'd want to be a good wife; look after the home; have your children. That's what wives are for.'

'Other women manage to combine career and home.'

'Not this one! Besides, it's also a matter of geography. I've got this marvellous new opening here in Surrey, and you're moving to the West Country. Distance alone is enough of an obstacle to any marriage. We've gone over all this before.'

'You could get a job on one of the local West Country papers.'

'No!' It was a shout. 'I've told you a dozen times. Don't you want to understand? I won't accept any old job. I want the one on the *Southern Examiner*. I'll be women's page editor there and that's a chance I must grab. I refuse to bury myself in some academic backwater.'

'I wouldn't call my new technical college an academic backwater.'

'I would. Look, we've discussed this so many times. For me, the *Examiner* will only be a stepping stone towards London. I've told you I intend to become a leading, national journalist. Anything less would be failure for me.'

Simon closed his eyes and groaned.

4

She could guess what he was thinking. He was casting his mind back over the years of their affair. Only once had they been away from each other for any length of time. That had been when she was a trainee reporter in her first job.

But apart from that, they had been together – a deeply loving, caring relationship. It had been tempestuous but always gratifying. There had been no one in her life before Simon. He had satisfied all her longings, emotional and physical. The great romance. The love story of all time. Now, it was over.

'I feel as if I've been kicked,' he said.

She understood; it was no less painful for her. She had to deny herself the happiness that he alone could bring. But she couldn't stifle the other voice, urging her higher and higher in her career. There could be no turning back, not even through love for Simon.

'I suppose we can go on seeing one another from time to time?' he said after a while.

It was her turn to be silent, not wanting to hurt him still further. 'That wouldn't be wise. I mean – ' She couldn't finish the sentence. Of course, she wanted to go on seeing him but each meeting would only cause them both heart-ache. It was better by far to make a clean break. 'I don't think we ought – ' Again her voice dried up.

'Please change your mind,' he said at length. His manner suggested he already knew what her answer would be. He made a move to rise from his chair. Immediately she was on her feet and sheltering behind her own. Seeing that she was keeping him at a safe distance, he accepted defeat and settled back once more.

'It's a grim outlook,' he went on. 'I don't have to tell you I couldn't live as a celibate. You know what'll happen? I'll find some mousey little woman and marry her.'

The very thought of it caused her anguish. 'Why "mousey"?' she managed to ask.

'Because any woman who came after you would be mousey.'

Sarah smiled. 'That was sweet.'

'No. The truth.' This time he did rise and walk towards her. She made a tentative movement away but gave it up as useless. His arms were around her, pulling her to him.

5

His voice was very low, caressing. He kissed her tenderly and, in spite of her resolutions, she responded. 'Darling, I love you so much. Please think again. Please!'

'I can't. You know that.'

'Do I?'

She flung herself away from him, angry at his persistence. 'You're being stubborn and unreasonable.'

'*I'm* not unreasonable. *You* are. It's such a bloody waste of our happiness, this grand gesture of yours.'

Her blood was up.

'What a typically masculine remark! Why is it that my wanting to follow a successful career up here is a "grand gesture", while your going to some piddling little tech isn't?'

'I didn't mean that.'

'Yes, you did. You said it with a sneer in your voice and I resent that. I resent it very much.'

'Anyone can see that your ancestors way back came from Ireland.'

'And what d'you mean by that?' She teased a lock of her hair. 'OK, OK. If you're reminding me that I have the temper of the Irish-Americans, you're dead right. I have. And I have as much right to a career as you.' She looked at him and his expression was so woebegone that her words stuck in her throat. She threw herself down in the armchair feeling frustrated.

Everything had gone wrong. She'd made an effort to keep her temper under control but had failed. The last thing she'd wanted was a heated exchange during what was to be their last evening together.

Simon was the first to apologise. 'Sorry, Sarah, you know I hate quarrelling,' he murmured, making a step in her direction. 'Are you definitely going to take this new job with the *Examiner*?'

'I've already taken it.' It was a struggle to make her tone sound normal.

'Oh! When do you start?'

'Just over a week's time – on the ninth of August – at the beginning of the silly season.' She forced a laugh to bring a little levity into the conversation.

He didn't respond in kind. 'I see.'

'When are you moving into your new digs?' she asked.

'In a few days. My sister and I are selling the family house now that Mum's died. I'll be putting it on the market tomorrow and driving down to Devon at the weekend.'

'So you're staying at home tonight, are you?'

He looked sheepish. 'Well, I was hoping – '

Sarah had foreseen this gambit. 'No, Simon, you're not going to spend the night with me. It wouldn't be a good idea.'

'Why not?'

'Well, I don't think it would be, that's all.' She couldn't tell him she was afraid of herself; that if he stayed, her resolve might be weakened.

Simon was close to her again, pleading eloquently with his eyes. She was trembling as she felt his hand in the small of her back, pressing her body against his. She gave up the struggle. She still loved him, still wanted him. Nothing had changed. Nor had she. It had been like that ever since they had first met during their student days.

He was already undoing her zip. She stopped him. 'Not here, darling, in the bedroom.'

'May I stay until morning?'

She could only nod.

'Shall I make some coffee?' he asked.

'Mmm?'

'Would you like some coffee?'

A drowsy voice answered, 'Coffee's a stimulant.'

'I know.'

'You don't need stimulating.' Her eyes remained closed.

It was true. He gave up the idea of coffee.

What a girl! An outgoing American girl, they all said. But he knew better than that. Behind the facade, she was tender and extremely vulnerable. He loved her.

Simon studied her peaceful face. Glossy black hair. Lustrous lashes resting on pale skin. Lips curved in a tiny smile. Quite beautiful! How could he let her go?

He kissed her gently and she responded with a sleepy murmuring sound. He pulled back the sheet, revealing her naked body. He knew it so well, in passion and repose.

He took hold of her firm breasts, fondling them and teasing the nipples. Again that languorous, murmuring sound.

7

'You know I can never resist you doing that.' She opened her eyes and lifted her head to be kissed. He needed no further encouragement.

Bodies in harmony. Sarah shuddered. She cried out. Her lips were on his, smothering him with kisses. Her arms hugged him tight, refusing to let him go.

'Oh, darling, darling, Simon.'

They lay there a long time, recovering, savouring their union. At last, he stirred. Looking down at her, he saw eyes filled with tears.

'Why must things be so difficult for me?' she sighed. She wriggled free of him, put on her négligé, slipped her feet into her mules. 'I'll go and get some breakfast while you're having your shower.' She bent down and kissed him. 'I wish to God I didn't love you so much.'

'In my opinion, you'll have no difficulty selling your house, Mr. Dowling. It is, after all, a seller's market at the moment.'

'And you don't think we're asking too much?' Simon sounded doubtful.

The estate agent grinned and made an expansive gesture with his hands. 'Good heavens, no. Prices are rising all the time. Very good for business.'

'Are they – prices rising, I mean? I'm not very commercially minded, I'm afraid. Oh, there's one other point. I'm moving down to Devon in a few days. My sister is a nurse and lives in the nurses' home here. That mean's you'll have to show prospective purchasers over the property.'

'No problem at all.'

Simon returned home to an atmosphere of chaos. But then, wherever his sister happened to be, chaos was never far away. True, they were moving their furniture out and that always involves upheaval, but Jenny never did anything tidily.

At this precise moment, she was turning out her bedroom, emptying it of the jumble she'd collected first as a child and then as a teenager. The collection of rubbish on the landing looked quite daunting.

On hearing Simon's return, she skipped round the pile and bounded down the stairs two at a time.

'How did it go?'

8

He told her what the estate agent had said and she listened with interest.

Simon was very fond of his only sister, a pretty twenty year old with hazel eyes and soft, auburn hair. At times, she could look sober and demure. This was largely illusory for Jenny could be capricious and quite volatile but a warm heart compensated for all her faults.

She went into the sitting room and he followed. Everywhere he looked, there were family effects waiting to be taken away. All this, coming on top of Sarah's decision, was hard for him to cope with.

'How's Sarah?' she asked, apparently reading his mind.

'She's fine. But it's not her health that's bothering me.'

'What d'you mean?'

He explained that she had chosen to break off their relationship. Jenny was shocked and fell silent for a long time.

'I think it's a crying shame,' she said eventually. 'You were such a romantic couple – stars in your eyes. It made me feel sentimental just to look at you.'

Simon sat down on the arm of a chair, thinking back.

'Still,' she went on, 'I do see Sarah's point of view. As a woman, I understand her wanting to go all out for an exciting career.'

'Actually, so do I. But I refuse to take her decision lying down. I can't. I love her too much.'

Jenny bent down and kissed him on the forehead. 'I know you do. Pity you're moving so far away.'

He nodded, acknowledging the truth of this. He'd been over it in his mind many times. 'It was a great mistake to take this job. But then, it was for me to choose lecturing in the first place. You've got to have a vocation to be a teacher and I don't have one, more's the pity.'

Once again, Jenny voiced no opinion. She'd heard him say this so often that she had no new comment to make.

He walked over to the mantelpiece and touched the marble clock with affection. When he was little, he'd opened the back to see what the chimes looked like. They'd never worked again after that.

In the corner of the room, there were some of their old toys recovered from the loft. And books. Dad's old pipe rack and Mum's needlework basket.

Tomorrow the family home would be emptied of all their possessions. Removal men would cart most of them off to the auction rooms. Only their most treasured pieces would be put into store. He felt he was in limbo.

He began taking off his jacket. 'Come on. It's no good daydreaming. We've got work to do.'

After Simon had gone, Sarah wrote a letter to him at his new lodgings in Devon. It didn't mince matters.

In spite of their night together, she confirmed what she'd said the previous evening. The affair was over. Putting it in writing made it seem more final. But as she sealed the envelope, she had a recollection of Simon as he'd left. She thought she would never forget how he looked then. Disbelieving. Dejected. Beaten.

Of course, she ought not to have let him sleep with her. That had been soft and foolish, making it more difficult for them at the final parting. Just the same, last night would remain with her as a lovely memory − more beautiful than any swan song.

She felt like weeping but stifled the urge. In general, she disliked weepy women. Besides, crying would only sap her strength and she couldn't afford that. In a weak mood she'd be on the phone telling him she hadn't meant what she'd said.

Her mind flitted into the past. That first night together, for instance, how he'd climbed in through the window of her ground-floor bedroom at college; how they'd repeated the escapade afterwards without ever being found out. She thought of their lovemaking over the years, of the depth of companionship they'd known, the fun they'd had. Oh, they were wonderful times!

She was suddenly angry with herself for indulging in nostalgia. She had to snap out of it. A suitable remedy was physical activity.

There was a good opportunity ready to hand. That afternoon, she was due to drive down to Sussex for a few days' holiday at her beloved Auntie Win's. Her clothes needed to be folded, toilet articles gathered together, the small valise dusted off.

When everything was in order, she ran down the stairs outside the flat and posted the letter in the pillar box by the main entrance.

It was when she was sitting with a cup of coffee on her return, that she was again struck by the horror of parting from Simon. She'd thrown away personal happiness. That was a very big price to pay for career advancement.

This time she did weep, shedding salty, stinging tears that were only partly a catharsis.

Having dried her eyes at last, she sat down at the dressing table, studying her face before repairing the damage to her make-up. She was not unaware of her attractiveness but often saw it as a disadvantage. Sometimes she wished she'd been born plain.

It would have made it easier to convince people that she had a mind and could reason with it. Moreover, people would know that any success she might achieve had been won on merit alone. The widespread belief was that attractive women were empty-headed. That rankled and she intended to prove them wrong.

She knew that the face she presented to the world was deceptive. It showed competence and self-assurance. Inwardly, she was insecure. She desperately wanted to be loved. A legacy of her childhood, no doubt.

That was another reason why Simon would leave such a void. He idolised her. Not only was he a lover who lifted up her spirits to the heavens, he was also her rock, her refuge. He had never, ever failed her.

And I've thrown him out like a pair of old shoes, she told herself. I must be out of my mind!

She glanced down at his photo on the dressing table. She herself had taken it at Beachy Head. Laughing eyes, curly fair hair blowing in the wind. He had very unruly eyebrows. Sarah had adored his eyebrows.

She leapt up from her seat. She was becoming morbid again. Dwelling in the past when what she had to do was to look forward. Be positive. The past was past. Only the future held any relevance.

With a decisive movement, she picked up the photo-frame and slipped it into the bottom of one of her drawers . . .

Out of sight but he wouldn't be out of mind. She didn't deceive herself about that.

Chapter Two

Winnie Seeberg laughed. It was a hearty, deep-throated, body-shaking laugh that made her sides ache . . .

Her amusement was caused by the sight of a pompous young man whom she'd never liked falling fully-clothed into the shallow end of her swimming pool.

'The stupid jerk!' she exclaimed, wiping her eyes. 'What possessed him to stand there dressed in his city suit?'

The elderly man beside her agreed. They watched as City Suit struggled to make the rail where he was hauled out, dripping and forlorn.

'My spectacles!' he wailed.

At that moment, everyone lost interest in City Suit. Several heads had swivelled round and Winnie followed their gaze. Sarah Castle, her brother's daughter, had appeared from the house and was advancing towards the poolside. She looked ravishing. The emerald bikini showed up her tanned skin and shapely curves. Glowing dark hair and eyes completed the picture.

Winnie cherished the esteem in which her niece was held. Sarah was the pride of her life – more like a daughter than a niece. Beautiful, forthright, sensual, in looks she was the image of her mother but, thank God, she hadn't inherited Ella's character.

Sarah waved to everyone and dived into the pool, cleaving the water as she swam its length. Instead of surfacing immediately, she retrieved City Suit's spectacles and returned them to the owner.

For Winnie it marked the end of a pleasant diversion. She sighed contentedly.

Fifteen years ago, the Seebergs had transferred their business from New York to London. Subsequently, following her husband's untimely death, she'd remained in Britain and bought Sandalwood, her Sussex estate.

It was near the coast, within easy reach of London, and Winnie's engaging personality made her an ever-popular hostess. She loved that role and her house parties were a byword among London's artistic and professional people.

'I like to see people enjoying themselves,' she said to her companion without moving her eyes from the swimmers.

'They've more energy than I have these days.'

'Still, we've had our time, Harry. I don't regret getting fat or growing old, do you? It's enough for me to see folk having fun.' She spread her hands to embrace everyone. 'I keep old age at bay by having youngsters around me.'

'Meaning Sarah in particular?'

'Yep. Meaning Sarah in particular.' As she spoke, she was watching her niece climb out of the water and begin towelling herself. 'I can't tell you what she means to me.'

'She's weathered everything OK.'

'Oh, she has but it was hell for her at the time. I'm sure you don't realise the half of it. When she was little, she was dragged around by Ella from New York to Los Angeles, not getting any proper love.'

'Except from you.'

'Yeah, well, that was the easy bit. The trouble was after we moved to the UK, there was the Atlantic Ocean separating us. But I had my way in the end. I sent her to boarding school over here and had her to live with me during the vacations.' She expelled her breath angrily. 'What makes me so damned sore is that Ella couldn't have cared less about her during childhood, but since Sarah's been grown-up her mother wants to organise her life.'

'Does Sarah intend to return to the States?'

'Shouldn't think so. She's twenty-six and, like me, she's well settled. Besides, her mother's over there.' Winnie guffawed again. 'That'd be enough to put Sarah off.'

They lapsed into silence. A servant was setting up the

14

barbeque and, on the patio, the butler was preparing pre-dinner drinks. Sarah was walking towards them.

'Hi, there. Having fun?' Winnie asked.

Sarah ran her fingers through her hair. 'I always do here,' she said as the butler came up carrying a silver salver bearing a glass for his mistress.

'Your usual, Mrs. Seeberg.'

'Thanks, Charles.'

'And Miss Castle? A dry Martini?' Sarah nodded.

Before the butler returned with the drinks, a large black Rolls-Royce appeared in the drive.

Inwardly, Winnie groaned. Sarah had become visibly tense, her mouth a tight line. The reason was all too obvious. Ella St. Clair, her mother, had arrived.

From the driver's seat emerged a tall middle-aged man with grizzled grey hair. He looked around him with a supercilious air before turning to help his companion out of the vehicle.

It was immediately obvious that Ella was a celebrity. Having stepped out on to the flagstones, she turned her head slowly to register that she had an audience, then removed her sunglasses with an elegant sweep as if uncovering her beautiful eyes for all to see.

She was dressed for stardom instead of an alfresco party. The electric blue dress clung to her figure and exposed to the thigh a flash of shapely leg covered in black nylon. She balanced on high stiletto heels, and several significant diamonds glittered on her fingers. In that setting, Ella St. Clair was an incongruity but remained blissfully unaware of it.

Sarah walked over to greet her mother.

It was an ideal evening for a barbeque. The heat of the day had given way to a cool sea-borne breeze.

Winnie's cook was an old hand at barbeques and knew exactly how to serve the steaks and kebabs to everyone's satisfaction. Laughter and chatter accompanied the supper but, for Sarah, much of the pleasure had gone out of the evening.

She'd been under the impression that her mother was safely ensconced in London where she was playing a short season in the West End and wouldn't be able to attend the party. She'd forgotten that the season didn't start until Monday. Today was Saturday.

So, instead of having a companionable evening with her friends, Sarah was forced to give her mother more attention than she felt she could spare. And she had to suffer the company of the tall, grey-haired man.

Sir Reece Brown was his name; an old friend of her mother's, he explained. And he had come especially to meet the stunning daughter of the equally glamorous Ella St. Clair. Sarah shuddered at the description. His eyes raked her, lingering over the curves of her body.

In spite of her dislike, Sarah had to admit that Sir Reece — with his finely-cut features and head of grey, curly hair — was not unattractive. In his mid-fifties, she reckoned. Very distinguished.

But his eyes were cold, calculating and insolent. A male chauvinist, clearly. And when he addressed her, it was in a patronising tone. This angered Sarah for she wouldn't be downgraded on account of her sex. To some of his remarks, she gave tart replies. Several times, he raised his eyebrows at her responses. This gave her a degree of satisfaction.

She'd been forewarned about Sir Reece. As a commercial tycoon, he was at the top of his world. His orders were obeyed without question. When, however, he was in the company of desirable women, he was prepared to waive his superiority in order to charm and to ingratiate himself.

'I feel your male business associates must have a difficult time of it.'

'Why?'

'How can they concentrate? They must find it hard to keep their eyes off you.'

She smiled an acknowledgement but said nothing.

'By the way, what do you do for a living?' he asked.

Sarah was determined to be vague. 'Oh, a little bit of this and a little bit of that.'

'Fascinating!'

'Oh, it is.'

Just then, Auntie Win appeared at their table with a young man and addressed Sarah. 'Des was saying he'd like to stretch his legs, honey, so why don't you two go for a stroll?'

The idea appealed. A walk would offer an escape from her present company. Knowing her aunt, she guessed that was precisely why she'd made the suggestion.

'Yes, why not?'

Ella intersposed quickly: 'We can all go.'

Winnie glared at her sister-in-law. 'In those heels, Ella? You'd never make it. Besides, I thought we older ones ...' she paused as Ella bristled '... could play a little bridge.'

Ella made no audible retort.

'Let's go,' Des said.

Sarah had enjoyed the walk. They'd been able to discuss their respective careers – hers in journalism, his in television.

Thanks to Winnie's parties, they were old friends and were easy in one another's company. But because he preferred men to women, their relationship was free of sexual overtones.

In her bedroom later, she was going over their discussion when her thoughts were rudely interrupted. The door was pushed open and her mother marched in. The mask of stardom had been removed; beneath it was a face that looked like thunder. There was no one here for Ella to impress.

'What the hell are you playing at?' she began. 'I bring Reece all the way down here to this rustic retreat to meet you. And what d'you do? You go off with that Des. He's gay, isn't he?'

Sarah concealed her feelings. She moved over and closed the door firmly before speaking. 'Now, look, Mom –'

'Don't call me "Mom". Can't stand it. I'm Ella to you, as you damn well know!'

'What if he is gay? I've known Des a long time.'

'Huh! What does he do for a living?'

'He's in TV. He's just become a producer.'

'Just become! So what? He's still a nothing. Reece is something – somebody – now. Now! Think of that. He's the president of dozens of companies. He's absolutely loaded and he's buying up papers like crazy. He could do a hell of a lot for you.'

'Really?' Sarah murmured without interest.

'What must Reece have thought of you, going off with that Des? Anyway, I smoothed it over, told him you were a journalist and said you'd be glad to meet him.'

17

Sarah was furious. 'You had no right to do that.'

'Listen to me. I'm only thinking of your good.'

'Really?'

'Reece is a tycoon, a real big shot, and he can smooth the way for you, make things easy.'

'I'm not interested.'

'With his money, he could do anything for you – help you meet the right people – Royalty perhaps. I guess he'd be more than willing to set you up in a flat, too.'

Sarah exploded. 'You want me to be a bimbo, is that your ambition for me? Let me tell you, Ella, you know nothing about me whatsoever. I'm not like you. Not a bit. Of course I want a successful career. But I'll do it my way.'

'Like I said, Reece will oil the wheels.'

'You just don't understand. Never will. Before I sleep with someone, I make sure I love him first.'

Ella sneered. 'You've been reading romantic fiction or watching old movies. Love doesn't exist. You haven't lived, Sarah. I tell you, what sophisticated folks get out of so-called romance is sex. Sex and money and power! That's all there is and don't you forget it.'

Sarah felt sick. 'Well, I disagree,' she said. 'And you can warn Reece that if he tries to proposition me, I'll tell him to get lost.'

'Why, you stupid bitch! Can't you see I'm trying to help you? And just bear this in mind – Reece *will* be calling you and you'd better be nice to him. I'm warning you.'

And with that, she flounced out of the room, slamming the door loudly behind her.

Sarah didn't move. Her mother's belief that she couldn't achieve success without sleeping with Sir Reece Brown was an insult. It was also a challenge.

Even so, what a holier-than-thou tone she'd adopted just now. She wasn't really a prig and regretted having spoken like that. On the other hand, she genuinely disliked the promiscuity with which Ella conducted her own love life. Surely there must be middle way? If so, Sarah was determined to find it.

If she'd had sneaking doubts about parting from Simon, she had none now. She had picked up the gauntlet that Ella had thrown down and it gave her a wonderful feeling of exhilaration. Of freedom, too. She might even start of a new affair if the chance of one presented itself. But there would be no strings. Definitely no strings.

Sarah moved over to the window. The moon had come out and the light was playing on the water of the pool. On the far side, a young couple were holding hands. Looking into each other's eyes. Whispering sweet nothings.

She thought again of Simon and her eyes misted over. She had a vision of the disbelief on his face when she'd ended their affair; felt a stabbing pain in her own heart. Neither the vision nor the pain would go away.

Against the odds Sarah slept well. In the morning she felt refreshed and her spirits were lighter. They lifted still higher during the day. Avoiding Ella and Reece as much as possible, she swam a lot and had fun with friends.

It was only in the late evening that things went badly wrong. Her car wouldn't start.

Des said, 'I think it's your plugs, darling.'

She was sure it wasn't the plugs but didn't say so. He was doing his best and she didn't want to discourage him.

They were standing on the drive at Sandalwood, staring down at the engine, hoping that − like the oracle − it would give them the answer. But it held on to its secret.

All that they did know for certain was that they couldn't get it to fire.

It couldn't have happened at a worse time. After an enjoyable weekend, she had to drive back tonight without fail. It was already becoming dark. By the time the breakdown service arrived, she'd be very late in getting away, and she didn't fancy driving through the night.

Des couldn't give her a lift because he wasn't returning to London immediately. She didn't know what to do.

Auntie Win's gardener came by. He touched his cap and offered to help. He tried the engine several times and gave his considered opinion.

'Your ignition's gone, Miss. Reckon 'tis the condenser. Might be wrong, mind, but that's my thinking.'

'Is it easy to repair?'

'Can't repair 'em, Miss. Got to get a new one.'

19

As she was turning over the possibilities, two powerful headlights swung round from the front of the house. A car was coming in their direction, the lights blinding them. No, not just any car . . . The Rolls-Royce slowed down and pulled up.

Reece called out: 'Having trouble?'

Sarah couldn't deny it.

Ella, sitting in the front passenger seat, said, 'We'll drive you up to town, won't we, Reece?'

'Delighted.'

Sarah hesitated but it was obvious she'd have to accept. At least she wouldn't be alone with Reece. That was something. For once, she welcomed her mother's company.

Having made arrangements about her own car and said goodbye to Des, she stepped into the spacious rear of the Rolls. She sank against its accommodating upholstery, enjoying the feeling of luxury which it gave.

Despite the circumstances, it was a pleasant drive. Ella wasn't disparaging towards her and Reece showed more friendliness than before. The time sped by.

When they reached the London outskirts, Reece didn't make for her home suburb, as requested. Instead, he drove straight on towards the city centre. She pointed this out but he just smiled. To have protested further would have made her seem gauche. She didn't want that so she said no more.

Over Waterloo Bridge, into the Strand. He parked outside the Savoy and alighted. A commissionaire opened the door for Ella and took her bags. Reece kissed her lightly and she gave a small wave in her daughter's direction. Was there a hint of triumph on her face?

So that was how they wanted to play it. Sarah put on her most blasé expression and moved into the front seat, vacated by Ella. She had no intention of giving her mother the satisfaction of seeing her at a loss. And if Reece was going to play games, he might get more than he'd bargained for!

'Where shall we go?' he said when they were on the move again. 'Somewhere discreet, of course.'

So that was the planned scenario. He did have games in mind, then. She, though, had no intention of playing.

'Nowhere, thanks, Reece. Just home.' She put as much force into her voice as she could.

He glanced at her, making sure she meant what she said. 'There's a nice little club round the corner. We could have a dance, something to drink. You'd enjoy it.'

'Thank you, Reece, but no. I must go home.'

'You do disappoint me.' He was angry. She could tell that by the way he sucked in his breath and swung the car round with only a cursory warning to the traffic behind. He didn't speak for some time.

At last, he said, 'You live in Bromley, don't you?'

'Yes.'

'You'll have to direct me to where you live.'

When they reached her block of flats, he carried her weekend valise up to her front door.

She'd already decided she'd have to ask him in for a quick drink. He accepted with alacrity.

Once inside, he started to remove the light jacket from her shoulders. In doing so, he slid his hands up her arms gently, seductively. He spoke in a whisper. 'Oh, my dear, you're very, very beautiful.'

This wasn't quite the moment for a showdown, she thought. With a deft movement, she was out of his grasp and stepping towards her small drinks cabinet.

'Now, what would you like, Reece?'

'A brandy would be very acceptable.' His voice had lost much of its velvet quality.

Over their drinks, she studied him and confirmed her first impression. Classical features. Undoubtedly handsome. But no warmth, no soul. An aloof, unsmiling man.

Not wanting to prolong the evening more than was necessary, Sarah drank quickly. And, taking his cue from her, so did he. That was to have been the extent of her hospitality but she relented. Upon reflection, she thought she'd better offer him another one.

While she was bending over to take his empty glass, he made another pass. This time, he took her hands and tried to pull her down beside him. 'I wish you'd let me be your friend.'

'I'm sure you already are my friend,' she replied lightly, trying without success to straighten up.

'But I mean like this.' He dragged her down lower. Her toe

21

caught on his foot and she fell on to his knee. His free hand was already slipping up her skirt.

Sarah thought quickly. She refused to give an impression of outraged modesty which would only have reduced the situation to farce. On the other hand, she had no intention of succumbing.

Instead, she adopted the tone of a stage school-ma'am. 'My goodness, Reece,' she said, at the same time clamping her hand over his to stop it exploring further. 'We barely know each other.' She twisted aside, slid off his knee and moved away.

Refusing to be beaten, he followed her. Sarah had had more than enough. Placing both hands on his chest, she pushed. Very hard.

He hadn't expected this. Rebuffs were not part of his experience, it seemed. He stumbled and lost his balance. He also lost his dignity. But he regained it quickly. Drawing himself up to his full height and straightening his tie, he glared at her.

What cold eyes! Ice blue. Unforgiving.

'I will bid you goodnight.'

How pompous he sounded! She wanted to laugh. She didn't, though, but thanked him politely for the lift home. He took his leave without another word. She didn't even watch him go down the stairs.

For her, closing the door was almost symbolic. She hoped it would mark the end of their association.

Chapter Three

Sir Reece Brown stretched himself in his chair and re-applied his mind to the work in hand.

His desk, consisting only of a large sheet of plate glass supported by tubular, chromed legs, had a futuristic appearance. On its surface were a phone, an intercom, a pen tray, a digital clock. Nothing more except the company report on which he was working. He read it studiously with pursed lips, sometimes raising his eyebrows as he pencilled notes in the margins.

Reece's office, on the second floor of his headquarters, reflected the bleak personality of the man. The rest of the furniture matched the desk. It was simple in design and extremely functional. There were no soft furnishings, no frills. The only concessions to art were surrealistic paintings on three of the walls. The fourth was taken up by an enormous picture window.

But Reece seldom even saw the paintings. He believed that an office was for work and nothing else.

Having finished the report, he pushed it to one side and paused awhile, thinking. His foray with Sarah on Sunday had been a failure. But no matter. He was disappointed but not entirely surprised. He would try again.

She was a young woman of spirit. He liked that; it would add spice to the adventure of chasing her. Think of the excitement when, in the end, he had his way. He would win eventually, of that he was certain. No woman could ever resist the lure of money. Neither would she.

He came to a decision and pressed the intercom. 'Come in here a minute, will you, Miss Clark?'

A moment later, a tall angular woman came into the room, notebook and pen in hand. His choice of secretary complemented his taste in office furniture. He believed that his women acolytes should be plain in appearance and strictly functional. Dalliance he reserved solely for out of office hours.

He pushed the report across to her. 'This has to be processed immediately. It's urgent.'

'Yes, Sir Reece.'

'Oh, and I want you to send two bouquets of flowers. Make them large ones, from the best florist. You know how I like these things done. The first is to be sent to Ella St. Clair at the Savoy. And the second is for Miss Sarah Castle. Her address is in my book. And find out Miss Castle's phone number from Directory Enquiries.'

'Very well. And what card would you like attached to the flowers? Your private one, I assume?'

'Of course. The one with my London address. There's no message. See that they go off first thing tomorrow, will you?'

'Yes, sir.'

'One more thing. Get my son on the phone and tell him I want to see him here in the morning at nine sharp. That will be all.'

Miss Clark nodded and left the room.

Reece remained in his chair and began reflecting upon his only son. His thoughts, though, were not coloured by loving paternalism. They never had been.

Reece accepted he was taking a great gamble in placing Max in the managing director's chair of his new company. But the Examiner Group was, after all, only a small one and Reece would be able to keep a close watch on what was happening there. And it was just conceivable that his only son might take naturally to the newspaper business.

If only a good physique and an engaging personality could guarantee success in commerce! Reece grudgingly admitted that his son had an abundance of charm. Women adored him and succumbed easily to his advances. What a pity his business abilities didn't match his prowess between the sheets.

Max had been a great disappointment to Reece. The trouble was he took after his mother. He lacked drive and was not dedicated to hard work. Moreover, he was disobedient, and that was something Reece could not tolerate. As supreme head of his corporation, he demanded absolute and immediate subservience from all his underlings, including his relatives. That any of them might have wishes and a mind of their own did not occur to him. As Reece saw things, everything and everyone within his purview was his to control as he thought fit.

The only exceptions to this rule were his mistresses who were placed in a slightly different category. With them he could be very indulgent – until, that is, the time came to move them on.

In the case of Alison, his current girlfriend, that question hadn't so far arisen. She hadn't been with him long and still had novelty value. That was not to say he didn't like to get away from her now and again. His recent trip to Sandalwood had been a case in point.

He knew she hadn't swallowed his excuse that he was going to a business conference in Wales. When he'd told her he'd be away, she'd just smiled in that enigmatic way of hers and said nothing.

Reece glanced at the digital clock on his desk. Fifteen minutes to six. Plenty of time for him to get ready for his evening appointment. He rose decisively and left the office.

On the way out, Miss Clark said: 'Oh, sir, I've tried Directory Enquiries and they say that Miss Castle's number is ex-directory. Also, I've contacted your son. He promises to be here at nine sharp.'

'Good!'

He dismissed her with a nod and strode out of the office without another word.

Half an hour later, he alighted from a cab outside the London flat which he used during most weekdays. Although he found the place a little restricting, it was more convenient than Glenhurst, the mansion in Surrey where he usually spent his weekends.

Alison was in the bedroom, sitting at her dressing table brushing her hair. She kept her eyes on the mirror but inclined

25

her head slightly so that he could kiss her cheek. She smiled at him.

His hands were on her bare shoulders. 'You're very beautiful. Is it any wonder that I love you?'

'Love? You don't know the meaning of the word, my dear.'

'Do you?'

'No.'

They both laughed.

Reece moved over to the window overlooking Mayfair. 'Perhaps you're right. But we both understand business. And we have a good arrangement, don't we? You enjoy a very good life style; you want for nothing and live in two elegant homes. In return, you –'

'Give you my body.'

He shrugged. 'I wouldn't have put it as crudely as that.'

'But I would.' She resumed her brushing. 'Not that I mind – as long as you don't regard me as part of your personal property, that's all.'

He chose to make no comment as he watched the passing traffic. 'I have to dine out tonight, I'm afraid.'

'Who is she?'

'It's a "he" – a very tedious industrialist who'll bore the pants off me. Still, I'll have to put up with that. He doesn't know it yet but I'm planning to buy him up soon. Then I'll be able to put him out to grass with the other old hacks, where he deserves to be.'

'That's all right, then. I don't mind you spending your evenings with businessmen.'

'Oh, good. I'm glad of that.' His tone was heavily ironic.

'But if it were a woman you were seeing, it'd be a different matter. Like this "conference".' She gave the word a special nuance. She half-turned and gave him a honeyed smiled. 'You won't forget, will you, Reece, that I'm not a chattel to be picked up and put down on a whim?'

She considered again her reflected image and smoothed her eyebrows in place. In the mirror, she saw him move towards her, felt his lips on her neck, his face in her hair.

'What is that perfume?'

'The one you bought me last week.'

'Ah, yes! Very seductive. We understand each other perfectly.'

She looked at him straight. 'Perfectly.'

Max Brown had always been afraid of his father, and the prospect of the interview at headquarters filled him with dismay. It was too much like being summoned to the house-master's study at boarding school and having to explain why he'd not done his prep. He tried to calm himself by looking out of the train window at the vista of suburbia as it flashed by.

He'd decided against driving up to London from Glenhurst because of possible traffic problems. If he arrived late, he would start off on the wrong foot because his father could not tolerate unpunctuality.

I'm not experienced enough, he thought, to be managing director of the Examiner Group. I'm only twenty-six after all. No matter if Father had his first company at twenty-two. I'm not him. I don't even want to be.

He's testing me, of course; trying me out. And he'll be breathing down my neck, seeing that I do things *his* way. It's going to be hell. Hope I'll be able to stand it.

Max sighed at the future he envisaged for himself.

His father was obsessed by his possessions — the companies he owned, the people who worked for him. Any of them could be purchased or discarded at will.

And he, Max, was one of those assets. As the only son, he was the heir. But that afforded him neither comfort nor sense of security. His father could disinherit him as easily as batting an eyelid.

He had a vision of his mother — beautiful and gracious. She too had been one of his father's choicest belongings until finally she'd rebelled and left him. Max had been too young then to understand much of what was happening. Years later, he learnt that his father had fought her in the courts and had won the custody battle.

With her departure, warmth and love had gone out of his life. A childhood spent with Father had been a poor substitute for what his mother had given him. As a child, he had always assumed this was his fault and that Daddy was displeased with him. So he tried to smarten himself up, to be helpful and bright.

27

But Daddy never seemed to notice. After a time Max gave up trying.

He realised that the train had come to a halt. Craning his neck through the open window, he discovered that they were near Vauxhall Station. A signal ahead showed red. He glanced at his watch. He was still in good time for his appointment.

But the minutes ticked by. Five. Ten. Fifteen. Max was becoming alarmed. Head out of the window again, he looked at the signal, willing it to change and let them through. At last it did, and Max sat back in his seat, praying there would be no more hold ups.

At Waterloo, though, there was a long queue at the taxi rank and he fretted at the enforced delay. But it was the rush hour and traffic was very dense.

In the end, he arrived at his destination, breathless and ill at ease. The clock in the entrance hall showed ten minutes past nine.

'Your father is expecting you, Mr Brown,' Miss Clark said as he approached her desk. 'Will you please go straight in?'

Max pushed open the door of the office. His father, standing by the window, whipped round.

'You're late.'

'I'm sorry. The train was held up.'

'Train? Why didn't you come by car?'

'I thought the train would be more reliable.'

'Well, it wasn't. You made an error of judgement. You should have allowed for hold-ups and caught an earlier one.'

'Yes. I'll do that next time.'

His father stood for some moments, surveying him with an expression that suggested he didn't like what he saw. Reece's bearing never varied. He was an aloof, humourless man with thin lips and cold eyes. The features could have been hewn from stone, Max thought.

'Humph! Now that you're here, we'd better get down to business. Sit down. No, not over there − here, facing me where I can see you.'

Max sat. Reece took his place at the desk and smoothed his hands over the glass surface. His exquisitely manicured hands said a lot about him. They revealed the innate fastidiousness which he exhibited in all things. Max had suffered from this all his life.

Reece cleared his throat and appeared to make an effort to be pleasant. He put a trace of warmth into his voice. 'Now, my boy, let's not start our discussion on a note of discord. We've important business to cover. In many ways, I envy you. You're starting your career with so many more advantages than I had at your age. After all, you've been to university and, since then, had some experience in management. It's time now to put into practice all that you've learnt.'

'I'm looking forward to it.'

'You are? Good.' Reece sounded surprised.

'It's a challenge.'

'It is, indeed. The Examiner Group is a very viable little company with its evening paper covering the southern home counties. Tell me, how do you envisage the group developing? It can't be allowed to remain static. We're going to change things – or you are. You must have given this matter some thought already.'

Max hadn't given it any thought at all. He had assumed his task was to keep the ship on an even keel and maintain its course. Faced with the questioning gaze across the desk, he floundered. His answer was unconvincing and he could tell his father wasn't deceived.

'Remember, Max, growth is the essence of good business practice. You'll have to give that a lot of consideration in the near future.'

'I will, Father.'

'You realise, of course, that one of our priorities must be to dismiss the present board and replace them with my nominees. I've drawn up a list of names and I'll let you have it tomorrow.'

'Fine.'

'Remember this – you are the management and your business is to manage. Stand no nonsense whatsoever from the journalistic staff.'

'They won't like that.'

'What they like or dislike is neither here nor there. They'll do as they're told. From the very beginning, show them your authority. And you are to let me have the names of all senior journalistic personnel. I want to have them vetted and to check whether I have anything against them.'

'Very well.'

His father swivelled his chair round and looked out of the window. It was some time before he spoke again. 'When I was a schoolboy, I collected stamps and cigarette cards. Now, I collect companies which cover a broad spectrum of industries – as you are aware. That in itself is satisfying but there's always been something missing.' He became silent and swivelled his chair round to face Max once more. 'So I bought the Examiner Group to fill that gap.'

'I don't quite follow.'

Sir Reece gave one of his rare smiles. 'No, I thought you wouldn't. My plan is that the Examiner should be just a start to my publishing interests. You see, I'm engaged in delicate negotiations at the moment to acquire another newspaper group – not a provincial one this time but one consisting of a couple of national dailies and a clutch of magazines.' He waited for this to sink in. 'Do you know why I'm doing this?'

'No, Father.'

'Because newspaper publishing can provide what few other businesses can offer – virtually unlimited power. Think of that, my boy. *Power*.'

Chapter Four

'Miss Castle?'

'Yes.'

'These are for you, Miss.' Sarah eyed with surprise the enormous bouquet the man was holding. 'Sign here, please. You can use my pen.'

'Thank you.' She did as directed and took the flowers.

'Right, Miss. Cheers.' The man gave her a cheeky grin and ran down the stairs, whistling.

When she'd closed the door again, one glance at the attached card made her start. Sir Reece Brown! Her immediate reaction was one of extreme annoyance. He didn't give up easily, did he? Couldn't he get the message?

But the flowers were certainly beautiful. Shame to waste them. She arranged them in a cut glass vase and looked around for a suitable spot.

To put them on the console table would partly hide a favourite miniature bronze. She couldn't bear to do that. And the top of the bookcase facing the door would be much too high for such a large bouquet. In the end, she settled on the Benares table by the window. There, the dove grey of her velvet curtains would be an ideal backdrop for the yellows and reds of the flowers.

Meanwhile, she had other matters to occupy her. Tomorrow, she was due to start her new job and she wanted to be mentally alert. She planned a lightly cooked supper, a leisurely evening watching television and then an early night.

By ten-thirty she was already in bed but far from sleep. Her mind was too active, dwelling on all the challenges that lay ahead. She picked up a book, hoping it would help her to doze off. It didn't.

She lay back on the pillow but didn't switch off the bedside light. The bedroom seemed wrong somehow. She'd noticed this for some days. Unfriendly. She couldn't say why.

Then the truth dawned. Simon's photo was no longer in its familiar place. Hadn't she herself hidden it away after their final night together?'

She slipped out of bed and retrieved it from her bottom drawer, dusted it with the palm of her hand and replaced it on the corner of her dressing table. Darling Simon. He would be thinking of her tomorrow, she knew.

She returned to her bed, gave the photo a last look and switched out the light. Reassured, she fell asleep.

The very moment she walked into her new office, Sarah decided she was not going to like Louise Gifford. There was an air about her new assistant that she could not immediately define. She only knew it made her uneasy.

Louise was about her own age and seemed reluctant to communicate. Short in stature, she had a round face, snub nose and fair hair that was carelessly brushed back behind her ears.

The women's page office was only a large cubicle partitioned off from the main reporters' room. To reach it, Sarah had had to run the gauntlet of the male staff, some of whom had ogled her on the way.

'Not very large, is it?' she remarked as she sat at her desk which was cheek by jowl with the one Louise used.

'Oh, you get used to it.'

'I shan't. We're almost sitting in each other's laps. Only one filing cabinet, I see. And what about reference files?'

Louise pointed to a small metal card index. 'That's it.'

Sarah was horrified. 'We'll have to do better than that. I shall aim at a comprehensive system – individuals, institutions, that sort of thing – all listed and cross indexed. We must have good, reliable references.'

'There are a lot of things *I'd* like.' Louise sounded prickly. 'I've been on my own for months, don't forget.'

'Oh, I realise that. That wasn't a criticism, Louise – just

an observation. Now, what stories have we got for our page? Anything interesting?'

'Well, there's a local woman who's just returned from a trip up the Amazon.'

'Great. We might lead on that – unless something else crops up. Can I see it?'

Louise rummaged on her desk and passed over three slips of copy paper. Sarah scanned through the typescript quickly. The style was turgid and uninspired. Her own taste was for good, punchy writing. Certainly she would have to make a change of style an urgent priority but sensed she might find Louise a reluctant convert.

A face appeared round the open doorway – a grinning, male face that possessed a lot of teeth and a pair of watery eyes.

'Hello,' said the newcomer. 'Glad to make your acquaintance, Sarah. I'm Kevin – sports page editor. Anything you want, just come to Kevin. Remember that.' His eyes swept over her. 'I'd be glad to be of service.'

'Kind of you, Kevin.'

Mercifully, the internal phone buzzed and he disappeared. Sarah picked up the receiver and heard a woman's voice. The editor's secretary, apparently. 'Miss Castle? Mr. Sanders would like to see you now if you're free.'

'Fine. I'll be right along.'

Bob Sanders greeted her warmly as she went into his room. 'Welcome to the *Examiner*, Sarah. I hope you'll be very happy here and stay with us a long time.'

'I'm sure I shall.'

Bob was a small, genial man with an easygoing manner which, Sarah guessed, concealed a highly disciplined mind. 'Coffee?' he offered.

'Love one.'

The secretary brought in two plastic cups from the coffee dispenser and returned to her own office.

'Sugar?'

'No, thanks.'

'Do I detect a trace of an American accent?'

Sarah laughed. 'Yes, Boston. I thought it'd largely disappeared by now. I'm American but I've lived over

33

here since I was a youngster. I'm almost English after all this time.'

'You still have the American self-confidence.' Sarah made no reply. 'You might be interested to know that was one reason why we appointed you – your dynamism. Probably your high-powered American blood.'

She laughed it off. 'Must be.'

'None of the other candidates showed the same drive as you.' He paused and re-adjusted his spectacles. 'A small point – one of those who applied for your job was Louise Gifford, your assistant. I thought you ought to know. She might be a bit touchy.'

'Thanks for the warning!'

'How long were you on your last paper, by the way?'

'Four years. I went there straight from college and did the usual grind – flower shows, district reporting and all that – before going on to women's features.'

'Your last editor spoke very highly of you.'

'I'm glad.'

They discussed the group's catchment area, the social classes of its readership, and editorial policy. Of the paper, and of the women's page in particular.

Those items dispensed with, Bob asked: 'Anything you don't like so far?'

Sarah smiled. 'Yes, plenty. My office for a start. I'd like a new one, please.' He blinked at her and leant back in his chair.

She told him of her objections. It was too small for one thing and was only accessible through the main reporters' room. 'And there's no privacy. That might inhibit people coming to see me.'

'OK, I get your point. It so happens, we do have a room free. I think we could let you have that.'

'Great.'

'Now, Sarah, I have something to ask you. I don't want a women's page just dealing with newsy items and feature snippets. I want something more and I know you can supply it. I want you to run a correspondence column devoted to women's personal problems.'

'Agony aunt stuff?'

'In short – yes.'

'Isn't that a bit unusual for a provincial evening paper like ours?'

'It is. But my philosophy is that anything the nationals do we can have a damn good crack at.'

She thought this over. 'It's quite a tall order and I haven't done anything like it before.'

'I know that. But I believe you can take it on – otherwise I wouldn't have asked you.'

'Well then, if you want me to be an agony aunt, I'll certainly need secretarial help and an editorial junior as well.'

Bob puffed out his cheeks. 'You're asking a lot, Sarah. I don't have an unlimited budget.'

'Without the tools, I won't be able to do the job.'

'It's that American dynamism showing through again. OK, I give in. Anyway, think about the whole project and let me know what you feel.'

'Actually, I've already made up my mind. I find it quite a stimulating prospect.'

'I thought you would.' Bob rose from his seat and she followed suit. 'Oh, before you go – there's one other thing you ought to know. We – the Examiner Group, that is – have recently been taken over. The new owners have their fingers in almost everything as far as I can find out but this is their first venture into newspaper publishing.'

'Will this affect us, do you think?'

'I doubt it. Our last proprietors owned a tin mine among other things and they never interfered with editorial matters. I don't suppose the new people will be any different. I just wanted you to be in the picture, that's all. Don't let it bother you.'

'Thanks. I won't.'

Late that evening, the phone rang at home.

'Damn!' Sarah wiped her hands on the kitchen towel and went through to the sitting room. She picked up the receiver.

'Sarah?' A smooth voice, silken in texture. She recognised it at once.

'Yes. Sarah Castle.'

'Hello, my dear. It's Reece.'

Trying to recover from her surprise and anger, she thanked him for the flowers. He assured her it was only a small token of his esteem.

'I must apologise for the other night, Sarah. Don't blame me, please. I simply could not resist you.'

'That's perfectly all right.'

He said he hoped they could be friends.

Trying to humour him, she said: 'Of course. By the way, my phone number is ex-directory — very few people have it.'

'I know. Your mother gave it me.'

Something else to take up with Ella!

He was still speaking. 'I'm ringing, my dear, because I'd be delighted if you'd have dinner with me one evening.'

She knew she had to speak plainly and put an end to this nonsense once and for all.

'It's kind of you,' she said, 'but I'm afraid I'll have to decline. There would be no point in our meeting. I'm sorry to have to be so blunt but really I — '

'You disappoint me.' His voice held a sharp edge. 'I'd expected you to be more sophisticated.' The doorbell rang loudly. 'It appears you have a visitor. It must be your chaperone. I won't detain you.'

Thankfully, she replaced the receiver and opened the front door to find Simon standing there. In the joy of seeing his friendly, familiar face she fell into his arms.

'What a welcome sight you are! Come in.'

Then, she remembered their parting. 'But what are you doing here? It's over between us.'

'Yes, well, I refuse to accept that.'

'Simon, we made an agreement.'

He swept her up in his arms and kissed her. 'I've decided I'm not going to stick to it.' Still carrying her, he moved over to examine the flowers by the windows. 'Sir Reece Brown? Who's he? An admirer?'

'He's odious. A friend of Ella's. I've just choked him off for pestering me. Are you going to put me down?'

'If you kiss me first.' She did so. 'OK, you may stand down.'

When she'd regained the floor, she clapped her hands over her ears. 'Oh, God! I've just remembered I've got something in the oven and it'll be ruined now.'

She ran into the kitchen, uttered a cry of dismay and returned to the sitting room. 'Well, my supper's a total write-off. It'll have to be bread and cheese, that's all.'

'No, it won't. I'm taking you out. How about the Chinese nosh house in the town? We'll go in my car.'

'Fine. You're very exuberant tonight, Simon.'

'And why not? I've escaped temporarily from my new lodgings – which by the way, are unutterably dreary – and I'm with the girl I love. Anyway, how are you getting on with your new job.'

'I'll tell you in due course. Right now, I have to tidy myself up. Won't be a minute.'

True to her promise, she reappeared a few moments later, jeans replaced by a skirt, and hair tidied. On her wrist, she wore a favourite silver bracelet engraved with her initials.

On the way to the Chinese restaurant she told him of the agony aunt project and he continued his lament over his move away from her.

The Pagoda, a favourite of theirs, was only a short drive away and they reached it quickly. The head waiter always greeted them as favourite customers and tonight was no exception.

While they were waiting for the dishes to be served, silence fell. Perhaps the dim lights and the subdued atmosphere inhibited speech. Other diners were talking quietly.

Meanwhile, Sarah had time for reflection. She'd been far too welcoming to Simon – throwing herself into his arms and talking non-stop. Not in the spirit of their separation at all. She ought to have been more offhand in her manner, however much it would have hurt her.

Perhaps she'd already given him the wrong idea; that breaking off their relationship had been a mere passing whim on her part. She mustn't let him think that.

With the uncorking of the wine and the arrival of the food, they had an excuse not to speak. Handling chopsticks, Sarah had always found, required concentration. It was not until the Chinese green tea arrived and she was nosing its bouquet, that she became aware that Simon seemed unusually quiet and his eyes were lowered.

'What are you thinking about?'

'Us, mainly.'

'Oh!' She slid her hand across the table and took his. It was a reflex action and she was immediately sorry for it. 'I really meant what I said the other night, Simon. It is all over between us. It has to be.'

He withdrew his hand as if scalded. As he spoke, he raised his voice. 'It is *not* all over between us.'

Suddenly aware that two diners at a neighbouring table had turned in their direction, he smiled at them briefly and looked away.

'What I mean is – ' He lowered his voice. 'Look, Sarah, you can't kid me. You love me just as much as I love you. Why torment us both?'

'I'm not doing this from bloody-mindedness, you know.' It was her turn to speak loudly. She glanced across at the other table but the diners were studiously looking into their rice bowls. In a whisper, she went on, 'This is something I've got to do. You used to be sympathetic to my ambitions.'

'Well, yes, but – '

'Don't shout!'

'I'm not shouting.'

Sarah was aware of an unnatural silence in the rest of the restaurant. People were listening to them.

The waiter came up and placed the bill on their table. 'Your check, sir.'

'Thank you.'

'I think he's hinting. We're making an exhibition of ourselves. You'd better take me home.'

'It'll be a pleasure.'

Once back at the flat, Simon was contrite and Sarah was glad to kiss and make up.

'Don't let's fight.'

'I don't want to. I'm sorry I shouted at you.'

'Well, I shouted back. Let me fix you a drink. Scotch?'

'Please.'

She gave him his drink and poured one for herself. Then she kicked off her shoes and sat on the sofa with legs curled up under her.

'So, you're regretting taking this job in the South West? I'm sorry about that.'

'It's humdrum. I hate everything about it. I can't wait to get back up here again. I've missed you like hell.'

Sarah was about to say that she'd missed him too but that would have been another tactical error. She'd already held his hand in the restaurant and shown him too much affection. Her entire behaviour had been a mistake. It was more prudent not to reply.

'You don't mind if I stay the night, do you?' he asked after a long silence, giving her an appealing look.

This was her moment for setting the record straight once and for all. She tried to speak briskly but lost her nerve, taking refuge in an excuse.

'I'm afraid it's the wrong time of the month for me, Simon.' This wasn't true but it offered a convenient escape. She dared not let him sleep with her because he played havoc with her feelings. Right now, she needed all the concentration she could muster for her new responsibilities.

'Oh!' He sounded very deflated. 'Better luck next time, maybe.'

'There mustn't be a next time.'

He lifted his gaze from his drink and looked at her sharply. 'D'you know, I believe you're actually glad – yes, *glad* – that I can't stay. For you it's the great let-out – isn't it? And how eagerly you grabbed it.'

'I didn't have to grab at anything. Surely to God I've made myself plain by now? But it seems I'll have to say it again.' Now, she was beginning to feel genuinely angry and didn't have to act any more. 'How can I ram it into your thick head that it's all over between us?'

He drained his glass at a gulp and stood up. 'Well, that's it then. You obviously still haven't got over this ridiculous obsession of yours.'

'Tell me something, Simon.' Her tone was one of sweet reasonableness. 'Why is it an obsession for me to refuse to move house and follow you? Would you have agreed to do that if I had asked it of you?'

'Well –'

'I remember how desperately you wanted this job in Devon. In the beginning, you were really quite obsessional about it, you know. In other words, you can have an obsession but I can't. But that's different, of course. *You're* a man.'

'You're being unreasonable!'

'There you go again. Simon, you're a bad case of rampant chauvinism. You make out you're so enlightened about women but you're not. You're as hidebound as the rest.'

'Look. What's got into you all of a sudden?'

'I'll tell you what's got into me! My eyes have been opened, that's what.'

'All these high falutin' ideas of yours! Remember, you might not even get the big prize you're seeking. Have you thought of that? Your head's in the clouds, Sarah. You think you're climbing a stairway to success, but it's only dreams. Come down to earth now before you're hurt by disappointment.'

She listened in stunned silence. She wasn't even angry any more. At last, she managed to say, 'What a lucky escape I've had.'

'I don't follow.'

'Can you imagine what our married life would have been like? Me stuck in the house doing the chores, chin-wagging with Mrs. Bloggs over the garden fence, talking about our hubbies. And then, in the evening: "Have you had a good day, dear? Here are your slippers, dear. Put your feet up and have a nice rest. You must be exhausted after your hard day's work, dear. Your supper's almost ready." Ye Gods, what a prospect! I'm glad I saw it in time.'

'After that little monologue, you're not the only one.' He was raising his voice again. 'Let me tell you, I wouldn't marry you now if you begged me to.'

'What makes you think I'd ever stoop so low?'

Simon sucked in his breath, astonished at the speed and vehemence of her retort. For a moment, he was at a loss for words. But the devil was in Sarah now. Her pride had taken a beating and she wanted her revenge. Suddenly, she remembered the bracelet. She undid the clasp and thrust it into his hand.

'And you can take this back!'

He stared at her, expressionless. 'My mother gave you that on your twenty-first birthday,' he said.

In the heat of the moment, she'd forgotten that. But it was

40

too late to retract. 'I want nothing that reminds me of you.' That she had deeply wounded him was obvious from his face. He turned on his heel and left without a backward glance.

The enormity of what she'd done hit her. Stung into action, she ran after him. He was already half-way down the stairs.

'Simon, come back!'

The only answer was the clattering of his footsteps. She heard him cross the tiled entrance hall and the slam of the front door.

After that there was only silence.

Chapter Five

'Do I like it, you say? Frankly, Louise, I think it's appalling.'

Sarah's assistant blinked two or three times, wondering whether she'd heard aright. 'What's wrong with it?'

'Well, quite honestly, there's not much *right* with it. It's just plain dull.'

Louise plumped herself down on her chair. 'Oh!' she said, making her displeasure very apparent.

Sarah knew she sounded tetchy − rude, even. She couldn't help it. She *was* tetchy and rude, ready to explode at any provocation.

The truth was she was feeling very sore about her treatment of Simon. Or, rather, conscience-stricken. And, whenever she knew she was in the wrong she was snappy with other people, as though it were their fault. It was not a very commendable trait. Sometimes, she hated herself for it.

Four days had elapsed since their row, days in which she'd had time to reflect and regret. No doubt about it, she'd been an absolute bitch. Simon hadn't deserved that.

Today, was the start of her first full week as women's editor of the *Southern Examiner* and she'd made a very bad beginning, taking it out on her assistant. That was no way to treat her staff. Or to get the best results.

She put on a smile and tried to repair the damage. 'I'm sorry, Louise, I'm a bit overwrought this morning.'

But she wasn't prepared to be mollified. 'Well, I think you've got a cheek to pick on me! I don't care a tuppenny cuss how overwrought you are. You're not going to take it out on me just because you got out of bed the wrong side. And if you don't like our page as it stands, that's too bad. I've been on my own for months, y'know.'

'I realise that. I wasn't criticising you personally, you understand.'

'Then what were you doing?'

This was a tricky one. Sarah searched around for an answer. 'Well, I – er – think that you were given the wrong brief for our page.'

'Do you?' Louise sounded marginally happier.

'Yes. At the moment our page is written mainly for the middle-class, middle-aged woman. I'm going to slant it towards the younger marrieds. A bit more trendy with a touch of glamour. So I'll be buying in some freelance work.'

'Cookery?' Louise asked, trying hard to be friends again.

'No, we'll keep out of the kitchen and the broom cupboards and go into the beauty salons and fashion houses. Don't you agree that's a good idea?'

'I don't know.'

'And we'll be launching our problems column.'

'I don't think our readers want an agony aunt at all. And the name – "Sarah's Postbag" – stinks.'

Sarah was about to thump her desk but stopped herself in time. 'Good heavens, Louise, why are you so defeatist? Do you always look on the black side?' She immediately regretted the rebuke and tried to put more warmth into her voice. 'Anyway, what have you got on today?'

'Only re-write work on press handouts we've received.'

'OK. I want you to drop them and go to this address.' She handed over a slip of paper. 'This woman has just been appointed chairman – chairperson, if you like – to an industrial outfit. Make your story featurish rather than newsy – how a woman has risen to the top in spite of male prejudice. That sort of thing. We'll lead on it tonight.'

Louise looked at her, open-mouthed. 'You mean you hope to use it today?'

'No, I *intend* to.'

'But there won't be the time.'

'Of course there'll be the time! It's only eleven now. You can easily nip over to the industrial estate, get your story and write it up before handing it to the subs.'

'I hate doing rush jobs.'

'It's not a rush job.'

'But —'

Sarah struggled to hide her impatience. 'Look, Louise, in newspaper journalism it's speed that counts. Tomorrow is always too late.'

'Well, if you say so. You're the boss.'

'I do say so. You'd better go straight away.'

'Very well.'

Left on her own, Sarah got up from her desk, feeling fretful and unsettled.

They'd already taken over their new office — a spacious room that overlooked the busy High Street. There were additional filing cabinets and a new electric typewriter for Sarah. And two other desks had been installed for the secretary and editorial assistant, yet to be appointed.

She strolled over to the window and looked down at the traffic. But the bustling scene didn't register. She was thinking about her deputy, knowing full well she was handling her badly.

There was no getting over the fact — Louise was sullen. She didn't like change, she said. Sarah did. She found it stimulating, especially now. Louise was, so far as she was concerned, dead weight. Sluggish in temperament, she showed no enthusiasm for office efficiency and her written work was well below par.

But of course, Sarah herself had exacerbated the situation a few minutes ago. It had been extremely tactless of her — and unjust — to be so harsh. She ought to have kept her temper under better control.

And yet, in spite of starting off on the wrong foot with Louise, should she have it out with her now? Let her know the standards that were required? If only Simon were here. He would advise her what to do ... On her own, she decided to put off the moment of truth.

And then there was the question of the problems column. Suppose Louise were right? Suppose the readers rejected the agony aunt idea and she fall flat on her face? That would not only be humiliating. In a new appointee it would be disastrous.

Here again, Simon could have given valuable advice. She was lost without him. Her old recurrent sense of insecurity returned. She was floundering again, astray on a sea of conflicting doubts. He'd always been her rock, her beacon. Whenever he'd needed help or guidance, he'd been there, showing her what to do, strengthening her resolve.

No longer. But it was no good whining. After all, she had a reputation for being decisive, hadn't she? What a hollow boast that was!

She glanced at her watch. Time for her session with the editor. Sarah found Bob, shirt sleeves rolled up, poring over several galley proofs on his desk.

'Ah, Sarah, come in. Shut the door. Take a pew.'

She sat down, adjusting her skirt and placing a notebook on her lap as she did so.

He wanted to know how she was settling in. She told him she intended to liven up her page. 'I'm going to buy in features on make-up and fashions.'

'That's fine — only watch your budget, won't you? The new management is scrutinising operating costs very carefully.'

'I'll only be using syndicated stuff — it won't cost the earth.'

'OK. How's Louise taking to the new regime?'

She told him, trying at the same time to be as fair as she could be.

He puffed out his cheeks. 'Sorry about that but I did warn you. If the friction continues you'd better let me know. Try and get her on your side. In the meantime, I shouldn't worry too much about it.'

'One other point — you did promise me secretarial and editorial assistance. When is it likely to come?'

'We're advertising this week, so it should be quite soon.'

'Good. As long as it hasn't been forgotten.'

'No, I assure you — it hasn't.'

She stood framed in the open doorway, silhouetted in the light from the corridor outside.

He could not see her expression for her face was in shadow but he had an impression of resentment, anger even. He wondered why and stood up as she entered.

'Oh!' she exclaimed.

'My name is Brown.'

'How do you do? Mine is Sarah Castle. Perhaps you have come to see me.' She swept into the room and her features were revealed for the first time. He caught his breath. Sarah Castle was a stunning beauty. This was very good news, and with hopes running high, he put on his most charming smile.

She appeared not to notice but turned instead to her assistant and took the printers' proofs which the girl was holding. 'Thank you, Louise. I'll take these.'

'I was just going to show Mr. Brown —'

'No, Louise.'

'But, Sarah —'

She sat down, very composed, placed the proofs in her drawer and cast her eyes questioningly upon him.

'What can I do for you, Mr. Brown?'

'This is just a friendly call. I was asking to see what you have in store for your readers.'

She gasped. 'Are you being serious?'

'Certainly.'

'Then I'll have to refuse.'

'Why?'

'It's never done. No journalist would show his work before publication to anyone other than a colleague.'

Max Brown tried to appear patient. He was getting angry but he kept his annoyance out of his voice. He wanted to remain on friendly terms with this desirable creature.

'Miss Castle — it's not a lot to ask.'

'On the contrary, Mr. Brown, it's a very great deal!'

'So you refuse to let me see the next edition of your women's page?'

'I don't wish to discourteous but, yes, I do.'

'And that is your final word?'

'I'm afraid so.'

'Very well.' He felt humiliated and angry. Not what he'd planned at all. 'We know precisely where we stand then, don't we? I'll bid you good afternoon.'

He strode out of the office, remembering just in time not to sacrifice even more dignity by slamming the door behind him.

Once in the corridor he stood stock still, trying to recover his composure. What had he done wrong? How would his father have handled the situation? It was a very bad start.

He marched forward, head down, a young man fleeing from the scene of his defeat. He knew he couldn't take this lying down or he'd be finished. A firm, forthright reaction was essential. Refusing to wait for the lift, he ran down stairs.

The editor looked up from his desk, startled at Max's sudden entrance and his glowering expression.

'Sanders, I want you to sack that woman.'

'What woman?'

'Sarah Castle − or whatever her name is.'

'You can't be serious. On what grounds?'

'She refused to let me see her page proofs.'

'Does she know who you are?'

'I gave her my name.'

A slow smile spread over the editor's face as he leant back in his chair, twiddling a pencil in his fingers. Then he laughed. Max bridled. Sanders ought to have got to his feet and apologised profusely. The fellow was far too casual, lacking in respect and discipline. His father wouldn't have stood for it.

'This is all rather amusing.'

'Amusing!' Max was outraged.

'Yes. You must admit that "Brown" is not exactly an uncommon name. So it's not surprising Sarah didn't connect you with the takeover.'

'That's no excuse. As you know I've assumed managerial control and I'm instructing you to dismiss the woman.'

'Impossible! We've just made her our woman's editor and I'm sure our circulation is likely to increase as a result. Do you really want to jeopardise our sales? Your father wouldn't like that.'

Max sat down, crossed his legs with deliberation and examined the tips of his fingers before giving his editor a slow, studied look. 'I can see I'll have to do some straight talking. In business, my father's will has always been law. And I intend to see it's the same with me. I shall insist on obedience. Is that clear?'

'Perfectly.' The editor leant forward, his elbows on his

47

desk. His expression changed. The languid, laid back look disappeared. The eyes narrowed, the brows were furrowed and his voice had become clipped. 'But I have something to make clear as well. We have a long-established tradition here of not suffering interference in editorial affairs.'

'Really?'

'As Sarah didn't know your identity, she had every justification for what she did. I support her in it. So will all our editorial staff. If you sack her, you could find yourself without a paper on the streets.'

'Don't you threaten me, Sanders!' Again, Max wondered what his father would do and was painfully aware of his inexperience. If he bungled this, his first managerial post, his father would remove him without compunction.

To insist on his rights could only worsen an already dangerous situation. So, he had no option but to make a tactical withdrawal and lose face. But even that was preferable to facing his father's wrath.

Sanders was speaking. 'I'm merely giving you the overall picture. Sarah is quite young for the job she's taken on, but she's got great talent. One of the national dailies is bound to claim her eventually but I want to hold on to her as long as I can – and I mean to do so.'

It was a clear case of having to eat humble pie. 'Thank you, Sanders. Perhaps I was over hasty. I'm prepared to overlook the lapse on this occasion. But next time, I shan't be so lenient.'

The editor's lips tightened. 'Frankly, Mr. Brown, you have no other option. Forgive me if I speak frankly. No discourtesy is intended. You have a great deal to learn about people in general and newspapers in particular. You will see that – like you – I believe in speaking my mind.' Max made no reply. 'Now, perhaps I can take you around the offices and introduce you properly to the staff – which is what you should have let me do in the first place.'

On the floor above, in the women's page office, there was complete silence. Sarah was brooding over her gaffe. Louise was looking amused, thoroughly enjoying the situation.

'Why didn't you tell me he was the new boss?'

'I didn't get the chance! I thought he was going to tell you himself but then you took the proofs and everything happened very fast after that.'

'Yes, sorry about that. I didn't mean to make you look small.'

'What d'you think he's going to do?'

'As far as I can see, there's nothing he *can* do. I'm certainly not going to lose any sleep over it.'

'He's very sexy.'

Surprised, Sarah glanced up from the doodle she was scribbling on her notepad. Louise didn't normally strike her as being interested in men. 'Oh, I don't know. Handsome, yes, but too full of himself. And I shouldn't think he has much up here,' she added, tapping her head.

'Anyway, he's certainly interested in you. From the moment you came in, he couldn't keep his eyes off you.'

'He didn't like being bettered by a woman, that's all.'

'Before you came in, he told me his father is the big industrialist, Sir Reece Brown.'

Sarah's mouth dropped open.

'I might have guessed – he has the same conceit, the same smarm.'

'Do you know him?'

'You could say that. Anyway, I don't suppose they'll interfere with us.'

Louise was silent a moment. 'I hate new brooms,' she said.

Sarah wanted to make a retort but refrained. Louise's face was inscrutable.

Max was feeling thoroughly chastened.

After leaving the *Examiner* offices, he'd driven far into the country, eventually stopping the car on a hill top near the South Downs. A good spot, he thought, to review the situation. In spite of the storm which was threatening, he got out and sat on a tussock of grass, thinking hard.

His opening gambit had been an unmitigated disaster. He had demeaned himself before Sarah Castle and in the eyes of the editor. He knew precisely why he'd behaved in that arrogant fashion.

It was his father's fault – or rather his example. The great

Sir Reece Brown never suffered fools gladly nor allowed his word to be questioned. His every wish was law.

Max was not made like that. He took more after his mother. And so he was playing a part, acting the great tycoon, and the role didn't fit.

The clouds were darker now. Some spots of rain fell on his face, large drops which stung his eyelids. And then the storm broke. Sheets of rain cleared the air, drenching his jacket. Running to the shelter of the car, he sat in the driving seat for some minutes before heading towards the main road and a small hotel he knew.

The dining room was almost empty.

'Will you take wine, sir?' the waiter enquired when he'd given his order for dinner.

'No, thanks.' Alcohol tended to cloud his judgement. 'Just some Perrier.'

'Very good, sir.'

He hardly tasted the meal. His mind was too taken up with the problems that lay ahead.

I can't be a carbon copy of father. I've got to run things my way. I want the staff to back me not fight me. Bob Sanders seems a nice guy and I'd like to have him as a colleague. And as for Sarah . . . Fantastic girl!

I know what I'll do. I'll send her some perfume and a note of apology. I'd like her to have dinner with me. I wonder if she would? I think I'll drink to that.

'Waiter!' he called. 'Will you get me a whisky, please? Only a small one − I have to drive.'

He sipped it slowly, feeling more relaxed. It was only later when he was heading the car towards Glenhurst that his spirits began to plummet once more. His father would be waiting for a report on the day's progress. Max didn't relish that prospect.

The butler met him in the hall.

'Your father is expecting you, sir. He's in the main drawing room.'

'OK. I'll see myself in.'

'Thank you, sir. Good night.'

Max pushed open the door of the drawing room. His father was standing at the far end by the open fire, clad in a maroon smoking jacket. There was no sign of Alison.

'Good evening, Father.'

'Hello, my boy. Drink?' He was in an apparently affable mood.

'Thanks.'

Sir Reece poured two large measures of scotch.

'No soda, I suppose?'

'No. Neat, please.'

'Tell me about your day.'

Max gave him an expurgated summary, glossing carefully over the contretemps. He desperately wanted to please, hoping for even faint praise for his efforts. None was forthcoming.

'I didn't do much more than settle into my office and get to know some of the journalists.'

'Did you, indeed? I can't say that's the right approach. You can't risk getting too friendly with staff. They are there to do precisely what you tell them, and they have to know their place.'

'Er – I was very careful.'

'I'm glad to hear it.'

Max handed over a sheet of paper. 'That's the list you asked for – the names of our senior journalists.'

'Ah, yes.' Reece read through the list quickly. At the end, he said: 'How interesting! How *very* interesting!'

'What is, Father?'

'The final name on this list – Sarah Castle.'

Max started. 'Why? D'you know her?'

Sir Reece smiled. 'Yes, I certainly do know her. Well, we shall see, won't we?'

After this enigmatic remark, he rose, bringing the interview to an end. He said goodnight and left the room.

Max remained in his chair a long, long time, wondering whether he would survive in his high-flying new role.

Chapter Six

On Monday morning there was a peremptory knock at Simon's door.

'You there? Can I come in?' It was Jenny's voice.

Simon leapt up from his seat, surprised because he thought his sister was in London. Though always glad to see Jenny, he wished she'd rung him first. She was never organised. That was one of the main differences between them.

'Sure. Come in.'

Dressed in slacks and a summer shirt, she swept into the room, her manner as unceremonious as always. Dropping her handbag in the middle of the floor, she hugged him.

'Why didn't you let me know you were coming?' he demanded. 'I could have made some plans.'

'I took a chance. Colin, my boyfriend, drove me down and we left London at the very crack of dawn. He's great fun.'

'Where is he now?'

'Somewhere in the town and I've arranged to meet him in an hour. I've got something to tell you – but later, over lunch perhaps. You're not doing anything for lunch, are you?' she added as an afterthought.

He smiled. 'No.'

'Just as well.'

Jenny threw herself down at the foot of the divan bed and kicked off her shoes. She looked around at his lodgings – the small table, the solitary easy chair, the wardrobe, the shelf with an electric kettle on it. 'Oh, Simon! Can't you do better than this?'

He shrugged. It was something he'd rather not discuss.

But Jenny wouldn't drop the subject. They were about to complete the sale of the family house, she reminded him, so he could afford to buy himself a decent flat. Why didn't he?

He shrugged again and was forced to give a reason. 'I doubt very much whether I'll be staying.'

She hadn't been expecting that. 'So you're still sorry you took this job? What don't you like about it?'

He sat at the other end of the bed. 'Everything. Term's not begun yet, of course, but I'm busy preparing projects and that sort of thing. I'm bored out of my mind.'

'Aren't you looking forward to the arrival of the students?'

He laughed. 'That's the rub! I gave up my last job because I thought the college was wrong for me. Now, I know differently. It's lecturing itself that I dislike.'

'Oh, that is bad.'

'I'm just not cut out to be a teacher, Jenny. That's all there is to it. I want something more fulfilling; something – oh, I don't know. Can't explain. Maybe, if I'm patient enough, the light may one day shine and I'll shout out "Eureka!" But at the moment, I'm completely in the dark.'

Jenny was at a loss for words. 'I can't help you, can I?'

'No. But I envy you, settled in your nursing in London.'

A guilty expression spread over her features. 'Well, actually, that's what I wanted to see you about. This is goodbye – or rather, cheerio. I've got a new job nursing in the Middle East.'

Simon was shocked and delighted at the same time. 'For how long?' he asked.

'The tour lasts two years but it can be extended after that.'

Two years! It seemed a lifetime. He would miss her.

'When d'you go?'

'Five days' time.'

'Phew! Why the rush?'

'Actually, I applied some time ago. There's this vacancy come up and I'm grabbing it. Colin's following next month. He's a doctor, by the way.'

Simon was trying to assimilate all this. Then suddenly everything hit him.

He experienced a great sense of loss, not just because his sister was going away. Her leaving was only one of many factors but a catalyst, nevertheless, that made everything stand out crystal clear.

It had all happened at once. The selling of their family home, the emptiness of his career, the departure of Jenny, and of course the devastating loss of Sarah. In a matter of a few weeks, his life had been turned upside down and made completely empty.

He was floating; no roots, no ties. Nothing.

Jenny said, 'You're very silent.'

'Yep.'

'Any word from Sarah?'

'No.'

'Anything I can do?'

''Fraid not, Jen.' He pulled himself together and jumped to his feet. 'Come on, we'll go and find your Colin. Let's get out of this dump.'

Passing through the hall on their way out of the house, Jenny pointed to the communal telephone. 'Why don't you phone Sarah? You've got her office number, haven't you?' He nodded. 'Then do it now.'

The idea was such an obvious one. He ought to have done it before. He checked the number in his pocket book and began to dial.

Louise was alone in the office when Simon's call was put through. She picked up the receiver.

'Women's page.' Her manner was brisk.

'Is Sarah Castle there?'

'Not at the moment. Can I help? I'm her assistant.'

'This is a personal call. Will you please ask Sarah to phone me back? Simon Dowling is my name. I particularly want to have a word with her. Tell her that, will you?'

'As soon as she comes in.'

'You won't forget?'

'I'll put a note on her desk straight away.'

Louise replaced the receiver and sat with her chin in her hands, thinking hard. It was an understatement to say she was discontented with the new regime. She hated Sarah; the more so because she had been so scathing about Louise's efforts. The fact that her own application for the post had been rejected still weighed heavily on her mind. She was turning all this over when Sarah came in some minutes later.

'Hello, Louise. Been busy?'

'Just finished that story on the child with the high IQ.'

'Good. Any calls for me?'

A slight pause. She looked Sarah straight in the eye. 'No. Nothing at all.'

Lunchtime came. Louise prepared to go out and picked up her handbag.

'Are you going near the post office?' Sarah asked.

'Yes.'

'Would you mind putting that in the box for me?' she said, handing over a handwritten envelope.

'Anything to oblige.'

Louise went out.

Approaching the post office later, she glanced at the letter in her hand. It was addressed to Simon Dowling at a place in Devon. The name immediately rang a bell. Of course! The man on the phone.

She stood by the post box for several minutes, deliberating. Her mind made up, she screwed up the letter and dropped it in the nearest litter bin.

Satisfied, she went on her way. She felt she'd partly settled a score.

'That's the third one you've thrown down in disgust in so many minutes.'

Simon looked up and grinned at his colleague. 'Well, it's an accurate reflection of my feelings.' It was a fortnight since Jenny's visit and the first week of term. He hadn't settled in and he knew he never would.

'Don't tell me you're hoping to find a spark of true scholarship among your students?' Webber asked.

'I was but it's a vain search.' Simon threw the rest of the pile of essays to join the others on the floor. 'Oh, what's the use?'

Webber, who was close to retirement, looked understanding. 'Those are my feelings after a lifetime in the game. It's all right for me to be cynical. But you!' He paused to brush off some cigarette ash. 'If you're feeling like that already, what are you going to be like when you're a crabby old sod like me?'

'You make it sound a grim outlook.'

'It could be.'

'The trouble is I've discovered I don't like lecturing at all,' Simon explained. 'In my first job, I put my restlessness down to the college itself. That's why I took this post. But I feel now just as I did then. I suppose that means – '

' – that you have no vocation. I'd agree with you. My advice is to find something else before the rot sets in as it did with me.'

'Yes, but what?'

Webber didn't answer immediately. He was too busy taking another cigarette out of his packet and putting it between his lips. 'Can't advise you on that, can I? Every man has to make up his own mind about what he wants to do in life.' He searched in his pockets. 'Have you a match?'

'Sorry, no. Don't smoke.'

'Damn.' He rose and made for the door. 'Must get some matches. Don't blame yourself too much for your disillusionment, old chap. Education isn't what it used to be, y'know. It's all politics these days. Politics everywhere. Even in cricket and athletics. Disgusting.' He gave a token wave of his hand and went out.

Simon considered his surroundings. The staff common room was a cheerless place and matched his feelings perfectly. Some hidebound armchairs and two small tables were its only furnishings. No curtains graced the windows. On one wall a noticeboard displayed timetables and fixtures.

Outside it was raining heavily and the sky was dark. He switched on the light and sat down again, deciding against marking any more essays.

He considered his lot. Loneliness weighed heavily. Would it never go away?

Three young women came in, two of whom he knew. The third was a stranger. She was dressed not in casual attire like most staff members but in a blazer, pleated skirt, stockings and shoes. She seemed too neat and tidy for a provincial technical college. The whole ensemble had an out-of-date look.

She was of medium height and Simon had an immediate impression of a pretty girl with brown hair; a girl who needed someone to show her how to make the most of her looks.

The three women gravitated towards the notice board. Having seen what they'd come to check, the first two departed with a nod in his direction. The third sat down on one of the armchairs. Like him, she too seemed to be at a loose end.

'New to the staff, are you?' Simon ventured.

'No. I'm only here for a few weeks, getting a bit of work experience.' She was very softly-spoken. 'My father knows the principal here, you see. I work for him − my father, I mean. What's your subject?'

'Sociology. And yours?'

'I suppose you could call it social studies. Not quite the same thing.'

'No.'

The conversation petered out for a while. Simon searched for another topic. He studied the ceiling as if hoping to gain inspiration there. He glanced across at the girl.

She was looking away, lost in her own world. She had quite pretty eyes, he thought, and her face had a pleasant expression.She had no style, though. But he was comparing her with Sarah which was unfair. No girl could compare with Sarah.

'You said you work for your father. Is he principal of a college?' he asked for want of something to say.

'Not exactly a college. It's a rehabilitation centre for accident victims. He manages it on behalf of a charity, helping people to come to terms with their disabilities and to lead useful lives.'

Simon was jolted. He was also interested. As a result of his promptings, she told him more − how their work really began after medical and physiotherapy treatment had ended. They taught a few basic trades and skills. Mainly, though, their task was to prepare people mentally for life in the world again.

Simon's imagination was fired and he wanted more details. His interest began to break down her reserve. He learned that the centre was a converted mansion and that there were a number of single-storey buildings in the grounds which acted as dormitories and lecture rooms.

'Where is this place?'

'Chiddington in Surrey.'

57

'Chiddington! I often drive through it. I also live in Surrey − or rather we had a house there.'

'A small world!'

'Yes, isn't it? What's your name?'

'Tina. Tina Phillips.'

'Mine's Simon Dowling.' He voiced what was in his mind. 'Do you think your father might have room on the staff for someone with a degree in sociology?'

Tina looked surprised. 'I don't know. I can ask him, can't I? Tell you what − why don't you come up with me at half-term next month to meet him? It'll give you a chance to have a chat. You'll like him − everyone does. I love him dearly. You will come, won't you?'

'That's very kind.' He laid his head against the back of the chair, studying the rain-washed windows, stroking his beard. He came to a decision and turned towards her. 'If you're not doing anything this evening, would you care to come out for a drink?'

'Tonight? Yes. I'd enjoy that.'

And so, as it happened, did he. Far more than he'd expected. They spent a pleasant time in a local pub, talking of this and that, getting to know one another.

Tina was good company, he discovered. After the initial barrier of shyness had been removed, she proved to be an easy conversationalist with a quiet sense of humour.

When Simon took her back to her lodgings, they paused briefly at the garden gate. There was no kissing, no cuddling, no hand-holding. Simon didn't see Tina as a romantic interest. She was just a nice girl and they were starting a simple platonic friendship. That was all.

'We'll have to do this again, Tina.'

'I'd like that.'

'Fine. Be seeing you, then. 'bye.'

After her first encounter with Max, Sarah had dismissed the Brown family from her thoughts altogether. Reece was sufficiently removed from her own sphere as to pose no problems. Admittedly, Max was closer at hand but he was ineffectual. He'd be no bother as far as she could see.

She'd been at the *Examiner* for six weeks now and felt on

the crest of a wave. New challenges faced her every day. She always rose to them. And then there was "Sarah's Postbag" which had already become established.

The workload was building up fast and she eagerly awaited the weekends when she could fully relax. One Saturday morning towards the end of September, she was glad to shut the door of her flat and be on the open road, Sussex-bound.

Auntie Win greeted her with the customary warmth and held her against her ample bosom.

'Why, honey, you look bushed.'

'I am a bit. It's been a hectic, exciting week.'

Sarah loved her aunt's house, oak-beamed and with an aura of history. Here she could unwind, get a new perspective. And Auntie Win was a darling. So warm and wise in her counsels.

'Where's your Simon?' she asked later when Sarah had unpacked. 'Don't say he's not coming again? This must be the third or fourth time he hasn't been with you.'

Sarah had to tell her the truth.

Her aunt was horrified. 'Sarah, you're crazy! Plumb crazy. And you'll be sorry for it. I liked Simon. Everybody did. And I'll tell you this — he's the man for you. You've really upset me. And why have you been keeping me in the dark all this time?'

'I don't know, Win. Because it hurt too much, I suppose.'

Sarah's aunt opened her mouth to say something further but closed it again. Obviously she'd decided on tact.

They were sitting by the french windows, gazing out at the patio and swimming pool. No other guests had yet arrived so it was looking deserted and forlorn.

Sarah told her about the advice column.

'Oh, not one of those!' Winnie sounded shocked. 'Over in the States, I knew an agony aunt who was married to a psychologist. What a pair! They thought that people could be neatly classified into pigeonholes.'

'You don't think I'll get like that, do you?'

But Win wasn't listening. Suddenly, she said, 'I think you're being extremely selfish.'

Sarah was jolted. 'Selfish?'

'Don't look so surprised. You know very well what I mean. I'm thinking of what you're doing to poor Simon.'

'But – '

'Don't interrupt me, honey. I will have my say. You're misusing him. You're lucky to have Simon. You don't deserve him. Just because you want to get to the top – '

'There's nothing wrong in that.'

'Sure there isn't. But you're playing fast and loose with him. That's not fair, Sarah. You're trading on his loyalty. You want him to leave you to concentrate on your job, and yet be ready to come running whenever you snap your fingers. You can't have it both ways.'

Sarah made no reply.

'Stop this stupid nonsense. Come to terms with the situation. There're plenty of women who combine a love life with a career. So can you.'

'I've already written to Simon asking to see him.'

'That at least shows you're not completely mad. Make it up with him – if he'll have you. And keep me posted. But it wouldn't surprise me if he told you where to go.'

Chapter Seven

Chiddington lay in the heart of the Surrey countryside and Simon knew it well. Or thought he did. He had driven through the village on many occasions in the past and had admired its green, the duck pond and row of stone almshouses.

At the end of the village, there was a road junction where he'd always turned right. But today it was to the left that Tina directed him. The signpost read: "St. Giles College." He changed down to second gear and took the corner slowly.

'I'm so glad you're spending your half-term with us, Simon.'

'Same here.' He smiled at her. Her eyes widened with delight.

He drove leisurely, his mind absorbing the tree-lined road and the fact that the leaves were looking quite autumnal. Still, he reflected, you have to expect that in late October.

He loved the setting – so remote from the hustling urban life with which he was familiar. He looked forward keenly to the weekend ahead.

'There, those large iron gates on the left. That's it.'

Simon swung the car through the entrance and found that they were on a long, straight driveway. At the far end, he saw a mansion – late Georgian, he reckoned – set in the midst of what had once been a country estate. He noticed several low buildngs close to the main house.

'Those are the dormitories and classrooms I told you about,' Tina explained in answer to his unspoken question.

The tyres made a crunching sound as he pulled up by the

front entrance. Having helped Tina out of the car, he carried their suitcases to the heavy oak door.

'Dad's known as the warden, by the way. I'm longing for you to meet him. You'll like him.'

Simon did. Mr. Phillips was a tall man with a stooping posture, and was much older than he'd expected. A trim goatee beard emphasised his strong chin but his cheeks were gaunt, with skin the colour of parchment.

'So you're Simon,' Phillips said on being introduced. 'Glad to know you. Bet you're tired. Roads busy?'

'Very.'

'No fun driving these days.' He turned to his daughter. 'Tina, show Simon his room, will you? I'll meet you here. Take your time.'

It was only a few minutes work for Simon to unpack. After a wash and brush up, he made his way back to the study, a large untidy room overlooking the drive. Tina, it seemed, was still upstairs. A severe-looking woman had now appeared and was sitting at a desk in the corner.

'This is Miss Macintosh,' Phillips said. 'She's the college secretary.'

They expressed mutual pleasure at the introduction. Simon looked around for a chair.

'Oh, before you sit down – be a good chap. Pull back the curtains, will you? Gets a bit dark in here. Sun's moved round to the west, y'see.'

Simon did so. He circumvented the central desk and the files stacked on the floor, pushed a tabby cat off a chair and sat down.

'That's right. Shove him off. Thinks he owns this place. Make yourself at home. No ceremony here. Smoke?' Phillips had the habit, it seemed, of speaking in clipped sentences.

'I've given up.'

'Sensible fellow. Hope you don't mind if I do?' He proceded to fill an enormous meerschaum pipe and lit it carefully. Through the clouds of smoke, he said: 'So – you've been seeing something of my daughter? Delighted to hear it. She's a rare girl. Tremendous support since my wife died.'

'I'm sure.' Simon hoped that Tina hadn't given the wrong

62

impression about their relationship. He might have to correct that later.

'So you're not happy in your job? What don't you like?'

Recovering from the suddeness of the question, Simon told him. It was not sufficiently fulfilling, he said. 'I think it's academia itself that I chiefly dislike. All statistics and theories and having to teach students who aren't particularly interested anyway. I want to do something more useful with my life.'

'Point taken.' Phillips removed his pipe from his mouth and gave Simon a shrewd look. 'Not interested in career advancement, then?'

'Not for its own sake, no.'

'Man after my own heart. Absolutely. I was a university don once. Gave up for the same reason. Came here. Never regretted it.'

'You must be doing a very worthwhile job, rehabilitating your patients – '

'Students, we call them. Nice of you to say so. It's satisfying. Yes. Very.'

Tina came in and stood behind her father, holding his shoulders and then kissing the top of his head. It was not a brief, perfunctory gesture but clearly an expression of deep mutual affection.

Simon felt humbled. No such depth of feeling had existed between him and his own father when he was alive, although they'd got on well enough. Tina's bond with her father was something much richer. He envied them.

At dinner and during the evening that followed, his impression that his hosts were different from him was reinforced. He thought about it in bed that night. How were they different?

It was not exactly that they were unworldly, but they seemed to live in a realm characterised by unselfishness and dedication to others. Father and daughter seemed remote from the self-seeking quality of 'normal' life. St. Giles College, its students and work, constituted their entire universe. For them, nothing else mattered. He wished he could know such peace and fulfilment.

Tina was a sweet, naîve little creature. He liked her. But as he lay back on the pillow, he thought lovingly of Sarah and his heart overflowed. Why hadn't she answered his phone call?

'What d'you think of St. Giles?'

'It's fascinating. I love it,' Simon answered, meaning every word.

Phillips smiled approvingly.

It was the second morning of Simon's visit and he and the warden were strolling round the grounds in the autumn sunshine. Several men were trundling their wheelchairs along the paths with great dexterity.

'They're off to work. Monday morning classes,' Phillips explained.

Simon already knew that the students were acquiring new skills or merely learning how to cope with doing ordinary domestic chores in spite of their disabilities. Phillips broke off several times from their conversation to exchange a few words with them.

While they were thus engaged, a young woman approached. She was tall and slim and, although she was wearing jeans, it was obvious she had long, shapely legs.

'Good morning, Mr. Phillips,' she said on coming up to them. 'A lovely morning. I hope you're well.'

'As well as can be expected, my dear. Stephanie, this is Simon, a friend of my daughter's.'

They expressed their mutual pleasure and shook hands. Her grip was firm and her touch warm.

Phillips turned to Simon in explanation. 'Stephanie teaches here, y'know. Computer studies.'

Simon was most impressed. Surprised, too, that such an attractive young woman could have chosen a technological subject like computers.

Stephanie was certainly a very pretty girl. She had long, flowing honey-blonde hair which swished on her shoulders when she turned her head. Her eyes were wide open and very blue with an innocent, amused look in them.

'Are you staying here long?' she asked him.

Phillips interposed: 'Just the weekend. He and Tina leave tomorrow.'

'Oh. I was thinking I'd like to have shown you my class at work.'

64

'I'd have enjoyed that but another time, perhaps.'

'Sure.' Stephanie smiled. 'Have a good trip. Hope to see something of you, one day.'

'That goes for me, too. 'bye.'

When she was gone, Phillips spent some moments relighting his pipe. Puffing furiously, he asked, 'Well, Simon? Like to join me here?'

'Very much.'

'You would? Need help badly. My health not good. Emphysema, y'know. Among other things.'

'I'm sorry.'

Phillips sighed. 'Yes, but there it is. Can't have everything, can we? I'd like you to come as my assistant warden.'

'*Assistant warden*? But my only experience is of college lecturing. D'you think − ?'

'Yes, I do think. I'm good at summing people up. You'll do, Simon. You'll do very well. Feel it in my bones. Have to let the committee know, of course. But they do what I tell them. What d'you say?'

'The answer's yes. I love it here.'

'Fine. That's settled then. Living quarters provided, of course. Meals *en famille*. Adequate domestic staff. A cook-housekeeper looks after us. The students have separate arrangements. We'll discuss salary details this afternoon.'

'I'll have to give a term's notice at my present college.'

'No need for that. I know your principal, Tim Clark. Great pal of mine. Leave him to me. I'll fix old Tim.'

'Thanks very much.'

'Driving back tomorrow, eh? With Tina?'

'Yes. First thing.'

'Hope the weather stays fine.' He glanced towards the house and waved. Simon followed his gaze. Tina was walking in their direction. 'My daughter's going to be pleased. Yes, very pleased,' he added.

She ran forward to meet them.

It had been a pleasant drive down to Devon with little traffic on the roads and sunshine most of the way. But darkness had fallen by the time Simon pulled up outside the old Victorian house where Tina had a room.

He deposited her small suitcase by the doorstep and she stood beside it. The street light shone down on her features, giving them a greenish hue. She seemed very uncertain and looked a bit waif-like. He was sorry for her.

'I'm so glad about everything,' she murmured.

'So'm I.'

'And when we leave here, I'll be seeing you every day. And living in the same house as you.' Her eyes opened wide in wonderment at the thought of it.

Simon didn't know quite how to reply. He was embarrassed. Tina hung her head as if aware she'd worn her heart on her sleeve. She scuffed the path with her shoe.

'Well,' Simon ventured after a while, 'see you tomorrow at college.'

'Yes.' Her voice was small and distracted. She was obviously weighing something up in her mind. 'You can come in if you like. Lots of the girls in the house do it − have boyfriends in, that is. Not that you're actually a boyfriend.' She gave a nervous little laugh and looked away.

'I ought to be going.'

'Must you really? I'd like you to see my room. I promise I won't keep you.'

Feeling that he could protest no further, he finally agreed, following her up two flights of stairs to the top floor.

'This is it,' she said, pushing open a door. 'Nothing very plush, I'm afraid, but then it doesn't really matter. I'll soon be returning to Chiddington.'

It was a dingy room − worse, if anything, than his. The furnishings were similar except that she had a dressing table. She insisted she make some coffee which was instant out of a tin. He sat on the only available chair while the water boiled. Afterwards, she perched on the edge of the bed and they drank in almost total silence.

Tina held no sexual attraction for him. He found her figure boyish and uninteresting. Her face, though, was appealing with its large saucerlike brown eyes. Her skin was clear and she wore no make-up. When she smiled, she had a habit of blinking at the same time. Physical attributes apart, there was an undeniable goodness about Tina that made Simon conscious of his own shortcomings.

He was turning over these thoughts and wondering how he could extricate himself and return to his own lodgings without hurting her. An inner voice told him it would need tact. He drained his cup.

'Tina, it's late. I think I ought to make tracks.'

'Oh!' She was sitting, head averted, knees together and hands twisting in her lap. 'I'm not in the least bit tired.'

'Well, I –'

'Please!' She cast her eyes upon him, winsome and entreating, willing him to say yes.

'Sorry, my love.' He had to be firm. Rising to pick up his scarf from the floor where he'd thrown it, he heard a small sound that threw him off balance. It was almost inaudible but nevertheless unmistakable. Tina was weeping.

For a split second, he wondered whether she was resorting to one of the oldest tricks in the book. But no, she couldn't be. She wasn't like that.

He went over to where she sat on the bed and put his arm around her shoulders, pulling her to him. 'What is it, Tina? Have I done something to upset you? Shall I make you some more coffee?'

For an answer, she pressed her face against his. He could feel her wet cheeks. She moved her hand over his chest slowly, luxuriating in the touch. When her fingers slid up and began ruffling his hair, her movements were dreamy, almost in slow motion.

She shifted in his arms. Her eyes met his and she immediately disengaged herself. 'You must think me terrible,' she said, sitting bolt upright.

'I've got to be honest with you. I wanted you to come up here. I – I thought it would be very romantic to entertain you in my room.' Her eyes were cast down and she was twisting a handkerchief in her lap. 'But I must have been assuming too much. I'm very new to this sort of thing. I don't think I'm cut out for having affairs.'

Simon took hold of her hand and squeezed it. 'What a silly thing to say! It was kind of you to invite me in. I've enjoyed your company.'

'You have?' She lifted her face, looking wistfully at him. Doe's eyes. Tears on her cheeks. Oh, God! Such a sad little waif. He could stand her misery no longer. He reached out and pulled her to him.

What occurred next seemed to happen to someone else, as though he were viewing events through the wrong end of a telescope.

Gently, he removed her clothes. She made no attempt to stop him, even helping him with fasteners and press-studs. It was only when he had divested himself of his own clothes that he woke up to what he was doing. There was no going back now.

Tina was lying naked on the bed, her arms thrown over her head, eyes averted, not daring to look at him. 'I've never done this before,' she murmured. He made no answer as he lay beside her.

She was obviously very inexperienced. There was no foreplay and it was all over incredibly quickly. She'd given a little cry but he couldn't be sure whether she'd enjoyed it. She gave no sign. But afterwards there was a look of contentment on her face and she kissed him warmly.

'Dearest Simon, my darling. I can call you that, can't I?'

He gave her a kiss on the cheek. 'Of course.' He had the absurd desire to apologise for what he'd done.

She was disappointed when he began to dress. 'Can't you stay? Have our first night together?'

But he wouldn't be drawn. Gently but firmly he said he'd have to go. Before he took his leave, she clung to him, begging him to come again soon and stay with her until morning.

Driving through the darkened streets back to his own lodgings, he turned over this new situation.

He hated himself. God knows he'd had women in the past. Before Sarah, that is. Skirmishes in the bushes; more decorous affairs in comfortable beds. Some of them only one night stands. But he'd never felt this way before. He was bitterly ashamed.

Although Sarah had broken with him, he still felt he'd betrayed her. And he'd violated Tina. And yet she'd seemed willing enough, hadn't she? Encouraged him, in fact. He took some comfort from that.

As he let himself into his own room, he was assailed by a new anxiety. Tina was not a woman of the world. She had taken what had happened as an expression of his love. How could he disentangle himself? Especially as he would be working for her father and moving into the house with them both?

And then there was Sarah. He wanted to see her. Couldn't live without her. And he would have to tell her everything. Oh, God, what a mess!

Chapter Eight

'Just look at it! I swear our mail gets bigger and bigger each day.'

Sarah picked up a handful of letters and flipped through them. A few were addressed simply to the women's editor but most had 'Sarah's Postbag' on them.

Her feelings were a mixture of satisfaction and despair – satisfaction because her agony column was a runaway success and despair because she was seriously understaffed. 'Looks like we'll be working late again tonight,' she said.

Louise shrugged. 'I've given up the idea of ever getting home at a reasonable time.'

Sarah sympathised. In the past month, she'd rarely returned before ten in the evening. After that, there was no energy left for anything except a quick meal. Then she'd doze in the armchair before dragging herself to bed in the small hours. The situation made her increasingly angry.

'I won't let this continue another minute.' She rose decisively and made for the door.

'Where're you going?'

'To do something about it.'

She walked briskly along the corridor. Kevin, the sports editor, tried to waylay her.

'Don't be in such a hurry, sweetheart.'

'Can't stop, Kevin.' Her heels made a clattering noise on the stairs as she ran down them.

The editor's door was already open. She swept in. He looked up from his desk and read the signs on her face.

'You look het up.'

'I *am* het up! "Incensed" would be a better word.'

Bob Sanders was good at pouring oil on troubled waters. 'Sit down, Sarah. Relax. What's the trouble?'

'I don't like broken promises.'

'I'm not with you.'

'When you asked me to do the agony column, you said I could have secretarial help and an editorial assistant. That was over two months ago.'

Bob was contrite. 'Yes I did, and I don't blame you for feeling you've been betrayed. Believe me, I made that promise in good faith. But since then – '

'Don't tell me. The new owners! That's it, isn't it? They've cut your budget?'

'Yes. But I'm still fighting them. That's why I haven't said anything to you yet. I ought to have done, I suppose.'

'It would have helped.' She was feeling calmer now but her sense of injustice was no less abated. She had no intention of leaving the matter where it stood.

'We mustn't give up hope, Sarah.'

She digested this for a moment. 'I see it this way, Bob. My agony column is a success.'

'And so is the rest of your page.'

'Thanks. OK, the readers like it. Hopefully, that'll mean more people will buy the paper.'

'They already are.'

'Great. So, if the owners want that to continue, they must give me the tools to do the job. That means extra staff. And I also need one or two tame experts – like marriage guidance people – to whom I can go for advice.'

'I'm with you all the way.'

'I know, but I'm not going to sit back and do nothing. I'm not made that way.'

Bob puffed out his cheeks and stroked the side of his nose. 'What do you have in mind.'

'First of all, I refuse to wait indefinitely – a few days. No more. If there's nothing positive by that time, then I'll quit.'

Sarah hadn't planned this. In the heat of the moment, she blurted it out. Was she being over hasty? But it was too late to change her mind now.

'You wouldn't do that, surely? In the time you've been with

71

us, you've become the most prized member of our team. You'd be a great loss.'

'Look at it this way, Bob. I'm a perfectionist like you. Without adequate staff, Louise and I will get overtired and become careless. Standards will deteriorate. We'll lose readers. And my reputation will be tossed into the bin.'

Bob was most unhappy. He'd phone the company secretary, he said, and explain the position.

Returning to their room, Sarah smiled and fobbed off Louise's questions with an enigmatic answer. Half an hour later the intercom buzzed. It was Bob. Would she please come and see him again?

Sarah went.

The editor looked uneasy. 'Well, I've been on to the company secretary and he's dug in his heels. No more money for extra staff.

It was as Sarah had expected. 'Then that's it, I'm afraid. I'll draft you a letter of resignation with a copy to the secretary. And I'm bitterly sorry.'

'So am I.'

'I'll give you two months' notice which will take us up to Christmas.'

'I wish you'd reconsider.'

'No, Bob, I can't. This is a matter of principle.'

'I understand.'

Entering her own office, Sarah put on a cloak of gaiety. She knew she sounded forced but couldn't help it. This time, Louise was tactful enough not to ask questions. Work was resumed.

Sarah arrived back at her flat after nine that night, tired, weary, and with spirits well below par. She was hungry and yet didn't fancy anything to eat. She prepared herself an omelette and a cup of coffee. Sitting on the sofa with a tray on her lap, she reviewed her situation.

What a mess! Yet there'd been no other choice open to her. She'd have to go through with her threatened resignation.

Then what? She would be back on the job market, writing round to editors again. This time she might not be so lucky. They would want to know why she had left her last post. Would they assume from the reason she gave that she was difficult to work with?

If only Simon were here! Why hadn't he replied to her letter? She had written him several pages, acknowledging her spiteful treatment of him and pleading for forgiveness. She'd told him everything she was doing, making it abundantly clear that she missed him. And he had not so much as answered. Not even a brief phone call after several weeks. That hurt.

She drank the coffee but left the omelette unfinished. Having cleared away, she went into the bedroom and sat at the dressing table.

Why was it that sitting there stimulated her mind? Brushing her hair or making up her face or merely looking at her reflection in the mirror helped to organise her thoughts. It was always the same. She couldn't explain it.

Her gaze was roving over the cosmetics, nail varnish and hair brushes, not really seeing them. Her eyes rested on a bottle of perfume. Max Brown had sent her that. Accompanying it had been a letter apologising profusely for their first meeting and inviting her to dine with him. He had been very wrong to behave like that, he'd said. Would she forgive him? She had done so but had declined the dinner invitation.

Once or twice since then, she'd passed him in the *Examiner* building and he'd always stopped to ask how she was getting on. He'd seemed pleasant enough on each occasion. They were, presumably, on friendly terms.

She realised he could be her saviour. She'd take a leaf out of her mother's book and use a man for her own ends. Why not? Men like Max's father didn't hesitate to play the game the other way around. She'd write to Max, not the company secretary, and ask for his support. He wouldn't refuse that, surely!

Feeling a little better, she glanced down at the photo of Simon on the corner of the dressing table. She studied again the laughing, friendly eyes, the trim beard and the fair, windswept hair.

So many memories! If only he would get in touch.

A business lunch Max had called it but it didn't make much difference to Sarah. There'd still be opportunities for her to use her feminine guile.

She had expected him to choose one of the restaurants close to the *Examiner* offices. Instead, he'd driven her about five miles out of town, to an exclusive establishment close by a stretch of common land. He'd reserved a table in the window. From their position, they could look out upon the grassland and the circle of beech trees that encircled it.

She'd already revised her initial opinion of Max Brown who was much nicer than he'd appeared at their first meeting. He possessed considerable charm and was most attentive, listening carefully to what she had to say.

Upon closer acquaintance, there was scarcely any resemblance to his father. He looked boyish and there were no lines on his face. And, unlike Sir Reece, Max smiled often.

But it was his physique that caught her attention. He would obviously excel at any kind of sport. His shoulders were broad and he held his head high. Once or twice, it crossed her mind that he'd make a marvellous lover.

When the coffee was served, he broached the subject on both of their minds.

'I bitterly regret that you want to leave us, Sarah.'

'I don't *want* to leave. I love the work on the *Examiner*. But I do feel I've been sold a pup. I was promised adequate staff. Since then, management has gone back on its word. I don't like that sort of thing.'

Max looked uncomfortable. 'That wasn't my personal decision, you understand. It was made by the board.'

'I still don't like it. Cutting back on essential staff is cheeseparing. In the end, the page will suffer and that'll reflect on my reputation. I won't stand for that.'

'Naturally.'

'Besides, I don't see why I should arrive home tired out each night just because management is too mean to give me adequate support.'

Max leant forward across the table. 'Look, Sarah, I sympathise. Your contribution to the *Examiner* is invaluable.' He was making a valiant effort to retrieve the situation. Sarah was not sure how much of it was just sweet talk. 'Let me assure you this is not the end of the matter.'

She asked him what he meant.

He drew himself up to his full height. 'Well, of course,

decisions such as these are made corporately. But I happen to be the managing director and, as such, my wishes carry considerable weight.' He was talking very grandly, she thought. How much substance was there in his words? 'There is only one person above me and that is the chairman.'

Ah, yes, Sir Reece Brown, man of steel. 'What do you propose?' she asked.

'I shall inform the board of my feelings and demand an increase in your budget.'

'Thank you.' She smiled at him and lowered her lashes. 'I have great faith in you, Max. I know you won't let me down.'

'I wouldn't dream of it.' He squeezed her hand. 'Just trust me.'

'Oh, I do. Implicitly.' She shot him another alluring smile. 'I honestly don't want to leave.'

'Then will you please withdraw your notice?'

'Oh, Max, I can't − not until my budget is decided. You do understand, don't you?'

His face fell. 'I suppose so.'

'But I'm relying on you to change the board's mind.'

'Of course. And I shall.'

But his voice didn't carry much conviction.

Max drove home to Glenhurst with trepidation. He had a number of irons to pull out of the fire and he was doubtful whether he could do it. He was aware that he had not fooled Sarah at lunch that day. That, too, made him sore.

It was Friday and Max never looked forward to weekends. For the next two days he would feel the deadening weight of his father's authority and Alison would act the mistress of the house, queening it over him. He resented that. When Monday mornings came round, he almost felt himself breathe more easily.

But the coming weekend was going to be worse then usual. He would have to explain the resignation of a key member of his staff. That would look like inefficiency.

And then there was Sarah herself and her opinion of him. His one hope of saving his face before her was to enlist his father's support. It wouldn't be easy.

He drove up the drive to Glenhurst and parked his car in the garage. On going indoors, a shower and a change of clothes boosted his morale a little before he ventured into the family circle.

When he went into the drawing room, Alison was alone, sipping sherry and reading a magazine. She greeted him civilly but without warmth. Max was used to that. He poured himself a drink and sat down, eyeing her. She continued reading.

Alison, who was only two years older than he, had been with his father for about a year. She was certainly a beautiful young woman, poised and well-groomed, and made a gracious addition to his father's entourage.

He recalled how much he'd fancied her when she'd first arrived. He was jealous, suffering tormenting dreams of his father making love to this glamorous creature. But she had never shown the slightest interest in him. He knew why, of course. He had no power, no standing, no wealth. His father had all three in abundance.

Since then, his own tastes had changed. It was Sarah who now filled his dreams. Her beauty was staggering. He fantasised about her constantly.

Sir Reece came into the room. Alison put her magazine away. The atmosphere changed. Over drinks, conversation was stilted and formal. During dinner, it was the same. Max took only a small part in it, letting the others talk across him. He didn't mind.

He waited until after dinner, when his father was mellowed by wine and brandy, before mentioning Sarah's resignation.

Fortunately, he was able to play on Reece's vanity first. Knowing that his father had just assumed control of a large national publishing group, he was able to offer his congratulations.

'I'm delighted about the success of your takeover, Father. You really deserved it.'

Reece raised one eyebrow and looked surprised. 'Are you, Max? I must confess I find it gratifying.'

Alison rose. 'If you two are going to talk business, I'll leave you to it.'

Reece made no response. Max thought it doubtful whether he was even aware she'd left the room for he continued speaking as if he hadn't been interrupted. 'Have I explained my precise reason for venturing into national newspaper publishing?'

'It offers power.'

'Exactly — power such as no other commodity can give. Remember that. Buying the Examiner Group was just an opening gambit. Now that I've acquired two national papers and several magazines, I'll have power to influence the entire population. Think of that, Max.'

'You must be very proud.'

'I am. Now tell me about the *Examiner*. Any problems?'

Max outlined the current situation in a tone that suggested he was not unduly worried by the outcome.

Sir Reece dismissed it in a few words. 'A storm in a teacup. These things happen. Forget it.' He turned to his cigar box, selecting a Corona and lighting it with care.

'But she's a key member of my journalistic staff.'

'What's her name?'

'Sarah Castle. You said you knew her.'

A grim smile played around his father's lips. 'Sarah, eh? I might have known. So she's making threatening noises. I will not be threatened. Call her bluff.'

'But if she does leave?'

'Then she leaves. That's all there is to it.' Again he gave a sour little smile. 'Besides, I would shed no tears over that. She's snubbed me more than once and that's something I find hard to forgive.'

'And that's your final word?'

'Positively. Pour me some more brandy, will you?'

Chapter Nine

For Simon, the shame of that night still lingered.

He was appalled by what he'd done. It wasn't as though he'd been tempted by a nubile young girl. That would have been understandable, even acceptable. But this ...

He wished fervently he hadn't gone into Tina's room. That had been his initial mistake. His second was to be moved by her crying.

Why had he succumbed? It wasn't because she offered any physical attraction. On the contrary, apart from her extraordinary eyes, she held no appeal for him whatsoever. The truth was he'd pitied her. And that only made him more ashamed than ever. His pity demeaned them both.

Tina was not made for casual liaisons. She was a naïve, unspoilt child and now he'd sullied her. Simon was sick with regret. He had to do something about it, tell her he'd been carried away and would she please forgive him and forget?

He cornered her in the college and suggested a walk in the recreation ground nearby. The choice of a public place would make things easier, he hoped. Tina said she'd like a walk.

The park was almost deserted and the late afternoon sun had already dipped behind some distant houses. The ground was littered with fallen leaves. A park attendant was sweeping them up, whistling.

They sat on a bench. He said it was beautiful weather for the time of year. She said, yes, wasn't it mild?

At last, summoning up his courage, Simon blurted out, 'Tina, I'm sorry about the other night. It mustn't happen again. I'm sure you'll agree.'

78

He'd expected floods of tears. None came. Nor was there reproach in her eyes when she looked at him.

'Oh!' she said. That was all.

'I want to apologise and beg your forgiveness.'

'No, it's I who ought to ask *your* forgiveness.'

'You?'

'I took much too much for granted. I was assuming that just because we – ' She was silent for some moments. 'It's another girl, isn't it?'

He faced her frankly. 'Yes.' He went on to tell her about Sarah and how they hadn't met recently even though they were still in love. 'She's obsessed with making headway in her career and I've agreed not to distract her for a while. But I can't get her out of my mind. Please try and understand, Tina.'

'I do. And I respect you for being so truthful.'

It was his turn to lapse into silence. When he spoke, it was in a low voice. 'In the circumstances, I'll have to write to your father and withdraw from the job he's offered me.'

'No!' There was horror in her face. 'Dad needs you. He's relying on you.'

He smiled. 'You do love your father, don't you?'

'He's all I have.' It was a simple statement of fact. 'And, yes, I love him dearly.'

Oh God, why did she always pull at his heart strings?

'But, Tina, don't you see? We would be living under the same roof. You'd be a constant reproach to me.'

'That's piffle.' Her voice had taken on a firmer, more resolute tone. 'I'm proud, Simon that you – that we – ' Her voice faded. 'I shall always cherish those few moments.'

He was feeling more and more of a heel but put on a brave face. 'Then you're not cross?'

'No. But I shall be if you go back on your promise to Dad. That's something I wouldn't forgive.'

Eventually, she convinced him. 'But there is one thing I must make clear,' he said. 'I want to see Sarah again. I couldn't give her up.'

'I wouldn't want you to.'

'And as soon we get back to Surrey, I'll make a date with her and explain what happened. I know she'll understand.' After a moment he added, 'So we leave the day after tomorrow, as planned?'

'Yes.'

'And your taxi will be bringing you round to my place at nine?'

'Yes.'

He was about to say something else but she appeared to be deep in thought. He decided not to disturb her. They walked back to the college without another word.

'I can't say I enjoy these weekly sessions,' Sarah observed. 'I come merely from a sense of duty.'

'My feelings exactly.'

It was a pleasant change, Sarah thought, for her and Louise to be entirely in accord. She looked around the bar which was regarded by the *Examiner* staff as an unofficial clubroom.

It was Friday. Tomorrow only a sports edition would appear so today marked the end of the week. Typewriters had been covered, unwanted copy put on the spike, pens and notebooks placed in drawers. Now was the time when the editorial staff let their hair down over pints of beer and gins and tonic.

Sarah and Louise were sitting slightly apart from the others, having a post-mortem on their page that day.

But Sarah was giving only part of her attention to the discussion. She was thinking of Simon and asking herself why she hadn't heard from him. It was two months now since she'd written and his silence upset her.

She asked Louise: 'I wrote to my boyfriend some time ago and he hasn't answered. That's most unlike him. He hasn't by chance phoned me at the office, has he, and you've forgotten to give me the message?'

Louise met her gaze steadily. 'No. I never forget things like that. Perhaps he's got another girl. You know what men are.'

'I just wondered, that's all.'

Sarah's thoughts were arrested by a voice at her elbow. It was Kevin, the sports editor. 'Are you girls ready for the meeting?'

'What meeting?'

'Naughty, naughty. You've forgotten, haven't you? We're

having a union meeting in the room upstairs.'

'Sorry, Kevin, I've got to go back to the office to work.' Sarah was glad of the escape.

'Work? What's that? How about you, Louise?'

'I'm coming.'

'Good.' He raised his voice and called everyone to follow him upstairs.

The mass exodus was greeted by sighs of relief from the few elderly regulars. They stretched their legs, spoke loudly and got out the dominoes.

Sarah crossed the road and let herself into the darkened *Examiner* building. At that time of night, the place had an eerie, ghostly feeling and she found herself tiptoeing along the corridors as if afraid of disturbing the spirits.

It was a relief to enter her own office, switch on all the lights and look out at the busy High Street below.

There was a pile of agony aunt letters to deal with. It was about two hours later when she called a halt.

Humming to herself, she walked briskly along the corridors and down the stairs into the dark entrance hall. About to leave the building, she stopped with her hand on the door latch. Across the road stood Kevin. He was turning his head, obviously on the look out for someone.

He was the last person she wanted to meet at that time of night. She decided to wait for him to go first. But he didn't move. Probably someone had offered to give him a lift home and had failed to turn up.

That put her in a quandary. Her car was parked behind the *Examiner* offices and Kevin would see her when she went for it. And what was worse, he would ask her to drive him home! It would seem churlish to refuse. On the other hand, she didn't fancy being alone with him in a car at night.

Debating on her best course of action, she suddenly froze. Footsteps on one of the floors above. Coming down the stairs. In her direction. Getting closer. In the dim light, she could see the figure of a man.

The figure stopped. 'Why, Sarah!' Max Brown exclaimed. 'What are you doing here at this hour?'

Relieved, she smiled up at him. 'Hello, Max. I've been working late.'

'So've I.'

'And I'm coming in again tomorrow morning.'

'Ha! Me too. It seems only women's editors and managing directors have to do that.'

'Look, Max, I'm about to go home and I'd be grateful if you'd see me to my car. Would you? There's someone out there I'd rather not meet.'

He agreed readily. As they left the building, Sarah caught sight of Kevin trying to attract her attention. He gave a small wave but she affected not to see and Max's presence choked him off.

The car park was only a few yeards away. As she got into the car, Max said, 'Maybe, I'll see you tomorrow.'

'Yes. Fine. Good night, Max. And thanks.'

She started the engine and moved off. He raised his hand in a salute. It was only when she was driving through the gates that she remembered she hadn't asked him whether her budget had been increased.

Sarah usually enjoyed working on Saturday mornings when the building was empty of staff. But today work palled and she found concentration difficult.

By nine-thirty she'd already done an hour's work and decided to phone Simon. This was a good time, she thought. He was bound to be in. She dialled the number of his lodgings. The burr-burr went on a long time and she was about to give up the attempt when it was eventually answered.

'It's Sarah Castle here. May I speak to Simon Dowling, please?'

'Mr Dowling? He's just gone.'

'When will he be back? Did he say?'

'Oh, he won't be back, m'dear. He's moved out, y'see.'

'Moved out? Where's he gone?'

'He didn't actually say — somewhere up-country, I reckon. Can't tell you more than that.'

'Thank you anyway.'

'It's such a shame, m'dear, you missed him by a whisker, as you might say. Only a couple of minutes before you rang, he left with his young lady.'

Sarah replaced the phone in a daze. His young lady! It was

impossible to come to terms with the idea.

Well, she'd only herself to thank. She couldn't blame him. She'd taken Simon too much for granted. Always had. And then she'd abused him to his face. She'd behaved like a bitch! She would never forgive herself for that, and now Simon was gone, out of her life forever.

She was sitting at her desk, head in hands, when she heard the door open. Max came in.

'Sarah, you look upset.'

She put on a smile. 'Just a bit of family news. It's nothing really.' She deliberately changed the subject as he settled on the corner of her desk. 'Now, how about my budget – do I get the extra staff as originally promised?'

His face clouded. 'I'm sorry to say – no. It's not my fault, Sarah. I honestly did try but, as I explained, mine is not the only voice on the board.'

She'd already expected this. 'You needn't apologise, Max. I realise it's not your fault.' She looked him straight in the eye. 'It's your father, isn't it?'

This caught him on a tender spot. He glanced away. 'Yes. He keeps a tight rein on all spending.'

Sarah sighed deeply. 'So it appears I'll be leaving the *Examiner* as soon as my notice expires just before Christmas. It's very sad. I've enjoyed working here.'

'For me it's a tragedy. I shall miss you.' He was looking at her steadily.

'Will you, Max? That's kind of you.'

He stood up. 'I'm sorry to have disappointed you over your budget just after you've had some bad family news. Look, are you doing anything tonight?'

She had to think a minute. 'Why, no.'

'Then come and have dinner with me. I insist. We can form ourselves into a mutual cheering-up society.'

'Swell idea. You're on.'

'That's settled then. I'll call for you about seven at your flat. How's that?'

'I'll look forward to it.'

Chapter Ten

The adrenaline was already flowing. The prospect of spending an evening with Sarah excited Max as no other date had ever done before.

Dressing was taking him longer than usual. Getting his tie just right was a real problem. After several failures, he'd re-knotted it yet again. Now, he was trying to get it straight, he hoped, for the last time. But he was impatient and his fingers wouldn't respond quickly enough.

Calm down, old son, he told himself. Trouble is, you're too hyped up to be bothering with ties.

He took several deep breaths which helped. At last, he got the knot right.

Sarah was a truly fantastic girl, beautiful and sophisticated. And sexy! God, she was sexy. He was a very lucky guy to be taking her out.

He was humming a tune as he ran down the stairs and let himself out by the front door. Luckily, his father and Alison were dining in town so he'd had no explanations to make. Not that it would have mattered if he'd had. He wasn't a kid any longer.

It was a clear, moonlit November evening with a hint of frost in the air. Max found it invigorating. He drove at speed along the country roads, savouring the good fortune that was undoubtedly his.

He'd never had illusions about himself. How could he, with his family background? From a very early age he'd had it drummed into him that he was inferior to his father. He accepted that he was morally weak and had no strength of character. That also had been instilled into him.

But in one sphere at least he prided himself on being supremely successful. At university, and later at commercial college, he'd always been able to bed any woman he wanted. He'd acquired a reputation for it. As a lover, he felt he had no equal. He was looking forward to the evening ahead of him.

Max found Sarah's block of flats without difficulty and parked his car outside. His hopes were running high.

Dining out had always afforded Sarah great pleasure. She liked the atmosphere of a good restaurant: the attentive service of the waiters, the subdued lighting, and the due deference given to the chef's skill.

Following the discovery that Simon had another girlfriend, she felt she deserved cheering up. Max had duly obliged and she welcomed the prospect of an evening out as an escape from her own thoughts. She was determined to enjoy herself in spite of the heartache.

It proved to be a pleasant evening for them both. The food was excellent; Max had chosen the wine with care and Sarah was enjoying his company. When there was a suitable break in the conversation, he apologised again about her budget, regretting bitterly that her resignation still stood.

What were her plans? he wanted to know.

'To get another job. I'm writing around to editors.'

'I shouldn't think you'll have any problem. Apart from the quality of your work, you're so self-assured.'

Sarah laughed, a brittle sound. 'Glad you think so. That's just an impression I give. It's an illusion, I assure you.'

He looked disbelieving. 'You're being over-modest.'

'It's true.' She wondered why she was being so frank. She didn't usually open her heart to comparative strangers. 'If you knew my mother, you'd understand.'

Max paused, wineglass in hand, recognising a fellow sufferer. 'Tell me,' he said quietly.

She explained about her childhood; that her mother, Ella St. Clair the actress, had regarded her as an encumbrance and that it was her Auntie Win who had virtually saved her.

'Deep down, I'm still insecure. A legacy, I suppose, from those early experiences.' Why on earth was she telling him all

85

this? Perhaps because she found it a release.

'You too,' he said slowly.

'What do you mean?'

'I've also suffered from a successful parent – in my case, my father.' It was his turn to tell her about his own upbringing and how he was always made to feel worthless. Afterwards he called a waiter.

'Will you bring us another bottle of that burgundy – number ten, I believe it was.'

'Very good, sir,' the man said and went away.

'Another bottle?' Sarah said.

'Certainly. We have to celebrate the discovery we've just made. D'you realise that we are two of a kind?'

When the wine had been poured, he lifted his glass in a toast. 'Here's to us both, and down with successful and overbearing parents.'

They both drank. Sarah found it comforting to meet someone who had suffered in the same way. She was warming to Max. He understood her. She liked him. Was the wine making her maudlin? She dismissed this. Sarah had always been able to hold her liquor.

Coffee and brandy followed, and for Sarah the time flew by. She was surprised when she glanced at her watch to find it was after midnight.

'Don't you think we ought to be going?' She wanted to invite him to her place but baulked at extending an outright invitation.

Max looked crestfallen. 'I'm in no hurry. The night is yet young. Let's have another brandy.'

'No, Max. You've got to drive home, remember.'

He was silent for some moments. 'OK.'

'But you can sleep on my sofa, if you like.' There, she'd said it, conscious of her true motives. 'It's a large one. You'll be quite comfortable.'

'I'm sure I shall be. Thanks. Let's go then.'

The central heating had been on so the flat felt warm when they entered. Sarah went to pour them yet another drink.

It was while she was doing this that she felt Max behind her. His hands went to her breasts, holding them firmly. She made no attempt to resist but leant back against him. She brought her own hands up to his and pressed them.

'God! You're beautiful,' he murmured.

Suddenly, she had turned in his arms and was kissing him with all the fervour of which she was capable. Eventually she pulled away, regretting her forwardness.

She tried to compose herself. 'As you'll be sleeping here — on the sofa — I might as well open another bottle. It's claret. Will that do?'

'Great. D'you mind if I put on one of your cassettes?'

'Help yourself.'

To the background of romantic music, they drank their wine, sitting facing one another. As Sarah crossed her legs, her skirt rose a little, revealing some of her thigh. She straightened it.

'That's a shame,' Max said. 'You've spoilt the view.' Sarah laughed but was flattered all the same. She was aware she had nice legs and was glad they weren't going unappreciated.

For a time they drank without speaking. Sarah tried to analyse her feelings. She didn't know what had come over her, inviting a near stranger to stay overnight in her flat. She'd never done anything like it before.

On her sofa, had she said? She had no illusions about that. And neither had he. She'd invited Max to sleep with her. Why? She was on the rebound from Simon, of course. But it wasn't only that. Having a handsome desirable man stay the night would do wonders for her morale, she was honest enough to admit.

The tape came to its appointed end and Max put on the other side. They had some more wine, drank one another's health again, and talked about nothing in particular.

Sarah was feeling mellow. Extremely mellow! And she was having a job focussing her eyes. At the same time she felt she was gaining a new perspective on everything.

Slowly, her inhibitions were being cast aside, bringing an exhilarating breath of freedom. And she gloried in it. She didn't care. That's what was so wonderful about it. *She didn't damn well care!*

It was in this mood of abandon that she went over to where Max was sitting on the sofa and put her head on his shoulder.

He needed no further encouragement and kissed her hungrily.

When he pinioned her down on the cushions and feverishly tried to undress her, she forestalled him, wriggling from beneath his weight.

'No, Max. Not like that. Let's undress.'

He agreed readily, casting off his clothes. Sarah, no less eager than he, went about undressing more decorously, draping her clothes on the back of a chair. She found she enjoyed teasing Max with her slow, deliberate preparations.

For a moment they stood looking at one another in their nakedness. Max's face was unlined and immature. But his body! How very different that was. Physically, he was a wonderful specimen.

With a swift movement, she lay down on the rug and looked up at him invitingly. 'Down here, Max.'

The invitation was unnecessary. His lovemaking was marked by a vigour that, by the end, left her sated and breathless.

When they had both recovered, she whispered, 'Let's go to bed.'

They did, but there was little sleep for them that night.

Towards dawn, Max fell into a deep sleep. While he was breathing steadily, Sarah's mind was still active, thinking over what had happened.

In memory, she could hear Ella's voice. 'It's sex, and money, and power,' she'd said. And what had she herself replied? She'd smugly declared she'd only sleep with a man whom she loved.

Well, she'd been wrong. There was no love between her and Max. She'd invited him in, knowing that, and knowing precisely what her invitation implied.

Perhaps it had been grief at losing Simon that had sparked off the situation in the first place. But after that it was sheer physical desire and she found she didn't give a damn. On the contrary, she'd enjoyed their night and had every intention of repeating the experience if she could.

She was past sleep by now. As the first rays of light filtered through the curtains, she slipped out of bed noiselessly. She didn't want to wake Max. In the kitchen, she put on a kettle to make some coffee.

Max surfaced slowly, shaking his head and rubbing the sleep out of his eyes. His vision cleared. Sarah was standing by him with a cup which she placed on the table beside the bed.

'Coffee,' she said, and bent over to kiss him. As she did so, the loose kimono which she was wearing gaped open at the top, revealing a pearly white breast. It was too much for him. He reached up and took hold of her.

She pulled away a little but not before he had undone the girdle around her waist. She straightened up. The kimono unwrapped itself and his senses feasted on the vision presented to him.

To his disappointment, she insisted on re-adjusting her dress and looked at him with mock reproof. 'No, Max. Not now. There's lots of time for that later – it's Sunday, after all, and we don't have to be at the office. I'm going to get some breakfast. What would you like – tea, coffee, cereal, or a slap-up English one with bacon and eggs?'

He halted the flow of words by lifting his hand. 'No, please. Just some toast and coffee.'

'OK. You can have a shower while I'm getting it ready.'

When she'd gone, he gulped down the coffee and inched himself out of bed, feeling fragile. But once under the shower, he began to recover. Turning the regulator to 'cold', he gasped and spluttered as the jet hit him. Having towelled himself, he had no intention of dressing fully. In the absence of a bathrobe, he made do with his boxer shorts and a shirt. He hoped Sarah wouldn't mind.

Apparently she didn't. As he went into the kitchen, she said, 'I like your shorts.'

As they breakfasted, Max had little to say, preferring to reflect upon the night that had gone, knowing that once again his prowess hadn't failed him.

Sarah was still en déshabillé. He thought she looked fabulous in her silky kimono. He was ready to take it off her and ravish her on the spot but he held himself in check. Like she said, they had plenty of time.

She refused to let him help her wash up. He didn't argue but sat beside the gas fire in the sitting room and soon dozed off.

He was woken suddenly by a loud ringing of the front doorbell. He started up, immediately conscious that he was dressed only in a shirt and boxer shorts. Instinctively, he ran his fingers through his hair to tidy it as best he could.

From where he was sitting he saw Sarah go to the door and open it.

She gave a sharp intake of breath. 'Simon!'

Max heard a voice say, 'Hello, darling,' and a bearded man stepped into the hall. About to kiss her, his eye caught sight of Max. He stiffened and lifted his head.

'Oh! I'm intruding.' His manner was brisk, his words clipped. 'I had hoped to have a private word with you, Sarah, but I see you're otherwise engaged. My apologies.'

With that, he turned on his heel and ran down the stairs. Sarah watched his retreating figure. It was only when his footsteps had faded away that she closed the door.

For some moments, she stood trying to regain her composure. Her shabby evening with Max was in its proper perspective now.

Sarah went into the kitchen. She didn't choose the kitchen because she had something to do there. In fact, at that moment, she wasn't capable of choosing anything at all.

Subconsciously, she wanted to get away from Max; avoid his probing gaze. Questions. There were bound to be questions and she didn't see why she should answer them. It was a personal matter. Not Max's business at all.

Her initial feelings were of intense shame. Her little affair with Max – how titillating it had seemed last night, how exciting, how daring! And now? It was just sordid.

The trouble was, she'd been found out. She'd wanted to run after Simon and plead. 'It's not what you think it is.' But that would have been futile. He had eyes, hadn't he? He could see how she'd spent the night.

A sense of shame spread over her, blinding her, choking her, preventing rational thought. She was physically shaking, unable to stop. Salty tears stung her eyes.

Simon would never look at her again.

What a fool she'd been!

Footsteps sounded behind her. 'Friend of yours?' Max asked.

What a redundant question! She could scarcely keep the scorn out of her voice. 'Yes.'

'You're upset.'

'Yes.'

'I'm sorry.'

'I know.'

'I'll pack my things. You'll want to be alone.'

Sarah nodded. She couldn't trust herself to speak.

After Max had gone, she spent the rest of the day in a dreamlike trance. She ate nothing; did nothing – except think. And that got her nowhere.

In the small hours, she took some sleeping tablets and dragged herself off to bed. But the whole night was torture. Release came only in the morning when she rose to go to the office.

A tepid shower refreshed her body but it did nothing at all for her bruised emotions.

Chapter Eleven

The week was starting off very badly. Following Simon's disastrous visit and its consequences for her well-being, Sarah arrived at the *Examiner* to find that she had an ill-mannered assistant to cope with.

'You've got great bags under your eyes,' was the greeting she received. Louise seemed to take pride in being uncivil.

Concentration was very difficult. Sarah's brain did not want to focus on the work lying on her desk. In her memory she was constantly looking over her shoulder, thinking back to yesterday. If only she could erase the pain on Simon's face when he'd caught sight of Max! She would have given anything not to have hurt him like that.

How ironic it was. Max was only a temporary diversion. Nothing more than that. She'd only allowed herself to become involved with him because there'd been no word from Simon. No one could possibly replace him in her affections.

Fortunately, the week ahead was a very full one which would leave little time for personal reflection. And every evening would be given up to writing letters to editors extolling her own virtues as a journalist. With each, she'd enclosed selected cuttings from her page.

At first, she avoided Max. But one morning, he stopped to talk to her outside her office and suggested they meet on the following Saturday.

She pointed to the half-open door to her room, nodded her head towards the end of the corridor and walked in that direction. Max understood and followed.

'I'm sorry about what happened on Sunday,' he said.

'It wasn't your fault.'

'Thanks for not holding it against me.'

She managed a smile. 'That's all right.'

'May I take you out to make it up to you?'

Sarah thought a moment. What was there now to lose? She'd already burnt her boats as far as Simon was concerned.

She was about to accept his invitation when she remembered she'd already promised to spend the weekend in Sussex. Why didn't he join her there just for the Saturday? she asked. Her aunt had a swimming pool and usually kept open house at the weekends.

Max thanked her and said he'd love to come.

Taking her seat at her desk a moment or two later, Sarah was conscious that Louise was giving her an old-fashioned look. So she *had* heard!

Driving down to Sussex on the following Saturday, two thoughts were uppermost in Sarah's mind. Both concerned men.

Max would fit in well at Sandalwood, she thought. Auntie Win would like him. As long as Sarah gave him no romantic encouragement, there should be no difficulty.

Simon was a different problem altogether.

For one thing, she no longer knew where he lived. He and his sister had sold the family home, and when Sarah had tried to contact Jenny at the nurses' home, she was told she'd gone abroad. How could she get in touch with Simon? She could, perhaps, write to him care of his bank.

Then what? Apologise for sleeping with someone else? Why should she do that? They were free, both of them. Besides, hadn't she been told he'd left his lodgings with 'his young lady'? Wasn't this a case of sauce for the goose?

Sarah didn't fool herself. She knew she was making excuses. Physically, Max was perfection. He was also good company. But that was all. He could never be a substitute for Simon.

As she approached Sandalwood, she guessed that her aunt would ask once more about him and whether Sarah resolved her problems regarding marriage and career. She would merely say that Max would be joining them in the afternoon, and hope that no more need be added.

On arrival, luck played into her hands. Scarcely had she unpacked and joined her aunt in the lounge, than she heard a car drive up to the front entrance.

The butler entered and coughed discreetly. 'Mr Desmond Mallon is here, Mrs. Seeberg.'

'Oh, show him in, will you, Charles? And then, you may serve the lunch.'

'Very good, madam.'

Des swept in and his exuberance immediately seemed to fill the room.

Sarah smiled. Whenever he was with Auntie Win, he 'camped it up', knowing that she expected it of him. He made his gestures exaggerated and his speech affected. When he was in this mood, no one minded. In any case, they either loved him or found him a star turn. No one disliked Des.

'Darling Winnie and beautiful Sarah – you both look adorable.' He kissed them on the cheek. 'How any man could possibly resist either of you, I don't know.'

As Des preferred men to women, Sarah had to suppress her smile. He was blissfully unaware that anyone guessed his proclivities.

Winnie asked him how he was.

'Well, darling, no better for this horrid November weather. I hate the winter, don't you? It's only the thought of Christmas on the horizon that keeps me sane.' He sat down, crossed one elegant leg over the other and regaled them with anecdotes from the world of television.

They listened avidly.

He had launched into a story about one particular star. 'She really is an awful hussy. A right bitch. D'you know, she and one of the extras on the set – well, let's say they were discovered by the vision mixer – ' He stopped suddenly. 'No, mustn't tell tales out of school, must I? That would be naughty.'

Sarah was longing to know more and Auntie Win was perched on the edge of her seat, waiting for the dénouement. She shrieked with frustration, her whole body quivering. 'Des! What a let down. I'll never ask you here again.'

He grinned at her. 'Darling, if I thought you meant that, life would be unbearable.'

94

The butler came in.

'Lunch is served, madam.'

'Thank you. Charles.'

They rose and began to make their way to the dining room.

Auntie Win took hold of Sarah's arm. 'There's one bit of bad news, honey. Ella's coming tomorrow evening.'

This was a blow. 'I didn't know she was even back in England.'

'She didn't tell you? Ah, well – that's Ella. And, I'm sorry to say, she won't be alone. That man Reece Brown is coming, and he's bringing his girlfriend.'

'Tomorrow, did you say? Glad it's not today.'

'Why?'

'Max, his son, is coming this afternoon. They don't get on too well.'

Sunday evening was a re-run of Ella's appearance a few months ago. The same performance; the same performer. The only modification was the absence of the sunglasses. But indoors, on a chilly November day, they would have been *de trop* even for Ella St. Clair.

Nevertheless she made a dramatic entrance, surveyed the assembled guests and, as it were, waited for applause. None came, of course. Immediately behind, Reece and Alison stood in her shadow.

Winnie welcomed her sister-in-law, kissing her perfunctorily. There was a handshake for Reece and an introduction to Alison. Sarah followed in her aunt's wake.

The butler came over to the newcomers with a tray and they each selected a drink. After that, the party seemed to sag somewhat. People stood around in groups, not certain whether they were allowed to speak or not.

It was Winnie who broke the spell. She shepherded Reece and Alison to the centre of the room, ensuring that they had someone to chat to. Ella needed no such assistance.

Alison, who made a glamorous picture in a white satin designer dress, had been button-holed by a hopeful young man. Sarah found herself with Reece.

He gave her a sardonic smile. 'Well, Sarah, we meet again.

I have to say I have a grudging respect for you. I like a woman of spirit.'

'That surprises me. I would have thought you'd prefer someone slightly more subservient.' She was smiling to take the sting out of her words. Nevertheless, she'd caught him on a tender spot. His eyes narrowed for a brief moment.

'And I admire your work. That son of mine shouldn't have accepted your resignation.'

'It was a question of finance. I'd been assured of a budget increase for extra staff but the promise wasn't honoured.'

'I realise that – Max should have increased it. I have reprimanded him.'

Sarah stifled a gasp. One of them was lying. She was certain it wasn't Max. 'Have you?' she managed to answer.

'I understand he has been escorting you lately.'

Again, Sarah had to control her expression. 'He told you, did he?'

'As a matter of fact, he didn't. I heard from another source.'

'Oh, yes?' Sarah wouldn't rise to the bait. Could it be Louise? 'My aunt's house parties are great fun, don't you think? Max entirely agrees – he was here yesterday, as a matter of fact.'

'Really?' Reece contemplated the amber colour of his fine malt and took a sip. 'You know, Sarah, in view of your – er – friendship with Max, it might be providential that you're leaving the *Examiner*.'

She answered with asperity: 'I hope you aren't trying to monitor my life.'

'Not at all, my dear.' His features creased into another mirthless smile. 'You see, I'm right. You really *are* a woman of fire – someone after my own heart. I'm glad you're leaving because you're worthy of much better things and Max would only hold you back. The fact is, Sarah, I have a proposition to put to you.'

At that moment, Alison glided up and, putting a proprietorial hand on Reece's arm, gave Sarah a glacial smile. Reece acknowledged her presence only with an impatient nod, brushing off the interruption.

'Perhaps you've heard,' he went on, 'I've recently acquired

several new companies which I've renamed the Brown Newspaper Corporation. One of my papers is the *Daily Sentinel*. I'd like you to join as its problems columnist.'

'Oh!' She noticed that Alison was becoming restless and there was a hostile glare in her eyes.

Reece continued, 'The salary – need I say? – would be commensurate with your outstanding abilities. You would have an adequate staff and – even more important to an ambitious woman like you – I'd give you columnist's status and high visibility. Your career would be nurtured by my promotions department.'

'I don't know what to say.'

'You don't have to, my dear – not here anyway. One should never make business decisions without due thought.'

'I shall certainly think about it and get in touch.'

Alison pulled on Reece's arm, claiming his attention. 'Darling, I feel we ought to be circulating around. There are so many interesting people here that I want to meet.'

His business finished, Reece agreed. With a look of triumph, she bore him off towards the other side of the room.

With practised fingers, Alison removed her artificial eyelashes and laid them down carefully on the small glass dish. She moisturised her face and wiped it off with several tissues.

She brushed her hair with smooth vigorous strokes. As she twisted her head, her tresses swirled around the nape of her neck. She enjoyed seeing the light scintillating on the waves when she did that. On the whole, Alison was very pleased with what she saw in the mirror.

She rose with languid grace, removing her peignoir as she did so and placing it carefully on a coathanger before hanging it up.

Reece came into the room, eyeing her figure approvingly. She said nothing.

'Have you enjoyed yourself this evening?' he asked.

'Not much. But you obviously have.'

'What are you implying?'

'That Castle woman. You have designs on her.'

'Designs? What nonsense is this? I want her to join the *Daily Sentinel*, that's all.'

'And you expect me to believe it'll end there? I know you, Reece Brown. You'll get her into bed before she knows what's happened.'

He moved over and slid his hands over her naked curves, taking hold of her breasts and holding them firmly. 'What a very beautiful body you have, my dear. Do you think I'd exchange this for another woman's?'

'Given the chance, you would. And if you do, don't imagine I'd stamp my little feet and have girlish hysterics, will you? If you ditch me, I shan't fight according to the Queensbury Rules. Just remember that, my sweet.'

'Hasn't Simon answered your letter yet? It must be at least two months ago that you said you wrote to him.'

'It's longer than two months. I wrote at the beginning of September.'

Sarah's face looked bleak. Winnie didn't press her further.

It was Monday morning and the two women were having breakfast together before Sarah left for town. All the other guests had departed the previous evening.

Outside, the dreary, November weather looked cold and uninviting. In contrast, the log fire in the grate crackled pleasantly and Winnie felt snug in the comfort of her dining room.

It was a time for exchanges of confidences. Winnie waited for some clarification on the Simon situation. But none came.

Sarah was pushing some cereal around her bowl. She looked up suddenly. 'As far as I can tell,' she murmured, 'he's got another girl.'

Winnie was disappointed but not entirely surprised. 'Oh, no!' she said. Then, after a pause: 'I don't want to rub it in, Sarah, but it is your own fault.'

She nodded and cast her eyes down. 'I know that.'

'Is Max a substitute?'

Sarah made no comment but shrugged. It was an eloquent gesture.

Winnie decided not to pursue the matter further. 'So Reece offered you a job on the *Daily Sentinel*, did he? That's interesting.'

Sarah visibly brightened at the change of subject and recounted what he'd said.

Winnie was impressed. 'Are you going to take it?'

'Not from choice – that's for certain. I don't like the man. But he doesn't want an immediate reply. So I'll sit on the idea and hope that something else turns up.'

'That makes sense.' Winnie thought awhile. 'Tell you what, honey, you could use his offer as an ace in your deck when dealing with other editors. Used like that, it could be quite valuable.'

'Yes, I see your point. It could be quite a strong card, if I play it. Yes, I think I'll do that.'

Chapter Twelve

Monday morning at St. Giles'.

The senior staff had just finished breakfast. The warden was engrossed in *The Times*; Simon was reading the *Telegraph*. Tina, having heard the postman, had gone into the hall.

'There's a letter for you, Simon, from the Middle East,' she said on her return. 'Perhaps it's from your sister.'

He took the flimsy air mail envelope and glanced at the writing. Jenny's scrawl was unmistakable. He grinned. 'At last! I wonder how she's getting on.'

'Is she enjoying it out there?' Tina asked when he'd finished reading it.

'By all accounts she's having a whale of a time, I'm glad to say. Here, read for yourself,' he said, passing the letter over and picking up his newspaper.

Tina read it with obvious interest.

'Simon — this bit about your friend, Sarah.'

He was immediately on his guard. 'What about it?'

'Jenny says she left in such a hurry that she didn't tell Sarah she was going.'

'Well?'

'She's asking you to give her the message.'

'Yes, I know. I read it. But there's no need for that. Jenny knows where Sarah lives.'

'Look, why don't you run over in the car and call at Sarah's office? After all, it's not far.' Tina turned to her father. 'That's all right, Dad, isn't it?'

'Eh?'

'That Simon should drive over to give a message to his friend?'

'Of course. Good idea. Why not?'

Secretly, the prospect appealed to Simon but he still had to be persuaded.

It was a pleasant drive and he found a parking space without trouble. That part was easy. The difficult part was still to come.

He recalled that terrible morning when he'd seen the other man in Sarah's flat. It wasn't going to be easy meeting her after that.

And yet, he wanted to see her. Always would. Nothing had really changed. And he knew he had to grasp the nettle if he and she were ever to be reconciled.

He went into the High Street and paced up and down outside the *Examiner* offices. He crossed the road, looked up at the building. So many windows. Which one was hers?

He hesitated. He turned. He walked away. His courage had failed him.

Sarah stood by the office window and looked down at the High Street below.

Suddenly she started. For one ridiculous moment, she thought she'd caught a glimpse of Simon, going round a corner. She shook herself. Couldn't be.

She must have been dreaming. Besides, the sun was very strong, shining on a tiled façade opposite. Much too bright really. It stung her eyes. She turned away.

Was that a knock she heard at the door? She didn't think so. Her senses must be playing her false today.

She thought again of the weekend at Sandalwood. On the whole, it had been a pleasant time. As expected, Max had behaved decorously and people had liked him.

Reece's offer intrigued her. Not that she had any intention of accepting it, but Auntie Win was right — it might be a good card to play later on.

Sarah heard the knock again. Louder this time, and the door was pushed open. One of the office cleaners put her head through the doorway.

'Excuse me, Miss, but can I have a word?'

'Yes, I can spare you a minute or two.'

The girl came in and closed the door. 'Sorry to trouble you, Miss, but I thought you could help – you running "Sarah's Postbag" and all that and giving advice, like.'

Sarah put on a bright encouraging smile but there was a sinking sensation in her heart. She felt helpless and inadequate. Most of the queries she received needed only simplistic answers and a referral to experts in that particular field. Giving a spontaneous verbal answer was a different matter altogether. It scared her.

'What's the problem, Joan? Your name is Joan, isn't it?'

'Yes, Miss. Well, it's like this – it's my hubby. He wants me to take him back.'

Sarah considered the girl standing nervously before her. She looked vulnerable and Sarah's heart went out to her. 'Tell me,' she said kindly.

The girl's story was as old as love itself. Infidelity followed by remorse and a plea for forgiveness.

'I was under the doctor with worry, Miss, when he went off with that woman. It was awful. Ever so bad, I was. Still am, really. Still taking my pills.'

Sarah said she was sorry. She was aware that the girl's reaction could have been caused by hurt pride rather than the actual loss. She had to find out. 'Does that mean you still love him?'

'Oh yes, Miss. I'll always love him.'

'But, tell me truthfully, do you really want him back?'

Joan hesitated a moment. 'I – I suppose so.'

'I think you do in your heart. Don't you?'

'Yes, Miss.'

'Then, you'll have to forgive him.'

'Yes, I must, mustn't I?'

'The aim should always be for reconciliation if possible.' Sarah was pleased. The word had the right sort of sound, the right nuance. 'So you will give him another chance?'

'Yes, Miss. I promise. And thanks ever so.'

She performed what looked like a curtsey and scuttled out of the room.

Driving home that night, Sarah thought back over the way she'd handled the interview. She had the impression that she'd gained more from the exchange than Joan.

She'd been faced with a real life problem that couldn't be shunted off to an expert. She had actually answered a domestic problem in a satisfactory manner and her professional morale was boosted.

The phone was ringing when she opened her front door. Throwing her handbag and gloves on to the nearest chair, she picked up the receiver.

'Hello, Sarah,' the voice said. 'It's Des.'

'Des! This is a surprise.'

'Sorry to bother you. Fact is, darling, I'm in a jam. I badly need your help. Are you doing anything tomorrow afternoon?'

'I'll be at the office. Why?'

'Can you escape for a few hours? I'd like you to come to the studios.'

Sarah sucked in her breath. 'Look, Des, you'd better explain from the beginning.'

'I'm producing this new discussion series on social problems, see? I'd signed up a certain woman's writer to appear but she's slipped a disc. Stupid bitch! So I've got to find a temporary replacement. I thought of you.'

Sarah tried to let all this sink in. 'I can't do TV work; I've no experience.'

'Bullshit! You're your mother's daughter, aren't you? If you can't handle the camera after that family background, then I don't know who can.'

'But would they want anyone unknown like me?'

'Look, sweetie, I'm the bloody producer. If I want you, that's it.'

She recovered her breath sufficiently to say, 'OK, Des, you're on. But don't say I didn't warn you.'

'Mind you, darling, it's not peak-time viewing. It goes out on Monday in a mid-morning slot. But it'll give you a little bit of exposure. We're recording tomorrow afternoon. Come and have lunch with me and then we'll go from there. Must go now. 'bye.'

The studio was much smaller than Sarah had imagined. She'd expected something like one of the big sound stages that she'd seen in Hollywood but it was nothing like that.

At one end, there was a small audience of earnest-looking people. Some had notebooks on their laps with pens ... poised for action. A bit intimidating that! Sarah hoped she wouldn't disappoint them.

At the other end, was a low dais on which the set had been built. As informality was the programme's keynote, this represented a domestic living room with chairs irregularly placed. An engineer was checking the hidden mikes and another technician was taking a final look at the props.

In the centre of the studio, thick cables snaked across the floor from the cameras, and their operators were busy making adjustments. A battery of high-powered lights shone down on the scene.

Sarah felt at home. All her nervousness had vanished, leaving only a residue of excited anticipation. It was as if she had been born to this – which, in a sense, she had.

Des had briefed her about today's theme which was to be 'stress in modern life'. Although the programme was going out unrehearsed, everyone had been told what questions to expect. Sarah was well prepared.

Now, she noticed that the other panel members were beginning to go on set and Sean Maguire, who was hosting the show, followed. Sarah did likewise.

The studio crew donned headsets and took up their positions. The floor manager raised his hand for silence. The seconds ticked away on the studio clock. The red light went on. As it did so, he dropped his arm and pointed at Sean as much as to say, 'It's all yours.'

Sean was a skilled presenter and handled the panel well, extracting from them a vigorous exchange of views on stress. Sarah made several contributions to the debate.

Eventually, Sean said, 'One of the factors causing stress in modern living must surely be the constant break up of marriages. Suppose, for instance, a woman discovers her husband has a mistress and is planning to leave her. What does she do? Divorce him, shut her eyes or plead with him to make a fresh start? What would you say, Sarah?'

She was on camera, the first to be consulted on this subject. This was her moment and she was determined not to muff it.

Knowing that she could handle the camera like an old friend, she left her delivery to instinct and concentrated on making as much sense as she could.

She realised with gratitude that, through the meeting with Joan, the Fates had provided her with a preliminary run-through for today. Her arguments were well marshalled and she had the attention of the studio audience.

Bringing her advice to an end, she said, 'The stress that's endured by the innocent party in a marital break-up is traumatic. Often the guilty party is weighed down by remorse as well. And then there are the children. The answer to all this stress has to be reconciliation. Must be! That's why I always advise my readers to seek reconciliation with their partners.'

There was applause from the studio audience. Sean asked for comments from the others. One panel member disagreed with Sarah but, for the most part, they were in accord with what she'd had to say.

The floor manager raised his hand and made winding up signals. Sean smiled benignly at the panellists and spoke to the camera. 'Well that, I'm afraid, is all we have time for today. But we'll be back next week at the same time. Till then, good bye.'

Sarah saw from the studio monitor that the credits were rolling. The floor manager made a cutting motion with his hand and the red light went out. It was all over.

Afterwards, in the hospitality room, they gathered for a post mortem.

Des came in. 'Well done, everyone. It went off splendidly.' He hugged Sarah. 'You were marvellous, darling, and so were you, Sean – as always.' To show his appreciation, he gave them both a kiss on the cheek.

In spite of the central heating, the flat seemed chilly when she returned. Sarah put on the gas fire, made a snack and brewed herself some coffee.

Sitting on the settee with the tray on her lap some minutes later, she reviewed the afternoon's events, wondering whether it would have any effect on her career.

She felt replete – not from the food but from satisfaction. Appearing on television had been a marvellous experience.

And yet, it was as though she had been doing it all her life. She was filled with elation.

It was in this state of mind that she dozed. When she awoke, it was nearly eleven o'clock and one of her legs had gone numb. Rising from her cramped position, she massaged it vigorously until the blood circulated once more.

It had been an exhausting day and she was very tired. She ought to take herself off to an early bed, she knew. But instead, she stood irresolute, gazing down at the glowing gas fire.

'Reconciliation'. The word was still very much on her mind. Reconciliation was the only sensible answer.

She would write to Simon through his bank. In her letter she would make a frank admission of her lapse with Max and ask him to forgive her.

Simon would listen and come back, wouldn't he? In the past, he'd always said that if she snapped her fingers, he'd come running. But things were different then. She recalled his landlady's remark on the phone. Suppose his 'young lady' had supplanted her in his affections?

That possibility was too awful to contemplate. In desperation, she switched on the late night movie. Anything to stop her thinking.

Chapter Thirteen

'Daddy! I don't believe you've heard a single word I've been saying.'

Brigadier Crawley, once the scourge of his troops, turned to his daughter and admitted his lapse. She didn't return his look. Monica was too busy concentrating on the road ahead.

'I merely remarked that, after his first month at St. Giles, Simon Dowling seems to have settled in well.'

'Ah, yes. He has. Fine feller. Should do well.'

The presence of two boisterous grandchildren on the back seat of the car caused the Brigadier to retreat once more into his own private world. He wished that Monica were more strict with them. But then, he thought, that was modern parenthood for you.

She was right about young Dowling, of course. In his opinion, the young man had arrived on the scene not a minute too soon. Poor Phillips wasn't a fit man and surely couldn't carry on as warden much longer.

Pity that Dowling hadn't a wife. Ideally, they needed a married couple to run the place. But, with help from Tina, Phillips had managed on his own since his wife had died. A very capable girl, Tina. She and Dowling would make an admirable couple.

But the Brigadier had some reservations about the current domestic set-up at St. Giles. There were only the three of them in that house. Admittedly, Phillips was a kind of chaperone. But, still, young people these days ...

He sighed. It was not a perfect situation by any means. And

suppose Phillips were forced to give up through ill health, what then?

If Dowling took over as warden, would Tina continue as his assistant? From the point of view of administration, it would be an excellent arrangement. But morally? Could their committee connive at an unmarried couple living in the same house under their patronage?

It posed a problem and one that would have to be given careful consideration in the near future.

The children began tickling his neck but he was spared prolonged torment because, just then, Monica drove through the gates of St. Giles. She pulled up in front of the house and he got out.

'I'll pick you up at four,' she shouted and drove off at speed, sending up a cloud of dust as she did so.

He was met on the steps by Dowling who conducted him into the study where Phillips awaited him.

'Brigadier Crawley,' he announced.

The warden was about to get up from his chair but Crawley forestalled him. Tina came in with a tray of coffee.

He always enjoyed their coffee − must ask them what blend it was − but the biscuits he never touched. For him, the next half hour was a pleasant time spent with friends.

Eventually, Tina cleared away and Dowling followed her out of the room. Apart from Miss Macintosh, he and Phillips were left alone for their business discussion.

Phillips tried to brush off enquiries about his health but the Brigadier remained concerned. There seemed nothing, however, that he could do. Phillips' management couldn't be faulted so the matter had to be left where it was.

After lunch, the warden had to rest on doctor's orders. Quite providential, thought the Brigadier. It offered the chance of a private talk with young Dowling.

'I hope you're happy here?' he began when they were in the grounds, out of earshot of the house.

'Very happy. It's all so worthwhile. I feel I'm really doing something with my life at last.'

'Good. I confess I'm worried about your warden. Mr. Phillips is a very sick man − as I'm sure you realise.'

'Yes, I do.'

'If it should come to the point where he could no longer continue, we'd obviously have to find a successor. That might not be easy. On the other hand, you've been trained by him – albeit for a short time. If the worst should come to the worst, d'you think you could step into his shoes?'

'I wouldn't have his experience, of course, but I share his ideals. I'd certainly have a good try.'

'Well spoken. I thought that's the line you'd take. You can rely on the committee supporting you to the hilt.'

'Thank you, sir. Still, I hope Mr. Phillips will continue for many years to come.'

'Ah, yes. So do I – so do we all.'

The Brigadier was about to make another point when he caught his breath. That young woman – what was her name? – always did make him catch his breath. She had just appeared out of one of the classrooms and was right in their path.

She gave them both an engaging smile that did wonders for an old soldier's morale. 'Good morning, Brigadier. Hello, Simon. Are you about to visit my class?'

'Not now, my dear. Another day, it'll have to be.'

She looked genuinely disappointed. 'I'll look forward to that.' Then, with another dazzling smile, she went on her way.

'What an extraordinarily pretty girl, that is!' the Brigadier murmured. 'I never can remember her name. What is it, now?'

'Stephanie Gilbert.'

'Of course it is. Teaches computer studies, eh?'

'Yes, with Doug.'

'Thought so. I must make a point of seeing her in action next time I'm here.'

'She's very well liked by the students.'

'I can imagine,' the old man replied with feeling.

They walked on some way in silence, each with his own private thoughts. The Brigadier had something on his mind and wondered how he could broach the matter without sounding impertinent. He summoned up his courage.

'Have you – er – any thoughts of getting married? You haven't any nice girl in mind?' As he spoke, he gave a little laugh to make the question sound less intrusive.

109

Simon took it in his stride. 'No, I haven't. I don't even have a girl friend.'

'Oh.' The Brigadier was disappointed but tried to hide it by the tone of his voice. 'Well, let me give you a word of advice as an older man to a younger one — marriage, Dowling, is a wonderful institution. I recommend it.'

Simon found it a very moving tableau.

He'd gone into the specially-adapted garden where students could tend their plants at wheelchair height. He'd stopped yards away from where Tina was talking to Alf Harris, a paraplegic. As planned, he kept discreetly out of sight.

She had just broken some shattering news to him. In great distress, Alf's mother had phoned. Her daughter-in-law, she explained, felt she could no longer cope with having a paraplegic for a husband. She'd decided to set up home with another man.

Tina had risen to the occasion magnificently and had shown great reserves of strength.

'It's easy to criticise,' she'd said. 'But how do any of us know how we'd react in similar circumstances?'

Simon nodded his agreement. 'But it's not going to be easy telling him.'

'I'll do it. It'll be better coming from a woman.'

'Is that fair on you?' he'd demanded. 'Mr. Phillips, what do you think?'

'Difficult task. Yes. Very. But Tina can manage. Has the comforting touch.'

So it was agreed. Simon was to keep a watching brief. He saw the look of incredulity, the abject misery as Alf's lips twitched. His eyes closed, face creased up. His whole body heaved. Alf Harris was weeping.

Tina was sitting on the low wall where only a few minutes earlier Alf had been happily tending his plants. She had taken his hands in his, talking softly.

Then, she put her arms round his shoulders, holding him tight. Alf pressed his face against her chest, sobbing bitterly. The sound of it tore at Simon's heart strings.

He slipped away. He felt he was prying. But that scene would probably remain with him always.

110

During the time he'd been at St. Giles, he'd changed his mind about Tina. Living under the same roof had given him the chance of getting to know her.

Once, he'd thought she seemed like a waif. She still looked like one. But Tina wasn't like that at all. She was a capable young woman with her feet on the ground.

He was glad of this. It meant his conscience was easier for he no longer felt he'd violated her. And she seemed to have taken that episode in her stride and hadn't mentioned it since.

One way and another, quite a remarkable girl, he thought, with so much love to give – not just for her father but for everyone.

It was Sunday evening and Simon hated Sunday evenings. For him they lacked stimulus and he was always glad when Monday mornings came round.

The trouble was he had no interest in the television. But Phillips was an addict and wasn't very selective. Simon was struggling to keep awake. Tina was dividing her concentration between the small screen and her father.

He was suffering the recurrent pain of a back injury he'd received during the war. In consequence, he was sitting with his legs resting on a stool.

'You sure you're comfortable, Dad?'

'I'm fine, Tina.'

'Can I get you anything?'

'Thank you, dear – no.' He returned his attention to the screen just in time for the commercial break.

Television adverts bored Simon. To him, they were banal. And, besides that, he wasn't interested in the play they were watching. He yawned and immediately apologised.

'I could do with a spot of air. I think I'll go for a walk down to the village and back.'

'I'd like to come, too.' Tina was already jumping up out of her seat. 'Do you mind?'

Simon smiled. 'No, of course not.'

'Wrap up well. Chilly outside,' Phillips advised.

Tina stood behind her father and kissed the top of his head, as he'd seen her do so many times. They went out.

It certainly was very chilly but a magnificent night

111

nevertheless. A keen wind was blowing and they were glad of their scarves and anoraks. There were no stars but a full moon could be seen hiding behind a bank of light clouds.

They walked briskly along the drive and on to the road that led to the village. They spoke little; Simon was enjoying her company without having to make small talk. And it was pleasant to savour the magic of the night.

The moon came out as they reached the village and almost immediately went in again. The only signs of life were lights at the cottage windows.

They sat on the seat provided where, during the day, villagers would gossip and watch the ducks on the pond.

Tina spoke in a small, hesitant voice. 'Do you ever regret what happened between us that time?'

Simon was glad he was able to reply truthfully. 'No, I don't. More to the point – do you?'

'Not a bit.' This time, her tone was vigorous and sounded sure. 'I feel proud that you loved me just for a few minutes.'

How could he answer that? Say that she'd misunderstood and that it wasn't just a few minutes? But that would give the wrong impression. It was safer to say nothing.

Even so, he did like Tina. He enjoyed her company and had an enormous respect for her. When he needed advice, it was usually her that he consulted.

He recalled the Brigadier's words. Obviously, the old boy wanted him to marry Tina. Perhaps Phillips did too. He felt he was being pushed in that direction.

She shivered. 'You're cold,' he said. 'We'd better return.'

'Do we have to?'

'I was thinking we could go back across the fields.'

'That would be nice.'

The grass was springy beneath their feet as they walked towards the stile in the far corner of the field. Simon took her hand. It hadn't been premeditated but came quite naturally. She said, 'Let's take our gloves off.'

They did so and her hand felt warm in spite of the night air. She hummed a little tune. When they reached the stile, he took up the refrain in his baritone voice.

'You sing very well,' she said.

112

'And so do you. Tina, may I ask you something? Are you happy?'

'Mmm, very.' She was leaning over the top rail, staring into the distance. The moon came out again, playing upon her features. With her big eyes and serious face she made an enchanting picture, simple and yet profound.

He climbed over the stile first to help her over on to the other side. She negotiated the first part then stood on the top step, looking down at him.

For a moment, he was unnerved. Then, taking her by the waist, he gave her a lift. She slid down against him and his arms remained about her, holding her off the ground.

He felt her shiver again. 'You're cold.'

'No.'

He kissed her and she pressed her body against his. It seemed an age since he'd last had a woman. He could feel his desire mounting.

'Oh, Simon, I've longed for you to do that. Kiss me again.'

He did so, harder this time. Slowly, he lowered her to the ground. Her arms were still around him, her hands sliding beneath his anorak.

'We ought to go back,' he said.

'Not yet. There's that old barn at the back of the house. Can't we go in there for a few minutes?'

He hesitated. It was tempting. But caution prevailed. 'Isn't that a bit sneaky with your father in the house?'

'He wouldn't mind − not if he knew I was with you.'

They went to the barn. The place smelt sweetly of the earth and everything pertaining to the world of nature.

There, in the light from the moon streaming in over the door and cushioned by a mound of straw, he made love to her again. This time, there was no shame.

He thought of his recent trip to Sarah's office; his cowardice at the last minute; his return without seeing her. Hadn't all that been in the stars? Wasn't it meant that he and Sarah should part after all? Wasn't Tina to be his destiny?

'Tina,' he began after a silence, 'don't you think we ought to get married?'

Her response was to kiss him fervently.

'Oh, yes! I thought you'd never ask. How could I possibly

113

refuse you, my dearest Simon? I'm yours for ever and ever.'

He kissed her again.

'I'm longing for Dad to know,' she went on. 'He'll be in bed now. I'll tell him tomorrow when he's settled in his chair. He'll be so pleased.'

The back injury continued to give Tina's father some pain but she was not unduly worried by this. The trouble often recurred but usually it was only of short duration.

It had been decided he needed at least another day's rest. Monday morning found him sitting in his favourite chair. Beside him lay a pile of the day's newspapers.

Tina came in, bubbling with excitement. 'Daddy, I've got something very special to tell you.'

He looked up. 'Have you, dear?'

She sat on his knee. 'I'm not hurting your back, am I?' He shook his head. 'Good.'

She kissed his forehead and snuggled her cheek against his. 'Daddy, I'm going to be married. To Simon.'

Tears filled his eyes and he was unable to speak at first. 'Marvellous,' he said at last. 'So − so very happy.'

'And you're not cross?'

'Why should I be?'

'That I'm taking a husband.'

'I'm delighted. Absolutely.'

Simon could be heard coming along the hall.

'I've told Daddy,' she said, slipping off her father's knee as he came in.

'Delighted!' Phillips murmured.

After that congratulations and wedding plans were the sole topic for several minutes. In the end, they all dried up, exhausted.

During the ensuing lull, Phillips said, 'Switch the television on will you, Tina? There might be something on.'

'You and your old TV!' She did as requested.

She and Simon tried to discuss their wedding but it was difficult against the background of the television.

'Ah, I like this chap − Sean Maguire,' Phillips said. 'He's a very good chairman.'

The programme was nearly halfway through. Tina heard

114

the name 'Sarah Castle' mentioned. It rang a bell.

'Sarah Cas − isn't that the Sarah you − ?' Tina froze. She'd caught the expression on Simon's face as he watched the girl on the screen.

In that moment, Tina knew the truth. She stifled a cry of anguish as she realised that, fiancée or not, she would always be second best for Simon.

Chapter Fourteen

The editor of the *Daily Courier* was Lamb by name but not always by nature. He was, in fact, anything but docile towards his colleagues. His temper was unpredictable and when raised, his voice could be heard several offices away. The only staff member who had no fear of him was his secretary.

But in the family circle, a transformation took place. He became tractable and it was his wife, Olivia, who ruled the home and made all the decisions.

Today promised to be a great event in Martin Lamb's life. He was to be presented to his new grandson at Heathrow when the child's parents arrived from the States. So he'd taken the day off from work. That in itself was unusual and showed the importance of the occasion.

Martin was an impatient man and the morning hung heavily on him. He had nothing to do. All the papers had been scrutinised by his experienced eye. None of the tabloids came up to the standard of his own *Daily Courier*, of course. He was a professional to his finger tips — the best editor in Fleet Street. No one knew that better than he.

He looked at the wall clock. Still over an hour to go before they'd have to leave for the airport. In frustration, he grabbed his handset and switched on the television.

At that moment, Sean Maguire was on screen hosting his new discussion programme. Martin knew Sean, had worked with him on one or two occasions, but his eyes were on the dark-haired young woman on the panel. A good-looker! Bright and intelligent. Lovely legs. Knew how to dress, too.

As far as he was concerned, no one else there was of any consequence. Her name, he discovered, was Sarah Castle.

What she had to say was well delivered with a trace of an American accent. And he liked the way she structured her argument so that the viewer could follow her reasoning.

Martin became her devoted fan. When his wife came in, he 'shushed' her and she went away aggrieved.

At the end of the programme, he switched off. He wondered where he'd heard that young woman's name before. Funny that. It certainly struck a chord in his memory. But, try as he might, he couldn't recall why.

The problem was still teasing his brain as he drove to Heathrow with his wife. It was not until they were in the airport that his subconscious finally jogged his memory.

'Got it!'

Olivia looked at him curiously. 'Got what?'

'I'll explain later.' Depositing her on a seat, he phoned his office from a call box. His secretary answered.

'Hi, Pat. It's Martin. Remember a few days ago, we had a letter from a woman journalist offering her services?'

'I've got it right here.'

'Fine. What's her name?'

'Sarah Castle.'

'Thought as much. Right. Here's what I want you to do. Write and say I'm willing to meet her − just that. Make it non-committal. Ask her to phone to make an appointment. Don't wait for my signature − sign it yourself per pro − and get it off today. Got that?'

'Sure.'

'Any problems?'

'One or two minor ones. But I've sorted them out.'

'Good girl. Cheers.'

He rejoined Olivia.

'Why are you looking so pleased with yourself?' she wanted to know.

'I'm hoping to acquire a valuable new member of staff. But I don't want to talk about it. As you know, I'm superstitious and that would only tempt providence.'

* * *

Sarah waited.

The editor's outer office was neat and tidy and obviously efficiently run. The secretary looked that sort of young woman. No nonsense about her. That was encouraging.

Even so, Sarah's old insecurity was making itself felt. She was also extremely worried on a personal matter and had been low in spirits for some time. If she didn't keep her anxieties under control, they might show through.

But she was quite adept at putting on an act, giving the impression that she was brimming over with self-confidence and joie de vivre. She would do that now. She *had* to do it.

A buzzer sounded on the secretary's desk.

'Mr. Lamb will see you now, Miss Castle.'

'Thank you.'

Sarah braced herself. Like her mother, she could make a good entrance when she chose. This was one of those occasions. She took a deep breath, held her head high and swept through the open door into the editor's office.

'Miss Castle. How d'you do?'

They shook hands and she took a seat facing the desk. She could tell she'd already made a hit.

Martin Lamb was of medium height with a high colour. Too much lunchtime beer, she thought. His manner was friendly but forthright and she had the idea he didn't suffer fools gladly.

The interview began with the usual pleasantries. She followed these with the observation that she admired the professionalism of the *Daily Courier*.

This pleased him. He expanded upon its quality and style. 'And that is why you want to work for me?'

'Yes.'

'And what makes you think you'd be suitable?'

Ah, now, Sarah. Don't hold your fire. Let him have your big guns.

'One reason only: I'm a professional like you and my work is the best. Ask my present editor. He'll tell you. You need someone like me for your women's page.'

He sucked in his breath. 'Well, that's frank. You realise, of course, that we have a woman's editor?'

'Oh, yes, but not anyone doing a women's problems

118

column. Your last one left a month or two ago.'

'Yes.'

'I can fill her place. I outlined in my letter my reasons for leaving the *Examiner*.'

'That they reneged on your budget?'

'That's right.'

He leant forward aggressively, his arms on the desk top. She realised she wasn't going to have it all her own way. They sparred for several minutes while he played the part of the devil's advocate. But she wouldn't give an inch.

At last, he relaxed and smiled. 'Very well, I think you've convinced me.' He outlined the salary and expenses they were prepared to pay.

'I'd want more than that.'

'Then it's no go, I'm afraid.'

She shook her head in sorrow. 'Such a pity. I do have another offer but I thought I'd see you first.'

'Who is it?'

Sarah gave him an arch look. She had no intention of telling him it had come from Sir Reece Brown. 'Oh, come, Mr. Lamb, surely, you don't expect me to reveal that? But I can tell you it's one of the leading tabloids.'

For some reason, this convinced him. 'So we come back to the question of salary.'

'Yes.'

He sighed. They bantered. They bargained. At last, a compromise was reached. Sarah was pleased. It was more than she'd expected.

'Very well. It's a deal. When can you start?'

'At the New Year. But before I agree, I have some conditions to make. There's my budget for a start. I must have a personal secretary, a research assistant, expert ancillary help, and I don't want to have to stint on office equipment. Can I have your assurance on those points?'

He laughed. 'You certainly know your own mind.'

She returned a smile. They seemed to be friends. 'Yes, I do. And there's one other condition.'

He was on his guard. 'And what's that?'

'With my other offer, I was promised star columnist status. I'd like the same from you.'

119

'Tell me more,' he said in a low voice.

'I need to be hyped-up – for the readers to be told that Sarah Castle is a real coup. And only eye-catching bylines, please. Also, I want to do more television. The *Courier* will gain by my exposure, but I need your co-operation. May I have it?'

He was some time in answering. 'Phew! Star columnist status, eh? Very well. Our woman's editor won't like it but it'll do the paper good. Now, Sarah, I never go back on my word and I'm sure you don't. When I say we'll support you and give you a lot of publicity hype, I mean just that.' He stood up and reached across the desk. 'Let's shake on that.'

'Gladly.'

She felt a little weak at the knees but a great surge of elation filled her.

The feeling didn't last long. By the time she'd reached home, her spirits had sunk once again.

An appointment with the doctor had been made for the next day and she was dreading it. For the past three weeks, she'd had a growing anxiety. At first, it had seemed unimportant and she'd dismissed it as a blip in her cycle. But the days had slipped by and still nothing had happened.

She was very overdue. Sarah had little doubt what the doctor would say.

Two days later, on the Saturday, Sarah rose late, had a leisurely shower and spent some time at her dressing table before preparing breakfast.

In the hallway, she noticed a letter on the doormat when she went to take in the milk. The writing was Simon's.

Trembling fingers opened the envelope, unfolded the paper, straightened it out. Her eyes skipped through it, not fully taking it all in.

'. . . will come as a surprise . . . getting married. When I called . . . saw you had other interests . . . better to make complete break . . . I'll no longer be a drag on your career . . . able to forget . . . Love, Simon.'

Sarah was shattered. They had been so close over many years. Their affair had been such a passionate one. They loved one another. No question of it.

She could not even envisage Simon belonging to someone else. Another woman calling him 'darling', cooking for him, sleeping with him ... No! But it was true. She'd have to get used to the idea. And she had no one to blame but herself.

And now ... God, what a mess everything was!

The doorbell rang. She opened the door. Max stood there, weekend case in hand. She didn't kiss him.

'Come in, Max. I have something to tell you.'

He sat down. She didn't soften the blow. 'I'm pregnant.'

He didn't raise so much as an eyebrow. Sarah had expected some expression of shock or anger or sympathy. Instead, no comment at all.

'I must say you appear remarkably calm.'

'What d'you expect? These things happen, Sarah. It's unfortunate, certainly.'

'Unfortunate for whom, Max?' She spoke quietly.

'Well – you.'

She studied him awhile in silence. 'What do you intend to do about it?'

'Me?'

He was floored. Sarah had the impression he hadn't realised something might be expected of him. 'If you're about to suggest I should have an abortion,' she said, 'forget it.'

He shifted uncomfortably in his seat. 'Well, for my part, marriage can be ruled out. I mean, these days couples don't rush off to the altar just because there's a kid on the way. Besides, I don't want to get married yet.'

'So you'd prefer to set up home with me, is that it? As you say, lots of couples do that nowadays. It's even quite respectable.'

'But living like that would be almost the same as being married. I mean, there'd still be domesticity and the child. I'm not geared up for that sort of life.'

Sarah gasped and sat down heavily. 'That's all you have to say?'

'Oh, look, Sarah. We've had lots of fun, you and I. For a while at least, we can go on having fun, can't we? We can't give everything up just because you're pregnant.'

He rose, gave her a swift kiss and picked up his suitcase.

'Where're you going with that?'

'Into the bedroom to unpack.'

'Listen, buddy — there's only one place you're going and that's out.' She pointed to the door. 'Get!'

His mouth dropped open. He didn't believe she meant it. But she went to the door and held it open. He slipped his hand round her waist, felt her breast, tried to kiss her. She turned her head and disengaged his fingers.

Max pulled away. He looked like a scolded schoolboy. He bit his lip and blinked at her. Then, without another word, he ran down the stairs.

Sarah softly closed the door.

In the sitting room, she picked up Simon's letter again and read it more carefully this time. '... no longer a drag on your career' he'd written.

Well, that was a laugh for a start. Recently, she'd kept Simon at arm's length because she was ambitious. He'd finally taken her at her word. Max had been nothing more to her than a temporary diversion.

Temporary had she thought? Now, she was going to have his baby. That certainly had the quality of permanency about it. And what effect would a baby have on her career?

Ella would laugh or sneer — or both. Might even be delighted that she'd fallen. Sarah could almost hear her saying, 'Serve the little bitch right!'

Sarah pondered the situation afresh. Other unmarried women had babies and still carried on with their careers. And became successful into the bargain. She would too. Nothing had really changed. She was already on the ladder and would continue to step up it until she had reached the top.

But explaining her condition to Martin Lamb wouldn't be easy. He'd be furious, try and renege on his promises, maybe. If he did that, it would be a battle royal between them. Sarah was damned if she'd be cheated of her chance a second time.

The main drawing room at Glenhurst, with its high ceiling, stone fireplace and square bay windows, breathed elegance. The sumptuous furnishings provided comfort and warmth. The curtains had been drawn to shut out the winter's night.

Max was ill at ease. Bewildered. Astonished at Sarah's

122

rejection. His pride had been hurt by what he saw as her unreasonable behaviour.

But his unease had a far more deep-rooted cause. He felt he was the pig in the middle, with Sarah on one side and his father on the other. And he was no match for either of them. He had no illusions about how his father would react to the news of a bastard grandchild. The more Max thought about it, the more frightened he became.

He had no alternative but to make a clean breast of everything and it had to be in the next few minutes. Tomorrow, Reece and Alison would be entertaining lavishly and there'd be no chance for him to have a private word with his father. Max couldn't face another week of this agony. Besides, Reece might hear from Sarah by then. That would only make matters worse.

Alison rose from her seat by the dying fire and stretched. 'I think I'll go up to our room, dear,' she said. 'You won't be long, will you?'

'Another half an hour or so.'

Max murmured a goo₫night and watched her glide across the room and go out. He listened for the click of the door catch.

The dreaded moment had come.

'Father,' he began in an uncertain voice, 'you remember Sarah Castle?'

Reece looked up irritably from the paper he was reading. 'Of course I remember her.'

'Her period of notice with us has almost expired.'

'I know that too.'

'She's got another job.'

Reece sat up, suddenly interested. 'She has? Who with?'

'The *Daily Courier*.'

Reece flung his paper to the floor. 'Damn and blast! I'd already made her a good offer to join my *Sentinel*.'

Max was surprised. 'But, when she first gave in her notice, I thought you said we were to call her bluff and let her go. I don't understand.'

Reece looked at his son as though he were dealing with an imbecile. 'I like to have the initiative in everything I do. Her resignation was a threat and I will not be threatened. Afterwards, the situation changed. At her aunt's house party, I

123

regained the initiative so I made her a most generous offer.'

'I see.'

'And she's turned n.: down. She prefers the *Daily Courier* to my *Sentinel*. Damn the girl! It's an insult.' He was breathing heavily, clenching his fists, leaning forward on the edge of his seat in exasperation.

Max also took a deep breath. He had reached the point of no return. 'But I'm wondering whether she'll be with the *Courier* very long.'

Reece looked up sharply, his senses keenly alert. ''Vhy do you say that?'

'She's going to have a baby.'

'Good God! And you − you've been going about with her. Don't tell me you're the father?'

'Yes.'

His father almost exploded. 'You blithering idiot! You ineffectual oaf! Isn't there anything you can do that is right?'

'I'm sorry, Father.'

'Why didn't you take precautions?'

Max had no answer.

'You'll be marrying the girl, of course?'

'Well, no − that is − '

His father got out of his chair, stood with legs astride and pointed a finger accusingly at his son. 'Listen to me, numbskull. Remember this. You are not the only one who has a say in this. I also have a substantial interest. Sarah's child will one day be my heir. And I will not allow my grandchild − my heir − be born a bastard. Understand?' He raised his voice and his face became livid with fury. 'I will not have it, do you hear? Get that into that thick skull of yours and learn to do as you're told.'

'Yes, Father.'

'You will go back to that young woman and you will marry her. Understand?'

124

Chapter Fifteen

Winter sunshine on the birches. People out with dogs. Children riding bikes. Families feeding ducks.

A typical Sunday afternoon. Sarah loved it all. The scene was so typically English. A brisk walk across the park in the sharp air envigorated her. Afterwards, she was ready to curl up on the settee with a good book.

As she let herself into the flat, she felt a return of her crippling uncertainty but tried to banish the feeling. This was no time for defeatism. She took off her coat and sat by the fire.

The phone rang. She picked it up.

A man's voice. 'Sarah Castle?'

'Yes.'

'Lamb here – editor of the *Daily Courier*. He sounded most unfriendly. 'I want to see you. You owe me an explanation.'

For a moment, she was lost for words. Not knowing what was in his mind, she said, 'Do I?'

'You know damn well you do! I'll see you in my office tomorrow – Monday – at eleven.' There was a crash as he slammed the phone down.

Sarah was in a daze. To make a business call on a Sunday afternoon was certainly unusual so he must have regarded it as urgent. And he'd sounded extremely annoyed. Why? There could be only one reason. He'd heard about her condition.

Who'd told him? It couldn't have come from Max ... but Reece? It could only be him. Max had probably confided in

125

his father and Reece had been motivated to do this from sheer spite.

She lay awake most of the night, turning everything over and over, her thoughts in confusion. When the dawn came, she felt haggard and worn. But a hot shower put some of the spirit back into her and by nine o'clock she was ready to face the world.

A phone call to Louise explained that she would not be in the office until lunchtime. Her assistant complained bitterly. Sarah apologised and said that she had no option.

With Sir Reece Brown as her employer, Moira Clark hated Monday mornings. Not a sympathetic man at the best of times, he was at his worst at the beginning of the week.

She heard his footsteps on the landing outside. The click of the door latch. One glance at his face told her that today would not be an exception to the rule.

She put on her most winning smile. 'Good morning, Sir Reece.'

He gave her a curt nod. 'Morning.' Without another word he went through to his own office and closed the door.

While waiting to be summoned to the great man's presence, she busied herself with trivial jobs. The phone on her desk rang and she answered it.

'It's Williams, the butler from Glenhurst. I'd like to speak to Sir Reece Brown. It's important.'

'Hold on.' She flipped a switch. 'Oh, Sir Reece, I have your butler on the line. He says it's important.'

'Damn! Put him on, then.'

Miss Clark didn't replace her receiver but listened in to the conversation. For some reason she was curious.

She heard Williams say, 'I beg your pardon, sir, for bothering you at the office, but I thought you ought to know. It's Mr. Max – '

'What about him?'

'Well, sir, he didn't come down to breakfast as usual. I thought it was a bit funny – '

'Get on with it, man!'

'I knocked at his door and there was no reply.'

'Probably oversleeping.'

126

'No, sir. I tried to open the door and found it locked. I asked Cook and the maids whether they'd seen or heard him and none of them had. I feel very worried, sir, and have a premonition that something terrible – '

'I'll return home at once.'

Hurriedly, his secretary replaced her own receiver when she heard movements from the inner office. The door burst open.

'Cancel all my appointments for the rest of the day, Miss Clark. I have been called away on family business.'

'Very well, Sir Reece.'

Miss Clark was delighted. It was going to be a more enjoyable start to the week than usual.

Sarah arrived at the *Daily Courier* office with several minutes to spare. The secretary showed her in immediately.

The editor half rose from his seat and sat down again. 'I must say you've chosen a bloody fine time to get pregnant, haven't you?' he bellowed.

The fact that he was in a temper put strength into Sarah. She faced him boldly.

'Let me make one thing clear, Mr. Lamb, I will not be shouted at. If you continue in that vein, I'll leave this office and wait until you're in control of yourself.'

He looked as if he'd been slapped. His eyes glinted angrily but were lowered to the desk. She'd won the first bout. He took several deep breaths and began to speak in a more reasonable tone. His manner, though, remained belligerent.

'You tricked me.'

'I'm not a lawyer, Mr. Lamb, but I imagine if you were to repeat that charge to anyone else, it might constitute slander. I'd certainly advise you against it.'

'Oh, look here – '

'No. *You* look here! I did not trick you. I did not know I was pregnant until after you appointed me. That's the truth. Whether you believe it or not is up to you.'

'Very well.' He was still hostile. 'According to our agreement, you would be hyped-up as God's gift to journalism – the greatest discovery since the invention of the typewriter. How can I launch you in public while you get fatter and

127

fatter around the midriff? Tell me that.'

'You're shouting again. And why couldn't you? TV presenters have managed under those circumstances. I'll carry on as usual. When the time comes, I'd take maternity leave – instead of a holiday – engage an au pair and go from there.'

'Too facile.' He was more subdued but still not entirely convinced. 'No, it won't work. Our deal's off.'

'That would be most unwise.' She was about to play her trump card. 'That other offer I told you about: it's still pending; I haven't turned it down yet. So if you force me, I could take it up after all.'

'And deceive them as you've deceived me?'

'Careful now. As a matter of fact, there wouldn't be any need to deceive them as you put it. They – or rather, *he* – already knows.' He stared at her, struggling to understand. She continued. 'It was Sir Reece Brown who told you, wasn't it?'

After a while, he nodded. 'Yes.'

'I thought so. Yes, it all makes sense. It so happens I'd prefer to work for you. I really mean that. But he would more than welcome me into his fold even though I'm pregnant – just to dish you.' Lamb was shaking his head disbelievingly. 'Besides, it would be keeping everything in the family. You see, Sir Reece will be my baby's grandfather.'

Lamb put his head in his hands. When he looked up at her again, a slow smile was spreading across his face.

'I'm beginning to understand. The cunning old bastard thought he'd pip us by letting on about your condition. He hoped I'd tear up your contract and so send you over to his stable.'

'Precisely.'

He held out his hand across the desk as he'd done on the earlier occasion. She took it warmly. 'Sarah, we've beaten him. What a triumph this is! And if you have any problems during your pregnancy, just let me know. I'll fix them. And I'd like to be godfather – if you'll have me.'

'Delighted – provided you don't shout at me.'

The staff memo that landed on Sarah's desk was very succinct. It said, 'Sir Reece Brown, chairman of the

Examiner Group, has announced that, with immediate effect, his son, Max Brown, no longer has executive status within the company. A successor will be appointed in due course.'

The news came as a blow to Sarah. She was sure Max's fall from grace was connected with her pregnancy but assumed a mask of disinterest when speaking of the change.

Louise received the news in her usual sanguine manner. 'Well, he's no loss. Not that it's going to affect you. You're about to leave us, after all. Two more days and you'll be saying your farewells.'

'Yes.'

'And then I'll revert to my usual role – keeping the women's ship afloat until another enthusiastic captain comes along to chivvy me around.'

Sarah's patience snapped.

'Why do you always have this chip on your shoulder?'

'Chip?'

'You know what I mean. You've resented me ever since I came here. Now, with me gone, you'll have a chance to convince Bob that you can do this job.'

'No. He'll choose someone else. I think that to get on in journalism you have to be a go-getter, like you. And it helps if you're prepared to sleep with – ' She stopped abruptly, obviously realising she'd gone too far. 'What I mean is – some do it, don't they?' she added lamely.

Sarah refused to be drawn into an unseemly argument which might sound like an admission on her part. Or even a defence. That would have been worse.

'We have a deadline, don't forget,' she replied in a level voice. 'I suggest we both concentrate on our work.'

Concentration, though, wasn't easy and Sarah finished her page with relief. She was glad to be out of the office and away from the silent reproach of Louise. Driving through the crowded streets was a slow process in the rush hour and her state of mind did nothing to relieve the tedium.

Had Max been dismissed because he'd made her pregnant? Had he resigned? Had he suffered an accident? And what was Reece's reaction – if, that is, he knew he was going to be a grandfather?

129

She didn't feel like having supper but forced herself to have a light snack which she ate at the kitchen table. And still the questions refused to go away.

It was while she was washing up the dishes, that she heard the front doorbell. She dried her hands hurriedly and flung open the door.

On the threshold stood Sir Reece, imperious and disdainful. She was startled and lost her tongue. Without waiting for an invitation, he marched through the hall and into the sitting room with the words, 'I have to talk to you.'

She offered him a seat but he refused. Instead, he took up a position on the hearth rug, feet apart, arms folded. The veins in his temples were throbbing.

'You've insulted me.'

Sarah gasped and sat down heavily. 'I have?'

'You rejected my offer − a most magnanimous offer, I might add − and preferred to go the *Courier*. Why?'

'Let me ask you a question. Why did you tell Martin of my condition?' For a second, he was knocked off balance. 'I'll tell you. You wanted to crab my chances.'

'I was thinking of your own good.'

'You weren't thinking of my good at all. You wanted to have me as your property − like all the other minions in your life. Like your son.'

'What rubbish!'

'You enjoy pulling the strings of your puppets but I refuse to be anybody's toy nor will I have people interfering in my life. I'm my own woman, Reece.'

He gave a slightly mocking bow. 'Interesting.'

'I have to say I would never work for you.'

He smiled. 'I wouldn't be too sure of that, young lady.' He stroked his chin and surveyed her for some moments. 'Now to this other matter. You're pregnant.' He pointed his finger at her and made it sound like an indictment.

'Should I have asked your permission first?'

He was forced to say, 'Of course not.'

'Oh, good. That's a relief.' Sarah's tone was heavily ironic.

'But the fact remains, it's most unfortunate.'

'For whom?' Reece Brown held no fears for her now.

He hesitated. 'Well, there's your career, for one thing, and – '

'My career is my own affair. Have you asked how Max feels?'

'Ah, Max!' Suddenly, the arrogance was drained from his face. He looked older, more careworn. He gave up his position on the rug and sank slowly into the nearest armchair. 'Max has gone.'

'Gone?'

'He's walked out. Emptied his wardrobes and drawers and drove off during the night. God knows where he is.'

Sarah sat down. She didn't know what to say. And yet it all fitted in with what she knew of him. Immature and irresponsible. The two words summed up Max Brown.

Reece continued. 'I shan't try to find him, if that's what you're thinking. He's an adult – although there are times when that is hard to believe. He won't starve. He has a small income from his mother's estate.'

'What will he do?'

'I don't know. I don't even care. When he was young, I thought one day he'd be my heir and take over my interests. Now, the very sight of him irritates me. But I'm angry he hasn't had the decency to legitimise his child. He should have married you.'

'Don't I have a say in this? Suppose I don't want to marry him?'

This came as a new thought. 'Don't you, then?'

'No.'

He digested this. 'So you don't mind having an illegitimate child?'

'It's not what I'd choose.'

'Well, *I* certainly mind.' His voice had regained its vigour and had a sharper edge to it. 'I mind very much about my grandchild being born a bastard.'

'I'm sorry but – '

He stood up. His tone was belligerent. 'I have a solution. *I* would marry you.' Sarah suppressed her astonishment as Reece went on: 'The child would have a name and you'd enjoy a good lifestyle.'

'The short answer is "no". But thanks for the offer.'

131

'I see.' He didn't seem unduly surprised. 'So we come to the second option. I'd provide maintenance for you and the baby providing you change your name by deed pool to "Brown" before the child is born. That, at least, would give the semblance of legitimacy.'

'I wouldn't even consider it. I am not on the bread line. Never have been. Besides, I like my independence and I mean to keep it.'

'And that is your final word?'

'That is definitely my final word.'

His face became hard; his brow thunderous. 'Well, it's not *my* final word.' He marched into the hall. With his hand on the open door, he turned. 'That baby is my grandchild and I'll never let you forget it.'

Sarah watched him pull the door after him; heard the click of the latch and the sound of his feet on the stairs.

She took a deep breath. She would never forget the look in his eyes nor the implied threat in what he'd said.

She shuddered.

Friday the twenty-first of December. The day when Sarah's notice expired at the *Examiner*.

She'd made a whistle-stop tour of the building for a last-minute chat with her colleagues. Everywhere good wishes had been showered upon her. Even Louise had had the grace to say she was sorry she was going.

In some ways, Sarah was sorry too. So much needed to be done; so many improvements to her page to be made. She regretted not being there to carry them through. On the other hand, a far more exciting challenge lay ahead.

But before starting her job at the *Daily Courier* in the New Year, she would be spending Christmas with Auntie Win. She was looking forward to that.

Now, she'd wrapped up her gifts, packed her suitcase, put on her coat. One last look around the flat. Gas taps turned off. Central heating OK. Lights switched off. Everything in order. She locked her front door and went to her car. Moments later, she was on her way.

Sarah's earlier doubts about the future had given way to supreme self-confidence. 1985 was going to be an eventful

132

year; an exhausting and stimulating one, she knew, but she would win through.

She was singing as she filtered into the traffic on the main road and headed towards the south coast.

PART TWO

Chapter Sixteen

In a corner of north-west London lay a small cul-de-sac called The Close. Situated near the shops and the tube station, it consisted of a recent development of town houses built in Georgian style.

Despite its proximity to the town, the small cluster of houses gave the impression of being peacefully remote. And yet, its location offered speedy access to Sarah's office in the *Daily Courier* building just off Fleet Street.

These were some of the reasons why she had chosen it, and in the two years she'd been living there, not once had she regretted the decision. Moreover it had been to number five, The Close, that she'd brought Rufus, her newborn son. That, in itself, made it home in a very real sense.

Rufus, a lively child with a will of his own, had inherited her looks and was developing fast. Helga, the au pair, was a vivacious nineteen year old from Heidelberg, perfect for Rufus and good company for Sarah. One way and another, theirs was a happy ménage.

There had been no word from Max. No one knew where he was; whether he was still in the country; whether he was alive, even. Sarah's thoughts about him alternated between two extremes. Anger at the way he'd treated her and pity for the weak character that he was.

At first, Reece had pestered Sarah about legitimising her son. He had cajoled and offered tempting inducements. But she'd remained adamant. She would not under any circumstances take the name "Brown" by deed poll. That, she said, was final. Reece made his displeasure very obvious. But at last, he gave up, recognising he'd met his match.

But she wasn't lulled into a sense of false security. She was certain that when Rufus became older and therefore more interesting to a man like Reece, he'd try to play a more dominant role. She'd have to watch the situation very carefully.

One morning in August 1987, she drank her orange juice, ate her breakfast cereal, hugged her son and said goodbye to the au pair at speed. She was short of time but the child tugged at her, begging her not to go.

'No, Rufus. Helga will see to you. Mummy is in a hurry.' She kissed his dark hair. 'God bless, darling. Be a good boy.' She turned to the au pair. 'I should be back about the usual time tonight, Helga.'

She grabbed her executive case and rushed out. In the office, she'd be faced with a mountain of work to get through. Sarah was under pressure as always. But she would not have it otherwise. It was only when she was hard pressed that she felt she was really living.

By mid-morning, though, there would be the chance to relax a little. She would be given a pleasant drive through the countryside for her most important appointment of the day. She was looking forward to it.

Sarah and the editor had been invited to lunch with the chairman. She had not the faintest idea what it was all about. She would soon find out.

Trees and hedgerows and old-world cottages.

Sarah leant back and watched the sights of rural Buckinghamshire glide by. Martin Lamb, by her side, was unaware of the scenery, absorbed by a pocket computer chess set on his lap. In the front seat, the company chauffeur sat ramrod straight as he concentrated on the road ahead. He might have been made of stone for all the movement he was making.

Sarah was beginning to find the silence oppressive. 'Why d'you think the chairman wants to see me?' she asked.

Martin looked up from his game and said he didn't know. 'Could be something or nothing. Lord Braidwood often keeps things close to his chest.'

'Well, I'm going to make an onslaught on him,' Sarah

remarked, still looking out of the window.

Martin lifted his head sharply, chess game forgotten. 'What's that supposed to mean?'

She laughed. 'It's all right, I'm not going to attack him. Only enlist his help to get me on TV more. I've had no exposure to speak of since I joined the *Courier*.'

'It was that duff agent you had.'

'Oh, I realise that. Now that I've got Margot to represent me – '

' – and she's good.'

'Yep, she is. This is how I figure it out – our chairman is a director of some television companies, isn't he? OK, I'm hoping he can bring pressure to bear. With his influence and Margot's skill – '

'I'll support you.'

'Thanks.'

'It wouldn't surprise me if he's already got something like that up his sleeve and is going to tell you today. On the other hand, it could simply be that his wife wants to meet you. She writes execrable poetry, by the way.'

'Glad you warned me.'

'She's bound to give you an inscribed copy of her latest volume.'

'I'll be duly appreciative.'

'He admires your work – and, remember, he's a newspaperman down to his fingertips. He's a rum old bird. You'll like him. There's no nonsense about Lord Braidwood. He loves the trappings of wealth but he's as proud as Punch of his northern working-class roots. He started life as a printer's devil and had his first paper by the time he was thirty. He'll tell you to call him "Sam", you mark my words.'

'What about his wife?'

'In spite of the poetry, I like Maisie. She's a pleb too. It's not unknown for her to help the servants clear the dishes, even at dinner parties.'

Before the chauffeur had pulled up at the entrance to the house, the burly figure of Lord Braidwood had appeared outside. In a gruff, forthright voice, he bade them welcome and ushered them into an oak-panelled hall. The butler, hovering there, was dismissed with a nod of the head.

'A good drive up, I hope?' said their host, shaking Sarah's hand.

'Very good, thank you, Lord Braidwood.'

'Call me "Sam", m'dear.'

Sarah caught Martin's eye. 'Thank you.'

'Now come in and meet Maisie. She always reads your column and is dying to know you.'

Sarah liked Maisie immediately. There was no artifice about her and she spoke with Yorkshire directness. Over lunch, it was she who conducted most of the conversation. She was eager to learn of Sarah's New England background and what it was like to live in the shadow of her famous mother.

Sarah said that as a child she'd found it difficult but had now broken free.

'That shows character, love. I knew you had spunk the moment you stepped in here. And I'm never wrong about folk.'

Sam Braidwood cleared his throat. 'And you're a damned good journalist, too.'

'I second that,' put in Martin to show he was still there.

'I write poetry,' Maisie said in a small voice. 'I'll give you a copy of my latest collection before you go.'

'That's very kind.'

'And you have a little lad, I believe?' Sarah nodded. Maisie cast down her eyes momentarily. 'Sam and I never had children.'

'I'm sorry.'

'How old is he?'

'Rufus? He's just had his second birthday.'

'Rufus! What a grand name. Oh, I envy you. However d'you manage to combine motherhood with your job?'

'I have an excellent au pair – a nice German girl, called Helga. I'd be lost without her. Also, I now live in St. John's Wood which is very convenient.'

'And I've seen you on television, too.'

'So have I,' Sam added.

'Have you? I've only appeared on Sean Maguire's programme three times in the last two years. And as it goes out mid-morning, I'm amazed anyone's seen it at all. I'm not exactly over-exposed.'

There was a tiny silence. She'd obviously touched upon a subject of some significance. She was both surprised and glad. Sam folded his napkin and inserted it in his silver serviette ring.

'That is something I'd like to talk to you about, Sarah – but not in here.' He rose, pushed his chair back on the parquet flooring and announced: 'We'll have coffee in the drawing room. Maisie, ring for the girl, will you?'

The drawing room was comfortable and homely. Like its owners, it was a bit untidy and without fussy overtones. The only pictures were a few family photographs. Large club armchairs and an assortment of newspapers and magazines on the carpet gave the room a lived-in appearance.

When the maid had served the coffee, Sam Braidwood lit a cigar and stood on the hearth rug with his back to the empty grate. Unceremoniously, he placed his cup and saucer on the mantelpiece.

'Well, Sarah, I don't have to tell you we're engaged in a circulation war with the *Sentinel.*'

'Sarah and I discuss it at our editorial meetings,' Martin pointed out.

'I'm sure you do. Because we're tabloids, the female readership is vitally important. You, Sarah, are one of the big guns in our battle with the *Sentinel.* And Sir Reece Brown is well aware of the damage you're causing his circulation.'

'Is that why he's appointed a new women's editor?'

'Yes. And just look at the spread he's giving her! He's got that new gossip columnist, too – what's her name? – Lady Virginia something. That shows he's worried about the way we've cornered the women's market.'

'You think we have?'

'I know it. Our latest figures prove it. Still, we have to go one better. And this is how we're going to set about it.' His wife was on the point of saying something but he stopped her with, 'Just a minute, Maisie love.'

'I was going to say your coffee's getting cold.'

'Oh, aye.' He took a sip and put the cup down noisily. 'Well, as I was saying, this will be our strategy – I want you, Sarah, to have much more television exposure.'

'That's fine. That was something I was –'

'Let me finish, Sarah, please. Apart from being a good journalist, you're an attractive lass and handle the camera well. We've got to exploit you.'

Martin said, 'That was the idea when Sarah first joined us.'

'Part of our agreement, in fact,' Sarah put in.

'It was,' the editor conceded. 'Sarah's first agent was useless so we've got her a new one who'll give us a break-through, we hope. Her name's Margot Frost.'

'Capital,' Sam said, 'I know Margot. And I can help too. After all, I am on the board of a couple of TV companies and not without influence. So far, m'dear, you've only appeared as a member of a panel, I believe? Now, I want you to front your own programmes.'

'That's exactly what I want, too. We've briefed Margot on that already.'

'Good. I've put the idea to one of our programme heads who's shown definite interest. When he heard you were Ella St. Clair's daughter, he couldn't wait to sign you up.'

'Fine.'

'The idea we've been throwing around is for you to present a kind of TV problems column. Details haven't been worked out yet, of course, but what d'you say to the general idea?'

'Sounds great!' Sarah spoke with enthusiasm. The self-doubt, she knew, would come later. Then she would lie awake in the still, small hours, wondering whether she'd be able to pull it off. This always happened and yet − paradoxically − she knew that she had no cause for concern.

'You'd better get your agent − Margot − to follow up this lead. She can take it from there.'

'Sarah will do very well,' Martin said. 'Having her present a national programme will be a great fillip for the *Courier* and it'll show in our −'

'− circulation figures. Precisely. And remember this, Reece Brown might be an astute financier but in the newspaper world, he's a raw beginner. And that's where we've got him beat. Sarah, it was a fortunate day when you came to the *Daily Courier* with all your obvious talents.'

'Hello, Helga. I'm back.'

Sarah closed the front door behind her and saw the lissom

142

figure of the au pair running down the stairs, blonde hair bobbing, eyes sparkling. A finger at her lips indicated that silence was called for.

'Rufus has just dropped off to sleep,' she said. 'I shouldn't go in to see him if I were you, Sarah. But there's a visitor waiting for you in the sitting room.'

'A visitor?'

Without enquiring further, Sarah pushed open the front room door.

'Jenny!'

They fell into one another's arms and collapsed on to the sofa, chattering without a stop. They had a lot to catch up on. There was Sarah's new status as a mother, for one thing, her exalted position in Fleet Street and Jenny's stay in the Middle East.

She immediately apologised for not having seen Sarah before she left to go abroad. 'Everything was done in such a terrible rush,' she explained. 'I originally went out for a couple of years but they let me extend the tour. I'm only on a week's leave, at the moment. But I'll be coming home for good in January − only five months to wait.'

'I've missed you.'

'I've seen Rufus,' Jenny went on. 'And I've cuddled him. He's adorable. You must be a very proud mum. He's got your colouring and your eyes, too. Phew! He's going to drive the girls wild later on.'

Sarah laughed. 'Hold on. He's only just two.'

'Time marches on, you know. Won't be long before you're a granny.'

'Give me a chance! What about you? Are you still enjoying the Middle East?'

'Fabulous. We've been living in sin, Colin and I. Oh! I didn't get the chance to let you meet Colin before I left, did I? Shame. He's very macho − a doctor, by the way. As I say, we've been living in glorious, unadulterated sin. Whoops! I ought to re-word that but you know what I mean.'

'Can you do that among all those Arabs − isn't cohabitation frowned on?'

'I don't know. Anyway, they think we're husband and wife. They've never found out the truth − at least I don't

143

think so. And if they have, they haven't said. I must say, Sarah, sin has a lot to commend it. I'd advise anyone to go in for sin. It's a lot of fun.'

'I'll have to remember that.'

'When we return in January, we plan to get a flat. We'll have a house-warming party, of course, and then, you'll be able to meet Colin and you'll see how gorgeous he is.

Jenny ran out of breath. It was Sarah's turn to say something.

'How's Simon.'

'Haven't you been in touch?'

'No.'

'I'm disappointed. When I was a teenager, you made such a romantic couple. You both had stars in your eyes.'

'I know.'

The door opened and Helga came in. 'Excuse me, please. Will Miss Dowling be staying to supper?'

'If Sarah will have me.'

'Of course.'

'I'll lay for three, then,' Helga said and went out again, closing the door softly behind her.

'How is Simon?' Sarah asked.

Jenny was some time in answering. She walked to the bay window, looking out over the Close, considering her reply.

'Well, he certainly enjoys his job. No doubt about that,' she said, turning to face the room once more. 'He absolutely loves it. Tina's father died and Simon's taken over as warden.'

'What's the wife like?'

'Tina? She's a little thing. Some would say she's a bit drab but I think she has quite a sweet face. She's got character and a lot of inner strength. But I think she's a bit pathological.'

'In what way?'

'Well, to say that she and her father were close is to put it mildly. She adored him. And his death has hit her hard. More than hard. Tina's a bundle of neuroses.'

'Sounds a bit sick.'

Jenny screwed up her face. 'I wouldn't go as far as to say that. But it's my belief she's trying to make Simon into a father substitute and I don't think he measures up.'

144

'Have they any children?'

'Oh, I forgot to say she's ten weeks' pregnant. The baby's due next February. Their first.'

'How about the marriage itself. Is Simon happy?'

'Of course not. Need you ask?' Jenny plumped down on to the sofa. 'Mind you − in spite of the father fixation − Tina loves Simon.' She paused awhile. 'At least, I think so. But you can never quite be sure with Tina.'

'And Simon?'

'Oh, he's a good husband. He's very thoughtful and attentive. Well, you know Simon. He's like that. But *love*? No. I'm sorry for Tina. I'm sorry for them both.'

Conversation lapsed. Jenny was exhausted by her own loquacity. Sarah was thinking about Simon as a family man. He would make a wonderful father. If only it had been he who'd fathered her child. But it was silly thinking like that. She shook herself.

'I was with him a couple of days ago,' Jenny went on. 'He asked if I'd seen you?'

'Did he?'

'I told him I'd be calling.'

'Oh.'

'He was very interested in your Fleet Street job.'

'Was he?'

'He said whatever happened I was to give you his love.'

Sarah glowed. 'That was sweet of him. Tell him I remember him with − with − love as well.'

'He won't need telling.'

'Has it occurred to you, Jenny, what a great divide there is now between us? Think of it − my glitzy world of the media and his world of good works. They are poles apart. Besides, I'm full of ambition; he has none.'

'That's always been true. But you worship each other. He knows that. You know it. And it is something that will never, never change.'

Chapter Seventeen

The *Daily Courier* building possessed an impressive entrance hall whose marbled columns, flooring and frescos gave it a pseudo classical look. It could easily have belonged to a municipal library or museum.

Some visitors were surprised that it looked so grand. But then, the *Courier* had not always been a popular tabloid read by the masses. Once it had been a dignified broadsheet beloved of the upper middle classes.

At the far end of the hall was a long desk made in heavy mahogany. Behind it stood a venerable-looking functionary wearing a blue and red braided uniform and a moustache that was probably one of the largest ever seen. On his chest were a number of Campaign ribbons from the last war.

Everyone called him 'Mr. Swallow'. When Sarah had first joined the paper, she'd thought it an incongruous name for such an imposing figure. But no one would have dared address him otherwise – except Lord Braidwood, that is. He called him 'Charlie' on account of having known him for over forty years.

Mr. Swallow had served the *Daily Courier* faithfully all his life. And it was said that when he retired, the paper would sink into chaos and oblivion. It was also common knowledge that his memory was prodigious and he never forgot a name or a face.

It was always a pleasure for Sarah to walk into the entrance hall at the start of each day and be greeted courteously by Mr. Swallow. 'Good morning, Miss Castle,' he would say in that rich sonorous voice of his. 'And how are we today?' 'Very well, thank you, Mr. Swallow,' she would reply before making for the lift to take her to her office.

The pattern seldom varied but today he added a request for her attention. 'Just a moment, Miss Castle, if you'd be so kind. May I have a word?'

Sarah went over to the large desk. He leant towards her and spoke conspiratorially. 'I think you ought to know there's been a young man enquiring for you. My suspicions were immediately aroused because he asked for your private address. Naturally, I refused to give it. I let him know that such details are confidential.'

'Quite right. Thank you, Mr. Swallow. What's he like? Can you describe him?'

'I'll try.' He collected his thoughts for a moment. 'Let me see. He was tallish – about six foot, I'd say. Athletic type. Looked like a rugger player. Fair hair, blue-grey eyes. Face – rather immature, in my opinion. Very charming manner though. Spoke like a gentleman. Well-dressed except that, when he walked away, I noticed his black shoes were not polished at the back. It let him down, I thought.'

'Phew!' Sarah was lost in wonderment. 'That's fantastic, Mr. Swallow. You must have a photographic memory.'

He smiled, pleased at the compliment. 'Just practice, Miss Castle. Just practice.'

'Well, you've given me a most accurate description of a man I used to know. I don't want to see him so if he calls again, I'd be grateful if you'd let him know that.'

'Of course. It'd be a pleasure. And I'll keep you informed if he does return.'

'Thank you, Mr. Swallow.'

As the lift took her up to her floor, Sarah tried to overcome her surprise. Why was Max hoping to meet her after such a long time? To see his offspring? Doubtful. To talk over old times? Possible. To take up with her again? More than likely.

Well, he'd be unlucky. With that, Sarah thought no more about him. She had much more important things to think about than Max Brown.

Once in her office, she rang for her secretary who came in carrying her notebook, a selection of pens, a box of tissues and Sarah's diary.

Sarah had liked Heather Walker from the moment she'd been interviewed for the job. About five years younger than her boss, she was ambitious, highly efficient and possessed a warm sense of humour. There was a real rapport between them.

As always, they began with Sarah's diary, checking her appointments for the day.

'You're lunching at the Mansion House with the Lord Mayor and Lady Mayoress. An informal affair. D'you want me to lay on anything special apart from the usual hire car?'

'No. I don't think so.'

'And don't forget we have the new research assistant starting today. I expect you'll want to spend some time with her this morning.'

'I can give her about half an hour. After that, I'll have to pass her over to Estelle.'

'Fine. When you get back from your lunch date, I've pencilled in an appointment for three-thirty. It's to meet a deputation from a northern women's organisation.'

'Yes, OK. How long d'you think it'll take?'

'Better allow for forty-five minutes. That'll give you fifteen minutes before your next appointment at four-thirty − that's when you're being interviewed for the launch of a new mag for social workers.'

'Is that the end?'

'No. You're meeting a couple of commercial radio producers for drinks at six in the Savoy.' Heather grinned at her boss. 'After that, dear Sarah, you can go home, tuck Rufus up in bed and sleep the sleep of the just.'

'Thanks very much.'

Heather put the desk diary to one side and had already opened her notebook, pen at the ready, by the time Sarah picked up her pile of correspondence. And she was still taking dictation an hour later when the office junior came in with coffee on a tray.

The inter-com rang. Heather answered.

'Sarah Castle's office.'

'Hi, it's Pat. The editor would like to see Sarah. How is she fixed?'

'Pretty busy. I'll pass you over to her.'

Sarah took the receiver. 'I'm booked right up today, Pat, except for odd moments. Tomorrow would be better. How about nine-thirty?'

Pat said it would do fine. Sarah rang off.

'Will you put that down for tomorrow, Heather?'

'I've already done it.'

'Good.'

'Did Pat say what Martin wants you for?'

'No. I don't think she knows. Nothing important, I imagine. Where were we . . . ?'

'What the devil d'you mean by it?' The wrathful voice of the editor rang through the closed door and down the corridor.

Sarah saw the door open and one of the sports subs scuttle out. Verbal abuse followed him like brickbats hurled at his retreating back. For some reason, Martin hated all sports subs. Nothing that they ever did was right. They must have found it discouraging.

The young man closed the door, caught sight of Sarah, made a grimace and put his fingers to his temples to indicate the horns of the devil.

As Sarah knocked on the door, she could hear him still fulminating. 'It's sheer incompetence, that's what it is. Oh, come in.'

Sarah entered as directed. 'Why is it that I have to suffer so many fools on the sports desk? Why? Take a seat, Sarah. Why is it? Tell me that.'

Pat Symes, his secretary, moved over swiftly and leant over him. 'Now, be quiet, Martin.' She knew how to handle him. 'Sarah doesn't want to hear your shouting, and, for that matter, neither do I. So behave yourself.'

He looked suitably chastened. But it took him some moments before he could speak in a reasonable tone. 'D'you know, in a bit of copy that sub showed me, there were no less than four mixed metaphors in the first para. Think of it! Four!'

'You wanted to see me, Martin,' Sarah said.

'Did I? Ah, that. Yes. You remember what Sam Braidwood said when we had lunch together? Well, he didn't let the grass grow under his feet. The upshot is his head of programmes is completely hooked on you fronting your own series next year. You'd better get your agent to follow it up.'

'Margot's already done that. The contract's being drawn up.'

Just for a moment, his jaw dropped. 'That's bloody smart work. Margot must be even better than I thought she was.'

'Right. And there's something else. It's not next year. The programmers have changed their autumn schedules and my first series will start in mid-October and be finished by Christmas.'

'Good God! You know a hell of a lot more than I do. So you won't need telling it's going to be fully networked throughout the country?'

'No.'

'But you probably haven't heard that a couple of his producers are vying for your services.'

'No, I hadn't, but I'm flattered.'

'And what's more, you've worked with one of them before − Des Mallon.'

'Des? An old friend. I've known him for years and years.'

'Have you? The situation gets better and better. I'll pass that on to old Sam.' Martin sat back and grinned at her. 'Y'know, this is going to do the *Courier* a hell of a lot of good. Your television kudos will brush off on to the paper and boost our sales like nobody's business.' He leant back in his chair and guffawed.

'What's the joke?'

'It'll be one in the eye for the *Daily Sentinel,* Reece Brown is going to be green with envy when he hears of this.' Martin's brow furrowed as his mind focused on a distant memory. 'I'll never forget how he looked last year at the christening of your baby.' He laughed again and blew his nose. 'There he was, full of pompous dignity, enjoying his role as the paternal grandfather. And there was I − his bitter rival in the tabloid war − actually becoming one of the baby's godfathers! Oh, he didn't like that at all.'

'He tried to conceal it, though.'

'Oh, yes, but I knew, all right. I enjoyed his discomfiture. Incidentally, does he ever try to interfere with the baby − throw his weight about as grandpapa, so to speak?'

'No he doesn't – at the moment. I think it's because Reece can't relate to babies. But when Rufus is older, I'll have to keep my eyes open. I'm not going to have him interfering.'

'Well spoken, Sarah. But, of course, in the case of a certain godfather, you have no such objection?'

'As you say, Martin, I have no such objection – providing he doesn't shout at me, that is.'

The restaurant in Soho was small, select and expensive. It was also favoured by executive women who sought to discuss business over their lunch with a minimum of fuss.

'How's old Sam Braidwood these days?' Margot Frost asked in her husky voice.

'I see very little of him,' Sarah admitted. 'As far as I know, he's fine. You know him then?'

'Wouldn't say that exactly.' Her agent unrolled a napkin and laid it on her commodious lap. 'But I have met him.'

Margot was formidable not only because she was heavily built with two dewlaps for cheeks. She gazed upon the world with an unsmiling face and her forthright manner intimidated Sarah among many others. But as an artistes' agent, she enjoyed a well-deserved reputation. She always achieved the best terms for her clients. As far as Sarah was concerned, that was all that mattered.

'I won't eat much,' Margot declared, laying aside the menu. 'I never do, actually – not that you'd guess, looking at me. So I'll plump for a salad. Ah, "plump" – did you notice the pun? It describes my figure.'

Sarah smiled although she didn't regard the pun as worthy of it. 'I'll have a salad, too,' she said.

Margot ordered two salads and a bottle of white Burgundy.

Over the meal, they discussed the 'Ask Sarah' series which was to be a TV correspondence column aimed at the younger woman. It was basically a simple idea. Sarah, as presenter, would be in the studio where selected viewers, their faces in shadow, would ask how to tackle their own particular domestic problems.

'I like the title they've dreamed up,' said Margot. ' "Ask Sarah" isn't exactly brilliant but it's simple, direct, and says all that you want to say.'

151

'I agree.'

'As you know, the first series starts mid-October and will take you up to Christmas. After that, there'll be a break before going into the second series. Altogether, this'll mean several months work for you, Sarah.'

'I'm most grateful for all you're doing.'

'Well, don't be!' Margot gave a deep-throated laugh. 'That's what you pay me for.'

Sarah asked whether the actual format of the programme had been raised in her discussions with the management.

'Not in so many words. That's for the production people to decide, obviously. But I do know they're hoping to go out live.'

Sarah was aghast. 'Live!'

The strain of presenting a live programme was very great, particularly for a newcomer. It placed a heavy burden upon the performer and allowed for no mistakes. But from Sarah's point of view there was an even worse danger. If the programme were not pre-recorded, she would be afforded no time in which to formulate her answers to the questions asked. She would have to give them straight off the cuff. And she'd have to be right each time!

On the *Daily Courier,* she had a few days in which to consider how to respond to the questions sent in, and there were experts to consult if she were unsure.

'How set are they on this?' she asked, hoping she didn't sound too anxious.

'Oh, quite keen. They came up with the usual guff. A live programme has more immediacy − which, of course, is just tele-talk.'

Sarah had no option but to put her cards on the table. 'I can't do it, Margot. Sorry, but there it is. If they don't agree to pre-recording, then I'm afraid the deal's off. Think of it: I'd lay myself open to all sorts of ghastly clangers. It could be professional suicide.'

Margot rubbed her chin. 'Yes, I see your point. Coffee?' Sarah shook her head. 'No. Nor for me.' She raised her hand imperiously. 'Waiter. My check, please. Okay, Sarah. Going out live is not on. I'll have to get that specifically stated in the contract and you'd better take it up with Des Mallon.'

'I'll do that straight away.'

Chapter Eighteen

The weekly staff meetings at St. Giles were informal affairs, and the agenda was as brief as Simon could make it. He was not a committee man by nature.

This morning he looked around to see if anyone was absent. No one was. The male tutors sat wherever they could – on a pouffe, on the floor, on a wooden settle. Stephanie Gilbert, the only woman on the teaching staff, was accorded an easy chair. Simon sat at his desk.

Tina didn't attend the meetings as the domestic staff and arrangements were her sphere of influence.

Since becoming warden, Simon had made a few changes. For one thing, the handicapped students now had easier access to him and Tina. The teaching rosters made better sense than hitherto. And, on a less important level, the study was tidy although the cat still regarded the room as its own domain.

So did Miss Macintosh, the secretary. She sat at her desk in the corner, surveying the scene with a proprietorial air, watching everything, missing nothing.

Everyone lived in awe of Miss Macintosh. Having been brought up in a Calvinistic home, she had narrow and rigorous views of what was right and seemly.

The discussion that morning proved once more how harmonious were relations at St. Giles. There were no inflated egos, no jealousies. They all worked as a team. And Simon was a strict chairman, not allowing any digression from the point at issue.

But the end of formal business was the signal for

relaxation. He enjoyed these periods. Simon was an outgoing man. He liked people around him, people he could talk to, laugh with, share experiences with.

He was on exceptionally good terms with his male assistants. Each was highly individualistic and could be characterised by a single adjective — boisterous or talkative or intellectual. And then, of course, there was Stephanie.

What epithet applied to Stephanie? As far as Simon was concerned, only one sprang to mind. Ravishing! But in the company of their colleagues, he had to be careful not to show his feelings. Even a hint of the truth would have been picked up by Miss Macintosh. And that would have spelt disaster.

Stephanie was always at her best in male company. And because staff meetings provided this environment, she scintillated. Today she was in very fine form, flirting overtly with every man in sight — except Simon. He understood. He knew she was laying a false trail and it suited them both.

From where he was sitting, he could see the light glistening on her honey-blonde hair. And her innocent blue eyes seemed to be amused at something one of her colleagues was saying. Before she turned once more to her notes, her gaze fleetingly met his.

When the conclave finally broke up, she gave an almost imperceptible nod in his direction. Simon got the message but showed no sign.

As they all strolled out into the drive, the sound of cheering some distance away made them turn. At the far end of the path, the occupants of two wheelchairs were waving their arms and shouting 'Yippie'.

The two paraplegics began to propel themselves towards Simon's group. Their advance had all the appearance of a neck and neck race. They came up, breathless, and halted their wheelchairs in a cloud of dust.

One of the men, known to his friends as Ginger, said, 'How's that? What chance d'you think we have in the 100 metres at the next paraplegic games?'

'Excellent, I'd say,' Simon agreed. 'But why the cheering?'

'We've just had our mail, Jock and me,' Ginger said. 'Here, sir, you take a look.' He extracted a letter from his top pocket and handed it over. 'Jock's is the same.'

Simon unfolded the letter, which had a printed company letterhead, and scanned it quickly. It was to confirm that they were offering Ginger a job as a computer operator.

'Congratulations. You deserve it,' Simon said and passed the letter over to Stephanie and the other tutors, who echoed his sentiments.

'Well, we couldn't have done this without St. Giles' training. Isn't that so, Jock?'

Jock, who was less communicative than Ginger, had to agree. 'Aye, we owe you a lot.' Then, apparently embarrassed at his show of feeling, he turned to his friend, 'Come on. Race you back there.'

Right! You're on!'

Simon watched their wheelchairs speed down the path and pass out of sight behind one of the buildings.

'They're like a couple of kids,' Stephanie remarked.

'They certainly are,' agreed Doug, another tutor.

'They make it so worthwhile,' Simon spoke with feeling. 'I'm very glad I took this job.'

Stephanie's eyes met his again. 'And that goes for me, too,' she said and looked away.

On his return to the office, Miss Macintosh was waiting for him before going to her lunch.

'A very good meeting,' he said.

'Excellent. But Miss Gilbert is quite outrageous.'

'Stephanie?'

'Yes. Miss Gilbert. The way she flirts with every man in sight. I find it embarrassing.'

'She means no harm by it.'

'Huh! She would never have been allowed to get away with that before Mr. Phillips passed away. He always kept her well under control.'

Simon had no intention of being dragged into an argument. 'Well, don't let it upset you, Miss Macintosh. I certainly won't. I'm going to lunch.'

As soon as she saw Simon, Tina could tell he'd had a good morning.

'Meeting go well?' she asked, already guessing the answer.

'Fine. And we've had two more job placements.' He told

her about Ginger and Jock. 'Doug and Stephanie get very good results.'

'Father always used to say that about Doug.' She paused awhile, looking thoughtfully at her husband. 'Y'know, he would be so pleased with the way you're running St. Giles.'

'I find it fulfilling.'

'I know you do. You're very much like my dad.'

He smiled. 'You're always telling me that. I'll begin to believe it soon.'

'It's true.'

It was while she was pouring the boiling water into the teapot later, that Tina thought over her last remark — one she'd made many times before. Yes, Simon was like her father. Was that why she'd wanted him to marry her in the first place? The one and only reason?

She and her father had always been extremely close, especially after her mother had died. Most of the time they even knew what the other was thinking. It was quite uncanny.

Was she making Simon into a substitute for her father? The possibility of this was very real. But it must be quite natural, she assured herself. After all, she was still trying to come to terms with his death.

The thought of her great loss made her feel sick. Sadness was like a giant hand squeezing her lungs. She struggled for breath, gulping in air several times before she could carry on with what she was doing.

Would she ever get over her bereavement? She was not sure that she even wanted to try. But when her baby was born, that would surely make a difference. And it ought to confirm her love for Simon. Anyway, she hoped it would.

Of course, in her own way she loved him. Tina had been attracted to him from the moment she'd first seen him in that dingy common room in 1984. But he would never be as close nor as dear as her father.

His voice startled her. She hadn't heard him come into the kitchen.

'I'll carry the tray in for you, Tina.'

She managed to say, 'Thank you, dear.'

During lunch, she recovered her spirits somewhat. She asked him about his morning. 'Who was at the staff meeting?'

He told her what they'd discussed and the decisions taken. 'And Stephanie was flirting madly as usual.' He tossed this off as an after thought.

'She's harmless.'

'She flirts with everyone except me. Not that it bothers me,' he added hastily.

Tina was thoughtful. 'Is that so? I wonder why?'

It was a rhetorical question only and she wasn't interested in the answer. Tina had no worries about Simon falling for Stephanie. He wouldn't do that. Not for Stephanie. But Sarah was another matter altogether. Tina was painfully aware that it was she who still held him in thrall. And it was the subject of Sarah that she was determined to drag into the conversation. It was almost a masochistic urge. She couldn't resist it.

'Oh, I forgot to tell you, dear,' she said casually, 'there was a letter from Jenny this morning. She mentioned her homecoming next January and was on about that housewarming party she's going to have.'

'What, again? She kept on talking about it when she was here. She won't be home for months yet.'

Tina laughed. 'You know Jenny. She can't wait.'

'OK. Sounds fun. But I don't suppose you'll be feeling in party mood at that time.'

'Oh, I'll be all right.' She paused and braced herself, ready to watch his reaction. 'Jenny says she's going to invite Sarah.'

His face lit up. He couldn't conceal it. But then almost immediately his eyes clouded over again. 'No, on second thoughts, I think it would be madness to go.'

'But why, dear?'

'Well, there'd be your condition and − and −'

'And what?'

That stumped him. Tina felt a perverse sense of satisfaction, as if she had proved something of immense significance. Which, of course, she had. Thinking of this, she hated herself. She was making him suffer. She was making herself suffer also. Why was she doing it?

'Well, I −' he began. Simon was struggling with himself. 'I don't think it would be right for us to go.'

Tina would not let him off the hook. 'But why not? Don't tell me you'd be scared of meeting Sarah?'

He tried to look defiant. 'No, of course not.'

'I mean, after all, it's all over between you and her, isn't it? So where would the harm be?'

He was some time in answering. 'No harm at all.'

Tina sat back in her chair and closed her eyes. Again that perverse sense of triumph. She believed she'd proved he still loved Sarah and was afraid of opening up old wounds. Why was she tormenting him and herself like this?

She didn't know. All she knew was that there was a sharp pain in her heart.

Simon was attempting to look bored. He wanted to go out and hoped that Tina would notice. He yawned audibly.

She looked up from her magazine. 'Why don't you go down to the Cricketers for a pint?' she suggested. 'It'll do you good, dear.'

He was glad that Tina had risen to the occasion once again. It made life so much easier if the idea came from her.

He got up from his seat slowly, not wishing to appear too eager to be out of the house. 'I think you're right. The walk will do me good.'

'Don't hurry back. And why don't you see that pal of yours and have a game of cards as you often do?'

'Yes. I might do that. I shan't be too late.'

He kissed his wife and went out. It was towards the end of September and the evening was warm and a little humid. The sun had disappeared behind the trees but some light clouds were burning gold and red above him.

He often felt the need to escape. The evenings were the worst part. He enjoyed the work, the challenge of his job. He liked the companionship of his colleagues. But when they returned home at the end of the day, there was for him a fearful void.

It was this same emptiness that he'd first experienced long ago — when they'd sold the family home, when Jenny had gone abroad and Sarah had broken with him. Since then, this sense of vacuum had never completely left him.

Ironically, it had been his loneliness that had driven him into marriage in the first place. The truth of that was inescapable. Only his wardenship at St. Giles offered any contentment and saved him from being completely bereft.

The prospect of seeing Sarah again − even though it was some months hence − thrilled him. He wanted to see her and yet he didn't. Would he be afraid? Yes, very. Afraid of showing his true emotions.

What if Tina were to discover how he still felt about her? That was something that had to be avoided at all cost. He would not knowingly hurt Tina.

He thought of the evening ahead of him with a surge of excitement. Meanwhile, it was not yet dark and he had to be very circumspect. They both had to be. Tina must never find out.

He reached the village after a few minutes' sharp walk, crossed the green, skirted the duck pond and stepped through the open door of the Cricketers.

Laughter. Chatter. The clink of glasses. Tobacco smoke. The smell of beer. Good company. Conviviality.

For a time, he immersed himself in the affairs of the local cricket eleven, and the proposal that an extra bus service would be run on Saturdays. For the villagers this constituted the stuff of life. For Simon, it was exactly the mundane distraction he needed.

After a time, he checked his watch and looked through the window at the sky. It was sufficiently dark, he decided, to venture forth. No one would see him now.

He skirted the front of the pub, passed through the village, walked up a lane and stood by the door of a small cottage. He rattled the letter box gently. Almost immediately, the door was opened.

'I thought you were never coming,' Stephanie said, and fell into his arms.

He kicked the door shut with his heel.

Tina was in bed, reading, when he returned. Hearing him, she called to him. He went to the bathroom, then joined her in bed.

He had no book to read, having forgotten to go to the library at the weekend. Tina was absorbed in her novel so he couldn't talk. He wasn't sleepy; besides, he couldn't have slept with the light still on. So he lay on his back, staring at the

159

ceiling, thinking. About Stephanie at first. How she satisfied his physical needs. What he would do without her, he just didn't know.

But he didn't deceive himself. Nor had he deceived Stephanie. He'd made it clear to her that she'd never replace Sarah in his heart. She understood perfectly. Stephanie was that sort of girl and they had that sort of relationship. They both recognised it couldn't last indefinitely. But while they were able to meet in secret, each filled a need in the other's life.

At last, Tina closed her book and switched off the light. 'I hope I haven't been keeping you awake, dear.'

He forced a laugh. 'Not at all.'

'Good night, dearest.' She kissed him and took hold of his hand, placing it on her stomach. 'Our baby is in here. Exciting, isn't it?'

He agreed it was exciting and tried to settle down for the night. An hour later, he was still awake when a sleepy voice said, 'I'm sorry I can't give you what you want.'

He asked what she meant although he guessed what she'd say.

'The doctor did warn me against intercourse for a time.'

Simon knew she wasn't sorry. It was so facile the way she spoke. 'Don't worry.' He said.

She roused herself and turned to face him. 'But you need sex. More than most men, I should think.'

It was true. Many men could abstain with comparative ease but he wasn't one of them. Sex, for Simon, was a necessity of life. Thank heavens he had Stephanie.

Neither spoke for a time. An owl hooted from the copse.

'You do love me, don't you, Simon?' said the sleepy voice after a long silence.

'Of course I do.'

'It's nice to hear you say that.' She snuggled her face against his chest. 'Good night, dear.'

'Sleep well. Sweet dreams.'

But there was no immediate repose for Simon. His mind was back with Sarah and he spent a long time wondering how he would react when − and if − they ever met again.

Chapter Nineteen

To Sarah, the old City of London, often known as the Square Mile, was sheer delight. Its streets — some of which had odd names like Cheapside, Mincing Lane and Poultry — had always set her imagination alight as she tried to visualise them in days gone by.

She enjoyed letting her imagination hold sway. In her mind's eye, she would see Samuel Pepys and Dr. Johnson, and visualise St. Paul's and Fleet Street as they once were.

Today had been a hard day for Sarah. Mondays, like Thursdays, always were. These were the days when she had to work very late, checking her column for the morning's editions. At the end of them, she felt exhausted.

But there were compensations. As soon as she'd finished her column, she could look down from her office on to the silent street below and let her mind wander. She loved that. Or else go for a walk along Fleet Street in solitude.

Tonight, she needed a breath of fresh air. She left her office, using the stairs rather than the lift. As she went through the building, there were different faces everywhere, the day staff having been replaced by the night personnel who were virtual strangers to her. In the entrance there was no Mr. Swallow. In his place was the night porter. Not the same at all.

Outside, it was a mellow September night. Apart from the clicking of her heels on the pavement, there was no sound. The great commercial houses were, of course, closed and all the office workers had returned to their suburbs. The City was deserted.

Everyone seemed to be asleep. But it was an illusion. The

journalists weren't. Neither were the printers. They were busy producing Tuesday's edition. And tomorrow, people would be reading what she – Sarah Castle – had written.

She was as happy as she possibly could be in her job. Had been for the past few years. She belonged here and the City was her professional home. It was sad to think that many of the great newspapers were moving out, bringing about Fleet Street's eventual demise. She prayed that Sam Braidwood would not be tempted to do likewise.

She turned off the main thoroughfare and went along a side road to a small pub that had an all-night licence. She often used it when working late. It was pot luck whether she drank alone or had the company of the night news editor and some of the subs.

Pushing open the door, she was met by the smells of English beer, furniture polish and old wood. For her, they were strangely evocative, reminding her of her student days with Simon. Odd to think that the smell of beer should remind her so strongly of him. It was unfair really. He was not a heavy drinker.

What was he doing now? Was he happy? Did he ever think of her? Would they ever meet again? If so, how would they react? And his wife ...? But she refused to dwell upon the improbable.

'Evening, Miss Castle,' the barman greeted her genially. 'Your usual scotch on the rocks?'

'Yes, please, Joe.' She indicated the empty bar. 'Where is everybody tonight?'

He laughed. 'Search me. Mind you, it's a bit early for the printers. They'll be in later.'

She took her drink and sat at an oak table in the corner. There, she opened her handbag and took out a pocket notebook. Several ideas had come to her during the walk and she wanted to put them down before she forgot.

A voice behind her. She froze. 'Hello, Sarah.'

She turned slowly, refusing to show her surprise. She looked up into the face of Max Brown.

'D'you mind if I join you.'

'The seats aren't booked if that's what you mean. I can't stop you.'

162

He sat down, a large brandy in his hand. He lifted his glass. 'Cheers.'

Sarah ignored the toast. 'If this is an attempt to resume relations, forget it. That's all I have to say to you.' She drank her whisky at a gulp, picked up her notebook and handbag and walked towards the door.

'Good night, Joe,' she said to the barman. 'I won't stop for another. In a bit of a hurry tonight.'

She'd only gone a few yards along the street when she heard feet racing after her.

'Sarah, please!'

She walked on. Max grabbed her elbow. She swung her free arm round and her palm hit him hard on the cheek. He hadn't expected that. He caught his breath, reeled and loosened his hold.

Her voice rang out, reverberating around the empty street Don't lay your hands on me again, buster!'

It had all been an instant reflex — not the way a woman of the world should behave. She immediately regretted her behaviour. Still, it had helped to get some of her anger against Max out of her system.

Ahead, she could see the night editor and a reporter walking quickly in her direction. Max dropped back.

'Was somebody pestering you, Sarah?' asked the night editor as they came up.

'Oh, it was some mindless jerk I once knew,' she said, hoping that Max would hear. 'He's of no account.'

'That's all right, then. See you.' And the two men moved on.

Sarah walked back with studied nonchalance. Up the marble steps. Through the enormous swing doors. Into the entrance hall. A picture of perfect poise and composure.

Inwardly, though, she was shaking. She went up to the night porter.

'Will you get me a cab in half an hour's time?' she asked. She'd had difficulty controlling her voice and hoped it didn't show.

'Very good, Miss Castle.'

'Oh, and would you tell the man to pick me up at the rear entrance?' she added as an afterthought, just in case Max had ideas of following the cab to her home. She felt she couldn't be too careful. 'I'll be in my office when he comes.'

She went up the stairs slowly. The reappearance of Max in her life was disturbing. Irritating rather than worrying, though. But she was too tired to give the matter much thought for the moment.

Besides, on her return to the office, she found one of the subs had left a proof of the entertainments page giving a review of the autumn television programmes.

A couple of paragraphs had been marked for her attention. Reading them hurriedly, she saw that "Ask Sarah" had been singled out for a mention. As far as she knew, this was the first publicity her series had received. She felt gratified.

A month had passed since the lunch with Margot when they'd discussed the series. Since then, everything about it had worked out well.

On the question of going out live, they'd reached an amicable agreement. It would not be recorded but Sarah would be given prior knowledge of all the questions. This meant she could check her facts and give the impression of spontaneity at the same time. It was a good compromise.

She thought momentarily of Reece. What would his reaction be when he heard about the series? He wouldn't like it, would he? She chuckled quietly in to the empty room.

Sir Reece Brown felt he'd been snubbed.

When he'd first heard on the grapevine that Sarah had been signed up for "Ask Sarah", he bristled with indignation. Now that it was being publicised, indignation turned to gall.

In the very first instance, he'd made his position more than plain. The television people knew precisely what was in his mind. They had no excuse. He wanted his own nominee to have a major series of some sort — especially as she'd already appeared in a couple of panel games.

As head of the Brown Newspaper Corporation, he had considerable status in the country. They ought to have heeded his wishes. But they had disregarded him entirely. It made him very, very angry.

The nominee he'd been putting forward was his gossip columnist, Lady Virginia Duval. Married to a man of impeccable pedigree, she was of doubtful lineage herself. But this didn't bother Reece. It was the title that interested him. It had snob value and he approved.

Her social connections enabled her to be invited to all the best house parties, race meetings and theatre first nights. In consequence, she knew everybody.

Personally, Reece couldn't stand the woman. He thought she was a bitch. But putting her in charge of his gossip column was very good casting. Gossip was what she knew best. Her pen was dipped in vitriol and her tongue was barbed.

He'd lobbied various TV executives about promoting her and they'd cocked a snook at him. It was an insult, pure and simple.

He paced up and down his office. He snapped at Miss Clark when she came in and told her to leave him alone.

Reece had had hopes of Virginia becoming a national celebrity through television. He'd wanted to out-gun Braidwood's *Daily Courier,* hoping to put up a rival to Sarah Castle and so boost his own paper. He didn't want Sarah to get all the exposure. But it hadn't worked out like that.

Irrationally, he held her responsible. She had been chosen and Virginia had not. So he resented her success.

In his more honest, candid moments he admitted – but only to himself – things might have been easier if he'd had greater experience of the media. It was undeniably true that, although a leading name in the business world, he was a newcomer to newspapers.

Sam Braidwood, on the other hand, had been in the press world since leaving school. So too had Reece's own editor, Charles Maynard. But Reece found it difficult to delegate to him or bow to someone else's judgement.

Brimming over with irritation, he snatched up the intercom on his desk.

'Miss Clark, tell Mr. Maynard I want to see him immediately.'

'Yes, Sir Reece.'

A few minutes later, she rang back.

'Oh, sir, I'm afraid Mr. Maynard is at an editorial conference and won't be free for another two hours at least.'

'I see.'

He replaced the receiver, his temper more frayed than ever.

165

Damn these journalists. Too independent by far!

His spirits picked up a little as he recalled that tomorrow he'd be presiding over a shareholders' meeting of one of his other companies. That was where he really belonged – dealing with commercial and financial matters.

He moved to his desk, picked up a report, skimmed through the first few pages. He sat down and began to put his whole mind to studying it. The television fiasco partly faded from memory.

The intercom buzzed. Miss Clark's voice. 'Oh, Sir Reece, Lady Virginia is here and would like a word if you're free.'

'Show her in.' All his earlier dissatisfaction came flooding back. He felt angry again.

She swept into the office and he invited her to take a seat.

As she settled herself, he watched her. He could never even begin to like Virginia. There was a studied gentility about her which irritated him. Small in build, she possessed pleasant features but they were marred by the enormous spectacles she affected. He thought they made her look ridiculous.

Perhaps that was why the television people had decided against her. No, couldn't be that. More likely her bitchy tongue had scared them off. They probably thought the camera would show her up for the cow she really was.

That was why a genuine and good-looking girl like Sarah had got the job. If only he could get her over to his camp – what a prize she'd be! And even more so when she'd made a name for herself in television. One day, he'd make another bid for her talents.

But, of course, what he'd really like to do would be to buy up the *Courier* itself, lock, stock and barrel. Kick out old Braidwood. Retain the best of the journalists, including Sarah. That way she'd be his anyway. He'd have to put out feelers with a view to a takeover ...

Virginia was speaking. The corners of her mouth were turned down which made her look sulky. Choosing her words carefully, she said she was disappointed that Sarah had been offered her own series while she had not.

'Oh, no matter,' Reece lied. 'It's no use worrying about it.'

'Well, I'm not a good loser. In my column, I'd like to give Sarah a few knocks. OK by you?'

166

Reece nodded. He thought it an exceptionally good idea but didn't want to show too much enthusiasm. That would have looked undignified.

Virginia seemed pleased. 'That's settled, then.'

'Was there anything else you wanted to see me about?' He intended to get the meeting over as quickly as possible.

'Yes, there is. I happened to run into someone at the weekend – someone you haven't seen for a few years.'

There was a half-smile on her face, and for some reason, he was put on the alert.

'Who?'

'Max – your son.' She gave him a saccharine smirk. 'I just thought you'd like to know.'

For a moment, Reece was unable to answer. He could feel his lips quivering. 'Tell me,' he said tersely.

'I was at a film premiere the other night and he was there.'

'I wasn't aware you knew him.'

She flicked a bit of fluff from off her skirt. 'It's my job to know people.'

He let that pass. 'What was he doing there?'

'He was with the production party, but his precise function I couldn't quite make out. I can follow it up if you'd like.'

His answer was brusque. 'No. He's of no concern to me. Forget him.'

With that, he rose to show that the interview was at an end.

Virginia was far less sanguine about Sarah having been offered a series than she'd admitted. In most things, she liked to keep her feelings close to her chest.

She left Reece's office and marched purposefully to her own room, head thrust forward, lips tightly closed, heels resounding on the wooden floor. Judging by the movements of her hands, it seemed there was nothing more important on her mind at that moment than stopping wisps of hair from falling into her eyes.

But this was misleading. With her it signified a particular thought process; a mannerism she unconsciously adopted whenever she was forming a plan of campaign.

Virginia had one aim in mind. She had never been able to accept defeat, and her vanity had taken a heavy beating this time. Now, her first priority was to hit back at Sarah.

In her office, she was met by one of the subs holding some of her typed copy. He thrust it into her hand.

'Look, Virginia, this story of yours on the bimbo – d'you mean what you've written?'

'I wouldn't have written it if I didn't.'

The sub sucked in his breath, apparently controlling his temper. 'It's a bit strong, isn't it?'

'I don't think so.'

'Well I do. And I can't use it without a few changes.'

'That's nonsense,' she retorted but knew it wasn't; that the sub was within his rights.

'You know our paper's policy on libel – we don't just go into court willy-nilly with our eyes closed. We only risk damages if the story is newsworthy; that is, if our lawyers are happy and if it's going to bump up our circulation. This story doesn't fall into that category. Sorry, Virginia, but there it is.'

She accepted the situation with bad grace. 'Oh, very well. I'll leave it to you to hack about as you think fit. I'm sure that's what you enjoy doing most.'

'OK.' He shrugged and went out, giving her a brief backward glance. Obviously, he didn't like her. Not that that bothered Virginia. The feeling was entirely mutual.

She sat at her desk and tried to compose her thoughts but concentration proved elusive. Her secretary came in, looking worried.

'Bad news, Virginia. This reception you're attending tonight – well, your escort can't make it.'

She fingered her hair in exasperation. 'Oh, bloody hell! This is a fine time to tell me.'

'He's only just phoned. But I've been on to Wilfred and he'd be delighted to escort you. Shall I say yes?'

'Of course. Get anybody. I don't care.'

Her office suddenly struck her as airless. Snatching up her handbag, she marched out of the building. At this hour of the day, her favourite wine bar was not too busy and she found a seat at the counter with ease.

'A glass of Chablis,' she ordered, and pulled a dish of cheese straws towards her.

She sat very still, looking straight ahead, avoiding catching anyone's eye. Just drinking, nibbling, thinking. Wondering what she could do or write about Sarah. It wasn't going to be easy. They'd only met socially on one occasion – and that had been two years ago.

Virginia drank quickly. She pushed her empty glass across the counter. 'Fill it up, will you? And give me some more cheese straws.'

'Certainly, madam.'

More drinking, nibbling, thinking.

Sarah appeared to be blameless. That was her trouble. But *nobody* was blameless. Impossible! Sarah must have an Achilles heel. *Surely she must!* And she would have to find it. Inveigle herself into Sarah's circle, get to know her friends – that sort of thing. She'd start right away.

Feeling more relaxed, she returned to the office. Picking up the phone, she dialled a Sussex number.

'Sandalwood,' a dignified male voice announced.

'I'd like to speak to Mrs. Seeberg.'

'Who shall I say is calling?'

'Lady Virginia Duval.'

'Very well, madam. I'll tell her.'

She had to wait only a few moments before Winnie Seeberg came on the line. 'Hello?' The American accent was immediately recognisable. Virginia put on her social voice.

'Winnie! How are you, my dear? Long time no see. It's entirely my fault, I'm afraid. But my social diary has been so very full.'

Winnie said that hers was also.

'What I mean is – ' Virginia went on ' – I wouldn't like you to think I'm neglecting you.'

'I hadn't thought that at all. You're always welcome here.'

'D'you know, I hoped you'd say that? I'd simply love to come. I've got my diary before me now. It so happens I'm free after lunch on Saturday the weekend after next.'

'That suits me fine. I'll look forward to seeing you then, Virginia.'

'Oh, do call me "Ginny". All my friends do.'

'Very well, Ginny.'

After a few more minutes of conversation that resembled

169

a game of ping-pong, Virginia rang off.

Her thoughts were still vague and her plans even more so. But a day at Sandalwood was surely a step in the right direction.

Chapter Twenty

At the beginning of October — about a week after the incident in Fleet Street — a letter arrived for Sarah at the office. Marked 'Private and Confidential', it confronted her one morning as she took her place at the desk. She recognised Max's handwriting immediately.

Because of the proximity of colleagues, she would have preferred to put off reading it until later but curiosity got the better of her. She skimmed through it hurriedly.

But even this cursory perusal made interesting reading. Max was filled with mortification for having deserted her. He had no excuses, he said. Only remorse. What was more, he sounded genuine. This surprised her.

Having escaped from the tyranny of his father, he had at last found his feet, it seemed. He was making an adequate living — he did not specify at what — and was hoping Sarah would grant him reasonable access to his child. He did not ask for more than that. He hoped she would be understanding and grant his request.

Other than this, there was no message, no writing between the lines as far as she could see. No hint of another woman in his life. No suggestion that they might resume their affair. Only the wish to see his child.

Had she the right to refuse him? Never mind the legalities of the matter — what about the moral argument? Would she be justified in forbidding him access to his son? Was it fair to prevent Rufus knowing his own father?

Oh, forget the moral argument! What about her independence? If Max were to make periodic visits to Rufus her autonomy and self-sufficiency might be under threat. Not 'might be'. *Would be*! She couldn't countenance that.

Sarah recognised her state of mind. She usually floundered like this when having to make a decision on a personal issue. Ironic, wasn't it? She was the professional who meted out advice to strangers without a qualm. But in her own life, it was she who needed guidance.

In the distant past, Simon had been at her side. When in doubt on any matter, she had consulted him. It had been the most natural thing in the world to talk to him about any problem. Never had his judgement been found wanting, and over the years she'd relied on him more than she ought to have done. Now she was paying the price for that reliance.

Thank God she was spending the weekend with Auntie Win. Tomorrow morning she would pack Rufus and Helga in the car and drive down to Sandalwood. They'd make an early start and be there before lunchtime. Then she'd take her aunt aside and explain her dilemma. Auntie Win would know what she ought to do.

Her reception at Sandalwood on the Saturday was unexpected and bizarre to say the least. As she drove up to the entrance, Charles the butler came out looking embarrassed. He held up his hand and stopped her.

'Mrs. Seeberg's compliments and apologies, Miss Castle, but would you please be good enough to drive round to the stables at the back? She will meet you there.'

Mystified, Sarah did as directed.

Auntie Win was crossing the stable yard when Sarah pulled up and got out of the car. Her greeting was not as expansive as usual and her manner a trifle dismissive.

'Keep Helga and the baby in the car, honey, until you've heard what I have to say. After that, you may not want to stay yourself.'

'Whatever's the matter?'

Her aunt spread her hands helplessly. 'Max is here.'

'Oh, God!'

'Well, you know how it is, Sarah. I like to keep Sandalwood as open house at the weekends and anyone within reason is welcome.'

172

'Oh, sure.'

'He turned up about an hour ago. It knocked the stuffing out of me – not having seen him for so long. I couldn't be unwelcoming, now could I?'

'Where is he?'

'Upstairs. He knows the situation and promises to stay there until you'd been told. He's behaved like a perfect gentleman. He's not staying the night but, if you refuse to see him, he says he'll leave immediately.'

Sarah groaned. He had certainly put the screws on her. How much of it had been by design and how much by accident? Instinctively she knew what Simon would advise if he were here. He would tell her to meet him. Get it over with; lay the ghost, if necessary.

She asked her aunt for her opinion.

'Well, dear, I honestly don't believe you have any option but to see him. Obviously, I don't approve of what he did to you and Rufus. That was a dreadful thing – to desert you like that. But he's weak rather than bad. Needless to say, I blame his father for the upbringing he gave the boy.'

'I guess you're right,' Sarah said reluctantly.

'I know how you feel, honey. And I don't blame you. But just let him see Rufus. Nothing more. And you can make it plain you don't want him pestering you in the future.'

Sarah was still undecided. 'It could be the thin end of the wedge.'

'Well, you've got to be firm, Be strong. Helga and Rufus can come into the house with me,' her aunt went on. 'I'll tell Charles to conduct Max to the library. You can see him in there.'

Sarah swallowed hard. 'Very well. As you say, I suppose I have no alternative.'

Max was watching the cameo in the courtyard from an upstairs window. He couldn't hear any of the words exchanged but their faces were very expressive.

Mrs. Seeberg was being persuasive. He could tell that. Max liked her; she was motherly and warm-hearted. Sarah was hesitant. Arguing, perhaps. He didn't blame her.

To see her again was an emotional experience for Max. She

173

was as stunning as ever. More so, if anything. The curves of her legs and the swell of her bosum took his mind back to happier days. But now his feelings didn't end with mere physical attraction. When she'd slapped him in Fleet Street, he'd made a discovery about himself; about her; about their relationship.

He'd realised then that Sarah meant more to him than merely a beautiful body that could provide a few hours' distraction. She was the mother of his child, a brave and self-reliant woman who aroused admiration in him as much as desire. It was a novel discovery.

He watched as Mrs. Seeberg and Sarah, talking animatedly, walked across the yard and into the house.

He would like to take up with Sarah again. Set up home together, perhaps. But not marriage. His mind still baulked at the idea of marriage.

But would Sarah have him? Very doubtful. How on earth could he convince her he was genuinely sorry for what he'd done? His regrets were real enough. His remorse was something that had grown in intensity over the last few years. Now, he wanted to face her; to put matters right.

His thoughts were interrupted at last by a gentle tap on the door.

'Come in.'

The butler appeared. 'Miss Castle will see you in the library, sir. If you will be good enough to follow me, I will conduct you there.'

Sarah was apprehensive. What little courage she'd possessed had now evaporated completely.

She heard two sets of footsteps crossing the parquet flooring in the hall. They stopped outside the library door. She held her breath. The door opened.

'Mr. Max Brown, madam.'

'Thank you, Charles.'

The butler withdrew. The door closed.

Max stood diffidently, waiting to be invited to take a seat.

'Please sit down.' The tone of her own voice sounded strange to her.

He selected a chair near the door, some feet away from

where she was sitting. 'Thank you for seeing me.' he said at last.

Sarah broke the silence that followed. 'What is it you have to say?'

He shifted his feet, opened and closed the palms of his hands, looked down at his finger nails. 'To say I'm sorry. But apologies don't come easily to me.'

'No. I suppose not.'

It was hard for Sarah to relate the young man before her with the vigorous lover she'd known. The immaturity of his features didn't square up to his physique. In many ways, he was a paradox.

Yet, despite this, he had aged slightly and looked better for it. His hair was already showing signs of receding. He was very young for that to happen, she thought. Perhaps baldness ran in his family. On the other hand, it could have been caused by worry.

Her mind had been wandering. She forced herself to concentrate on what he was saying. Max was apologising profusely, begging her to let bygones be bygones.

She heard herself say, 'Forgiveness is a lot to ask.' There was pain in his eyes but she forced herself to ignore it. Did he expect her to forgive him with ease? How could she do that after what he'd done? Even so, his remorse appeared to be genuine enough.

He asked about the baby. She told him he had a son.

Max was delighted. 'What have you called him?'

'Rufus.'

'Nice name. What's he like?'

She found herself becoming lyrical about the boy's looks, his progress, his mannerisms. Her reserve was being broken down. Sarah forgot she was supposed to be angry with Max. She was speaking in a tone that was almost friendly.

She pulled herself up. This wouldn't do! Be firm; accept his apologies, let him see his son and be done with it. And their meetings from now on would be strictly formal.

'May I see him?' Max asked.

Although she'd already tacitly accepted the situation, her reply was choked and unwilling. 'Very well.'

Sarah began twisting her hands in her lap but stopped

immediately. She lifted her head high, trying to bely the impression that she wasn't in complete control of the situation.

'But I cannot allow you to believe there's any chance of us resuming our former relationship.'

'No. I didn't expect that.' It was a lie, she could tell. His eyelids had drooped a little and he'd glanced down. Max was disappointed.

'But there is one thing I must insist on,' he said.

Insist? Max wasn't in a position to insist on anything. But she made no comment.

He continued, 'I must insist on supporting the child.'

'Oh, no!' Sarah wasn't having that. She had maintained her baby without outside financial help for two years. She didn't need it now. Besides, what about her independence? If she were not careful, Max could pose a threat to her freedom.

'I'm not well of,' he said, 'but I'm making a reasonable living and I want to help. It's my duty.'

Sarah dug her heels in. 'The answer's still no. And it's too late for you to be talking about duty.'

This had hit him below the belt but he recovered. She could see him weighing up the situation. 'Very well, I'm not going to argue. But you can't stop me opening a bank account for Rufus and paying something in each month, can you? And that's what I intend to do.'

She sidestepped this and rose abruptly, bringing the conversation to an end. 'You'd better come and meet your son.'

As she made for the door, he rested a hand on her arm and whispered. 'Thank you.'

She pulled away. 'I'd prefer you not to touch me.' The sight of his deep blush gave her no satisfaction. 'Please follow me,' she said, leading the way out of the room and up the stairs to where Helga minded the child.

Rufus seemed very unimpressed with his father. Max was allowed to pick him up but the boy showed no response to his attempts at conversation. He held out his arms for Helga to take him.

The first meeting between father and son hadn't been very encouraging. Sarah tried to cover this by explaining that Rufus was in a strange environment. 'You ought to see him at

176

home — full of life,' she said. 'Always chattering.'

Why had she said that? She wished she hadn't. Max looked lost and Sarah felt sorry for him. It was quite ridiculous, of course. Feeling sorry for Max? After what he'd done to her?

'Perhaps next time will be better,' he suggested.

'Perhaps. Yes.' She didn't want to discuss the next time.

Feeling suddenly claustrophobic, she walked away. 'Now, if you will excuse me, I must go and freshen up before lunch.'

He gave a little bow. 'Of course.'

Sarah left him without a backward glance. Once in the privacy of her own bedroom, she threw herself on to the bed and tried to recover her equilibrium.

As she examined her own behaviour she reached an unwelcome conclusion. She had been ungracious and boorish. Surely Max's coming to seek forgiveness had shown he had guts? And all she'd done was to throw his remorse back in his face.

Why was it sometimes so easy for her to behave like a bitch?

He would be at Sandalwood for the rest of the day and so she resolved to make it up to him in some small way. But, of course, she'd be treading a fine line between remaining courteous and keeping him at a safe distance.

She felt it would not be particularly easy.

In fact, it proved to be not such an ordeal as expected.

Auntie Win helped greatly. When Sarah mentioned her problem, her aunt had held her arm and given a very shrewd, knowing look. It held the suspicion of a wink.

'I reckon you've got to think about this very carefully, honey. When I look at Max, I see only a great hunk of manhood. Boy, what a body he has! I think he's the answer to any maiden's prayer.' She gave one of her characteristic guffaws. 'You know — the type maidens always hope to find underneath their bed.'

Sarah laughed. She didn't need to have the point underlined.

The warm, sunny weather enabled them to use the pool. This in itself broke down barriers. Both Sarah and Max were good swimmers so they had the chance to talk in the water and at the poolside without having to touch upon sensitive topics.

Moreover, Auntie Win was adept at smoothing over awkward moments and making people feel at ease. Often during the afternoon, she engaged the two of them in conversation, feigning ignorance of the problems that beset them.

There was only one discordant note. Sarah had been surprised by the arrival soon after lunch of Lady Virginia Duval. Sarah assumed she'd come trawling her nets, soliciting gossip for that column of hers.

During the afternoon, the two women did little more than brush shoulders with one another. And when they did speak, they went no further than observing the social graces.

Sarah had heard of Virginia's growing reputation at the *Daily Sentinel* and had no wish to be friends with a professional rival. They had met socially only once before — here at Sandalwood — and that had been enough.

The time went by more quickly than Sarah had anticipated. In spite of Max's being there, it was more enjoyable too. Fortunately, the weather continued mild for the time of year and they'd been able to enjoy a barbeque on the patio.

When the servants were clearing away later, someone called out, 'I'm going for a swim.' This was followed by a general exodus from the tables. Tracksuits were hurriedly peeled off to reveal swimming wear beneath.

Although it was already dark, the water was still warm and Sarah and Max swam several lengths. She was the first one to tire. She climbed out, towelled herself, put on a bathrobe and sat on a bench.

After some moments, he joined her. Neither apparently felt the need to talk. Sarah idly watched the other swimmers getting out of the water and drifting towards the patio where the butler was serving drinks.

Soon, they had the poolside to themselves.

'You've changed,' she said after a silence that lasted several minutes.

He shrugged. 'Have I? I thought the leopard doesn't change its spots.'

Briefly, her hand touched his. She withdrew it hastily. 'That's silly,' she said.

'Not really.'

'Sorry I was bitchy.'

'You weren't.'

'Couldn't help it.'

'I deserved it.'

'You'll be seeing Rufus.'

'I'm glad.'

'But nothing more. I mean – '

'Naturally.'

'You understand, then?'

'Of course.'

He stood up suddenly and slipped off his bathrobe. 'Before I leave, I'm going to have one last dip. Are you joining me?'

'No, I don't think so.'

The pool lights had not yet been switched on but the lights from the house showed up Max's body in silhouette as he poised to dive. Sarah noted the firm muscular physique. Max had a beautiful body. It had always fascinated her. It fascinated her still.

Her own bathrobe came off and a moment later, she was swimming in pursuit.

At the rail, he turned and saw her, came over and trod water by her side. Wiping her eyes, she spluttered, 'It's lovely.'

'Yes.'

'Come on – race you to the end.'

'OK. You're on.'

He was a strong swimmer and he beat her – but only just. She splashed his face and he tried to duck her. She escaped by swimming under water where he followed. He caught hold of her. And when he kissed her, she didn't resist. It was only shortage of breath that forced her finally to regain the surface.

They were both laughing as they came up. Sarah had found it a stimulating experience. And judging by the expression on his face, so had he.

He leapt up on to the poolside and offered her a helping hand. She accepted gratefully. As he pulled her up, she found herself in his arms. It seemed the most natural place to be. And he was kissing her hungrily and she was pressing her body against his.

179

She slid her hand languorously over his chest, savouring the touch of his skin, wanting him. 'Oh, Max!' she whispered. Eventually, she pulled away. 'Someone will see us.'

'I suppose so.' He sounded regretful.

'I'll be in touch,' she murmured.

'Make it soon.'

'Oh, I will. I will.'

Chapter Twenty-One

The first thing Des Mallon did each morning on arrival in the office was to look in his diary. Not that it was necessary for he never forgot appointments. But he checked just the same. The entry for eleven o'clock today was marked: 'Briefing for "Ask Sarah" – number one.'

Having worked hard in the planning stage, he was full of enthusiasm for the series. And the format that had been finalised pleased him. He was also satisfied with the compromise reached on the question of going out live.

Sarah would have plenty of time to study the questions and prepare her answers. The transmissions would be live broadcasts and the questioners, sitting in shadow, would read out their agreed queries. Sarah, who would have a guest panellist with her for back-up, would give what appeared to be off the cuff answers.

Des had high hopes for the programme and was delighted to be working with Sarah again.

For some moments, he twirled a pencil in his fingers and began doodling on his desk pad, thinking. Suppose if he'd been made differently, what would it have been like? Would he have enjoyed being caressed by a woman, making love to her?

He doubted it. He didn't really understand women. They represented a threat which he couldn't explain. But Sarah was different. In a completely unphysical way, he loved Sarah. He cherished her, wanted her happiness, and was glad to watch over her interests.

She was highly photogenic and handled the camera like the

professional that she was. Clearly, much of her talent had been inherited from her mother. Now, under his tutelage and guidance, she would blossom as a great television performer. He was convinced of that. It was going to be an exciting partnership.

Having checked his diary again, his second task was to scan the papers as it was essential to keep abreast of everyday affairs.

While reading the daily offering of one of the women columnists, he mentally jumped, spread the paper more firmly on his desk top and read it again.

'The bitch!' he said aloud to the empty room.

Des glanced at his watch. Only fifteen minutes to go before the briefing session. As it was the first programme of the series, everyone would be hyped-up – particularly Sarah. It was only to be expected.

And now this! Des thumped his fist on the offending paper and came to a decision. He called out to his secretary: 'Marie, be a sweetie will you, and get everyone in here, pronto. I want to have a word before Sarah arrives.'

'Will do.'

Des re-read the offending paragraph. 'The bloody bitch! It's done out of spite. And she's deliberately chosen today. God, I could kill her for this.'

A few minutes later, the 'Ask Sarah' team filed into the office. Des passed the paper around for everyone to read.

'You all see the point, I'm sure,' he said. 'That's been put in today deliberately. The idea is that Sarah should read it before doing the programme and so give a bad performance. It's sabotage.'

The crew murmured their agreement.

'Now, remember this everybody,' Des went on, 'this must not be mentioned to Sarah. With luck, she hasn't seen the papers – that's my hope, anyway. After we've wrapped the programme up, I'll have to break it to her gently.'

He had scarcely finished speaking when his secretary announced Sarah.

He watched her carefully as she swept in. She seemed in good spirits so perhaps she hadn't read the write-up. Thank God for that!

182

'Hello, everybody,' she said.

Des kissed her on the cheek.

'All right?' he asked.'

'Fine. I'm looking forward to this.'

'Good. So are we all."

Sarah and Des sat down and the production crew followed suit.

Des cleared his throat, picked up his notes and the meeting began.

The shooting of the first programme went exactly according to plan. Better if anything. Des was delighted with the overall result and was sure 'Ask Sarah' would one day climb into the ratings charts.

Sarah surpassed herself, showing no apparent nervousness at going out live. True, she already knew what the questions were but even so it was a good performance. Not once had she hesitated or fluffed a line. In fact, Des had noticed an extra quality about her – a new verve and an added sparkle. He felt that she was finally coming into her own.

Instead of using the hospitality room afterwards, Des steered Sarah into his own office and opened the drinks cupboard.

'Your usual Scotch on the rocks, darling?' he asked.

'Not today, Des. I need a good, large brandy.'

'And so do I.'

'It's been a gruelling ordeal for me,' Sarah admitted when the drinks had been served.

'You gave no sign.'

'Didn't I? Perhaps it's because I'm basically an actress.'

'Well, whatever you are, you're a professional.'

'Bless you.'

They drank in silence for some moments. Des paused, having second thoughts about the wisdom of saying what was on the tip of his tongue. Eventually, he felt he had no option.

'I think you ought to see this, Sarah – from Virginia Duval's column. It's not very nice, I'm afraid.'

Looking a little mystified, she took the cutting that he'd handed over and read it.

> Who is the dark-haired agony aunt
> who was indulging in clandestine
> kisses at a house party in Sussex the
> other night? I will not reveal her name
> for my lips are sealed.
> But I know her secret. She and her
> amour were enjoying high jinks by the
> poolside after dark when good living
> folk were a-bed. And kissing under
> water, forsooth! A bit kinky that,
> surely − even with the lady's
> rapacious taste for the unusual. Oh,
> tut tut!
> I wonder how her television viewers
> would react to such naughty
> behaviour if they knew?

Sarah passed the cutting back and breathed out through pursed lips. 'It stinks.'

'It does. It's what I've always said − Virginia is a right bitch. And she's got her claws out for you, darling. She's spitting mad because you've got a major series and she hasn't. Watch her. She's dangerous.'

'It's so silly anyway. The guy I was with on that occasion happened to be Max, my baby's father. He turned up quite unexpectedly at Auntie Win's party. All day I held him at arm's length. But by the poolside my resistance broke down a bit, that's all. It means nothing.'

'You're not thinking of taking up with him again, then?'

For the briefest of moments, she hesitated. 'No − and for two reasons. No one could replace Simon in my affections, and with the column and now this I can't really spare the time for boyfriends.' She caught the questioning look on his face. 'Oh, all right − if Max were to ask me out, I might succumb. But I don't think I'd go further than that. I wouldn't want any serious involvement.'

'I understand. You know, I'm surprised you were so calm about that piece of spitefulness. You didn't seem upset by it at all.'

'I'm not. If Virginia Duval wants to goad me, she's chosen the wrong woman. My private life is my own affair. And I'm going to keep it that way. That sort of journalism just seems petty and pointless.'

'It might be petty, Sarah. It certainly isn't pointless. That bitch is out to get you. I implore you to watch your step.'

Martin Lamb had a problem.

In spite of his fearsome reputation on the *Daily Courier,* he disliked having to reprimand his staff. He could only bring himself to do it by shouting at them. Early in life he'd discovered that adopting a bellicose voice provided him with the Dutch courage that he needed on such occasions.

But having to censure a senior woman journalist went against his natural chivalry. Besides, he knew that if he used that tone with Sarah she would walk out of the office.

He was faced therefore with the problem of admonishing her without having his customary prop of aggressiveness to help him. He wasn't looking forward to the coming interview.

Martin reconsidered his position. Upon reflection, how could it possibly be a reprimand? It was more of a warning, wasn't it? Just that. A friendly warning. But would she take it as such?

Sarah was a spirited woman. And proud. She wouldn't take kindly to what he had to say, however carefully he dressed it up. She'd regard it as an intrusion on her privacy. Which, of course, it was.

He turned to his secretary.

'Pat – when Sarah comes in, d'you think we ought to open the drinks cupboard?'

'No. She'd suspect something at once. I know I would. But I've got some coffee perking.'

'Fine. We'll offer her a cup. Then, when you've served it, take it as your cue for leaving the office.' A tap at the door. 'Come in.'

Martin caught his breath as Sarah walked in. She always had that effect on him. Stunning looks combined with poise and an undoubted sexuality. How he wished he were younger. And how he would have liked to avoid the next few minutes.

Pat served them their coffee and, with a glance at the editor, went out. He was left alone with Sarah.

'You wanted to see me, Martin. I have a feeling it's something serious.'

Why was she always so direct? 'Well, I – er – what makes you think that?'

'I thought it was a bad sign when Pat left the room.'

'Very intuitive!' He decided he had to make a clean breast of it. 'Look, Sarah, this isn't of my choosing.'

She laughed shakily. 'What is it, for heaven's sake?'

He took out a newspaper cutting from a drawer and pushed it across to her. She took it and scanned it hurriedly.

'Oh, *that*! Is that all?'

This floored him. He hadn't expected her to take that line. 'All?' he repeated lamely.

'I've already seen this. Lady Virginia obviously has it in for me. She's peeved because I've got a major TV series and she hasn't.'

Sarah was missing the crux of his argument and he had to put her right. 'But is it true what she claims?'

She gasped and there were danger signals in her eyes. He knew he'd said the wrong thing. 'Are you checking up on my private life?' she flared at him.

'Well – no – not exactly.'

'You are! And I won't have it. You've got an infernal cheek. What I do in my own time is my affair. I will not be quizzed on it.' With that, she rose swiftly and made for the door.

Martin stood too, leaning over the desk, pleading. 'Sarah, please. Listen to what I have to say. Just hear me out, that's all.'

She hesitated but the expression on her face remained unchanged, and her tone unfriendly. 'Very well.'

Martin tried to look relaxed. He felt anything but.

'It's like this. If the chief crime reporter or the political editor or the sports editor, say, wants to indulge in orgies or go on the rampage, then that's his affair. But the agony aunt has to be whiter than white – or at least, *appear* to be whiter than white.'

'But I don't indulge in orgies or go on the rampage.'

'I'm not saying you do. But even something as innocent as kissing by the poolside at night can be made to sound raunchy by someone like Virginia Duval.' He studied her. She was taking in what he'd said. He felt he was beginning to win her round.

186

'I accept that,' she said reluctantly and sat down. Martin did likewise.

'Believe me, Sarah, I don't want to pry or interfere. All I'm saying is, for God's sake be careful, that's all. I hope Sam Braidwood hasn't seen this cutting because he'd be very upset by it, I can tell you. He'd never countenance his agony aunt being mentioned in the gossip columns.'

Sarah was silent a long time. 'I know you're trying to help me, Martin, and I'm grateful,' she said at length. 'I suppose I'll have to regard this as the price to be paid for being in the public eye. I promise I'll be discreet in the future.'

'You'd better be. At the moment, Sam thinks you're the tops. I don't want him to be disillusioned and for you to lose his support.'

'Neither do I – especially now that 'Ask Sarah' is proving to be a winner.'

'I thought it would be. And it wouldn't be a bad idea for you to drop Sam a note to thank him and say how much you're enjoying doing the programme.'

'I was going to do that anyway.'

'That's it – keep the old boy happy.'

Sir Reece Brown had read in his own entertainment pages that Sarah's programme was being well-received by the critics. That made him more piqued than before, and he felt he was justified to hold it against Sarah herself. She was largely to blame, after all. If she hadn't joined old Braidwood in the first place, his corporation would now be enjoying the kudos from her success. It made him feel very bitter against her.

Apart from feeling vexed with Sarah, Reece was also bored.

He'd noticed that recently his threshold of boredom had become much lower. Not, of course, in his working hours. That was unthinkable and would have spelt disaster. He couldn't have survived if he'd been bored by his business.

But his free times, spent mainly in the company of Alison, irked him. During the week, the evenings at the West End flat were often short because of business commitments. They didn't present much of a problem. Weekends at Glenhurst, however, were a different matter altogether.

Sometimes, if the weather were fine, he would go for a

country walk and have a drink at the village pub. But those occasions were rare. He found the conversation of the other customers banal. Besides, they were beneath him socially.

He and Alison had joined a local golf club. Her game, though, wasn't up to his standard and she tired easily. They entertained lavishly at Glenhurst but her conversation he judged to be uninformed. She liked to have the young jet set around her. He favoured the business fraternity.

When they were on their own, he preferred to read; she liked the television. At meals, they never spoke unless they had guests.

Why had he kept her so long?

He laughed inwardly. The answer was really quite simple. She was elegant in appearance and very good in bed. Couldn't have been better, in fact. Alison knew all the tricks. She could keep any man happy.

But the question was: how much longer could he go on like this? His patience was wearing very thin.

And there was another matter that had been occupying his thoughts in recent months. This afternoon he thought of it once more. He missed Max. It wasn't so much the actual company that he missed. They had after all never been close.

It was something else. The absence of a son in his life made him afraid. When he became old, he would have to face the spectre of loneliness and possible infirmity. That such things could happen to him − Reece Brown − petrified him.

He had always hoped that his son would be near him when he became old and could take over the Brown commercial empire. But since Max had chosen to cut himself off, there was no one. No one of his own, that is. Except young Rufus. The trouble was he was two whole generations away. It seemed an unbridgeable gap.

Reece had never been able to relate to babies. Unsociable, unruly creatures, without the ability to communicate. Messy and noisy besides. So, apart from remembering his grandson on his birthdays, Reece had kept a low profile where the chil was concerned.

But the situation was rapidly changing. Rufus was over two years old, and in about a couple of months' time it would be Christmas. Why shouldn't he take Sarah and the child out?

Give Rufus a treat. In any case, Sarah was already aware that he intended to play his part in the boy's life. Surely now was a good time to start.

How would Alison react to the idea? She'd probably remain aloof. On the other hand, she could sometimes be touchy – even suspicious. You could never quite be sure with Alison.

He decided to broach the subject at once.

'Oh, Alison, my dear, I've been thinking about Rufus.'

She regarded him over her copy of *Vogue,* clearly irritated by his interruption. 'What about him?'

Briefly, he outlined his plans. She wasn't interested.

'I take it, then, you'd have no wish to accompany me?'

She laughed. 'None whatsoever.' She returned her attention to the magazine. But after a moment or two, she lifted her eyes and a sly look came into them. 'Unless you have designs on the mother rather than the son?'

Reece appeared suitably shocked although the idea had occurred to him. Once, he would have enjoyed having an affair with the glamourous Sarah. She had always attracted him and still did.

But he'd never forgotten how she'd rebuffed him in her flat some years ago, then turned down his invitation to dinner. And she'd rejected his generous offer of employment at the *Daily Sentinel.* He was much too proud a man to risk any more snubs.

' "Designs on the mother"?' he repeated. 'What a thing to say! Of course, I haven't.'

'That's rather short-sighted. You ought to give that possibility some thought now.'

'What on earth do you mean?' As he spoke, he had a premonition.

She looked at him over the magazine, a delicate smile hovering on her face. 'Can't you guess?'

It annoyed him that she was able to dangle him on a string like this.

'No,' he said, although he was beginning to have a fair idea of what was in her mind.

'Well, you see – ' Alison broke off to examine the nails of her right hand before patting her hair in place ' – I'm leaving you.'

189

So his premonition had been right. He was enraged that he couldn't think of a suitably casual riposte. 'Really?' Heavy sarcasm; sneering lips; raised eyebrows. Alison was unmoved. 'May I enquire when and, perhaps more to the point, with whom?'

She brought up an exquisite finger and stroked her cheek before replying. 'Let's just say that a girl does have to watch her own best interests, Reece. That's a good enough reason, I reckon.'

More sarcasm. A trenchant tone. 'Naturally. That goes without saying. It will be soon then?'

'In a few days − as soon as I've got my things together. Meanwhile, I'll be sleeping in another bedroom. You understand, of course.'

'Of course.'

Deep inside he was seething. Not because his affair with Alison was over. After all, he himself had been considering telling her to go for some time. No, Reece was angry because she had got in first. She had dispensed with him. That was something unique in his life.

Her voice broke his train of thought. 'There's one other thing to be discussed − my settlement. I've instructed my solicitor to contact yours. They can settle a sum acceptable to us both.'

He inclined his head in her direction. 'Agreed.'

'I'm sure the new arrangement will suit you very well. You'll be able to go after Sarah Castle at last. I know you've been wanting to get your leg over her for a very long time.'

Chapter Twenty-Two

Sarah was learning about herself fast. A new picture was emerging.

Until recently, she'd been merely a journalist – communicating to readers from her ivory tower. Her name was well known; that was all. When she went home or shopping or to a theatre, no one would have guessed her identity. Off duty, she was incognito.

But not any more. Her face was now familiar to thousands. People were beginning to recognise her: in the street, in cafés, in trains. And she gloried in it.

Sarah discovered that she liked having a large audience. It wasn't a question of personal vanity; it was simply that she was by nature a performer. She was her mother's daughter, after all.

There was, of course, the other side of the coin. It wasn't all adulation. She had to face some criticism, a consequence of appearing before a mass audience. No performer could escape it.

Also, having a public meant that your private life was no longer your own. She had already found this to her cost. But having been caught out once in this respect, she wouldn't let it happen again.

'Ask Sarah' had been running for five programmes. Its first series was nearly finished and was a runaway success. And the *Daily Courier* was reaping the benefit through increased readership figures. Everyone was delighted, and Martin was particularly pleased.

Sarah and Des had invited him to the studios for the last

programme of the series. Lunching in the studio canteen prior to the transmission, they were enjoying an animated discussion on the media. Des believed passionately in the power of the visual image. Martin reluctantly agreed that it had impact but stoutly defended the written word.

He was emphasising this point when a slim young woman approached their table.

'Mind if I join you?' she said. 'This seems to be the only seat available.'

'No, of course not.'

The two men jumped up. Des introduced the newcomer. 'Sarah and Martin − meet Patsie Wyeth.'

Sarah had seen Patsie on the screen many times but, until now, had never met her. She had soft brown eyes and a gentle mouth. Sarah responded to her warmth and liked her immediately.

Martin was most enthusiastic and pumped her hand vigorously. 'My wife is a great fan of yours. She loves your programme − er −' He struggled desperately to recall its name.

' "People and Places",' Patsie added, coming to his rescue.

'Of course. My wife likes the way you talk to the people and the upbeat presentation.'

Patsie arranged her lunch on the table. 'I'm glad she likes it. But you've got to thank the producer for the presentation.' She grinned and nodded her head in the direction of Des. 'It's all his idea. I just do as I'm told.' She paused and added as an afterthought. 'You're lucky to have him, Sarah. He's the best in the business.'

'Oh, I know that. By the way, when's your next series going out?'

For a moment, Patsie hesitated. Des answered for her. 'We're due to start recording the third week in January,' he said. 'At the moment, though, we have some minor problems but they'll be straightened out in the end.'

'I'm not worried,' Patsie said.

Des nodded in agreement. He looked at the clock on the canteen wall and addressed Sarah. 'I reckon we'd better be going, darling. Suggest you come up in about half an hour, Martin.'

192

'Right.'

Sarah and Des rose to go and began to walk away.

'Good luck,' Patsie called out after them.

'Thanks.'

It was Christmastime. There was a spirit of jollity in the air and everyone was in festive mood.

'Ask Sarah' was over − at least, the first series was. That meant she could relax just a little. She felt free but it was illusory. The more she got back fully into the old newpaper routine, the more she realised how much she owed her staff. She wanted to show her gratitude.

So on the Wednesday of Christmas week, there was a bottle of perfume on each of their desks. For her sub, she sent down a bottle of scotch. He responded by giving her a lingering kiss which Sarah found a pleasurable experience. She would look at him with greater interest in the future.

At midday, they opened two bottles of sherry in the office and toasted one another. Sarah thanked them for their loyalty and diligence. They replied by saying they enjoyed working for her.

At half-past one, the bottles were empty. The staff were content. They look around, stacked away the remnants of the party. At two o'clock they all went home, full of Christmas cheer and bonhomie.

On her return to St. John's Wood, Sarah checked the telephone pad in the hall. There was just one message. "Max Brown phoned midday. Please ring him back when convenient."

Sarah sighed. For a few moments, she stood irresolute. What ought she to do? She could, of course, put off replying until the last possible minute. She discarded that possibility straight away. That would be mean and unfair.

Impulsively, she picked up the phone, dialled the number on the pad and took a deep breath.

'Hello. Max? It's Sarah.'

He was surprised she'd rung back so soon. It was very good of her, he said, and hoped he wasn't being a nuisance.

'Not at all.' Sarah tried to keep her voice level and dispassionate.

193

As it was Christmas, Max said, he'd bought a gift for Rufus. Could he call round with it tomorrow?

Sarah had partly expected this. 'Oh, Max, that's very kind but tomorrow is fully booked. My au pair is spending Christmas in Germany and I'm taking her to the airport, and after that we're leaving for Sandalwood. And this evening I'm giving a dinner party.'

'Oh!' He sounded very disappointed. 'This afternoon, then. I won't keep you.' He paused awhile. 'And I won't embarrass you.'

His hurt tone tugged at her heart. 'Very well, Max. This afternoon then. But I'm afraid Rufus won't be here. The au pair has taken him to a children's party.'

'I understand.'

He was as good as his word. He arrived with an armful of gifts, all gaily wrapped in festive paper, and prepared to leave almost as soon as he arrived.

Sarah made him sit down, insisted he have a Christmas drink with her, determined to be sociable. Max accepted but remained diffident. He made repeated apologies for intruding on her time.

That was typical. Sarah remembered that in the past he'd constantly apologised for something or other. Max assumed he was always in the wrong – a legacy, no doubt, of his upbringing. Reece Brown would have that effect upon any sensitive child.

She told him that his father had called the week before with Christmas presents for Rufus.

Max looked startled. 'He doesn't know I've seen you again, does he?'

Sarah smiled. 'Don't worry. I wouldn't tell him. But in any case, he arrived, deposited his gifts, patted Rufus on the head and left again. His visit was over in a matter of a few minutes.'

'You don't have to tell me.' His eyes clouded over, recalling the past.

She felt sorry for him. His superb physique concealed the true Max. Hidden inside the virile frame was a conciliatory creature who was desperately anxious to be accepted. Sarah assumed that, as a child, he'd tried to please his father and failed. There was a quality about Max that made her strive to be gentle with him.

She was also curious. She wanted to ask him about his present life; what his job was; how he lived. But she refrained, maintaining an emotional barrier between them.

He sensed this and, after some polite conversation, rose to go.

At the front door, he turned to her almost desperately and the words tumbled out in a rush. 'I know how you feel about me and I don't blame you. But when we met by the pool – remember? – you promised to keep in touch. You seemed quite keen then. But that was over two months ago.'

Her conscience hit her hard. 'Oh, Max, I am so sorry but I really have been busy.'

'Oh, sure.' She wasn't certain whether he believed her. 'Well, I'd like to take you out – to dinner maybe or a theatre. Won't you let me – please? I want to do that so much.'

Sarah was torn asunder. One part of her was eager to accept. But in her current situation *vis-à-vis* the *Daily Sentinel,* she saw it as a recipe for disaster.

'It's sweet of you, Max, but I do have to be very careful these days.'

She told him of Virginia's write-up and how they'd been seen kissing. He was immediately contrite again, accepting full responsibility for her embarrassment.

She was weakening fast but pulled herself together. 'No, Max. It's too risky.' An idea had already presented itself. 'But Virginia Duval doesn't have her spies watching my home, as far as I know. Perhaps sometime in January you could have dinner here one night with us – that is with Helga and me?' She added this, not wanting him to entertain too many high hopes – .

His eyes flickered and the tightening of his lips registered disappointment. Then he smiled.

'I'd love that,' he said.

She put her arm around him and squeezed. 'And so would I.'

He kissed her on the cheek and then on the lips. 'Happy Christmas,' he murmured.

'Happy Christmas, Max. I really will be in touch this time. I won't forget.'

She was feeling uplifted by the encounter and was glad he'd called. Pity he couldn't have stayed longer. She watched him stride along the pavement to his car; saw him step inside and drive away.

Where would Max be spending his Christmas? She almost wished he were spending it with her.

The festive season at Sandalwood was in stark contrast to the weekends usually enjoyed there. Winnie Seeberg believed in the old-fashioned family gathering. No hangers on. Only close friends were invited to share the traditional roast turkey and plum pudding. Afterwards, they would sit round the blazing log fire, sipping port, cracking nuts or, quite simply, falling asleep.

This year, the company was even smaller than in the past. Apart from Sarah and Rufus, she'd only invited Harry Smith – an old business associate – and his wife, Beatrice. Both of them were now slumped in winged armchairs opposite her. Sarah, with the heat from the blazing fire on her face, was making a valiant effort not to doze off.

Winnie, on the other hand, had to remain vigilant. She was not used to having young children in the house, especially without a nursemaid. She was on edge, thinking with alarm of her precious objets d'art. She regretted that Sarah didn't have better control over her child.

During the morning, Rufus had been no trouble, much too busy, playing with his new toys. Since they had finished Christmas dinner, though, his fingers had been into everything. When he tried to pick up a Venetian glass bowl, Winnie sped across the room and rescued it. She was only just in time. That was the last straw.

'No, Rufus!' He put on a sulky face and tried to take it from her again. This time she spoke to him sternly and he looked as if he'd been slapped.

'I think he could do with a sleep,' Sarah remarked, suddenly, aroused by the fracas.

Winnie was relieved. 'I guess you're right,' she said, hoping she didn't sound too anxious to be rid of the child.

Rufus, however, had different ideas and protested vociferously. 'Want Helga,' he lamented as he was borne away upstairs, sobbing bitterly.

196

It was some minutes before Sarah returned, looking distrait. Even her hair was a little awry and she was plucking at her pearl necklace.

She flung herself down in a chair and passed a hand across her brow, glancing across at the other two guests as she did so. Harry was snoring gently. Beatrice's chin was resting on her chest and her eyes were tightly closed.

'I suppose you could say I'm not a good mother.' Sarah sounded defeated. 'I do try to be but I can't seem to cope as well as Helga.'

Winnie had seen evidence of this before, had noticed how Rufus played up his mother. She had never remarked on it lest she sound interfering. Now she spoke very gently, determined to be kind. 'It's because your talents lie elsewhere, I guess.'

'Nice of you to say so, Auntie Win. But it's not a real excuse, is it? I thought that giving birth automatically endowed a woman with these extra gifts. But it doesn't seem to have worked in my case.'

She glanced across at the other two guests again. Both were still sleeping. Having satisfied herself on this point, she faced Winnie challengingly. 'I know what you're thinking. You're worried that history is repeating itself.'

It was not in Winnie's nature to mince her words. 'Yes, honey, I am,' she agreed.

'What should I do about it?'

Winnie spread her hands despairingly. 'You ask *me*? You've got to take yourself in hand, that's all.'

'That's fine in theory but − '

'And in practice, too. You studied and sweated to be a good journalist and you suceeded. You've got to bring the same dedication and determination to motherhood. That's all.'

Sarah leant back in her chair, closed her eyes and sighed deeply. It was some moments before she spoke. 'I'll try,' she said, 'But it's not going to be easy.'

The noise of Harry's snoring only seemed to emphasise the silence that fell between the two women. It probably hadn't been easy for Sarah to be so frank about her shortcomings. Winnie wanted to change the subject.

'Have you had any more nonsense from that dreadful woman, Ginny?'

197

Sarah studied her aunt's face thoughtfully. 'Not so far. But she's had a profound effect upon my way of living. It's like being in a form of purdah. After that bitchy write-up appeared, I was carpeted by the editor — given a warning ... An agony aunt, I was told, has to appear to be whiter than white.'

Winnie gave one of her body-shaking guffaws. 'I could tell you a thing or two about the agony aunt I knew back in the States. Whiter than white? Geez!'

'Well anyway, I've had to accept the warning. It means I've to be very careful about who I'm seen with. I feel constantly under surveillance. And, frankly, it's getting me down.'

'Well, honey, don't get obsessional about it. It's not worth it. Maybe you should take a leaf out of your mother's book.'

Sarah sat up suddenly, eyes alert. 'What are you getting at?'

It was Winnie's turn to be surprised. 'You mean you haven't heard the lastest?'

'Heard what?'

'It seems she's gotten herself mixed up in some sort of sex scandal and doesn't give a rap. She's given the gossip writers a field day, the stupid bitch! It's in all the papers over there. A buddy of mine who lives in LA wrote and told me about it.'

Sarah was staring before her, shaking her head disbelievingly. 'Incredible, isn't it? And yet it's all in character. I only hope to God the story doesn't find it's way into any of the English papers that's all.'

'So do I.'

'If it does, it won't do me any good.'

There was a snort from one of the chairs opposite as Harry woke with a start. 'I wasn't really asleep,' he said.

'That's all right, Harry,' Winnie said, 'We didn't think you were.'

Chapter Twenty-Three

The coming of the New Year – 1988 – brought with it a number of problems. Circumstances conspired together to rob Sarah of her most essential commodity: time.

She'd been booked for a number of speaking engagements which necessitated a good deal of travelling, and her researh assistant was having time off to have a baby.

Sarah secretly wished the girl could have chosen a more convenient time for her confinement. It meant she'd be forced to leave her research in the care of a newcomer, and that worried her.

Of course, being temporarily free from television work helped to a limited degree. But, even so, the pressures remained and she felt she needed more hours in the day. When Sam Braidwood phoned to invite her to his country home, she was hard put to accept in a gracious tone of voice.

On the way out to an early appointment, she knocked on the editor's door. Martin looked up from his work, prepared to shout at the intruder, but seeing Sarah, he allowed himself a smile.

'Hey, Martin, Sam's invited me over to lunch today. By a stroke of luck, I happen to be free. Have you any idea what it's all about?'

'Not a clue. Maybe Maisie's produced another volume of poems and wants you to write a foreword.'

'Don't be facetious.' Laughing, she went out and closed the door.

Because of the ever-present time factor, she decided to go to the Braidwood estate by train, taking her laptop word processor with her. Every moment had to be productive.

Sam greeted her from the top of his steps as before. His large red hand enveloped hers in welcome.

'Good of you to come, m'love. Come in and say hello to Maisie. She's been looking forward to seeing you again. And then we can get down to a bit of business over lunch.'

He didn't say what was on his mind until the maid had brought in the cheese and biscuits. Then he put his case very bluntly.

'It's like this, Sarah. We'd like you to take on another television series.'

She was taken aback. 'Another series? Well, I don't know. This has come as a surprise.'

'Help yourself to biscuits,' Maisie put in.

'It's short notice, I'll grant you that. But we'd like you to do it.'

'Why short notice? What sort of format? I'd like to know more.'

Sam Braidwood seemed at a loss for a moment. 'Course you would. It's quite a long story. Oh, look, Maisie, let's take our coffee into the drawing room. Bring your cheese with you, Sarah. We can talk there in comfort.'

Patsie Wyeth was upset.

That a film company should slap an injunction on her with all the attendant publicity was bad enough, but the risk of losing her TV series to a rival was a far greater worry.

Patsie had always regarded her series as a doddle. No scripts to learn, just appear on set and play to the camera in her own inimitable way. What could be better? Especially as she was paid for it. Not a lot, of course, but it was bread and butter money. Films provided the jam.

Now, it looked as if her nice, safe little number would be snatched from her. And it was all because filming schedules had been altered a dozen times. The timetable of her next film clashed with the TV series. The film company claimed she was under contract to them and couldn't accept any other work at the same time. Hence the injunction.

It was a straightforward legal argument, her solicitor had assured her, and could be easily settled. But not in time for the television work. That was the rub.

And they would have to find a substitute, wouldn't they? That really bothered her. When Patsie had rung the head of programmes, his mouth was shut like a clam.

Her one fear was that her place would be taken by the dreaded Lady Virginia Duval, whom she distrusted.

Patsie had good cause for disliking her. Serveral times she'd been mentioned unkindly in Virginia's scurrilous column. And the possibility that she might be in the running for Patsie's own series – might already have been signed up, heaven forbid! – made her want to spit.

She could no longer face the torment of not knowing. In desperation, she picked up the phone and dialled Lord Braidwood's London number.

She told him of her fears.

'Aye, I was sorry to hear about the injunction.'

'Has anyone been selected in my place?'

He hesitated. 'Well, I couldn't rightly say, love, at this moment in time.'

'Oh, come on, Sam. Don't hold out on me.'

'It's not that, quite.'

'Put me out of my misery, please. It's not Virginia Duval, is it?'

'Well, I – ' He was breathing heavily at the other end of the line. He was coming to a decision, she could tell. 'I suppose there's no real harm in telling you.'

'Of course not.'

'I can assure you it won't be the Duval woman.'

'Then who?'

More huffing and puffing. 'It's been offered to Sarah Castle and she's considering it.'

Patsie was relieved. 'The agony aunt? Ella St. Clair's daughter? Oh, better than expected. I don't so much mind her taking over – she's a professional. It's these amateur upstarts like Virginia that worry me.'

He chuckled. 'Somebody did suggest Virginia but she was turned down flat. Still, Sarah hasn't agreed to do it yet. But if she does, can we say you'd be reasonably happy?'

'Well, no one likes losing a series, Sam, and I couldn't claim to be happy about it. But in the circumstances – '

'That's all right, then, I'd hate you to be upset.' She heard

201

him chuckling again. 'I know someone else who won't be very happy.'

'Who's that?'

'Reece Brown. Virginia is his gossip writer, don't forget. He's not going to like this at all.'

'That's true. Thank you, Sam. That thought has cheered me up no end.'

Sir Reece Brown was angry but not solely on the grounds of Sarah's continuing success.

He was presiding over a meeting in which a general spirit of acrimony prevailed. The circulation figures of the *Daily Sentinel* had dropped, Reece was displeased and a carpeting was in progress.

He was reading the riot act but his dry, acidic tone seemed to be having only a marginal effect upon his hearers. Charles Maynard, his managing editor, was a strong man who wasn't easily intimidated. The other executives too seemed un-abashed by his verbal onslaught.

Maynard even had the temerity to answer back. 'I told you when you first took us over, Sir Reece, that your policy was wrong. I know our readership, and – with respect – you don't. The circulation figures prove my point.'

'You've also cut down on the women's pages,' said one executive. 'That was a great mistake.'

'And our sports coverage needs to be much better,' said another.

'Besides, we don't have a well-known name writing for us – apart from Virginia Duval. But she's not in the same class as Sarah Castle. And she lacks popular appeal.'

'And look at the TV exposure Sarah's getting,' Maynard pointed out. 'I hear she's been offered Patsie Wyeth's series.'

'I am aware of that, thank you, Maynard,' Reece's speech had become more clipped.

'Of course,' Maynard went on, 'she might turn down the extra TV commitment.'

'Can't we get her to join us?' said the circulation manager. 'Make her an offer she couldn't refuse?'

Reece was forced into a defensive position. 'Do you think I haven't tried?'

'I'm told she's very loyal to the *Courier*.'

Reece sneered. 'Loyalty! How old-fashioned! The offer of money will always flush away so-called loyalty.'

The discussion dragged on. Maynard was becoming heated. Reece tried to counter his arguments but failed. Others took up the cudgels and he, the great Sir Reece Brown, had to retreat.

He was aware of the reason. The managing editor knew his job; had been in the newspaper business for years. Reece hadn't.

Maynard was too valuable a man for him to lose. Instead, Reece had to humour him and accept his proposals. But humble pie had a bitter taste.

A mile away, another meeting was in progress. No acrimony here; just good humour and constructive discussion.

The meeting had all the appearance of a council of war. They were discussing their offensive and Sarah was one of their big guns in the circulation war.

Sam Braidwood was in the chair. Martin and his deputy editor were on either side of him. Sarah sat slightly apart from the others, looking disinterested as though the agenda had nothing to do with her.

She was, however, acutely aware that the final decision was hers. She had to balance between what might be desirable and what was practicable. And she was not at all sure which side she would come down on.

They argued for some considerable time. Eventually, Sam said, 'Let's remind ourselves of the facts − Sarah's problem column is a sure-fire winner. We know how it's increased our readership.'

'But so is her television work,' Martin put in. 'The more she's before the public eye, the more we like it. So the chance for her to do this other series, can only help us in our circulation battle with the *Sentinel*.'

'That's obvious.' Sam agreed readily enough. 'But we can't force Sarah to take on this extra series.'

'I'm not trying to force her.'

Sarah stepped into the fray. 'It's not that I don't want to do Patsie's programme, "People and Places". I do. But the next series of "Ask Sarah" will be starting at the end of March. For a time, they'll overlap and I'll be doing two series at once. On top of that, I'll still have my work to do on the *Courier*.'

'We realise that, Sarah. You won't have any spare time at all.'

She gave a mirthless laugh. 'I wasn't thinking of spare time. I also have a number of speaking engagements lined up. But I refuse to let my column deteriorate.'

'Well, spoken, m'love.' It was Sam. 'We don't want that to happen either.'

Martin had been looking very thoughtful. He turned to Braidwood. 'I've just had an idea − d'you remember Felicity who used to work on the women's page before she got married? Felicity was a damned good journalist. She'd love to come back for a few weeks, I'm sure, and help Sarah out.'

The idea didn't appeal. Sarah preferred to select her own staff. She stated her point firmly but the others talked her round.

Martin said, 'She's really good, I promise.'

Sarah capitulated in the end. 'OK. OK. If you're really sure, then I'll have her. And I will do Patsie's programme − but only for the one series.'

Sam was jubilant. He jumped up from his seat and lapsed into his native Yorkshire as he sometimes did. "ee, that's champion, lass.'

Sarah took a deep breath. She fervently hoped she had done the right thing.

But it would only be for the one series. That, as far as she was concerned, was final.

At first, the demands on Sarah built up fast. Tying up existing commitments in the office; fitting new filming engagements into her diary; attempting to do a dozen jobs simultaneously.

But now that the initial indecision was past, she was glad she was taking over 'People and Places'. It would be stimulating; it would bring her interviewing skills more to the fore and she'd be getting out and about.

Her perspective had changed. This was largely through Felicity who'd welcomed the idea of joining her. An experienced journalist, she'd be taking over some of the editorial responsibility.

This relaxed Sarah somewhat. She'd begun to eat better and sleep more soundly at nights. She had, moveover, been able to fulfil her promise to Max. She'd invited him to dinner in the second week of January.

And the evening was a great success. Helga was captivated from the moment he'd arrived. During dinner, she positively sparkled, talking to him about Germany and praising his son.

Sarah, too, was happy – far more than she'd expected. Despite her good resolutions, her mind went back to their brief affair.

What fun it had been! How exciting! And, above all, satisfying. She remembered so clearly the first occasion they'd made love.

There'd been no man in her life since Max. It wasn't natural, living like a nun. If she wasn't careful, she'd become bitter in her old age. A crabby old woman!

The evening was drawing to a close and Max was speaking. 'I ought to be going, Sarah,' he said. 'It's been a wonderful evening.'

'Oh, is that really the time?' she heard herself say. How bourgeois she sounded! But she knew she'd said it as a kind of front. If it hadn't been for Helga sitting there, they might have gravitated towards the bedroom.

Sarah conducted him to the door. In the darkened porch, Max shed his inhibitions. Swiftly he proved that his technique was still without equal. He had lost none of his expertise and neither, for that matter, had she.

Physically, they were a perfect match. At the end of the brief encounter, Sarah was left breathless, dishevelled and hungry for more. She clung to him, kissing him, refusing to let him go.

'When can we be together?' he asked when she paused for breath. She placed her finger on his lips to silence him. Helga had been heard moving about in the lounge. But he wouldn't be put off. 'When?'

She thought quickly. She wanted to say tonight or even tomorrow night. But it was still the weekend and that would have needed a bit of explaining to Helga. A weeknight offered more scope for a plausible excuse to be away from home.

'How about Monday?' It seemed an age away.

'Fine. At my place then?'

'All right.'

'Don't forget.'

'I couldn't.'

He kissed her, slipped his hands up her skirt. Another kiss. Then he turned on his heel and walked away.

Sarah watched him out of sight. Then she took a deep breath, straightened her clothes and returned to the lounge with as much aplomb as she could muster.

It had the resemblance of a cloak and dagger spy novel and, in spite of the excitement flowing through her, Sarah had the desire to laugh.

She didn't believe for one moment that the *Daily Sentinel* had its spies watching her front door. Nevertheless, just to be absolutely sure, she did look up and down the cul-de-sac carefully before getting into her car and driving off.

She was elated. On the seat beside her, was her small case containing only the bare essentials for an overnight stay. Having rejected pyjamas, she'd packed a nightdress in the belief that Max would prefer it. But she had a shrewd suspicion she wouldn't need even that.

She found the large converted Victorian house without difficulty, and Max's welcome was warm and enthusiastic. It left her in no doubt as to how he hoped to spend the next few hours. This was just as well for she had similar intentions.

Sarah scarcely had time to divest herself of her outdoor clothes. She had a brief glimpse only of his bachelor flat, a fleeting impression of masculine comfort, and heard the strains of soft music coming from a music centre.

The next thing she knew she was being swept up into his arms and carried into the bedroom. Her heart was beating fast, glad that her years of celibacy were coming to an end.

The sight of Max's superb body sent shivers of pleasure through her. She had to touch him, to slide her fingers over his torso. Fantastic! Sensual and satisfying. Never before had she been so conscious of the sheer masculinity of a man. It was so powerful that she felt almost frightened of her own desire.

206

That he too had comparable feelings soon became clear. His hands were moving over her body, teasing, fondling, until she could stand the agony no more.

She lay down and gave herself to him eagerly. Neither of them could wait and their lovemaking had the quality of urgency to it. Sarah had forgotten how wonderful such physical union could be.

Max was a tireless lover and would not let her go. She didn't want to go and was glad when he took her again and again.

It was some time before, in a small voice, she murmured, 'I could do with some coffee.'

'Great idea,' he agreed.

They had some coffee, and some bread and cheese.

After they'd eaten Max said. 'Let's go back to bed.'

Sarah smiled. 'I'll tell you something, Max, you need never be out of work. You could always set yourself up as a stud – put up a brass plate saying "Lonely women satisfied".' She flung her arms around him and kissed his cheek. 'Come on, you wicked man, let's go.'

Next morning, she was feeling definitely jaded.

Just then, she would have liked to be anywhere but in her office, having to listen to her colleagues. Bringing a balanced judgement to the proceedings needed a considerable effort and she couldn't wait for the meeting to end.

Felicity, her assistant, was speaking but Sarah was having difficulty in following her line of reasoning. Mercifully, the phone rang and she answered it.

'Hi,' said a woman's voice. 'Sarah? It's Jenny. I'm back in the UK – or rather we are, Colin and I. There's so much I've got to tell you.'

Sarah said hello and welcome but explained she was in the middle of an editorial meeting. Jenny wasn't listening. She was in full spate, as usual.

'D'you remember I promised we'd be having a party when we returned? Well, it's on. Next week – in our new flat. And you've simply got to come.'

'Look, Jenny, can I ring you back this evening?'

She apparently didn't hear, continuing as though there'd been no interruption. 'I'll be very put out if you don't come.

207

If all goes well, Simon will be there, too. Won't that be marvellous? I can't wait to see you together again.'

Sarah felt weak but hoped it didn't show on her face. 'That's great,' she managed to say. But she wasn't at all sure whether it was.

After she'd put the phone down, she found concentration even more difficult than before. She wanted to see Simon very much indeed. But would it be wise?

She'd have to give the invitation some very careful thought.

Chapter Twenty-Four

The world of Jenny Dowling was still characterised by unpredictability and muddle. Her spell in the Middle East had made her worse, if anything. But people accepted her as she was. It was all part of her charm.

One morning at the end of January, she awoke with a start and shook Colin, her boyfriend.

A sleepy voice said, 'What's the matter?'

'Today's the day,' she replied, and leapt out of bed. 'We're having our party. No time to lie a-bed.'

'Oh, God, so it is.'

And so began a day of feverish activity for them both. Hoovering. Dusting. Shopping. Preparing. Fortunately Colin possessed a more orderly brain than she did. She needed a director and mentor and he performed both functions admirably.

They went to the supermarket together and returned with a trolley-load of food and drink. Thank heavens for convenience foods! Jenny thought. She was no cook. Not even a very good housekeeper.

But still she loved looking after Colin. And he was happy. That was all that mattered, wasn't it? It would be fun, tonight. She was looking forward to it.

Heavily laden with their purchases, they let themselves into their new flat. As they did so, Jenny heard the phone ringing and rushed to answer it. The caller was Simon and his tone was apologetic.

'Jen? I'm afraid it doesn't look as if Tina and I will be coming tonight. Sorry to give you short notice like this.'

Jenny was bitterly disappointed. She adored her brother and had greatly missed him while abroad. 'Why not?' she asked. 'Is it Tina? She's not feeling bad, I hope?'

'No, it's not that. As you know, she's only got a few weeks to go and she's very pregnant – absolutely enormous. It makes her self-conscious and not really in the party mood.'

'Well, it's a shame.'

Jenny didn't admit she'd hoped the party would be a means of bringing him in touch with Sarah again. She didn't see why the fact of his marriage should prevent them meeting. Just meeting! What harm could there be in that? Jenny was a romantic and wanted to be the one who brought it about.

She argued with Simon, using her feminine guile. She was very persuasive. Slowly, he weakened.

'I certainly want to come,' he said, 'and so does Tina, deep down.'

Jenny pressed her point. 'Well, then, there's no more to be said. Tell Tina, it won't be a boisterous affair and you'll be able to go home as early as you like.'

There was a long pause and Jenny could almost hear his thoughts turning over. 'Will Sarah be there?' he asked.

Ah! So that was it.

'She's been invited but I doubt whether she'll accept.' This was a lie but she didn't care. She's been given a new television series, y'know, and that's taking up a lot of her time.'

'I'll tell Tina,' he said.

"Tell Tina," eh? Now the real reason was beginning to emerge.

'I think maybe I'll be able to talk her round. Hope so, anyway.'

'So do I, Simon. A housewarming party wouldn't be the same without you.'

At his end of the line, Simon replaced the receiver without moving away from the phone.

The Victorian glass lustres on the sitting room mantlepiece were tinkling in the draught from the open door. The swaying prisms caught the afternoon light, casting it in sparkling purple fragments around the room.

The sound was pleasant and soothing, like cowbells on a

mountainside. Simon watched the dancing lights on the carpet, the furniture, the wallpaper. With half his mind, he was fascinated. The other half was occupied by more cogent thoughts. Could he persuade Tina to go to the party? He himself desperately wanted to, but didn't wish to appear too eager.

And yet, she had originally been keen to accept the invitation. In the first place, it had been he who'd hesitated. Their roles had since been reversed.

The root cause of their respective feelings was apprehension. Tina was probably worried about how he'd react to seeing Sarah again. That was only to be expected. He was concerned with precisely the same issue. It would be a very trying and testing meeting for him. For them both, perhpas.

Now, the news that Sarah might not after all be at the party had come as an anticlimax. Simon went in search of Tina and found her in the kitchen.

'I've just phoned Jenny, dear. She's very disappointed that we're not going. Oh, incidentally, she says Sarah will be too busy and is unlikely to be there.'

'Oh?' Tina hit the ball back into his court. 'What do you think we ought to do?'

'I feel we should go.'

'Very well, dearest. We will. We needn't stay late.'

'Exactly. And I'm sure the change will do you good.'

Simon and Tina weren't the only ones who'd been uncertain. Sarah was, too. Quite ridiculous, of course. It made her angry with herself.

She was, after all, a modern young woman, used to the ups and downs of the professional world. Experienced, sophisticated, intelligent. She was her own woman, answerable to no one for her actions.

Why then did she feel this way about going to an ordinary, run-of-the-mill party? Why was she behaving like a tongue-tied schoolgirl with a crush on the form master?

For the past few years – ever since she and Simon had broken up – she'd been trying to put the memory of him behind her. She'd never succeeded. Each time she thought

211

she'd exorcised him, memories would return to haunt her.

She knew the reason only too well: Sarah was still very much in love with him. Her feelings for Max were different. A fortnight ago, for instance, when she'd spent the night with him, she'd been driven by a great physical hunger. Nothing more than that. But her relationship with Simon was on another plane altogether. It always would be.

Sipping a brandy one night before going to bed, she began to fantasise.

Suppose — just suppose for argument's sake — that she found herself alone with Simon in romantic circumstances? They would become lovers again and there'd be no sense of guilt regarding Tina because they belonged to one another. It was as simple as that.

She knew that it was so. So did Simon. The writing was on the wall.

Why then was she uncertain about going to the party? Perhaps it was because she was not sure that the time was right. But one day it would be and all the barriers would disappear. Simon would be hers once more and she'd find true happiness.

With a swift movement, she picked up the phone and dialled Jenny's number.

Tina had long ago decided that there wasn't much fun in being pregnant. Apart from the various discomforts and disabilities, there was the distended shape to consider. She objected to that. And then there were the puffy ankles which made her legs look fat.

She felt overweight, ugly and clumsy, and that made her self-conscious. So, on their way to Jenny's flat that evening, she was forced to put on a false display of gaiety for Simon's sake.

He needed the break. For many months — since the death of her father, in fact — he'd been working much too hard with very little time off. His only contacts had been with the staff and his friend in the village with whom he played cards.

He never complained, though. He was the most amenable, the most gentle man she'd ever met — apart from her father, that is.

212

He loved the work at St. Giles, he said, and she believed him. Certainly, his relations with the students were excellent and he'd made many minor improvements.

Was he happy, though? Happy in his marriage and home life? If pressed on this, he would say he was. But, Tina wondered.

They were sneaking thoughts to which she was reluctant to give credence. Whenever they crept into her mind, she would dismiss them summarily; she didn't want to dwell on them.

She didn't really believe Sarah would stay away tonight. Coming to the party, therefore, was a testing time for her. She was keyed up for the moment of Sarah's arrival and her first meeting with Simon.

Then, all Tina's senses would be keenly alert, watching carefully. Being a perceptive and intuitive young woman, she would know precisely to whom her husband's heart belonged.

With this in mind, she rang the bell and they were ushered in.

'Hello, Tina. Lovely to see you. It was sweet of you to come. And, Simon, darling, thank you for bringing her.'

'Tina! Nice to meet you. I'm Colin. Jenny has told me so much about you. Now come in and meet some people.'

It was a warm welcome and Tina felt cheered. Soon, one of the men had found her a chair and everyone was cosseting her, making sure she was comfortable. She felt wanted, and relaxed in the happy atmosphere.

The other guests seemed a pleasant crowd. Some showed interest in her condition, asking when the baby was due. Tina was beginning to enjoy herself — until she remembered that Sarah would soon be arriving.

She had never met her rival but she'd made a point of seeing her on television. Suddenly, above the hubbub of conversation and the tinkle of glasses, she heard the doorbell.

The front door was opened. Voices in the hall, Sarah's among them. It would be interesting to see if reality matched up to the screen image.

A chic, raven-haired beauty swept dramatically into the living room. Tina caught her breath. Sarah was even more stunning than she appeared on the screen. People stopped talking, turned their heads. And Tina had been so taken up by

213

the arrival that she'd forgotten to watch Simon's reaction as she'd intended.

For the time being, Sarah was involved with greetings and introductions.

Tina glanced at her husband. He was looking in the opposite direction, affecting not to notice Sarah. But his ears were attuned, she could tell, listening to what was being said. And she sensed him holding his breath for the imminent reunion. There was no mistaking the excitement coursing through him.

Tina's instinct hadn't failed her.

'Well, hello, Simon.'

'Sarah. I didn't think you'd be here.'

None of it fooled Tina. She saw it as a theatrical, larger-than-life, gesture on both their parts. They advanced on one another, arms outstretched. A perfunctory hug, token kisses on the cheeks. All an exercise in carefully rehearsed restraint.

Her heart felt as if it would break. She looked away, trying to conceal the anguish. But it was only for a moment. Sarah advanced on her, exuding warmth and friendship.

'Tina, at last! I've wanted to meet you for so long. I think Simon's a very lucky man. And he's going to be a father. What more can he possibly want?'

'We're both lucky,' Tina said.

'Of course you are. And how are you? I must say, you look extremely well. You ought to have seen me when I was carrying Rufus, towards the end of my time. I looked like an old bag.'

Tina laughed. Strange to say, she felt at home with Sarah. 'I simply cannot believe that.'

'It's true, I assure you.'

Sarah's manner was disarming. Tina liked her and temporarily forgot her anxieties, ready to chat about babies and their attendant problems.

But as the evening wore on and the time came near for their departure, Tina gained a different perspective. She'd been fooled by the disarmingly friendly approach. The tinted glasses were now removed and she saw things plainly.

Simon and Sarah belonged together. Yes, they did. Not

Simon and Tina, *but Simon and Sarah*. Simon and Sarah. Simon and − !

She turned to her husband. 'Simon, will you take me home? I'm feeling rather tired.'

Reluctantly, he agreed. They said their goodbyes. Sarah hugged them both but lingered longer with Simon. They couldn't fool Tina. She wasn't born yesterday.

Let me out of this place; away from all these people; let me be alone with Simon where no one can steal him.

Once in the car, she felt a little better but overwhelmed with a desire to nag him. She'd never done that before. Why did she have the urge to do it now?

It must be because of Sarah. She was jealous and wanted to take it out on him. It was her only means of retaliation.

She didn't let up on him. On and on she went. He was getting rattled. His voice became hard, his manner taut.

Suddenly she could see she'd pushed him too far. He turned to her, taking his eyes off the road only for a few moments. But it was enough.

The car swerved. Too late, she saw the traffic bollard appear as if from nowhere; felt the impact as the car smashed into it.

After that − nothing.

Sarah decided to leave the party early. The fact that Simon had gone home had taken the edge off her enjoyment, anyway and there seemed little point in remaining. She would slip away, she hoped unobtrusively.

Jenny was in the kitchen, placing some vol-au-vents on a platter, when Sarah found her.

She had to make a very early start tomorrow, Sarah explained, and ought to be on her way. Did Jenny understand? Of course she did.

'Thank you for a wonderful party,' Sarah said.

'So pleased you came. Especially glad you and Simon were able to meet.'

'So was I.'

'Wish it were permanent.'

'That's subversive.'

'Suppose it is.'

'Goodnight, Jenny.'

'Goodnight, dear.'

As soon as she arrived home, she realised there was a minor crisis with Rufus. Her son had woken up, crying bitterly after a nightmare. Helga was comforting him.

Sarah held out her arms invitingly.

'Go to Mummy?' Helga suggested. Rufus shook his head. 'Please, darling.'

Another violent shake of the head. 'Want Helga.'

Sarah caught the au pair's eye and nodded. Accepting the situation, she tiptoed out of the nursery.

Although it was a mild night for the time of year, her own bedroom seemed bleak. Rejected by her son, without a regular man in her life, she felt lonely.

Usually, Sarah enjoyed getting ready for bed but tonight, she went through the ritual in a mechanical fashion and without conscious thought. Sitting at her dressing table, she concluded that her life was very empty.

Seeing Simon again had emphasised the inadequacy of her present emotional life. It was a wasteland. He had given her a tantalising glimpse of that other world where all was beauty and sunshine and love. Simon's world.

Hers was very different. Hers was one of striving and attainment, competition and unrelenting pressure. Yes, and often of false values, too. It was also the world that she herself had chosen.

There were times when she felt mummified, as though her emotions had been frozen. Like now. One day, perhaps, she might be resurrected and have real blood flowing through her veins again.

She was being cynical, she knew. Even so, much of it was true.

It had been wonderful to meet Simon after such a long estrangement. Physically, he hadn't changed. His eyebrows were as unruly and his beard as neat as ever. His smile was just as warm and his manner as spontaneous.

Would Simon ever be in the position to ring her? For an innocuous chat if nothing else.? Would Tina let him? It would be so wonderful.

Sunddenly, she jumped. The phone by her bed was actually ringing! She snatched it up eagerly.

'Sarah?' the voice said. 'It's Jenny. I'm afraid, there's been an accident.'

216

Chapter Twenty-Five

'You can't park there, miss,' the porter said. 'That space is reserved for ambulances. The visitors' car park is round the back.'

Sarah bowed her head in acceptance of the rules. Frustrated, she roared round the building to the darkened parking lot. Braking hard, she pulled up, switched off the headlights, slammed the door shut and half-ran, half-walked, to the main entrance.

When Jenny had phoned, the only detail they'd been given was the name of the hospital. Apart from that, they knew nothing.

Ignorance was a tormentor, eating away at her like a canker. The thought of her beloved Simon being disfigured, perhaps, or unable to walk again, tore her apart.

'Oh, God, protect him,' she muttered out loud. 'Make him well again. And Tina. And the baby. Let the baby survive. Please let the baby survive.' She wanted to weep and yet she was too distraught.

In the hospital reception area, a number of people were sitting in rows on tubular chairs, some looking anxious, others merely uncomfortable. There was no sight of Jenny. Nor was there anyone whom Sarah could ask for information. She looked around, feeling lost, biting her lip.

It was oppressively hot and the fluorescent lights stung her eyes. She hated the smell of antiseptic and the way everything around her appeared so sterile. The nurses and doctors who flitted by in their white coats seemed to belong to another planet.

Sarah wanted to know what was happening. She wanted someone to assure her this was only a bad dream after all. At last, she saw Jenny speeding down a corridor in her direction.

'What news?' Sarah asked.

Jenny took a moment or so to recover her breath. 'As a nurse, I pulled a bit of rank and saw the casualty sister. Tina was hurled against the windscreen – is concussed and badly cut about the face, I'm afraid. Smashed her right arm too. They're trying to save the baby.'

Sarah closed her eyes, to shut out the horror. 'And what about Simon?' She hardly dared hear the answer.

'He's still being examined. All I know is that the steering wheel hit his chest.'

'Oh, God! How serious?'

'Could be quite serious. Depends on whether any broken bones have pierced his lungs. All we can do is wait and see.'

Wait and see! How desolate it sounded.

They sat down on the uncomfortable chairs, not moving, not speaking. What was the point? Words would only add to their anxieties, not alleviate them.

But nothing could stop the agonising thoughts that were welling up in Sarah's mind. They were like flood waters that could not be held back. She guessed Jenny was suffering in the same way.

Time hung very heavily.

She watched new patients being brought in, all of them casualties of the night – other road victims, men caught up in gang fights, and drunks who had fallen foul of their own inebriety. Not an edifying sight.

'That's the sister,' Jenny said suddenly as a blue-uniformed nurse appeared.

She jumped up from her seat and ran across the room. Sarah, following a few yards behind, heard the sister say: ' – so they're both under sedation now. There's no point in your waiting any longer. We should have some positive news tomorrow.'

'I understand. Thank you, sister.'

Sarah took Jenny's arm and, together, they left the hospital, a sad, dispirited pair.

Jenny fixed her hazel eyes upon Sarah and attempted a

smile. 'I suppose your au pair will be in bed now?'

She nodded. 'Fast asleep long ago, I imagine.'

'Well, you can't go home and sit alone, waiting for news. You follow me in your car and come back to our place. Colin can make us some coffee and sandwiches. How's that?'

'Sounds wonderful.'

Des looked at the clock on his office wall and noted with surprise that Sarah was late for her appointment. That wasn't like her at all.

He was on the point of ringing her office when she arrived, breathless and ill at ease. It was immediately obvious that something was wrong.

'I've just come from the hospital,' she said, and went on to tell him about the car accident.

'Your lovely Simon?' Des was devastated. 'Don't tell me he's been hurt! I can't bear it.'

'He's got three broken ribs but fortunately his lungs are intact. He's badly bruised, of course, and he's still in shock.'

'It wasn't drink, was it?'

'Oh, no. Simon's always been most careful about that. His wife, who was pregnant, is in a pretty bad way, poor soul. She was concussed and badly cut about the face and will need plastic surgery. She also has multiple fractures in her right arm.'

'What about the baby?'

'Couldn't save it, I'm afraid. Stillborn – a little boy. It's very sad. I'm so sorry for them.'

'Oh!' he said. It sounded like a groan, an expression of deep anguish. Des, a sensitive soul, was always upset by the sufferings of others.

After some moments of silence, Sarah asked him when the script conference was due to begin.

He consulted his watch. 'In about half an hour. But I was thinking that with all your anxiety, perhaps you'd like to postpone it.'

Sarah spoke decisively. 'No, Des, thanks all the same. This business is like the theatre – the show must go on.'

'I knew you'd say that.'

'But as soon as the conference is over, I'll make a bee line back to the hospital. I'm hoping to be able to see Simon and Tina this afternoon.'

Sarah chose to visit Tina first. Why she made this decision, rather than seeing Simon, she could not exactly say. Perhaps, subconsciously, she was eager to get the interview over.

When she was shown into the small private ward, she could scarcely recognise the patient. Tina appeared lifeless with not a vestige of movement. And yet she wasn't asleep. She didn't seem to know she had a visitor. Or maybe she didn't care.

Her forehead, nose and left cheek were completely covered by surgical dressings. And the parts of her face that were visible were black and blue. Her right arm, encased in plaster, lay like a discarded object on the bed covering.

Sarah shuddered. 'Hello, Tina.'

No response.

She touched her free hand. 'It's Sarah, dear. I've brought you some flowers. I'll put them on your side locker.'

She looked down at Tina hopefully. There was a slight movement of the head. That was all.

'You remember me, don't you? We met at Jenny's party.'

Jenny's party! God! It seemed a lifetime away. But it was little more than twelve hours ago.

A small voice from the bed. 'Sarah? Is it Sarah?'

'Yes, dear.'

She seemed to be having a struggle to say something. Sarah bent over the bed to make it easier for her.

Tina repeated Sarah's name several times.

'Yes, Tina. What is it, dear?'

A long, long pause. 'My baby – dead.'

Sarah summoned up all her strength. It was not easy to be comforting and encouraging at the same time without sounding trite. She struggled to find the right words.

'I'm so sorry, Tina. You and Simon – you'll have to try for another baby – as soon as you're well again.'

At that, the frail litle figure turned to face Sarah, her large liquid eyes opened wide. There was indescribable torment in them. Sarah could barely look without flinching.

'You must have another baby – soon.'

Tina's response was a slow shaking of the head. Again and

again she did it. Then she closed her bruised lids and her breast started heaving.

Dry-eyed, she was weeping in total silence. Her chest was moving up and down in deep convulsive spasms. It was agony to watch.

Sarah sat on the edge of the bed, still holding the hand which was cold to the touch. She wondered whether she was being of any comfort. She doubted it. At the party, Tina had struck her as a girl with immense inner strength. Now, it seemed, all that strength had been drained. There was nothing left.

Besides, Sarah felt that even if she'd been able to offer real help, it would have been rejected. What could she do now?

The sobbing had become shallower. Sarah knew that it was time for her to leave. She wanted to show that she cared, but the cold hand was removed from her grasp. The bandages and the bruising made it impossible to give Tina a kiss. There was nothing further she could do.

Almost thankfully, Sarah whispered her goodbyes and tip-toed out of the room without looking back.

'Oh, nurse.' The sister hailed the probationer in a peremptory manner. 'Take Miss Castle to Mr. Dowling's room, will you?'

'Yes, sister.'

The probationer fell in beside Sarah and walked with tiny steps as they progressed along the corridor. She was a bouncy sort of girl with a lilting voice and Sarah took to her at once.

'Here we are, Miss Castle. That's Mr. Dowlings's door there. He's got someone with him at the moment but she won't be long, I understand. When the young lady comes out, you can go straight in.'

'Thank you, nurse.'

Sarah sat down on the hard wooden chair and watched the girl tripping along the corridor out of sight.

Seeing Tina had been a traumatic experience. Sarah had felt useless, redundant. Tina was grieving deeply and not a single drop of comfort had she been able to give.

Now that she was out of the room, Sarah was able to breathe again. That, in itself, made her feel callous.

The news regarding Simon was a little better than expected.

He was comfortable and in a stable condition, she'd been told. And the visitor with him now must be Jenny, she decided. That was fine. Jenny would certainly cheer him up.

Simon's door was being opened and Sarah got up, prepared to meet Jenny. But it wasn't her. Instead, an extremely pretty girl stepped into the corridor. She had long, fair hair that touched her shoulders.

The girl fixed blue eyes on Sarah and smiled disarmingly. 'I'm so sorry you've been kept waiting. Simon is ready to see you now.'

So, it was 'Simon', was it?

Sarah summoned up all her self-possession and smiled back. 'That's quite all right. I'm in no hurry.'

She felt intense jealousy, and a sense of injured pride. Who was she? And what was she doing here?

The stranger held the door open for her and Sarah went in. She heard the door click behind her.

Simon was half propped up in bed, his pyjama jacket open down the front, revealing the strapping on his chest.

'Darling!'

He smiled. 'Hello, Sarah.' He held out his hand.

She ran to him, smothering him with kisses. She was weeping, cupping his face in her hands. She loved him! Oh, how she loved him!

She wanted to hug him tight. Show him the depth of her love. But she mustn't. Even the act of breathing was difficult for him because of his broken ribs. She had to content herself with holding hands, stroking his cheek, smoothing his hair.

For several minutes, they scarcely spoke. Words weren't necessary. For them both, touch sufficed and the simple fact that they were together, at last.

She and Simon belonged to one another. There was no doubt of that. But where did that leave the poor creature in the other ward, the sad little woman married to him, who'd borne his dead child? What about her?

Sarah had a feeling of great poignancy and a fearful guilt. In showing her love for Simon, she was trespassing on Tina's preserves. It was a form of stealing.

Then, he said the words that made everything all right.

'I love you, Sarah.'

222

Immediately, the shame and guilt disappeared. The tears were trickling down her cheeks once more and she was kissing him.

'And I love you, my darling.'

The door was opened. A nurse appeared and the mood was lost.

'I'm sorry, madam, but Mr. Dowling ought to rest, now.'

'Very well, nurse.' She prepared to leave. Turning to Simon, she said, 'By the way, who was that girl who left when I arrived?'

'Oh, that was Stephanie – one of my staff. She's helping to run the place in my absence. She's an absolute brick.'

Sarah made light of it. 'I think we'll have to watch you.' But she felt another stab of jealousy just the same.

The nurse was becoming restive. 'If you don't mind, madam –'

'Of course. I'm sorry.' She went over to Simon. 'Don't forget what I said, darling' she murmured.

He squeezed her hand hard as she kissed him. 'I shan't.'

Sarah was singing softly as she walked out of the hospital building into the grounds. And even the recollection that Stephanie had seen him first couldn't diminish her happiness.

Chapter Twenty-Six

In the next three weeks, the general condition of Simon and Tina improved, but Sarah was sure they'd been discharged from hospital too soon.

It was modern health service practice, she knew, to reduce in-patient time to a minimum, but it didn't stop her from disapproving.

The St. Giles' committee had felt as she did. They'd sent the two patients to a convalescent nursing home by the seaside. This meant that Sarah's visits had been reduced to weekends only, thus giving her a chance to catch up on her work.

Her agony aunt column was as demanding of her time as ever. And having to incorporate extra television sessions into her existing schedule wasn't easy. This was especially difficult when they were filming Patsie's former programme on location. But in spite of problems, she managed to achieve a relative harmony between the two.

The first edition of this new series had already been transmitted and the critics' response had been favourable. They accepted her readily as a replacement for Patsie. This was a relief to Sarah but Des had taken it in his stride. He'd always known she'd be a success.

'People and Places' had an element of surprise about it which Sarah liked. Interesting people and projects were the stuff of the programme. She was never quite sure what would come up next. The research staff were highly innovative, constantly on the lookout for suitable subjects. And Sarah thrived on it.

One day, while having a snatched lunch in the studio

canteen with Des, she asked him what he had in store for her next.

He continued buttering a bread roll before answering.

'Sorry, darling, I was miles away. You were asking what's on the drawing board. Well, the next two programmes are studio jobs − quite fascinating people coming in. One's a bricklayer who's hoping to sail round the world, and another is a nun who's going to cut a pop disc.'

Sarah laughed. 'Great stuff − oh, the things that some people choose to do.'

'In a few weeks, my love, we have a location job − not far − only down in Surrey. And that's quite interesting in its way. It's a rehab centre − rehabilitation, to you − for accident victims.'

Sarah felt a frisson.

'It's not St. Giles, Chiddington, is it?'

'Sure. You know it, then?'

'You could say that. Simon is its warden and − '

'Simon? But that's *fantastic*. I hadn't realised.'

'Does he know yet?'

'I've no idea. We fixed it up with their committee secretary − a Brigadier Crawley. A very helpful old buffer, so I'm told.' A new thought struck him. 'I suppose Simon's going to be fit enough to appear?'

'Well, he's still strapped up but he and Tina are going home tomorrow. Not actually to work, of course.'

'How's the wife?'

'Not very well, I'm afraid. Her arm's in plaster and her face is a terrible mess − covered by horrible red scars. It was very badly lacerated. But that's nothing compared to her state of mind. I suppose it's a combination of post-natal depression and sadness at losing the baby. Lots of things, I guess. She's in a very bad state. I don't know how long it'll take her to snap out of it.'

'If she does snap out of it!'

Sarah looked at him sharply. 'Yes. If she does.'

'Poor Simon.' Des was silent a while. 'Now, about his appearing on the programme − if he's not well enough when the time comes, we'll switch dates, that's all. No problem.'

The discovery that she'd be interviewing Simon gave Sarah

a boost. When she went into the studio for the afternoon session, she felt heady. The filming went without a hitch. No fluffs. No retakes. It was as though the angels were on her side.

Afterwards, she had to return to the office for a couple of interviews. Heather, her secretary, had prepared the ground well and they gave no trouble. She didn't finish, though, until nearly seven o'clock.

Rufus was in bed when she arrived home. Helga said he'd only just dropped off to sleep so it would be better for her not to go in to see him. Sarah was disappointed. She liked at least to say goodnight to her child, if possible.

Sarah counted herself very lucky to have Helga. But she had one recurring anxiety. She was a young girl, making her way in the world. She wouldn't want to remain an au pair indefinitely. Someday, she'd be moving on. Sarah dreaded that moment. And Rufus would be bereft.

They washed up the supper dishes together, chatting of their activities during the day. Sitting down later with the coffee pot between them, Helga suddenly said, 'Sarah, I must talk to you.'

Oh, God, this is it! thought Sarah.

Helga struggled for words. 'It's – it's about Rufus. I'm worried.' She lifted her head and met Sarah's eyes.

She was uneasy. 'What is it, dear?'

Further hesitation. 'I'm – I'm scared that he might start loving me more than you. And – and –' She stopped, covered in confusion. Her cheeks were burning. 'It's just that – he's with me much more than with you.'

Sarah understood perfectly. She closed her eyes and passed a hand to her brow. History was repeating itself. Ella had neglected her and she was doing the same to Rufus.

'You're absolutely right, of course. But I'm sure it's something we can overcome.' Sarah tried to speak easily but she was far from calm inside. 'For the moment, I was afraid you might be going to leave me.'

'That was the other thing I wanted to talk about.'

'Oh, no.'

'It's for Rufus' sake as much as for my own. I think he's become too attached to me. It's not good for him.'

226

Sarah knew this was common sense. Reluctantly, she accepted the situation., She had no alternative.

Together they worked out a programme whereby Sarah would spend more time with the boy each week. In this way, he would be acclimatised to the eventual departure of Helga.

That night in bed Sarah lay thinking over what they'd discussed. Of course she'd neglected Rufus. And that was something she would have to rectify.

The question was − how? Her diary was already stretched to the limit. Wherever possible, she would have to stagger her work load. Late one evening; early, the next. That way, she would get to know Rufus better.

Get to know him?

Good heavens, what an admission for a mother to have to make! She was chastened.

Even after she'd switched off the bedside light, her mind still dwelt on the situation. It appalled her that she'd allowed it to develop this far.

She would mend her ways in the future.

'Will you come in for a drink?' Sarah asked, as the Rolls-Royce purred up to her St. John's Wood house. She felt that was the least she could offer in the circumstances.

Reece gave her an oblique look which was meant to be a smile. 'Thank you. I'd be delighted.'

Helga, sitting in the back of the car, was the first to alight. She lifted Rufus out and Sarah went on ahead to unlock the front door. Immediately, the au pair disappeared upstairs with the child and Sarah was left alone with Reece.

It wasn't easy to make him feel at home. There was nothing relaxed about Reece at any time. He sat on the nearest chair, his back straight, his head tilted slightly to one side. 'Stiff' was the only adjective that described him.

'What can I offer you?'

'Scotch, please, with soda.'

Sarah poured out the drinks in silence, thinking about the outing that had just ended. It had not been an unqualified success.

Reece's phone call a few days before had come as a surprise. And when he'd complained about seeing too little of

227

his grandson, Sarah had had mixed feelings. She wondered whether he had an ulterior motive.

However, she'd agreed to their being taken for a visit to Regents Park zoo. It would be a novelty for Rufus who'd never seen wild animals before. But during the trip, her apprehension had mounted as she watched Rufus' reaction.

He was excited at being taken to the zoo, but quickly showed his frustration at the pattern of their visit. Grandpa, it seemed, hadn't envisaged showing the child what would interest him most.

Reece regarded the pushchair as an encumbrance and failed to understand that small legs tired more easily than his. When Rufus became fractious, he made no attempt to hide his displeasure.

That, for Sarah, summed it up. The outing hadn't been designed with a child in mind. It was more of a grown ups' day. A child, by coincidence, happened to be a member of the party. That was all.

As always, Reece was aloof. This was not deliberate, Sarah was sure. Quite simply, he didn't know how to unbend. At one point, Rufus had tried to have a game with Grandpa. A puzzled expression had appeared on the older man's face and, discouraged, the child had given up.

Suddenly, she had a flash of understanding. She could see clearly what it must have been like for Max when small. Was it any wonder that his emotional development had been retarded? She felt renewed pity for him.

To Sarah, the outing had been an embarrassment. She was relieved when the zoo visit ended and they returned home.

Sipping his drink now, Reece was looking around the sitting room. She couldn't make up her mind whether it was with approbation or not. 'A pleasant little place you have here,' he said.

Sarah hated his patronage. 'I think so,' she said. 'And it's very convenient for getting into Fleet Street.'

'Ah!' He seemed to stretch the word to its fullest extent. 'Fleet Street! The *Daily Courier*.' He took a sudden gulp of his drink. Replacing the empty glass on to the Benares table with a clatter, he stared into space.

'Can I pour you another?'

'No thank you.' Another long drawn out exclamation. This time it was 'Oh!'

Sarah waited.

'Sarah,' he began at last. 'I dislike intensely the fact that we are in opposing camps.'

'Opposing camps?' she echoed innocently, knowing full well what he meant.

'Yes, this circulation war – the *Daily Sentinel* versus the *Daily Courier*. It's a fight to the death.' He was over-dramatising the situation and it amused her. He picked up his empty glass. 'I will have that other drink after all.'

'Of course.'

She poured it out in silence and handed it to him.

He drank absentmindedly. 'It's quite wrong that you're on the other side.' She, on the contrary, thought it eminently satisfactory but didn't say so. He put the glass down noisily. 'Sarah, I'm prepared to do a deal.'

'Oh.' She watched him, guessing what was coming.

'If you'd join my *Sentinel,* I'd be prepared to pay you any salary you ask. In addition, I'd give you a generous gift of shares of the company.'

In spite of everything, it was a tempting offer; much more than she'd expected, and for a moment she was nonplussed. When she answered, she picked her words carefully. It was like stepping through a minefield.

'I appreciate your kind offer very much. But I'm afraid I'll have to refuse.'

He was aghast. 'Refuse? An offer like that? Why, for God's sake?'

'I enjoy working on the *Courier*. Also, Sam Braidwood and Martin Lamb have always been very kind and supportive. I do feel a loyalty to them. I couldn't leave them now.'

'Loyalty! Sentimental rubbish!' He'd risen to his feet and was glaring down at her. 'And that's your final answer?'

'I'm afraid so.' Her voice was a murmur.

'You'll regret this.'

Sarah rose to her feet, angry at his pugnacity. He still towered over her. 'Are you threatening me?'

He hadn't expected to be challenged and was disconcerted. He shifted his feet. A lowering of the eyes. A change of

229

tone. 'Of course not. Don't be so juvenile.'

'You're the one being juvenile.'

Reece gulped in air hungrily. 'I will not be spoken to like that, young woman.'

'And neither will I, Sir Reece.'

For a brief moment, he appeared to be transfixed . Then, with a decisive movement, he swung round and left the house. From the lounge window, she watched him climb into his Rolls and drive away.

She was still trembling. The very sight of Reece Brown filled her with anger. All she wanted at the moment was for him to stay out of her life for ever.

Later that evening, Sarah was dozing in front of the television set. Rufus was tucked up in bed sound asleep, exhausted after his visit to the zoo. And, as it was Saturday, Helga was out with a friend.

The phone rang, strident and insistent.

Sarah leapt up from her chair and went to answer it, stumbling over a pouffe in her haste. Not yet fully awake, she picked up the receiver. 'Hello.'

A man's voice. 'Sarah?'

'Speaking. Who is that?'

'It's Max. You were going to ring me. When you spent the night at my place, you promised. Remember? But you haven't done so. Hope you haven't changed your mind about us.'

Oh, God! The simple answer was, yes, she had. Since that night, she'd been reunited with Simon and that had altered everything.

She struggled to find a suitable explanation. There was only one thing for it − tell him the truth, or at least, part of it.

'It's like this, Max. My former boyfriend and his wife have had a serious car accident and I've been visiting them in hospital.'

He was immediately solicitous. 'I'm so sorry about that.'

She explained about their condition and he offered his best wishes. There was a long pause at the other end of the line. 'Can I see you soon,' he asked eventually. 'How about tonight?'

'Oh, no, Max. I can't, really.'

'Let me come round, then, just for the evening.'

'Tonight? Actually, I was asleep when you rang.'

'Sorry I disturbed you. So the answer's no, I take it?' He sounded very crestfallen and it made her feel mean. Already, she was weakening.

'It's been a strenuous day and I'm very tired. Your father took us all to the zoo.'

'Good God! Did he? How did it go?'

'Well, it was a bit stiff and starchy. Reece couldn't unbend with a young child.'

There was another pause. 'You don't have to tell me that.'

Sarah had a renewed vision of what it must have been like for Max when a child. Her heart softened still further. 'Look, Max, suppose you come round for a short time − a very short time?'

'Thanks. I promise not to keep you.' There was new life in his voice. 'See you in a few minutes, then.'

It was, in fact, fifteen minutes. When she opened the door, his welcome was again overwhelming. As before, he picked her up, kissed her and carried her into the lounge. It was only after he'd kissed her again that he set her down on the settee.

She regained her breath, pushed a few strands of hair back into place and tried to dampen his ardour. 'You mustn't be so forceful, Max. I'm not fully awake yet.'

'Ah − you're at your most luscious when you're still drowsy. You make lovely murmuring noises. Did you know that?'

These were disturbing memories. Sarah didn't want to hear them. Since having comforted Simon in convalescence, her perspective had altered. 'You must stop talking like that, Max.'

'Why, for heavens' sake? It was only just over a month ago that we spent that marvellous night together. I had the impression you enjoyed it as I did. Don't tell me you've forgotten.'

Sarah was reluctant to meet his gaze. Memories of that night crowded in upon her. It would be so easy to weaken but she had to be firm.

She took a deep breath and faced him squarely. 'I know. I'm sorry, Max. I want you to know that for me it was wonderful, as well. I mean that. But since then, things have changed.'

'Such as?'

'Let's just put it down to my mercurial temperament.' She was being unfair and she knew it.

'Oh, no. That won't do.'

Sarah had to make a clean breast of it. 'OK. The fact is I've been seeing a lot of Simon and − well − please try to understand, Max.'

'So you're saying it's all over between us?'

She nodded. 'I'm afraid so.'

'I can't take that lying down.'

She laid her hand lightly on his forearm and spoke quietly. 'I'm afraid you'll have to, Max. And, believe me, I'm sorry.'

Some welcome noises could be heard issuing from the entrance hall. The click of the front latch. Footsteps, Helga came in.

To Sarah, she was a most welcome sight.

With the coming of Monday morning, Reece was no less angry with Sarah than he'd been on Saturday. But he didn't show it.

That was characteristic of him. His anger was never volatile like the explosion of a volcano. It was something he could push down deep inside him, holding it until he felt ready to retaliate with maximum effect.

He did that now, while preparing himself for the week's work.

He thought of Sarah; thought back over the years since he'd known her, of the times she'd snubbed him. He remembered them so clearly. Indeed, he had a prodigous memory for any affront to his dignity. And from Sarah there had been many.

She had turned down all his advances, even physically pushing him on one occasion; had rejected his business offers, preferring to go to his deadly rival instead. Nor was that all. She had steadfastly refused to take his name by deed poll to legitimise his grandson. That was particularly insulting.

And, in addition, there was that supreme blow to his ego, one that he'd never forgive or forget. Although she'd refused to have anything to do with him physically, she'd nevertheless

232

allowed that son of his to make her pregnant. That was something that choked him.

Reece had had more than enough. He'd been extremely patient in the face of Sarah's truculence. Now, he wanted to destroy her and he would. The weapon was to hand.

He picked up the intercom and asked for Virginia Duval to come and see him. After a few minutes, he heard her voice in the outer office talking to Miss Clark.

How he hated Virginia! All things being equal, he would have liked to sack her, get her out of his domain. But all things were not equal. She was much too valuable.

He could use her pen as a poison dart against Sarah.

A knock on his door.

'Come in.' The door opened and his gossip writer appeared. 'Ah, Virginia. I have a job for you. Sit down and I'll tell you about it.'

Chapter Twenty-Seven

Brigadier Bernard Crawley straightened his back and felt a twinge. Several more twinges followed and this made him ponder a recurrent problem. Would it have been better to plant his new corms kneeling down or standing up?

Either posture caused him pain. The only difference was the precise location of the pain. Breathing deeply, he stretched his back several times before throwing the trowel down into the wooden trug. He'd done enough for the afternoon.

In any case, his wife had called him several times, she said, to tell him she'd made a pot of tea.

Having carefully removed his muddy boots, he slipped on a pair of house shoes and went through the conservatory into the drawing room.

'The tea cakes are nice and hot,' Elena said. 'I thought you'd like tea cakes for a change.'

'Thank you, dear. Most welcome.'

'I do hope our roses will give a better show this year than last. By the by, did you see the black spot I told you about?'

Bernard hadn't actually noticed it so he evaded giving a direct answer. 'I'll have to prune them all very soon,' he said.

'I'll help you.'

He nodded his head without really listening.

'You seem very preoccupied this afternoon, Bernard. There's nothing wrong at St. Giles, is there?'

'Not *wrong* exactly. But I can't help feeling a little concerned.'

'You mean Mr. Dowling?'

'No. He's doing quite well. It's his wife I'm worried about.

She's not making a good recovery. After all, it's several weeks since the accident so she should be showing signs of improvement by now. Damnéd shame. Good worker normally. Nice girl, too. But fearfully depressed, so Dowling told me.'

He thought this over and nodded again as though agreeing with himself. When he'd drunk his tea and eaten a second tea cake, he said, 'It might be a good idea for me to run over to Chiddington and have a talk with young Dowling. I'm sure the poor chap must be worried out of his mind.'

'Very well, Bernard. But don't be late, will you? Remember the Woods are coming round for bridge tonight.'

'I hadn't forgotten,' he lied.

When he arried, a stillness had fallen over St. Giles. This was customary in late afternoon as the teaching was over for the day and the students were relaxing prior to their evening meal.

He found the warden talking to a few of the staff in the entrance hall of the main building. On seeing him they made a move to disperse but he dissuaded them.

His heart was immediately warmed by that remarkably pretty girl – what was her name? He always forgot it. Ah yes! Stephanie Gilbert. He liked the way she caressed him with her eyes! Very friendly. He wished he were younger.

Dowling was speaking. 'Stephanie has been wonderful, Brigadier. So has Doug. And, of course, Miss Macintosh in the office. Between them, they have kept the place going while we've been off sick.'

'I realise that and we're extremely grateful,' the Brigadier said. Stephanie was looking at him in that special way again as if to say, 'I only did it for you, Bernard.' He found himself weakening.

She laughed a beautiful, musical laugh. 'Anyone would have done the same,' she said.

Crawley turned to Simon. 'You seem to be making good progress, old chap.'

Simon said he was lucky and would soon be back to full duties.

'Jolly good show. And how's your wife?'

Dowling dropped his eyes but it was only for a moment. He recovered quickly and put on a display of chearful optimism. But Crawley wasn't deceived.

'I think the answer is, as well as can be expected,' he said. 'After all, she's suffered two bereavements in quick succession – her father and the baby. She's also trying to come to terms with her facial injuries.'

'And how's her arm?'

'She had the plaster off today, but she's lost all sensation in her fingers.'

'We are all most terribly sorry.'

'Thank you.' For a moment, he seemed to be struggling with his emotions, at a loss for words. 'I'll go and fetch her. I know she'd like to say hello.'

He went upstairs in search of his wife. The other male staff also departed to return to their respective duties. The Brigadier was left with the delectable Stephanie.

Despite her charms, Crawley's thoughts were partly elsewhere. He was thinking about Mrs. Dowling. When would she fully recover? Would she indeed ever recover?

Apart from the personal tragedy, where would that leave St. Giles? The fact that the Dowlings were on a joint husband/wife appointment could not be overlooked. Besides, he was duty bound to put the college before all other considerations. The Brigadier fervently hoped he would never have to make such an invidious choice.

Simon discovered Tina in the bedroom, sitting beside her dressing table. Immediately, she rose and walked over to the bay windows without acknowledging his presence.

'Didn't you hear me calling?' he murmured.

'Yes.' She didn't turn.

'Are you all right?'

'Oh, fine!' The words were weighted with irony.

'The Brigadier's downstairs.'

'I know.'

'He'd like to say hullo.'

'Is Stephanie there?' she asked in a faraway voice.

'Yes.'

'Apologise for me and tell the Brigadier I'm lying down.'

Simon groaned inwardly. This sort of situation with Tina had become frequent of late and it worried him desperately. She was withdrawing herself more and more from social contacts.

236

'Please, Tina — just this once. Come down and pass the time of day with him.

'Why should I? I look such a ghastly mess.' She swung round to face him. As she spoke, her hand went up and brushed some of the scars on her face. He moved over, put his arm around her and kissed her softly.

She said, 'I find it amazing that you can bring yourself to kiss anyone with a face like this. Don't you find it repugnant?'

'Tina, please! Don't talk like that.' On an impulse, he deliberatly kissed one of her most savage scars. 'There — that's my answer to what you've just said.'

She just looked at him, her large doe-like eyes opened wide. Suddenly, she flung herself into his arms.

'Forgive me, Simon. I can't help being a misery — can't help it!'

He kissed her again and gently disengaged himself. 'I'd better pay your respects to the Brigadier.'

She gave no sign of having heard but turned to gaze out of the window once more. When she spoke, her voice was almost inaudible, drained, it seemed, of emotion. 'Simon, what's going to happen to us?' She choked, struggling with an inner conflict. 'I — I don't think I can take much more of this.'

He moved over and held her tightly. 'Yes, you can. You must; you will. I'm here to help. Together, we're going to beat this.'

She buried her face in his shoulder, sobbing uncontrollably. It was some minutes before Simon felt he could return to the Brigadier.

He tiptoed out of the room as though it were a funeral parlour.

Sarah had a small problem.

Prior to a recording session, she would arrive at the studios or location with plenty of time to spare. There were moves and positions to be checked, the substance of the interview to be gone over and many other details to be ironed out.

This was also the period when she liked to meet the people she'd be interviewing. With the projected programme at St. Giles, however, the situation was different. She knew two of

237

the main participants — one of them, intimately — and that would put certain constraints upon her.

She discussed it all with Des.

'Go and see Simon and his wife, darling, a day or so before the filming,' he said. 'You can make it part of your normal warm-up but treat it as a social call. They'd prefer it that way, I'm sure.'

She did as Des suggested.

Two days before the recording, she was sitting in the Dowlings' lounge, sipping a sherry, covertly watching Simon whenever she felt that Tina's attention was elsewhere.

'We won't be going out live so there is nothing to worry about,' she was saying. 'Just take your cue from me.'

'I'm not worrying; looking forward to it, if anything,' Simon said. 'It'll be out of the ordinary run of daily life.'

'You make our life sound extremely dull,' Tina observed.

'I didn't intend that. All I meant was that to have the television cameras visit you at work is out of the ordinary. That's what I said.'

'Yes, I heard.'

Sarah's eyes flitted from one to the other. She sensed an undercurrent of friction and was disturbed. Tina seemed unmoved. Simon looked as if he'd been slapped.

As a distraction, he poured out more sherry all round. Sarah commented on the attractive gardens of St. Giles; on the excellent work they were doing for the disabled. She spoke brightly about the coming programme. There was little response from Tina apart from a polite smile and a few murmured affirmatives.

Most of the time, Tina's eyes were fixed on a spot on the wall. Her left hand was attempting to hide some of the scars on her face. A futile gesture.

It was Simon who saved the situation. He outlined some of their new plans for training the students, suggesting that these might be featured in the programme. Sarah agreed and said she'd mention it to Des.

'I'd like to interview some of your staff.'

'Glad to hear it.'

Tina's voice broke in. 'Be sure to include Stephanie. She's every man's pin-up.'

Tina had made the innocuous remark sound spiteful. Again Simon put up a front. He laughed to take the sting out of her words. 'It's true. She flirts with every man in sight – including our noble Brigadier.'

'She sounds a "must" for the programme.'

'While you're making up your cast list,' Tina said, 'you can count me out. I'd stick out like a sore thumb.'

The silence that followed weighed heavily. Sarah would have liked to make a comforting remark but nothing sprang to mind.

She decided instead that this was as good a time as any to take her leave.

At the front door, Tina said in a small voice, 'I do wish my father could have been here for the filming.'

'I second that wholeheartedly.' In his enthusiasm, Simon sounded over vehement.

Tina addressed Sarah. 'Dad was a marvellous man.' Gesturing towards the complex of St. Giles' buildings, she went on, 'It was he who made this place what it is today. It seems so unfair that he won't be here to receive the accolades.'

She spoke with unmistakable passion. No longer was she a wistful slip of a girl. Sarah was surprised at the change. Her voice had taken on a sharper edge, her brows were contracted and there was an intensity in her eyes.

'You admired your father, didn't you, Tina?'

'Admired him? What an understatement! I did much more than admire him.' Her voice was rising in pitch. 'I loved him. He was absolutely everything to me.'

'I'm sure.'

'I'd hoped that our baby would have taken after his grandfather – a sort of reincarnation. But, of course, that was a false hope.'

'I'm so sorry. And I assure you, Tina, that when we do the programme, I'll steer the interview so that Simon can give your father the credit he's obviously due.'

She was ridiculously grateful. Tears welled up in her eyes. She even placed her hand on Sarah's forearm. 'Oh, would you, Sarah? That's very kind.' Sarah was surprised to see her so demonstrative.

The women said their goodbyes on the step. Simon saw

Sarah to her car which was in full view of the front door. She wondered what would have happened if she'd parked round the side out of sight of the windows.

He was obviously anxious for her to get into the driving seat. To spare him embarrassment, she lost no time in doing so.

'Good night, dear,' she murmured, putting up her face to be kissed. 'Sweet dreams,' he whispered.

Sarah let in the clutch and moved off. St. Giles had a claustrophobic effect upon her and she was glad to be away.

After seeing Sarah off, Simon was greeted by a Tina who seemed to be limbering up for a fight. She faced him, head erect, chin thrust forward, a defiant look in her eyes.

'She really is beautiful, isn't she? It must have been quite an experience for you − I mean, sitting between beauty and the beast.' She spoke accusingly as though the situation were his fault.

His temper was frayed beyond bearing. 'Shut up!' he shouted, and thumped the nearest thing to hand which happened to be the table. 'Shut up, Tina, d'you hear? I can't bear you talking like that. If you do, I'll go out.'

'You can stay out for all I care. It won't make any difference − I won't be any more alone than I am now.'

'That's bloody unfair.'

'It's true. And don't swear at me. If only Dad were alive, I'd be able to cope.' Suddenly, she collapsed in a chair, sobbing bitterly. Simon regretted his outburst. He went to her, kissed her, embraced her, tried to heal her mental wounds though he was powerless to help the physical scars.

Eventually, the tears subsided, the sobbing eased. But as she lifted her head to face him, the rancour showed through again.

By the time the evening had come, her mood was little changed and the atmosphere continued to be taut. Simon couldn't suffer it much longer. He simply had to escape.

He glanced over at her. The television was on but he could tell she wasn't really watching it.

'Shall I switch off the TV?' he asked.

'No. I'm enjoying this programme.'

'OK. If you don't mind, Tina, I'll slip down to the village for a pint.'

'Why not? Do you good to get away from me for a bit. I'll probably be in bed when you get back.'

'Very well. I shan't be late.' He kissed her on the forehead and left the house.

Outside, it was remarkably warm for March. Striding out over the fields made him even warmer.

Stephanie greeted him in her customary way – closing the door first in case anyone saw, pulling him to her and kissing him with great tenderness.

For once, he seemed unable to respond. Instead, he threw himself down into one of her armchairs and looked around, collecting his thoughts.

Recognising his state of mind, she was immediately solicitous. She sat on his lap, stroked his hair and smoothed his brow with her lips. It was relaxing and he began to unwind.

He told her what had happened that day, how Tina had refused to see the Brigadier.

'That, in itself, is a small thing, I suppose. But it's her general state of mind that worries me stiff. I can't see what the future's going to be.' He was silent a long time. 'I just don't know what to do.' Then, he threw his arms in the air in desperation. 'I don't bloody well know what to do!'

Her nearness had a soothing effect. Just being in her company made him feel better. Eyes that smiled and understood; lips that were soft and warm. There was so much comfort in Stephanie.

'What is to be done about Tina?' he asked, knowing it was a rhetorical question.

'Surely once the plastic surgeons have done their work, she'll feel better, won't she?'

'It's going to be a slow job. But that's not the main worry. It's her state of her mind that bothers me. She's had a hell of a lot to put up with. Besides everything else, there's the loss of her father as well.'

'And that's hit her hardest of all.'

He looked at her quickly. 'Meaning what?'

'Just this – Tina would have coped better with everything if her father had still been alive.'

'I agree.'

'I've always felt that her love for him was obsessional. A bit kinky, really. Sorry, I shouldn't have said that.'

'That's OK. You're right. I've thought it too.'

'And his death has completely thrown her.'

'Yes. She needs a psychiatrist, that's for sure. But would she go? Of course not! Even if the doctor insisted, she'd still refuse. Tina's convinced she'll never be cured and won't be budged.'

'We mustn't give up hope, Simon. There must be something – someone – .'

He brightened. 'I've just had a brilliant idea. Sarah's a professional agony aunt, isn't she? Surely, she'll come up with something if we ask her. After all, she's giving advice to all and sundry, day after day.'

'True.'

'As soon as we've done the TV programme, I'll ring her and suggest we meet. I think that's a terrific idea.'

'Perhaps.' Stephanie didn't sound too sure. She changed the subject. 'You remember I told you I was thinking of selling this cottage?'

'Sure.' He smiled slightly. 'I'd be sorry, though. This place has happy memories for me.'

'For me, too. But I've been told there's quite a nice property on the market. It's only over at Everleigh. I might have a look at it.'

'Why not?' He closed his eyes. He didn't want to pursue the matter any more.

They lapsed into silence for several minutes. Eventually, she took his hand and slid it inside her jumper.

His cares began to fade. To feel the fullness of her breast, to fondle and tease it, took his breath away. He needed no further encouragment to go upstairs with her.

His affair with Stephanie had begun unexpectedly, spontaneously. She had broken off with her boyfriend and Simon had been going through a particularly bad patch with Tina.

Looking back, he supposed it was inevitable that they should have found comfort together. Neither had any illusions. They both accepted that it could not continue indefinitely. Meanwhile, they'd made a pact. It was agreed

242

that, whatever happened, Tina should not be hurt.

Tonight's lovemaking was as wonderful as ever. Tender, and yet full and satisfying.

The thought of leaving her and returning home cast a temporary shadow over Simon's mood of contentment but he knew it had to be faced. He slid out of bed and dressed quickly.

Downstairs, he took his leave of Stephanie, as usual in the darkened passage. He opened the door and was about to step outside when she grabbed his shoulder.

'Stop!' she hissed. She pulled him back inside, closing the door quickly. 'Didn't you see who was on the other side of the lane?' He shook his head. 'Miss Macintosh.'

'Oh, my God! Did she see me, d'you think?'

'She must have done. Couldn't have missed you — especially as the moon's so full tonight.'

Simon couldn't bring himself to speak for several moments. His head was too full of the possible ramifications.

Stephanie read his mind. 'Are you thinking she'll tell the Brigadier?'

'It's more than likely,' he said. 'What then? You'll be compromised and I'll be asked to resign. And Tina will be so hurt, God knows what she'll do!'

She held him tightly, her cheek against his.

He put on a brave face which belied his true feelings. 'Oh, well, I refuse to let it worry me. And I don't want it to worry you either.'

In the shadows, they kissed again. He looked carefully up and down the lane this time then took his leave.

As he made his way homewards across the fields, his mind was in a turmoil.

What was the future to be for them all?

Chapter Twenty-Eight

'That's it, everybody. Wrap it up.'

The release of tension that followed this directive was almost a physical thing. It was audible too. Until that moment, senses had been sharpened, nerves on edge, the entire TV crew determined to do their best. Sarah was proud to be one of their number.

Now they were able to stretch their legs, unwind, indulge in good-natured badinage. Chatter and laughter filled the air. Equipment was carried away and stored in the waiting vehicles.

Des Mallon went over to Sarah. 'Nice work. I think this'll turn out to be one of the best in the whole series.'

'Glad you think so, Des. I know Simon put a lot of effort into it.'

'That's true. But don't forget your own contribution. Very polished. It's a pleasure to work with you, darling.'

He drifted off in search of Simon. Sarah had intended following him but had caught sight of Tina in the front of the house, looking lost. She seemed to be debating whether to join the crowd or disappear inside.

Her craving for privacy won. She made to go indoors and Sarah quickened her pace. 'Wait a minute!'

Sarah ran to her taking her arm in a display of friendliness.

'I want to say how much I've enjoyed it here. For me, it's been a great experience learning so much about the good work you've been doing. Your father must have been a remarkable man to have laid such foundations. We did try to do him justice in our programme.'

Tina thawed immediately. 'Oh, I'm sure you did and I'm grateful.' She then explained once more about his work at St. Giles over the years. Sarah noticed how, instead of facing her directly, Tina had angled herself so that the worst of her scars were concealed.

Sarah decided to take her in hand. 'You haven't met any of the crew yet, have you? Come over with me and I'll introduce you.'

Tina disengaged herself. 'Oh, no. I've deliberately kept away from the action. I was just observing from the sidelines. I don't want to intrude.'

'You won't be.' Sarah refused to give up. 'Anyway, here comes Simon with our producer. You can't disappear now. I know Des wants to meet you.'

Covertly, Sarah watched her. Tina was bracing herself for the coming ordeal. Again she turned her head to lessen the visual impact of the scars. But when the two men came up and Simon performed the introductions, she handled the situation quite well, Sarah was surprised to see.

At the far end of the drive some people had emerged from behind one of the buildings. A couple of amputees in wheelchairs were accompanied by a small retinue consisting of two women and three young children.

'Is it visiting day?' Sarah asked.

'Not exactly,' Simon said. 'Those wives can't come on the official day for visitors so they've chosen today. I'm glad because I think your cameraman managed to get a shot of them all.'

'Good.'

While Des chatted with Tina, she and Simon watched the group coming slowly up the drive in their direction. One of the children was playing with a ball.

'Norman,' one of the mothers called out, 'mind what you're doing. Careful, now. Do what I say.'

The child was doing no real harm – which was just as well for he took no notice of his mother.

The group drew near. The child became more daring, kicking the ball towards the steps where Sarah and the others were standing.

'*Norman!* Do as I say! Come on away from there,' the mother called. In vain.

The ball bounced against the house door and fell at Tina's feet. She handed it back to the child who snatched it without a word.

'Norman,' said the mother, 'where're your manners? Say thank you to the lady.'

No response. Sullen looks. He scampered back to his parents, glad to be away.

The mother gave Tina an ingratiating grin. 'Sorry, Mrs. Dowling. He's such a shy little monkey.'

'That's all right, Mrs. Hughes,' Tina called back.

The group moved on a few paces. The boy was heard to say, 'Mum, why has that lady got that horrible face?'

Total silence engulfed them. It lasted only a second yet it seemed an eternity. Then everyone tried to talk at the same time. Sarah, Simon, Des, had each conjured out of nowhere a bland remark, about the weather, about the programme, about St. Giles.

Tina rose magnificently to the occasion. To Sarah's relief and astonishment, she lifted her head high and smiled on her immediate circle. It was a forced smile but it served its purpose. The ice was broken. Normal conversation was resumed.

For several minutes, she held sway. It was a remarkable performance and Sarah was full of admiration. From the timid withdrawn creature of half an hour earlier, she'd become the first lady of St. Giles.

The time came for them to leave. Des and the technicians departed first, leaving Sarah with the Dowlings on the top step.

'Are you sure you won't have some tea with us, Sarah?'

'No, thank you, Tina. I have to get back to the office.'

She kissed Tina on the cheek. She had the distinct impression that note was being taken of whether she flinched or not. She didn't.

While his wife went indoors, Simon saw Sarah to her car. He opened the door for her and she sat in the driving seat. She knew instinctively he was about to say something of significance.

Keeping his voice low, he said, 'Sarah, we must meet. I have to see you. I've simply got to.'

Sarah caught her breath. 'Oh, Simon! Would that be wise?'

246

'Yes, it would.' He sounded desperate. 'As soon as I can manage it, I'll give you a ring.'

The events of the last few moments had upset Sarah and her mind was full of questionings as she drove through the main gates on to the open road. It seemed she was about to be faced with a new challenge.

And she was not at all sure how she would respond.

When he'd said goodbye to Sarah, Simon entered the house by the front door without waiting for the car to disappear out of sight.

Indoors, it was dark and gloomy. Unfriendly. He couldn't say why. It had never struck him that way before. For the first time since he'd been at St. Giles, he wanted to return to the garden. The house seemed stuffy. Outside, it would be fresh and sweet-smelling; outside, he would feel free and un-constrained.

No, on second thoughts, he wouldn't find it like that at all. Outside would be just as bad as inside.

The truth was, Simon was very worried. Ever since Miss Macintosh had seen him coming out of Stephanie's cottage, he'd been waiting for the storm to break.

With every post, with every phone call, he'd expected to be summoned to the Brigadier to account for himself. But so far nothing had happened. He was aware, though, that it was only a matter of time. He harboured no false hopes that Miss Macintosh would hold her peace. He knew her much too well for that.

He wanted to escape. He knew he couldn't.

He sought out Tina. He called her name several times. No answer. Where was she?

He called her name again. Went upstairs. Into the bedroom. The other bedrooms. The bathroom. He even looked in the linen cupboard. Stupid of him, he knew, but it was a reflex action. Not a sign of her anywhere.

He found her at last in the old scullery, of all places. She was slumped against the great oaken table, weeping her heart out.

'I've been calling for you. Didn't you hear me?'

No reply.

247

He went over to her, put his arm around her shoulders, held her tight.

'Please, Tina, let me help you. Please! We're in this together.'

Suddenly, she came to life; swung round on him, eyes blazing. 'We're not in this together. I'm in it alone. I always have been.'

He spoke gently. 'I know it was difficult for you this afternoon. You behaved superbly. I was very proud of you.'

At that, her spirit seemed to fail her. She buried her face in her hands, sobs racking her entire body.

Slowly, they subsided. She lifted her head and looked him straight in the eye. 'I've never felt so alone as I do at this moment. I wish I were dead.'

Simon didn't get in touch with Sarah for a few days and for this, she was glad. It wasn't that she had no wish to see him. But there'd been a hint of the clandestine about his words and she preferred all her dealings to be open. The idea of deceiving Tina was wholly repugnant to her.

It was on the following Saturday, shortly before she expected friends for dinner, that she picked up the phone and heard his voice.

'Hullo, darling.'

'Simon!'

'I'm calling from the phone box in the village so I can't be long. As I said, I've got to see you.'

'Will you tell Tina?'

'No.'

'Would it be wise for us to meet? I don't like deceiving her.'

'I can't help that.' He sounded desperate. 'I'm at my wits' end. I need you, Sarah.'

She came to a speedy decision. The *Daily Courier* building offered the best place for a meeting; it would be open, above board, and should not give rise to gossip.

'We have one or two interview rooms at the *Courier*. I could meet you there. Monday morning at ten?'

'Not before?'

'It's Sunday tomorrow.'

'Oh, of course.' He was obviously disappointed. 'OK.

Monday, then. Can't stop now. Tina will wonder what's happened to me, 'bye.'

Sarah replaced the receiver, greatly troubled. Simon had always been so strong; had been her rock. Now, he seemed a shell of his former self.

She wanted to cry but the front doorbell rang, heralding the arrival of her visitors. She put on a smile and went to greet them.

The choice of one of the interview rooms for her meeting with Simon made Sarah feel secure. It was an austere room with a central table and tubular stacking chairs. And, because of the large windows in the partitioning, it was exposed to view. Nothing covert could possibly happen there.

She was not surprised by the story he had to tell: that Tina was in a precarious mental state and that he was worried out of his mind. It had all been crystal clear to her when she'd been at St. Giles.

'Obviously, I'm no expert,' he said, 'but I reckon she's suffering from some kind of depressive neurosis. She's even threatened to take her own life.'

Sarah closed her eyes. 'Well, I'm told that when they *threaten* suicide, they're making a cry for help. It's clear she needs expert guidance.'

'I'd hoped you'd be able to help − to be more positive.'

Sarah spread her hands helplessly. 'Oh, Simon! How?'

'Have a talk to her, maybe. Persuade her.'

'She wouldn't listen to me. She'd resent me − tell me I was interfering. I'm only a journalist, not a psychiatrist. But you've got to get her to the doctor's by hook, or by crook.'

He was silent a long time, tapping the table with his fingers. 'You disappoint me,' he said in a low voice.

She caught her breath. He'd never spoken to her in quite that tone before.

He was still speaking. 'You've changed. I don't think you're interested in real people any more. A dedicated career woman, that's all you are, now. You've lost touch.'

Sarah couldn't believe she was being spoken to like this. And by Simon! It was as though he'd been wound up and couldn't stop. She struggled for breath. 'But − '

249

'You live in a fantasy world with only cardboard figures around you.'

She was badly shaken. From somewhere she summoned up a modicum of dignity. 'Well, my readers wouldn't agree with you.'

'Wouldn't they? They know the advice in your column is just a big con. They look at what you've written just as they read their daily horoscope – it's a kind of fun thing but they don't believe any of it.'

'That is not true!'

'Isn't it? Why is it, then, that when I come hoping for sound advice, you're complely stumped?'

There was nothing she could say. Her own sense of pride forbade her from arguing. Simon appeared to realise he'd shot his bolt. His chair made a scraping noise on the floor as he got up.

'That, I think, is that,' he said, and with a curt nod, left the room.

For several moments, Sarah sat staring into space. The anguish, the pain in his eyes were seared into her memory. Faced with a dreadful, domestic problem, Simon had sought her help and she'd failed him.

That was what really hurt. She'd failed him.

How could she let him go like that? She was jolted into action. Pushing the chair aside, she sped out of the room, along the deserted corridor.

No use waiting for the lift. Too slow. Running down the stairs, colleagues looking at her, wondering. She was past caring.

Into the entrance hall. Not a sign of him. Mr. Swallow said a gentleman answering the description she'd given had just passed through.

'Which way?'

'Towards Ludgate Hill, Miss.'

Into Fleet Street. Spots of rain. Wind blowing. Running. Heels clattering. People staring. There he was, fifty metres ahead.

'Simon!'

No response. Too much traffic noise.

Running faster. Breath giving out. She was making an exhibition of herself. Who cared?

250

'Simon! Stop!'

At last, he paused, turned and saw her. He waited.

Coming level with him, she sacrificed every shred of pride she possessed.

'Look, Simon, I must talk to you,' she pleaded. 'Round the corner there's a little pub I often use when I'm working late. It'll be almost empty now. We could go there.'

His eyes had softened. 'But you're all wet.'

'Forget that.'

He studied her a moment, then smiled and took her arm. 'Let's go,' he said.

This little cameo was immediately forgotten by everyone who witnessed it.

Everyone, that is, except one person. Lady Virginia Duval, who happened to be walking nearby, found it extremely interesting.

To see the elegant and highly professional Sarah Castle chasing a man in public made her stop and stare. She watched the couple closely. It seemed they were making up after a row. Making up? Interesting! And then they just walked away, arm in arm.

The man's face was vaguely familiar. Where had she seen it before? She racked her brains. Some time ago, she thought.

Suddenly, it came to her. Four or five years ago, that was it. Win Seeberg's party — the first time Virgina had been invited. Sarah had been there with this man — what was his name? She couldn't remember. No matter. She'd look it up as soon as she got back.

What a good thing she always kept notes of her social engagements, wasn't it?

As expected, the pub was empty. They sat on wooden benches at a table in the corner, screened from view.

Simon was immediately apologetic, pleading for Sarah's forgiveness.

'Of course,' she said. 'It all happened in the heat of the moment. You were disappointed. You thought I'd let you down. I'm sorry if I did. But one thing is clear — Tina needs expert psychiatric treatment. I can't help you there. You must get her to the doctor.'

'Yes.' He sounded despondent.

'What I can offer you is friendship and moral support. In the past, you always gave me strength, Simon. I wish I could do the same for you and Tina.'

He held her hand tight. 'I realise that and I'm grateful.' He paused a moment. 'I love you very much. You know that, don't you?'

Yes, she did know it. And she felt the same way but she didn't want to be told it. Not now, with Tina in such a sad state. It made her feel furtive and sneaky and that wasn't playing fair. Gently, she pulled her hand free.

'Simon, listen to me.' Her voice had taken on a firm, businesslike tone. 'There must be no more hole-in-the-corner meetings. It's not fair on Tina. If we're to see one another in the future, then it can only be if she's there as well.'

Momentarily, he lowered his eyes. 'You're right of course.'

'But, at the same time, I'm sure Tina has no wish to see me whatsoever. It might even help her to get better if she knows that I'm right out of the way.'

He shrugged. 'Maybe.'

'I think it would be advisable for us not to see one another at all. It'll give Tina a chance; give you both a chance.'

Once again, she was presenting him with his marching orders. Her mind flitted back over the years, to the time when she'd broken with him in order to further her own career. The present circumstances were very different but the overall effect was the same.

She met his gaze. His expression was the same now as it had been then. Bleak; despairing; without hope. 'I understand – really, I do.' He smiled painfully.

She wanted so much to kiss him but she had to be strong. He finished his drink quickly. She left hers untouched.

'I ought to get back,' he said.

She nodded.

They both rose to go. He opened the door of the bar for her. She followed him out on to the pavement. They stood looking at one another, not speaking for a time.

'Well, this is it.'

'Yes.'

She put up her face to his. He kissed her on the lips. He smiled a loving smile.

'You'll keep in touch, won't you?'

'Of course.'

He backed away a pace or two before turning and walking swiftly along the side street. At the corner, he waved. She waved back.

Then he was gone.

Chapter Twenty-Nine

'There y'are, ducks.'

Heather Walker winced. She hated being called 'ducks' but didn't like to protest. The elderly office messenger was a nice man and meant no offence.

She watched him dump the pile of newspapers on the table beside her desk. 'That'll keep yer busy fer a bit,' he said and went out, whistling tunelessly.

Not too busy, she hoped. Reading what the opposition had written was one of the first chores of Heather's day. But she refused to let it become burdensome. She merely skimmed through the various women's columns, marking those that might be of interest to Sarah.

The lead story on the *Daily Sentinel's* diary page made her sit up. In it, Sarah was actually mentioned by name, and Heather read with mounting astonishment what Lady Virginia had written.

> Fleet Street stopped dead in its tracks yesterday. The mighty presses were hushed, newsboys lost their voice, seasoned journalists put down their pens. Any why? An agony aunt was seen running after a man, that's why! Down the street. Through the wind and rain. Think of it. Chasing a man.
>
> Sarah Castle – no less – was determined he shouldn't get away. And who was the man in her sights?

Simon Dowling is his name – an old
flame of the pursuer, so I'm told. And
I can believe it. Their reunion in the
street was most touching.
It certainly brought a tear to my
eye.

Heather gulped. She circled the passage with a blue pencil
and took it across to Felicity who shared the same room with
her.

'Typical bloody Virginia!' was her reaction. Felicity was a
young woman who knew her own mind and expressed it
freely. 'I shouldn't think this will do any harm, though. But
we've obviously got to show everyone.'

'Sure.' Heather folded up the paper and took it into Sarah
forthwith.

'I've just come across an unpleasant story on Virginia's
page. You're not going to like it.'

'Oh – *her* again!'

Heather passed the page across the desk. She watched for
reaction but Sarah's face was impassive. She actually gave a
little laugh when she came to the end.

'It beats me,' she said, 'the things that woman dredges up.
The facts are basically true.' She flipped the page with her
finger. 'I did run after an ex-boyfriend in the street. Not very
dignified, I know, but there it is. I badly wanted to see
him.'

'Virginia sounds bitter.'

'She is. This story of hers has no point at all except personal
vindictiveness. It has no news value – scarcely any interest
value, even. I mean, how many readers are going to be grabbed
by the report that Sarah Castle ran along the road?'

'You mean, she's just out to make trouble for you?'

'Exactly. My best reaction would be to ignore her.'

'All right, then. Oh, by the way, your Paris trip this week –
when are you actually leaving?'

'I'm finishing off my column a day early and going on
Thursday.'

'And you'll be back next Monday?'

'Returning London, Monday – back in the office first

255

thing, Tuesday. Felicity will be standing in for me. On Wednesday, we're starting the new series of "Ask Sarah".'

'I've got it marked up. Are you ready to go through the rest of your diary now?'

'Not quite. Give me a few minutes so that I can take this – ' she indicated the cutting ' – down to sir.'

Martin was in excellent mood. Affable and relaxed. Sarah thought it a highly propitious moment to show him the offending news story. And she was right.

When he'd read it, he also laughed. 'Ye Gods, the *Sentinel* must be hard up for material to resort to junk like this.'

'My opinion precisely.'

'All it shows is professional envy. Virginia's as jealous as hell that you have a better following than she has, and so she resorts to poking fun at you. When rivals start lampooning you, Sarah, you can bet your life you've arrived.'

'Thanks, Martin. That's all I wanted to hear.'

She left the editor's office, however, feeling less sanguine than she'd led him to believe. The fact that her name had appeared was of no importance whatsoever. What did matter was that Simon's had been mentioned.

Everything depended upon whether the Dowlings read the *Daily Sentinel*. Admittedly, it was not their type of newspaper. But, in an institution like St. Giles, most of the daily papers would probably be delivered every day.

It remained, therefore, a serious possibility that Tina would see it. If so, where did that leave Simon?

Her immediate reaction was to try and warn him. But how? There was only the telephone, and the chances of her talking to him without his being overheard were very remote.

All she could do was to cross her fingers and hope for the best. But the more she thought about the possible consequences, the more concerned she became.

'Hope I'm not intruding,' Simon said as he entered the sunny computer classroom.

'You know very well you're not,' Stephanie said, smiling as only she could smile.

Instantly Simon felt better. He wanted very much to kiss her. 'Where's Doug?' he asked.

256

'Gone to get some extra manuals. He won't be long.'

'I looked in to see if you've tried out the new software yet.'

'Doug's going to instal it this afternoon.'

'Let me know if it's OK.'

'Sure.'

When he took his leave, she walked with him to the d⌐⌐r. Outside, she asked, 'Any threatening noises from the Brigadier yet?'

'None so far, but don't think I've been lulled into a sense of false security. I'm just waiting for the world to explode around us.'

She surreptitiously touched his hand. 'Have you seen today's *Sentinel?*'

'No, why?'

But she was unable to answer for Doug came up at that moment.

'Did you have a good trip up to town, yesterday?' he wanted to know.

Simon thought Doug gave him rather an odd look and wondered why. 'Not bad. But I'm always ready to get away from the noise and bustle.'

'How's Tina today?'

This struck him as a strange question as Doug saw Tina on most days. Even so, it was kind of him to ask. But what could he say? His answers to this recurrent query were mostly bland. He sought to give the impression that Tina was making progress. The alternative would be tedious explanations and well-meant commiserations. He couldn't face that.

As he approached it, the main house looked forbidding. It had appeared that way for some time. Nowadays he had to brace himself − as he did now − before entering its portals.

Miss Macintosh greeted him with the words, 'Mrs. Dowling would like to see you when you have a moment. She's in the kitchen, I believe.'

Simon went in search of his wife. He found her apparently bemused by the array of vegetables on the kitchen table, looking at each in turn and then passing on to the next.

'You wanted to see me, Tina.'

'Did I? Oh, yes! Did you have a good trip up to London yesterday?'

'You asked me that several times when I got back. Yes, it was OK.'

'And you got the software – a database, I believe – for the computers?'

'I've already told you, yes.'

'And a spreadsheet as well?'

'Look, Tina, we've discussed all this already.'

'The computer shop is in North London, you said?'

'You know it is. We've been there together in the past.'

'So we have.'

'Look, what is this about?'

She picked up the cauliflower again, studying it thoughtfully. Replacing it with exaggerated care, she lifted her eyes and faced him.

'You didn't tell me that you saw Sarah?'

His mouth was suddenly dry and all the breath left from his lungs. Struggling to control his voice, he managed to say, 'Didn't I? I ran into her in Fleet Street.'

'You don't have to tell me. It's in the paper.'

He was aghast. 'The *paper!*'

'Yes. It appears you both had a touching tête-à-tête before disappearing from view.'

'Look, Tina, you've got it all wrong.'

'Have I? Then perhaps you'll explain how it was that you were in Fleet Street when your business was to take you to North London. I suggest you went there expressly to see her.'

He jumped up, paced up and down the room and swung round to face her. 'Oh, all right, I did go there to meet Sarah – but not for the reason you're imagining.'

She tossed back her head placing both her hands on the table top, daring him to tell her the truth. His mind was a blank but only for a moment.

'I arranged to meet Sarah because I hoped she'd be able to help – give you some advice, that is.'

She let out a shrill, hysterical laugh. It reverberated round the kitchen, chilling him.

'I simply don't believe you,' she said. 'I simply do not believe you! You arranged that meeting because you've never got her out of your system, that's why.' Her voice was faltering. 'To you, she'll always be your beloved.'

She dropped down on to a chair and buried her face in her hands. The hysteria had passed. In its place was a grief that racked her whole body.

Simon moved to her and put his arm around her. She leapt up as if stung. 'Don't touch me! Do you think I want your phoney love, your fake caresses? They're a mockery. They cheapen everything.'

'Dearest, please – '

'Don't you "dearest" me!' She was backing away from him as though he were about to attack her. ' "Dearest" indeed! I've never been your dearest and you know it. Sarah's always had that honour.'

'That's not true,' he said. But he knew it was.

'Has it ever occurred to you how alone I am? I have no one. *No one,* d'you hear? I lost my very dear father. My baby didn't live. And you!' She made a derisory noise 'You've never been part of my life. I am totally, irrevocably, absolutely alone.'

He made no attempt to refute it. Nor did he run after her when she fled upstairs. In her present mood it would only have made her worse.

Miss Macintosh gave him some strange looks as he returned to the office. She had obviously heard enough to know what the trouble was, and was probably connecting it up in her mind with what she'd seen the other night.

Tina avoided him for the rest of that day. Most of the time she spent in the bedroom with the door locked. When he went upstairs to bed, the key was still turned in the lock. His pyjamas were outside, neatly rolled up on the mat.

He settled in one of the spare bedrooms but there was no sleep for him at first. He sat up in bed, trying to read, hoping it would make him drowsy. It was a vain hope. In desperation, he switched off the light.

He lay there in the darkness, his mind in turmoil. Thoughts tumbling over one another, vying for his attention: Tina's sickness, their marriage, their job.

Would she ever be better? Would they have to resign from St. Giles?

Exhausted, he dozed off at last. Suddenly, he was awoken by a noise he couldn't at first identify. He sat up in bed, fully alert. He heard it again from somewhere outside. The garage. Somebody was opening the garage doors.

Tina! It could only be Tina.

He leapt out of bed. Ran downstairs, on to the front path.

He was too late. With a roar of it's engine Tina drove their car out of the garage, along the drive, through the main gates.

Stupefied, he watched the tail lights disappearing down the road. There was nothing whatsoever that he could do. Even if he'd had another car, he couldn't follow her. He didn't know what road she'd be taking. All he could was to sit and wait for her return.

Upstairs, he found their bedroom door unlocked. He went inside.

Tina drove like someone possessed. She had never done anything like this before but it was a most satisfying feeling. Normally, it was Simon who was the driver and she the passenger.

To be on the open road in the still of night was magical in itself. But actually to be at the wheel of a car, driving fast like this, was exhilarating. Even her bad arm wasn't paining her for once.

She felt like a goddess. In charge of her own destiny. And what exactly was that to be? She wanted fulfilment and peace. Ah, peace! She needed that more than anything.

Funny, she thought, how everything had a sharper perspective, more three-dimensional than ever before. Those trees, for instance, on the side of the road – how very round and tall they seemed. And in the moonlight, the colours were more intense. And the canopy of the sky was even more vast than usual.

She herself had a greater awareness, as if she'd acquired an extra sense. When she called her own name out loud, it echoed above the noise of the car.

She experienced a bounding sense of freedom. Simon and St. Giles already seemed a million miles away. Odd, that! She'd never felt this way before.

She wasn't very clear about her immediate plans but the car

seemed to know where it was going so she let it have its head. That way, she didn't have to think; just sit back and enjoy the new enhanced sensations.

She had no idea how long she'd been driving. It might have been hours. Maybe minutes. She couldn't tell. She wasn't in the least bit tired. Stimulated, rather.

Eventually, she found herself on a rough track. On either side were stretches of tussocky scrubland. It was vaguely familiar, like something she had once known – something out of another life.

Changing down to bottom gear, she moved slowly off the track and on to grassland ahead. She recognised the place now. Long, long ago, when she'd been a little girl, her father had brought her here for a holiday.

Memories crowded in upon her. Ahead of her was the sea, shrouded now by mist. Down below were the rocks and the pools where they had caught baby crabs and put them in jam jars. They were almost transparent, she remembered.

And when the tide was in, her father had taught her to swim. And the water wings kept on bobbing up and hitting her on the nose. That had made them both laugh.

Such happy times! How much she missed him.

She became restless, feeling the need to stretch her legs. She got out of the car and walked to the cliff edge where she sat down. Thinking. Reminiscing.

Remembering the past was easy. But, no matter how hard she tried, she couldn't look ahead. The future was just an amorphous void.

As she thought on this, the mist rolled back. The moon reflected now on the waters of the sea. It was so tranquil, so beautiful, so peaceful.

She walked back to the car, started up the engine, let in the clutch and opened the throttle wide.

Chapter Thirty

The hum of the aircraft's jet engines seemed far away and there was no sensation of flight. Sarah found it relaxing and sat back, eyes closed, dreaming.

The instruction to 'Fasten seat belts' brought her back to the immediate present.

The plane changed course slightly, causing sunshine to flood the cabin, burnishing her black hair with coppery overtones. She gazed out at the blue sky which contrasted sharply with the dun-coloured cloud below.

They were losing height rapidly. Her stomach was turning over and she instinctively clutched her seat belt. Though a seasoned air traveller, she had never quite got over her early fear of flying. It was silly, she knew, and forced herself to relax.

The aircraft plunged into the leaden mass of cloud and they were enveloped in gloom. The cabin lights were a poor substitute for the sun and it took some moments for her eyes to become acclimatised to the change.

They came in to land. Sarah held her breath, as she did every time. Only when she heard the reverse thrust of the engines, did the tension disappear. She knew then that the worst was over.

Sarah was travelling light. With only hand baggage to retrieve, she was at the front of the queue at the customs desk. The officer recognised and greeted her as a celebrity. 'Did you have a good trip, Miss Castle?'

'Well, it was short but, yes, it was pleasant.'

'You can't have much time to yourself, what with all your TV work and such like.'

'How right you are!'

Passing a newstand, she caught sight of a placard for the midday edition. It read, 'Sex romp star arrives in UK – pictures'.

It was nothing more than idle curiosity that prompted her to buy a copy. On glancing at it, she flinched. There on the front page was a picture showing her mother on the arm of a young man. Much too young for her, Sarah thought.

Her mind flitted back to what Auntie Win had told her at Christmas. She didn't have a chance to look at the story properly, however, until she was being driven home. In the back seat of the taxi, she spread the paper on her lap.

> The one and only Ella St. Clair arrived at Heathrow this morning with an unnamed companion. Miss St. Clair was passing through London on her way to Cannes. When questioned, she described as "absolute nonsense" allegations that she had indulged in sex orgies, and that her ex-husband was suing her for a million dollars.

Nonsense, was it? Sarah had her own ideas on that. So Auntie Win's fears that the story might break over here had materialised. It wouldn't do her – Sarah – much good, would it? Especially now, with her new television series about to start. Funny how every time Ella appeared in her life she caused disruption.

As expected, she arrived home to an empty house. This was because Helga had taken Rufus to Auntie Win's during her own absence in Paris. She had scarcely unpacked her bag and put the percolator on when the phone rang. It was Ella.

Sarah's greeting wasn't very gracious. 'Oh, it's you.'

'Where have you been? I've been phoning on and off all day. I even tried your office.'

'Sorry, Ella. My au pair's down at Sandalwood and I've just returned from Paris.'

'Paris, eh? I'm told those Frenchmen aren't all they're cracked up to be in bed.'

She refused to be drawn. 'Have you seen anything of Reece since you've been here?'

'That creep?'

'I thought you liked him.'

'He's too old for me, honey. I told him to take a running jump. Not my type anyway.'

It was on the tip of her tongue to suggest that Ella preferred toy boys. She resisted the temptation.

'When are you going to Cannes?'' she asked.

'Not for a few days. I'd like us to meet up.'

Sarah tried to put some enthusiasm into her voice. 'Sure. We'll have to fix something.'

'Yep. We'll do that.'

The matter was left unresolved. That suited Sarah. She hoped her mother might forget about it altogether and she'd be let off the hook.

She'd hardly replaced the receiver when it rang again. Jenny's voice this time. She sounded overwrought.

'Sarah? Oh, thank God I've got you at last. I simply must see you. It's very urgent.'

'Look, Jenny, I've only just returned form Paris. Can't you explain on the phone?'

'No. I've simply got to come over and talk to you. Straight away.'

'Won't you give me the gist, for heaven's sake?'

'I'd rather not. I've got to see you.'

There was a click at the other end and Sarah was left holding a dead phone.

The tone of Jenny's voice, the urgency, sent shivers of apprehension through Sarah.

She did, at least, make herself some coffeee. But she didn't enjoy it. Could hardly drink it. She was too much on edge. She paced up and down the room, wondering what had caused Jenny's anxiety. And when she wasn't pacing, she was standing at the front windows, watching for her arrival.

At last she saw her swing round the corner of the cu-de-sac and pull up sharply by the house. Jenney jumped out and ran to the front door, not even bothering to lock the car.

Sarah was there to greet her. Jenny fell into her arms, unable to speak. Her eyes were red.

'Come in,' Sarah said.

In the lounge, she poured out a brandy. 'Here, take this. You look as if you need it. Now tell me what all this is about.'

Jenny gulped down the drink gratefully. Sarah sat opposite her, trying to appear composed. She felt anything but.

'A terrible thing – ' Jenny began. Her voice trailed off into incoherence. She made a great effort. 'Dreadful! Poor Simon!'

Sarah spoke sharply. 'Jenny, please tell me what's happened.'

'It's Tina. She's – she's – dead.'

'Dead! Oh, God! How?'

Jenny was summoning up the courage to speak. 'She – she – committed suicide. Drove over a cliff.'

Sarah was speechless. She thrust her fist into her mouth, stifling a cry.

'Drove over a cliff? I can't believe it!'

'They found her next morning – had to winch her up out of the wrecked car. Took her to hospital. Dead on arrival. Back broken. Simon had to identify the body.'

Sarah was bereft of speech, of feeling. She just sat there staring into space, not seeing.

At length, she spoke. 'I suppose we were all quite blind. If we'd had the nous, we'd have seen this coming. She was hyper-sensitive about her disfigurement; in a bad mental state ever since the accident and the loss of her baby.'

'And the death of her father,' Jenny added.

'Yes. Oh God, poor Tina.' Sarah got up and walked about. 'Just imagine the state of mind she must have been in. It doesn't bear thinking of.'

'No.'

'And how's Simon'

'Shattered.'

'I must go to him.'

'Please! The sooner the better. But there's something else. It's not very nice, I'm afraid.'

Sarah sat down, placed her hands in her lap and faced her guest. 'Tell me,' she said quietly.

'Tina left a note for Simon. In it she said how completely alone she'd been since her father had died, and that Simon had never loved her because it was you he'd always loved.'

'Oh, Lord.'

'And then she read in the paper that you'd met him in London. That finished her. She said it meant you were planning to seduce him away from her.'

'That is simply not true.'

'I know that. We all know it. But her mind was unbalanced. Unfortunatley, after a lot of probing, Simon was forced to show the letter to the doctor. Now, I'm afraid, it's in the hands of the coroner.'

Brigadier Bernard Crawley was on the point of giving his lawns their first mowing of the season. He'd not actually planned this but he'd received a most disturbing letter form Miss Macintosh so he hoped a routine task like lawn-mowing would help his mind to absorb the shock.

He badly needed to think, to consider the fearful accusations made in the letter. Not young Dowling surely, and that pretty girl? Miss Macintosh must be fancying things. Perhaps not, though. They were both young and personable.

How should he deal with the allegations? Inform the committee immediately or bide his time? Confront Dowling at once? That seemed the best course.

The Brigadier was turning all these questions over in his mind when he was called to the phone. It was Dowling's sister on the line. He listened in stunned silence to the news that Mrs. Dowling had been found dead.

After a hurried explanation to his wife, he went straight out to the car. He drove automatically, his mind in a welter of disbelief and sorrow. He hadn't even changed out of his gardening clothes.

He was filled with horror and shock. Such a nice woman. A good worker, too. And Dowling. Did this tragedy shed a new light on what Miss Macintosh had said about him? He hoped to God it didn't.

At any rate, he'd have to defer speaking to him about Miss Macintosh's allegations. He'd wait for some time after the funeral. But, in the long run, what would the future be for St. Giles?

The Brigadier was a worried man. The wardenship was a

husband and wife appointment. Even assuing that Dowling was innocent of any infidelity, where did that leave him now? They surely couldn't engage another woman to take over his wife's duties. The committee would never countenance an unmarried couple in the house ...

The Brigadier pushed the vexing questions from his mind. His first priority was to give some comfort to Dowling – whatever wrongs he might have committed. The poor chap must be in a dreadful state.

Sarah also lost no time in driving down to St. Giles. But the roads were badly congested and it was early evening when she arrived. The door was opened by Miss Macintosh who greeted her with a curt, 'Ah, Miss Castle. This way, please.'

'Thank you.' Sarah found Miss Macintosh intimidating. She never smiled and her manner was cold.

'Will you please wait here?' she said, indicating a wooden chair in the hall. 'Mr. Dowling is engaged at the moment.' With that, she disappeared into the study.

A bit like taking a seat in the dentist's waiting room, Sarah thought. The chair was hard, causing her to change her position every few minutes, and the only illumination came from a small pendant light with a parchment shade.

After what seemed an age, an elderly gentleman with a military bearing came out of the sitting room. 'Good evening,' he said with a little bow before going out.

Some minutes later, the door opened again and out stepped that pretty blonde girl, Stephanie. It was just like that time in the hospital.

'I'm sorry you've had such a long wait, Sarah, but Simon will see you now.'

She forced a smile. With as much dignity as she could muster, she muttered, 'Thank you,' picked up her bag and swept into the sitting room. The door closed with a loud click behind her.

Simon was on his feet as soon as he saw her and at once they were in each other's arms. Not a word was uttered. Physical touch conveyed all that was in their hearts.

It was Sarah who pulled away first. She deliberately chose a seat facing him because she wanted to watch his reactions.

She blamed herself bitterly for what had happened, she said. If she hadn't run after him in the street, Tina would still be alive.

But Simon refused to accept this. 'Tina's suicide was inevitable. I can see that now. It was written in the stars all along. She was in a fearfully neurotic state and had been getting worse. If it hadn't been that newspaper article, something else would have triggered it off. I'm absolutely certain of it.'

His words were comforting; just the same, her sense of guilt remained. They talked a long time. Except for that terrible tragedy hanging over them, it might have been like the old days.

Her mind drifted back. Theirs had been a tempestuous relationship but always gratifying. She thought of their love-making over the years, of the depth of companionship they'd known, the fun they'd had. Even some of the rows!

Now – as in the past – there was no constraint between them. The old rapport remained strong. But the grisly spectre of Tina's suicide would be there for a long time to come.

Understandably, Simon was looking tired and worn and she knew she ought to go. 'I'd like to attend the funeral,' she said as she stood up to leave.

This embarrassed him. 'That would only be asking for trouble I mean – '

He didn't have to finish. She saw the wisdom of what he was saying 'All right. I won't make the situation worse than it is.'

He pulled her to him, hugging her until the breath was squeezed from her body. 'Thank you, Sarah.'

'You always lifted me up when I needed help,' she said. 'Now, it's my turn to support you.'

He disengaged himself. 'And I need that very badly. But it's not going to be easy.'

'In what way particualrly?'

'Well, there's that letter Tina wrote for one thing. I had no option but to let the doctor see it. The coroner's bound to refer to it in his judgement.'

She was a long time in answering. 'I suppose so.'

'I don't think we ought to be seen together, do you? Not until this whole affair has died down. Otherwise the media will make a meal of it. It wouldn't do you any good.'

'How right you are! And besides, there's your position here. We'll both have to be very careful.'

Their forecast regarding the letter was proved correct.

One morning she heard on the radio news that Sarah Castle, the journalist and television star, had been mentioned at a coroner's inquest the day before. She was named, the announcer explained, in a suicide note written by the deceased woman.

That was all. No whys or wherefores. No accusations. Just a plain statement of fact.

She caught Helga's eye across the table but said nothing. Having finished her cereal and fruit juice, she kissed Rufus, said goodbye to Helga and left for work.

But on arrival in the office, her equilibrium was jolted further. Both Heather and Felicity met her with a sheaf of cuttings from other newspapers. Fearing the worst, she sat down and began to read.

They all went into more detail than the radio report. Tina's allegations about Sarah enticing her husband were repeated, together with the fact that the coroner had rejected them. Of course if he'd had any doubts, she would have been called to give evidence. She hadn't though, and her name was technically in the clear. That, at least, was some comfort.

Nevertheless, this didn't stop other newspapers from gloating over her embarrassment. Each of the dailies – except her own paper – carried the story. Some were tolerantly amused; others treated it as a straight news item.

The papers from the Reece Brown stable, however, were spiteful, vicious, and mostly inaccurate.

Some of the things written about her were pure invention, but by no means all. The link with Ella St. Clair could not by any means be disputed.

Virginia had seized on that eagerly. 'Like mother, like daughter" was her underlying theme. How coincidental, she said innocently, that they should both be facing allegations involving men and their private lives.

Sarah gasped: 'How dare she!' Angrily, she got to her feet. 'I'm taking these down to Martin – see what steps we can take.'

269

But the editor was almost sanguine about the attacks. 'Look, Sarah, we're in the jungle where dog eats dog. Journalists love this sort of fighting — knocking their rivals. Most of it isn't meant personally.

'I find that hard to believe! Have you seen Virginia's piece?'

He hadn't so she showed him. He whistled. 'She's implying you're not a fit person to be an agony aunt.'

'Her timing's perfect — just when my new series of "Ask Sarah" is getting under way'.'

'Yeah, you're right. Virginia's trying to knock your career. You could get hefty damages for what she's saying. Would you be prepared to take it to court?'

She spread her hands and sighed.

'I don't think so.' She sounded uncertain. 'At the moment, I haven't the stomach for it. But if their campaign continues — who knows? — I might have to do it to clean up my reputation.'

'OK. We'd back you. Meanwhile, we'll have a word with our lawyers and watch the situation carefully.'

Winnie Seeberg was surprised when the butler announced, 'Miss Castle, madam.'

It was almost nine o'clock and she didn't normally have visitors at that hour on weekdays. Even so, it was always a pleasure to see Sarah.

As soon as she entered the room, Winnie could see that Sarah's face was drawn and she'd lost her sparkle. She sank into an armchair and gave a sigh that seemed to come from the depths of her soul.

Her aunt said 'Tell me about it, honey.'

Sitting there together in the quiet of the evening made Winnie realise once more how much she loved this niece of hers. They were two of a kind.

Sarah explained how her running after Simon in the street had come about.

'It was undignified, I know,' she admitted.

Winnie shrugged. 'Maybe. But why shouldn't you? Don't be inhibited, Sarah. Simon's a good catch for anyone. You shouldn't have let him get away in the first place.'

270

She listened with growing anguish to the tale of Tina's suicide and the letter implicating Sarah. She hadn't realised the scope of the journalistic muck-raking. There was also the linking of Sarah's name with her mother's. Winnie was horrified by the situation.

'Are you going to sue?'

'We may do.'

'Humph!' By this one exclamation, Winnie showed her dissatisfaction that there should be a moment's hesitation. 'They deserve to be taken to the cleaners!'

Sarah shrugged her shoulders. 'The question of going to court or not doesn't bother me so much.'

'What does then?'

Sarah told her. She loved Simon, wanted to take up with him again. 'But I can't − not for some time, at least.'

'Why not, for Christ's sake?'

'All the gossips will say, "Ah, I told you so. Where there's smoke, there's always fire".

Winnie stabbed her finger at her niece . 'Since when have you been a quitter?'

'I'm not.'

'You are. I'm ashamed and disappointed in you. Are you going to let these schmucks dictate what you should and should not do?'

Winnie watched her niece carefully, saw the factors being weighed one against the other, noted the lifting of her chin and the stiffening of her resolve. She was more than satisfied.

'You think I should see Simon and let them go to hell?'

'I do.'

'But they might crucify us.'

'Then they'll crucify you. Show 'em you're not afraid of 'em. Prove to everyone you're a gutsy women and don't give a damn. That way, you'll come out on top.'

A moment's hesitation, then: 'Right. You're on. When the funeral's over, I'll fix something up with him.'

'Now you're talking.'

Chapter Thirty-One

They buried Tina on a cold, windswept day at the beginning of April.

Simon would have preferred the old churchyard for the funeral because it was tree-lined and situated in the lea of the Saxon church, but it had seen no burials for over a century. So there was no alternative but to use the council cemetery, a bleak, impersonal plot.

Only a very small group attended the ceremony. Jenny was there. The Brigadier represented the committee, and Stephanie came on behalf of the staff.

As arranged, Sarah hadn't come. It was only sensible. Just the same, he would have liked to have her by his side.

No one from Tina's family was present. No friends, even. Strange that. It seemed that in life, as in death, she was alone. At the end, Simon was all she'd had and he had failed her.

He shivered.

The officiating priest was reciting the words of the committal expressionlessly. No one was looking at him. They all stood, heads bowed, clad in sombre clothes as befitted the occasion.

Dry eyed, Simon watched the coffin being slowly lowered into the ground. He tried to summon up the emotions he should be experiencing. His heart ought to be breaking but it wasn't.

Of course, he felt sorrow at the death of a dear person, a courageous young woman for whom he'd had great respect; sorrow because she'd always been unfulfilled in her hopes and ambitions; and sorrow, too, because she'd been driven to take her own life.

272

And what irony there was in that! Tina had never known about his affair with Stephanie. Her suicide had been prompted by his meeting with Sarah in Fleet Street, and that had been entirely innocent although it was Sarah he loved.

What mental torment his wife must have been through. If only he'd been able to give her what she desired the most — his love. But that had always belonged to someone else.

The parson was saying something. Words of comfort which washed over him. Simon murmured his thanks and almost immediately had his hand pumped by the Brigadier. He muttered a heartfelt 'I'm terribly sorry, old chap,' before taking his leave.

Stephanie took his hand and pressed it, fixing her eyes upon him. 'If there's anything I can do, Simon, you know where to find me.' With that, she gave him a half-smile and went along the drive to where she'd left her car.

Abstractedly, Simon watched her retreating back until she disappeared from sight.

He heard his sister's voice. 'We can't stand here all day, brother mine. Aren't you going to drive me to the station?'

That pulled him up. 'Sorry. Yes, of course. Come on. Let's go.'

As they moved away, they were surrounded by a group of pressmen who had materialised from nowhere.

Simon tried to reach his car but found his way blocked. The journalists were crowding in upon him. Everyone talking at once. A barrage of questions. Lenses clicking, lights flashing.

'Any truth in the suggestion that your friendship with Sarah Castle contributed to your wife's death?'

'Did your wife know of your relationship with Miss Castle?'

'Did she ever threaten suicide?'

'Do you feel that you were in any way responsible for your wife taking her own life?'

'What effect will this have on your job at St. Giles?'

Stonewalling them, he pushed his way with Jenny through the crowd. Opening the car door was a problem but he managed it at length. The two of them scrambled inside and he drove off at speed.

Everleigh Junction was only three miles away and within

minutes Jenny was alighting from the car in the station forecourt.

'Thanks for coming,' he said.

'Forget it.'

'Yes, but — '

'Nuff said.' Jenny blew him a kiss, told him not to worry, and promised to give him a ring. With that, she ran into the station building and disappeared from sight.

Seeing her had done him good. He felt a little easier in his mind. But as he approached St. Giles, the weight of his sadness returned.

Driving up to the main gates, he saw a few more journalists there but managed to pass them without being forced to stop. Moments later, he was pleasantly surprised to find no more pressmen waiting by the house. The doorway was clear and he went inside without hindrance.

Immediately, the atmosphere of the house descended on him like a pall. It was stifling. He wanted to open all the windows but that would have been foolish. Besides, it wouldn't have done any good. The feeling of oppression was not a physical thing. It was in his mind.

The office was empty. Miss Macintosh had gone home. Thank God for that! He couldn't have faced her just then. In fact, he couldn't face anything — the house, the atmosphere, the job itself.

He walked into the sitting room, looking around as if he'd never seen any of the furniture before. Tina's sewing box and reading glasses; her ballpoint pen and the notebook she used for shopping lists, seemed to stare at him accusingly.

He felt exhausted. He flung himself down on the settee, put his feet up and closed his eyes.

When he awoke, the room was dark. His body was stiff and it was difficult to orientate his mind. His tongue was dry and his throat parched. In the fridge, there was a can of beer which he drank gratefully. But the thought of food was anathema.

Feeling more refreshed, he donned an anorak and went outside. The wind had dropped now and a full moon shone in a clear sky. A good night for a walk, he decided. In any case, he wanted to think and, above all, to get away from this house of reproach.

274

That's what it had become to him. He ought never to have married Tina. Of course, he'd always known that, hadn't he? But then, he oughtn't to have seduced her in the first place. In doing so, he'd sealed his own fate.

It was odd that all along he'd had that sense of having violated Tina. Even after marriage, he'd still felt the same each time they'd made love. Why was that?

And this feeling lingered on in the house, as though the place were imbued with her presence. It was as if she were rebuking him from the grave.

He turned his back on the house and walked away briskly. There was no sense of direction, no sense of time. But after a while, he was dimly aware of springy turf beneath his feet. Without conscious thought, he made for the stile and sat on its top rail.

Thinking. Looking back. Trying to look forward.

From his position, he could see the silhouette of the house and the clump of trees on the skyline. One thing was certain: he'd never be able to live there again, and that would mean resigning as warden of St. Giles.

It was sad but he had no alternative.

How would Stephanie take that? He hoped not badly. They'd agreed that there should be no long-lasting commitment between them. He would miss her, of course. Miss her like hell. But that was life, he supposed.

And then there was Sarah, his true love, the one who would always have his heart. What chance had they now of taking up their old life? None whatsoever, it seemed to Simon.

Whichever way he looked at it, a great chasm existed between them. She was an ambitious career woman, in the public eye. He was just an obscure do-gooder without any ambition at all. Their two worlds were totally different and, he believed, irreconcilable.

They might be able to maintain their friendship, conduct an occasional affair even. But that would be all. They could never live together, marry, have children.

It was while he was thinking of Sarah that he saw a figure walking across the field in his direction. It was a woman. The moon glinted on her blonde hair. He recognised her immediately and his heart leapt. He got down from the stile, ready to greet her.

She came up to him. They didn't kiss. Stephanie said, 'I thought I'd find you here.'

'I'm glad.'

'I guessed you'd be brooding. I thought it might help to talk to someone.'

'Oh, it would.' He spoke from the heart. 'Take a seat,' he said, indicating the stile.

'Delighted.'

Simon helped her on to the top rail and climbed up beside her. He put his arm round her shoulders, pressed his cheek against hers and kissed her.

'I hope Miss Macintosh isn't hiding in the bushes over there,' she said.

They both gave a little laugh, releasing some of the tension.

'Are you going to cope?' Stephanie asked.

'Oh, I can cope but I don't want to. It's as simple as that.' He took a deep breath. 'Stephanie, listen to me – I'm handing in my resignation.'

She whipped round. 'You mustn't do that!' She was looking at him pleadingly. 'You belong here, Simon. I won't let you resign.'

He could smell her perfume. It was delicate and subtle. Very feminine. He wanted to stroke her lustrous hair, feel the touch of her lips, hold her. She was seductive, beautiful. And, oh God, how tempting! She'd give him temporary oblivion, but an innate sense whispered that now was not the time.

He had to break the spell. He jumped off the stile and gave her a hand. As she slid down, he felt her body against his. It reminded him of that night when he'd proposed to Tina. Ages ago, it seemed.

He spoke with an effort. 'I ought to be getting back.'

'Do you have to? It's only just after eleven.'

That surprised him. It felt more like the middle of the night. 'It's getting chilly,' he said, searching for an excuse to remove the temptation that she offered.

But temptation was not so lightly dismissed. As they walked back, Stephanie took hold of his hand, pleading with him not to resign.

On the front steps, she asked if she could come in. He said she could, thinking at the same time that he was making a mistake. He offered her a drink but she refused. She only wanted to talk, she said.

But Simon talked first. He told her about the journalists and their implied accusations.

Stephanie thought things over. 'I don't like the sound of that. I only hope that if there's a storm, Sarah is strong enough to ride it.'

Simon nodded uncertainly. He was not at all sure how she would react and wanted to be by her side. But, for appearances sake, they would not be seeing one another for a time. She'd be on her own. It concerned him.

'And there's you,' Stephanie said. 'Any adverse publicity could brush off on to St. Giles. It wouldn't go down well with the committee.'

'That's for sure.'

'Besides, we can't forget Miss Macintosh. D'you think she's told the Brigadier about us?'

Simon made a despairing gesture with his hands. 'I honestly don't know. I'll have to meet any trouble head on, that's all. But what about your reputation?'

'Don't bother about me. You've done so much good work here that I don't want to see you lose out. You belong here.'

'In one way, I feel that too. But, who knows? Events might force the issue. I might be thrown out on my ear for conduct unbecoming the warden of St. Giles.'

Stephanie pursed her lips and looked away. 'But quite apart from that − I know why you want to quit. You can't face living in this great mausoleum of a house any more, can you?'

'No, I hate the place.'

'Well, I've a suggestion. I've changed my mind about that property at Everleigh I told you about. Why don't you buy it? Then you could persuade the committee to let you live there instead of here. After all, it's only three miles away.'

This was positive thinking. Already Simon's imagination was racing ahead. 'And they might consider converting this old house for the use of more students?'

'Why not?'

They discussed the possibilities for some time, Simon

becoming more enthusiastic by the minute. At last, conversation was exhausted and Stephanie rose to go. Simon escorted her on her way.

'I can't tell you what you've done for me,' he said. For a moment, he looked down at the ground. 'I was sorely tempted. I wanted to ask you to stay the night.' The grip on his hand tightened. 'It was a struggle.'

'I could tell. And d'you think I didn't want you to invite me?' She disengaged her hand and stroked his cheek. 'But tonight of all nights − after the funeral, that is − would have been wrong. You would have gone down in my estimation, darling Simon, if you'd done that.'

He looked at her, nodding silently.

'Simon, you're so sweet. You mean a lot to me. I'd love for us to continue just as we've done for the past few months. But it could never be. I have to be realistic about the opposition.'

'Opposition?'

She laughed. 'Yes. And its name is Sarah! I bet you as soon as I've gone tonight, you'll be worrying yourself sick about her.' He smiled wryly. 'There, I'm right, you see. What's more, I really like her. And I have a horrible feeling that tomorrow the papers are going to give her a nasty mauling.'

Sarah was awakened by the ringing of her bedside phone. Trying to pull her wits together, she picked up the handset.

'Hello.'

'Sarah? It's Martin. Sorry to wake you up so early but I had to speak to you. Fact is, Bill, our night editor, has just been on the blower. Got me out of bed to warn me.'

She groaned. 'Break it gently, Martin.' By now, she was fully awake and on the alert for bad news.

'The early morning editions were delivered to the office as usual, right? Bill looked through them. All our rivals carry stories about you and that woman who died, linking you with her husband.'

'Bitchy, are they?'

'Not all, but Reece Brown's *Sentinel* has really gone to town. A three-column story with pictures. Most of the copy, I'd say, is pure fiction. And certainly libellous. I'm going to the office straight away to see for myself.'

278

Sarah was already out of bed, putting her feet into her slippers and feeling with her free hand for her négligé. 'OK, Martin, see you there, 'bye.'

On the way to the tube station, she picked up a copy of the *Daily Sentinel* at a news stand. At that early hour, the train was nearly empty so, once seated, she was able to open her paper in comfort.

She gasped at the story. There it was on one of the news pages. You couldn't miss it. It positively leapt out at you. 'Written by Virginia Duval'. Who else? And there was a picture of Sarah aged seven, with a missing front tooth, standing with her mother. Where on earth had they raked that up from?

Disbelievingly, she skimmed through the tissue of lies. The *Daily Sentinel* could reveal, it said, that Sarah Castle had had many clandestine meetings with Simon Dowling. His wife had pleaded with her to give up seeing him and she'd refused. Utterly distraught, Mrs. Dowling had taken her own life.

This information, it was claimed, had come from an informant who preferred to remain anonymous. You bet! Any lie can be hidden behind the cloak of anonymity.

Such blatant dishonesty! It was not even distortion but pure invention.

She and Simon were being publicly blamed for Tina's suicide. Sarah stared at the printed page, unable to comprehend the sort of mind that could be so vindictive.

It had been written by Virginia but, surely, had only been published with Reece's connivance and approval. Virginia was undoubtedly cruel but it was Reece who was Sarah's most ruthless enemy.

Discovering the extent of his animosity towards her made her tremble. Not from fear but from anger. She choked and could feel salty tears pricking her eyes. But she couldn't make an exhibition of herself in a train. A discreet dab with her handkerchief and a good nose blow managed to avert the fit of weeping.

The editor was already waiting for her when she got to the office. They went into session immediately.

'Listen, Martin,' she said vehemently, 'nearly all of this is a monstrous lie.' She brought the palm of her hand down

279

upon the offending story. 'The only time I've been alone with Simon in years was when I ran after him in Fleet Street. And that's the honest-to-God truth!'

Martin placed his hand on her shoulder and squeezed it gently. 'OK, OK. I believe you, Sarah. I'm sure we all do. What we have to decide is what we're going to do about this piece of gutter journalism.'

'Yes,' she murmured, sitting down.

'I'd swear that this is libellous – not so much because they've besmirched your character but because they've taken a dig at you professionally. They've implied that you're not a fit person to be doing agony aunt work, either in the paper or on TV. And that could mean damages.'

'I'm only interested in clearing my name.'

'I've already been on to Sam and we've summoned our solicitors here for a meeting at ten o'clock.'

'Suppose I don't want to go to court?'

'Remember, we've suffered through this as well. It could hit our circulation. The same goes for your TV people.'

'So I don't really have a say?'

'That's about it, Sarah, I'm afraid. Sorry and all that, but there it is.'

For Sarah, it was a long and gruelling day.

On her return home, she found Helga in the kitchen, giving Rufus his supper. The child hugged his mother and put up his face to be kissed.

'He'd like you to read him a bedtime story,' Helga said. 'D'you feel up to it?'

She nodded none too enthusiastically. But in fact it proved to be precisely what she needed. Recounting the adventures of Thomas the Tank Engine was a wonderful antidote to the stress and anxiety she'd suffered during the day.

'Mummy read nuther story,' he pleaded when she'd come to the end of Thomas.

'Not tonight, darling. Tomorrow.' Firmly she tucked him up, kissed him goodnight and tiptoed out of the room.

Over supper, Helga said she'd turned down a post as nursemaid in her native Germany.

'Oh, Helga.' Sarah felt weepy with relief. 'Why? Did you do that just for me – for Rufus?'

Helga cast down her eyes. 'I don't want to leave.'

Sarah knew this wasn't strictly true; that she was doing this because of all the trouble. 'Thank you, dear. I appreciate it very much.'

Helga was embarrassed and changed the conversation. 'Max phoned today. He said would you ring him sometime?'

Recent events had served to clarify Sarah's mind. Hitherto, she'd vacillated on the subject of Max. Not any more. She knew positively now that she had no wish to have any further liaisons with him. Her life was complicated enough without having him around.

She would write to him and explain the position. He would understand. He would simply *have* to understand and accept it. Knowing Max, he probably had a number of women in reserve. Perhaps her own name was merely one among many?

She was glad Helga had raised the subject of Max and that she'd made this decision about him. But her other burdens remained – the media pressure, the slurs upon her good name, and the effect all this would have on her career.

And then there was Simon. She wanted him back in her life. Auntie Win had urged her to see him. But what would the outcome be if she did?

If they were to meet, wouldn't it compound the present situation? Almost certainly, the *Daily Sentinel* would find out and splash it across their columns. That would make her feel guilty again; as if she really had driven Tina to suicide. She couldn't bear that.

Sarah looked up and saw that Helga was staring at her. The girl smiled.

'You were in – how d'you say in English? – in a brown study. I didn't want to disturb you.'

'I've a lot of problems on my mind at the moment.'

'I understand. I've read the papers.'

'It's not true what they say about me.'

Helga was indignant. 'Of course not. That awful Virginia!' She pursed her lips contemptuously. 'You must take no notice of them. Those people are nothing. They are rubbish.' She snapped her fingers to emphasise her point. 'You must not listen to them; listen to Helga. You must do what's in your heart.'

281

'Do what's in my heart?'

'Yes. Go to the man you love.'

Sarah was thoughtful a long time. 'D'you know, I think perhaps I will? Yes, I'll do what's in my heart. Thank you, Helga. You've made up my mind for me.'

Chapter Thirty-Two

Helga's display of loyalty had greatly lifted Sarah's spirits and she'd even slept reasonably well that night. But the next morning, she was in despair again, a feeling that was heightened the moment she stepped into her office.

Heather greeted her with some clippings. It wasn't necessary to ask about them. The expression on the secretary's face was enough.

And yet, reading through them, Sarah thought Heather had been unduly pessimistic. For one thing, the cuttings were fewer in number and the quality papers had dropped the story altogether. It was only the popular press that was continuing to show interest, and most of them, she thought, were running out of steam.

The one exception was, of course, the *Daily Sentinel*. But then, their campaign was a personal vendetta. Virginia's contribution was as virulent as ever, almost beyond belief. Sarah caught her breath at what she was supposed to have said and done.

The allegations put her on the defensive, but she couldn't protest too much lest she be misunderstood on that count alone. Her close associates and friends had faith in her. But what of other people? And her public? They were probably ready to believe anything.

It was all so unfair. She was the victim of a spiteful, vicious campaign and all she could do was to hold her head high and preserve a dignified silence.

But she would certainly do that, by God! Hold her head high, that is. She would show them! She would ride the storm!

Perhaps it might even do her good; might reveal that she had reserves of strength undreamed of until now.

Her feelings of hurt had given way to anger. How dare Reece and his minions subject her to such treatment? Sadism, that was what it was – pure sadism.

Auntie Win and Helga had urged her in their respective ways not to be browbeaten by the stories. On the question of Tina's suicide, her conscience was completely clear. Therefore to refrain from seeing Simon was to give way to blackmail. She wouldn't do it.

Her mind made up, she gathered the cuttings together and left the office, hoping to speak to Martin about her own future tactics.

Reaching the floor below, she saw the editor's secretary escorting a young woman along the corridor. Outside Martin's office, they paused and Pat opened the door. The visitor turned to enter and Sarah caught sight of her full face.

It was only a momentary glimpse before the door was closed again, but it was long enough for Sarah to feel they'd met before although she couldn't immediately place her. As she retraced her steps back to her own office, her brain was teased by the enigma. Who was Martin's visitor?

She tried to dismiss the matter from her mind but the riddle remained.

Sir Reece Brown arrived late at his office which was unusual for him. He was also in high spirits – another departure from the norm.

The truth was that he'd had a good evening and an even better night.

Her name was Françoise, a cabaret singer with a penchant for very revealing costumes under which she displayed her beautiful legs. Her voice was less notable but that barely mattered. It was her finer qualities that interested Reece.

A note sent to her dressing room inviting her to join him after the show had had the desired effect. Françoise had indeed joined him, not only at his table but later between the sheets at his West End flat.

But Reece was a highly disciplined man. Although behind schedule this morning, his mind was well organised,

284

immediately ready to cope with the business of the day.

He rang for Miss Clark and dealt with her summarily, dismissing her eventually with an abrupt gesture of the head.

Next he called for Virginia Duval. As instructed, she was harrying Sarah Castle with zest and expertise. Precisely what he wanted.

The first thing he did was to congratulate her. She'd respond to that, he was sure. Most women loved any form of flattery. But all she allowed herself was a slight raising of the eyebrows.

They discussed how they could step up the campaign. And then, to his surprise, she showed a crack in her armour.

'What about libel?' she said. It came out of the blue and Reece wasn't expecting it.

'What about it?'

'Well, aren't they likely to take us to court?'

'Yes, they probably are.'

'But the damages?'

'I'm not bothered. I'm adequately covered, and so are you. Even if they win the case, Sarah will still be discredited. Let a spotless plaintiff go into court and she'll come out a bit tarnished. It always happens.'

'So we go ahead with what we're doing?'

'Of course! We're not going to stop now. Step it up, if possible. It's doing our circulation a lot of good.'

The desk phone buzzed. He picked it up and heard Miss Clark say, 'Oh, Sir Reece, I've got your solicitor on the line.'

'Put him through.' A click and a man's voice came on. 'Morning, Smithson.'

'I'm afraid I have to see you, Sir Reece.'

'Oh. Is Sarah Castle begging for mercy?' He smiled across the desk at Virginia to see if she'd enjoyed his little joke. Her face was impassive.

'It's nothing like that. I can't explain on the phone. This is a personal matter.'

'Personal? Shall we say tomorrow morning at eleven, then?'

'No, sir. That'll be too late. This is extremely urgent. I must talk to you immediately.'

'Oh, very well then. I'll see you in an hour's time. But it's extremely inconvenient.' Reece slammed down the receiver with ill-concealed irritation.

He turned back to Virginia. 'We'll continue our discussion later.' Inclining his head towards the door, he added, 'I'll call you when I need you.'

After she'd gone, he sat back in his chair and wondered what on earth Smithson wanted to see him about. It was really very tiresome.

'Miss Castle in Studio 7B, please,' said the voice on the Tannoy.

The make-up artist had just finished her work and Sarah was ready to go on camera.

'Thanks, Jill,' she said, sliding out of the reclining chair and removing the protective bib from around her neck. 'See you later.'

In the studio, Des greeted her as she stepped among the familiar paraphernalia of cameras and lights and cables that snaked across the floor.

'You're looking a little peaky, darling,' he said as he kissed her on the cheek. 'Don't tell me you're worrying about all this garbage in the *Daily Sentinel?*'

'Well, it won't exactly do me or the "Ask Sarah" series any good, will it?'

Des scratched his chin meditatively. 'If I were you, I wouldn't be too bothered. Even adverse personal publicity needn't be damaging to the programme. Remember – it's still bringing your name before the public.'

'Yes, but Virginia has written some scurrilous things about me.'

'Yup, that's true. But I think we in the media over-estimate how much Joe Public is interested in our goings on.'

'You think so?'

'Sure of it. Anyway, they forget quickly enough. What grabs your own particular public is the fact that you always give a good performance. And that, darling Sarah, is what you're going to do now. The best you've ever given. Right?'

'Right.'

She did just that.

All during the shooting, she'd felt on top of her form,

cocking a snook at her detractors. And the moment she'd signed off the programme, she knew she'd done well. The best ever, as Des had predicted.

Everyone was delighted. Even the floor manager, a taciturn Scot with a bite to his tongue, commented, 'That was bloody good.'

As she entered the hospitality room afterwards, Des's PA came up to her.

'Sorry, Sarah,' she said, 'but your editor's secretary has been on the line. He'd like to see you as soon as poss. I gather there's been a new development.'

Sarah's heart plummeted. All her newfound optimism evaporated. 'Thanks, Marie. Will you order me a taxi?'

'Will do.'

In the cab, her mind was prey to a confusion of conflicting thoughts. A new development ... For the best, she fervently hoped.

Outside the *Courier* building, she paid off the cab driver, not even noticing how much she was tipping him.

Into the entrance hall she received a greeting from Mr. Swallow. She barely heard it. No time to wait for the lift. Up the stairs to the first floor. The editor's door was ajar. Good. He wasn't engaged. Sarah went in.

Martin smiled at her.

'Sarah! Glad you could make it so quickly.'

She sat down. 'What's happened?'

'Everything.' He sat on the edge of the desk, swinging his legs gleefully. 'Does the name Alison Wallis mean anything to you?'

'Alison Wallis? No, I can't say it does. What about her?'

'She is − or rather *was* − Reece Brown's girlfriend.'

Recollection came flooding back. 'Ah, yes, of course.' The young woman whose identity had escaped her earlier! 'I saw her being shown into your office this morning and couldn't place her.'

'Well, she left Reece and he promised her a handsome settlement. He later reneged on it, and so she came to see us.'

Sarah looked at him, wide-eyed. 'Don't tell me, let me guess. She's offering us a kiss-and-tell story?'

'Bang on the nail. And we're buying it. She thought it a

good way of getting her own back on the miserable bastard.'

Sarah could scarcely believe their good luck. Forgetting decorum, she jumped up and kissed him. 'That's marvellous!'

'You can see the scenario, can't you? Reece will refuse to be humiliated by us. He'll be forced to call his hounds off your back. The rest will be up to the lawyers. They'll meet and have a pow-wow. A deal will be struck and we'll all be happy.'

'One more thing, though. I demand a full retraction of all the allegations they've made against me. And it's got to be visible to the reader — not a snippet tucked away at the bottom of some obscure column.'

'Don't worry. Our lawyers will see to that.'

Sarah strolled over to the window and looked out on her beloved Fleet Street. 'The nightmare's almost over, then? I can't believe it.'

'You'd better. It's true, right enough.' He pressed the intercom and spoke to his secretary. 'Oh, Pat, I think we've got a bottle of bubbly in the drinks fridge, haven't we? Bring it in, will you? We've got something to celebrate.'

'I'm glad for you, Sarah,' he said when he'd replaced the phone. 'I know it's been hell these past few weeks. Now you'll be in the clear — free to lead your own life as you want.'

'I hope so.'

'When all the hoo-hah has died down, perhaps you'll be able to marry this chap of yours?'

'Ah, if only! I'd like to, of course. But I don't think you understand. His life style and mine are worlds apart. He's dedicated to his job and lives at this rehabilitation centre.'

'You've got to have a true vocation for that sort of thing.'

'And he's got it. I haven't. Never will have. I'm very much a career woman, as you know. My job with the *Courier* and my appearances on TV are vital to me. it's not just the success that I need. To me, the work itself is the very stuff of living. I'd never give it up.'

'Would you have to if you married this guy?'

'I think so. Simon's job is really a husband and wife appointment, you see. And he has tied accommodation — a vast mansion on the estate. I could no more live in that house than go into orbit.'

The door opened and Pat came in with the champagne.

Martin uncorked the bottle and poured out three measures. He lifted his glass and looked at Sarah.

'Here's to you. Reece'll be calling in his hounds and your immediate troubles are over. Ours too. Let's drink to that.'

Reece made it a practice never to drink in the office, but he did keep a bottle of brandy hidden away for emergencies.

He reached for that bottle now and poured himself a glassful. He drank it quickly and hid the glass. He couldn't allow any of his staff to think he'd been drinking in office hours. It would give the wrong impression and create a bad example.

The mellow liquor warmed him and he was sorely tempted to have another one. But he resisted it.

He felt a little stronger although his anger had not abated one whit.

The perfidy of the woman! Fancy Alison going behind his back and selling her story in that unprincipled way. A most dishonourable thing to do, and it would have made him a laughing stock in the City.

The *Daily Courier* would have printed the story if he hadn't stepped in promptly with counter proposals. Of course, he'd had to agree to drop the Sarah Castle campaign and agree to an out-of-court settlement. And a full retraction! That went against the grain with him but he'd had no option.

Virginia wouldn't be pleased at the new developments. He buzzed for his secretary. 'Oh, Miss Clark, get me Virginia Duval, will you?'

He waited impatiently. At last, the nasal voice of his gossip writer came on the line. He spoke peremptorily. 'I want you to drop the campaign against Sarah Castle with immediate effect.'

'But my copy's all ready for tomorrow's edition.'

'Then spike it and find something else.'

'I don't understand ...'

'You're not paid to understand. You're paid to do as you're told.'

'Very well,' she said reluctantly.

But Reece wasn't listening. He'd already hung up.

Chapter Thirty-Three

Brigadier Crawley usually liked to take things easy on Saturday mornings. He regarded it as his "pottering" day.

But not today. Ahead of him, lay a most unpleasant task and he was anxious to get it over with as quickly as possible. Still, he reminded himself, he was the committee's representative, and as such he had to ensure that everything was straight and above board.

Nevertheless, it was with a heavy heart that he left the house very early and drove to St. Giles. He wondered if he was in fact too early and whether Dowling would have finished his breakfast yet.

At least by calling at this time, he'd be sure not to see Miss Macintosh. That was his intention anyway.

Dowling opened the door himself. Crawley thought that the fellow looked a little alarmed at seeing him at that hour. He could have been mistaken, though.

Once in the study, the Brigadier came to the point immediately. He was not a man for beating about the bush.

'I'm sorry to say,' he began, 'that I've received an allegation of misconduct against you. It also involves another member of your staff.' He coughed delicately. 'Clearly, as committee secretary, I have to satisfy myself that the charge is without foundation.'

For a moment, Dowling said nothing. Then he lifted his head boldly and looked at his accuser. 'Miss Macintosh?' he asked unexpectedly.

The Brigadier was floored. He could only answer in the affirmative.

Dowling was speaking. 'I have to admit that I did have an affair with Stephanie. I'm not making any excuses for myself. I regret deceiving my wife, but I assure you it had nothing to do with her suicide.'

'Quite, quite. I accept that.'

'I expect you'll be wanting my resignation?'

The Brigadier hesitated, playing for time. 'Let's not be hasty.' He thought of the woman in the case – Stephanie. How could any man be blamed for succcumbing to her charms?

His mind flitted back to the summer of '45 when he'd been a member of the British Army of Occupation in Germany. A young fräulein, blonde with blue eyes – just like Stephanie. So pretty, so vivacious.

His gut feeling was to give Dowling the benefit of the doubt. The poor chap had had a harrowing time since he'd married Phillips' daughter, after all. Surely, he deserved a break. He spoke kindly.

'Listen, old chap. We're both men of the world. I understand how this could have happened. We'll keep this a secret between us.'

The younger man gasped. 'That's very good of you.'

'But on one condition only – that you bring no scandal to St. Giles; that you keep any romantic affairs off these premises. Do you understand?'

'Absolutely. Thank you, sir.'

The Brigadier rose and shook his warden by the hand. 'And the very best of luck to you, Dowling. I hope you find happiness, one day.'

Saturday morning at St. John's Wood. A late breakfast for Sarah. The daily papers. No scurrilous attacks. No pressures. A chance to relax. She was enjoying herself.

She looked across at Rufus eating his corn flakes. He was growing up fast and had very winning ways. Everyone adored him. She was extremely proud of her small son. Life seemed very good. How lucky she was. And a sweet girl like Helga to look after him. A happy household! There was only one thing missing. A husband.

Thinking of this caused a shadow to cross her mind.

Marriage to Simon belonged to the realm of make-believe. A fairy-story. 'And they lived happily ever after.' Indeed? Only small children could believe such nonsense.

She thought of Simon with longing. Their mutual love was not in doubt. There had never been anyone in her heart but Simon. And likewise she knew she filled his affections in the same way.

But their repective life-styles were irreconcilable. He was as dedicated to his work as she was to her career.

However, certain constraints had been removed. Now, there was no reason at all why they shouldn't see one another, enjoy holidays together maybe.

That was the very most for which she could hope. No good railing against Fate, though. She and Simon were what they were by birth. Nothing could change their characters − his dedication to good works and hers to a successful career.

Suddenly, Sarah's mind was made up. She wanted to see him today! Never mind about ringing him up first. She'd drive down there later in the morning. He'd be delighted to see her.

As soon as she'd attended to her tasks in the home, she was driving through London, en route for Surrey. Despite the traffic on the roads, there were few hold-ups and she was passing through the gates of St. Giles by midday.

To her disappointment, the door was opened for her by the redoubtable Miss Macintosh. Sarah was surprised to see that she worked on Saturdays. From the outset, it was clear the older woman wasn't disposed to be pleasant.

'Mr. Dowling is out,' she said brusquely. 'He left about an hour ago.'

'Have you any idea where he's gone?'

Miss Macintosh was affronted. 'Really, Miss Castle! I am not his keeper.'

Sarah left.

On the way to where she'd parked the car, she saw one of the tutors whose name she'd forgotten. She asked him whether he had any idea where Simon had gone.

'I believe he drove into Everleigh.'

'Isn't that the next village along the road?'

'That's it − about three miles away. If you go there, it

might be a good plan to look in the King's Arms. Simon sometimes has a lunchtime beer there.'

'Thanks, I'll do that.'

She drove out of the grounds, full of anticipation. He would be so surprised to see her.

But it was she who received the surprise. Driving towards the King's Arms, she caught sight of Simon coming out. And he had a companion – Stephanie.

Sarah's first impulse was to drive on. She had no intention whatsoever of sharing Simon with anyone, least of all Stephanie.

But she was too late. Simon had seen her. He called out, waving frantically and running towards the grass verge. She had no alternative but to stop and get out.

Stephanie or no Stephanie, they kissed warmly. Simon was clearly delighted to see her and kept his arm around her waist in a proprietorial way. And Stephanie greeted her warmly.

Sarah felt better.

The next few minutes were spent in chit-chat and displaying their social graces to one another. Bringing the ritual to an end, Stephanie glanced at her watch, saying she'd have to go. She smiled at them both. 'Not that you'll be sorry. You won't want me around.'

'No, please, not on my account,' protested Sarah, not meaning a word of what she was saying.

Stephanie explained, 'I'm off to meet a friend in London and I've a train to catch.'

'Trains – round here?'

'Why, yes. Quite a good service to Waterloo.' She bestowed a dazzling smile on Sarah. 'Well, see you around.'

'Where's the station?' Sarah asked.

'A little way along the road.'

'I'll drive you there.'

'That would be kind.'

A few moments later, Sarah was pulling up in the station car park and Stephanie was preparing to get out.

'Thanks, Sarah. That was a help.' Then, to Simon sitting in the back, she added, 'Oh, you'll need these,' and handed him a couple of keys. Another smile in Sarah's direction. Without explaining, she got out and walked towards the booking office.

Sarah couldn't conceal her curiosity and asked Simon outright about the keys.

'Drive back to the village and I'll show you.'

Mystified, she did as she was told. On his direction, she parked her car behind his and got out. He took her arm and conducted her along a lane.

'See that?' he said, pointing to a cottage at the end. 'I'm buying it. Stephanie was considering having it but she's changed her plans.'

Sarah could scarcely get over her surprise. 'But whatever for? As an investment? Are you going to let it out then?'

He laughed delightedly. It was the first time she'd heard him laugh like that since they'd parted. 'No. I'm going to live in it. Moving in today, in fact. It's furnished, you see.'

He said he'd had a long talk with their committee secretary that morning. As a result, there would be certain changes. One of these was he could now live off the premises. Secondly, to replace Tina as deputy warden, they would appoint a male assistant who'd occupy part of the old house.

'It sounds a much better arrangement.'

'Oh, definitely. And Stephanie is leaving.'

'Is she?' Sarah couldn't help being delighted.

'She's decided she wants to return to London and is looking for a new job there.' Then, indicating the cottage, he said, 'Isn't it lovely?'

'Like a picture postcard. You'll be telling me there are roses round the door next.'

Again that laugh. 'There are — or at least there will be in the summer.'

She began to walk ahead, pulling him along in her haste. 'I want to see it. Show me, Simon. It looks so romantic.'

He ushered her into the front garden and unlocked the front door with a flourish. It opened on to the sitting room, with its timbered ceiling and ingle nook fireplace.

Sarah was ecstatic. 'This is heavenly! Maybe it's my American blood but to me this is a genuine bit of old England.'

'It's all been modernised. It even has central heating.'

'Anyone would think you were an estate agent selling it to me. And you'd have a sale, I can tell you that. It's a dream place.'

He fell into the game readily. 'Oh, yes, madam. A des. res., two recep., kit., three beds, all mod.cons.'

'I'm glad about the mod.cons.'

Together, they explored the house which continued to delight her. She showed the same enthusiasm for the garden.

'And look at that gorgeous apple blossom. Isn't it pretty? It's sad it's beginning to fall. I love apple blossom, don't you? And there's even a child's swing. I haven't been on a swing since I was a kid.'

She went over and sat on it, swaying gently, her feet off the ground. 'Aren't you lucky,' was her eventual comment.

'You mean you actually like it?'

'What d'you mean – "actually like it"? I love it. Why d'you sound so astonished?'

He was embarrassed. 'I'd have thought all this was a bit unsophisticated for you, that's all – I mean, you with your modern town house and being a famous journalist.'

'Oh, Simon, don't you know me better than that? I only live in St. John's Wood because it's convenient – not because I particularly like it. And what's being famous got to do with it?'

He had no answer to that. He was contemplating the ground, thinking hard. There was a look on his face that suggested puzzlement or indecision. She studied his gentle, compassionate eyes.

Oh, how she loved him!

When at last he spoke it was in a low voice, almost expressionless. He didn't look at her.

'I don't have to tell you how much I love you; how much I've missed you. There hasn't been a day when you haven't been in my thoughts. I realise that sounds very disloyal to Tina and it makes me ashamed but it's the truth. I'd be dishonest if I were to say otherwise.'

She stopped swinging and took his hand in hers. 'I know – and it's been the same for me.'

He smiled as only he could smile. A smile full of understanding and love and spontaneity.

'Now that I'm going to move in here, living off the job, so to speak, would you – d'you think we – ?' He was unable to continue.

295

'Are you proposing?'

'Yes.'

'Oh! But would it be wise for us to marry? I mean, our lives are poles apart, Simon. What could be more dissimilar than our two jobs?'

'Sure, I agree. But our home here would be neutral ground. We'd be an antidote for one another at the end of the day.'

She was a long time in answering. 'You realise, darling, I still couldn't give up my career.'

'I wouldn't want you to.'

'My work is very, very important to me. It is extremely creative and it *fulfils* me.'

'Are you trying to tell me in a gentle way that your work is still all-important like it was in the beginning – that our marriage would come a poor second?'

She threw herself at him, her arms enfolding him. 'No.' She hugged him to her. 'It's not that at all. When I was starting at the *Examiner,* I wouldn't have made it as women's editor if I'd been married. Today, I've achieved my goal. Now, I want to marry you more than anything in the world. *Want to –* d'you hear?'

She couldn't finish because he was kissing her fiercely. At last, she was able to speak. 'Can we be married soon? The papers have lost interest in me as an item of gossip. But what about your side – the St. Giles people?'

Simon pulled a face. 'I've got to be a bit circumspect. There's still the committee to consider but I've got the Brigadier with me. By the way, he doesn't believe those stories in the *Daily Sentinel,* thank God. And I'm sure I'll be able to talk him round to the idea of my marrying again. He admires you on television, apparently.'

'Does he? That's something. And can we have a quiet wedding?'

'Whatever you want, darling.'

'And a honeymoon in Rome – go to the Colosseum. I've always wanted to see the Colosseum.'

'Of course. One day, I'd like to –'

But she wasn't listening. Her eyes were traversing the garden, the sides of the cottage, the timbers on the wall. A breeze whipped at the apple blossom and some petals fluttered to the ground.

'Oh, I'm going to love living here,' she said. 'And Rufus will have a real garden of his own instead of having to play in the park.' She paused as a new thought struck her. 'I hope you don't object to having a ready-made family?'

'Delighted. I'm looking forward to meeting him. Hope he approves of me, that's all.'

She kissed him lightly on the lips. 'He'll adore you – just as much as I do.'

He smiled, pleased at what she'd said. 'And you won't mind commuting up to London?'

'Not really. This cottage will be our bolt hole, darling.' Her imagination was already working fast, visualising the bliss that would be theirs. 'After work, we'll come home here and be together. Nothing else will matter; only us. I'll shed all my cares and you'll escape from – from Miss Macintosh.'

They laughed at this but only for a moment. Long ago, this vision of an idyllic life had filled their longings and hopes, only to be dashed. Now, it was within their grasp never to elude them again.

Their eyes met, reading one another's thoughts. Together at last. The depth of their love was beyond measure. Nothing would ever part them. He was hers to have and to hold for ever.

Sarah slid her hand to the back of his head and gently pulled him to her. Tenderly, lovingly, she kissed him.

As she did so, some petals of apple blossom swirled around them and rested on their shoulders.

Sarah picked one of them up. 'That's an omen,' she said. 'We're going to be very happy. As if we need telling!'

You have been reading a novel published by Piatkus Books. We hope you have enjoyed it and that you would like to read more of our titles. Please ask for them in your local library or bookshop.

If you would like to be put on our mailing list to receive details of new publications, please send a large stamped addressed envelope (UK only) to:

Piatkus Books, 5 Windmill Street
London W1P 1HF

PIATKUS

The sign of a good book